THE END OF EDEN

A SWAG TALES BOOK

First published as Marah Chase and the Fountain of Youth in the United Kingdom and United States by Pegasus books in 2020

This edition published as End of Eden in the United Kingdom and United States in 2024.

This edition published by Swag Tales, Glasgow, G40 4TR.

All works copyright Jay Stringer 2019, 2022, 2024.

Cover design by Jay Stringer.

Paperback formatted in Affinity Publisher.

Ebook formatted in Atticus.

Standard Paperback Edition ISBN: 978-1-0686074-3-1

Ebook Edition ISBN: 9781916892392

ALSO BY JAY STRINGER

"A bartender and a thief climb a mountain..."

ONE

August Nash was ready. He'd been waiting for this moment, impatient for his chance to make history. He began to move as dawn broke across Lake Tana, counting out steps across the large, flat rock.

One.

Two.

Three.

Taking up the correct position, he turned toward the sun rising above the Simien Mountains on the far shore. A distant red glow, filtered through a smoky brown haze, marked the spot where Erta Ale, a large volcano, had been erupting for the past few weeks. The increased activity was making people nervous, fearing it was a sign of something bigger to come.

The sun broke through the dust, and a line of golden light ran across the surface of the water toward Nash, dividing the lake into two halves.

Nash unfolded a bloodstained parchment. A small disc was drawn on the top corner of the page, sticking out above two mountain peaks. Thin yellow lines led outward from the disc, with one large line pointing straight down in the six-o'clock position. Nash held the paper out ahead of him, lining up the images of the sun and light with the real thing. Other rays on the map pointed out at three, four, and five o'clock. The thickest of these was at four, which led down to a painting of a small island with a stone building at its center.

Further markings ran down one side of the paper and across the bottom. For eight hundred years, the document had been seen as a piece of art. An early landscape portrayal of a lake or coastline. The image didn't match up to any known location. Tana had been discounted, because the lake had many more islands than were shown in the picture.

Nash was the first to see it for what it was: a map, with a grid reference along the edges. There was only one island shown, because only one of them was important. Nash's destination.

Nash didn't show it, but he was worried.

This had been almost too easy.

Nothing in his line of work came without struggle, but he was only moments away from the greatest archaeological find in history. And, aside from the map's previous owner's, no blood had been spilled. He couldn't shake the feeling that the worst was yet to come. There were legends about the demons carried on the wind, summoned to kill anyone who stepped on the island.

Things could be about to get very interesting.

Behind him, the mercenaries stirred. Gathering together their weapons and supplies. Talking in whispers, preparing for the signal to move. They didn't know what Nash was looking for, but his money was good, and his reputation was better.

Between the invasion of Iraq, the fall of Syria, and the uprisings in Egypt, the black market for antiquities had exploded. Any local with a shovel could head out into the desert and start digging, free from the laws of collapsed governments. But the real money—and the real glory—went to the relic runners, a select band of treasure hunters who would cut any corner to get what they wanted. The mortality rate was high. The pay was even higher.

August Nash had been in the game longer than everyone else. He was a legend in the field. A name whispered in bars around the world, along with only one or two others. But after today, he'd be world-famous, going down in history for what he was about to find.

He held the map up to the sky again, putting the image of the sun over the real thing. The mountains weren't in the right position. Or, rather, the sun wasn't high enough in the sky in relation to the peaks drawn on the page. He waited. Following the sun as it moved. When everything finally matched up, he traced his finger down along the four-o'clock line and let the paper fall away to see where he was pointing.

Tana Kirkos.

A small island near the eastern shore, with the large silver dome of an Ethiopian church showing above the trees. But that couldn't be right.

Tana Kirkos had been searched before, countless times. If the item ever had been there, it had been moved long ago. The map was eight hundred years old. For the first time since finding it, Nash started to think he was wrong. The map was too old. Out-of-date. He closed his eyes for a moment. Breathing in and out, preparing to tell his men the job was over. As his eyes opened, Nash caught the last moment before the sun completely cleared the mountains. Darkness still shrouded the edges of the view. On the far shore, he could see the many local churches starting to shine. The single beam of light had widened, spreading across the water's surface, ready to vanish as the sun climbed higher and morning light filled the area. In the last second, right before the beam faded, Nash saw something.

The hard edge of the beam had gone past Tana Kirkos to fall on a smaller island, closer to the mouth of the Blue Nile. And, caught in the ray's last moment, Nash saw the square roof of a temple.

That was it.

Had to be.

Nash pointed to the island and shouted commands to his team. Romain, a bald Moroccan sailor, grunted an acknowledgment. He liked to play tough and almost never spoke. But Nash had once caught sight of a Mickey Mouse tattoo on his right biceps. There had to be a good story behind that, but Nash had never asked. Romain ran down to the water's edge and pulled the cord on a small black cube. With a long hiss, the cube began filling with air and unfolding into a boat.

Bakari, a former gunrunner from Senegal, finished packing their bags and headed down to the boat. He was a tall man with a sloping gait, his broad shoulders rocking lazily from side to side as he moved.

Nash glanced to his right, where the lights were starting to blink on in the port city of Bahir Dar. Neither Bakari nor Romain knew this, but there was another member of the team. When Nash found what he was looking for, a rubber boat wouldn't be enough. He had a helicopter waiting on an abandoned airstrip to the south of the city. Once the pilot received Nash's signal, he would home in on their position to lift the prize out by air. There wouldn't be enough room on the chopper for Bakari or Romain, but Nash would deal with that problem when it came up. From there, the pilot would head straight for a small airstrip hidden away in the Mile Serdo Wildlife Reserve. Nash hadn't decided whether to let the pilot join him on the secret road into Djibouti. That could wait, too.

The trio climbed into the boat and started off across the lake, their wake sending large ripples across the calm surface. Romain pulled a plastic hood, specially designed to muffle the sound, over the outboard engine. Even still, Nash could hear every tick and rev. He was convinced they could be heard for miles around, and anyone waiting on the small island would be ready for them. He touched the knife strapped to his calf and checked that his Glock was loaded and ready.

Nash kept his eyes on the surface, watching for crocodiles. Every expert he'd spoken to said there were no crocs in Lake Tana, but with rivers and lakes starting to dry up across Africa, and increased volcanic activity along the Great Rift Valley, Nash knew predators were starting to show up in areas they'd never been before. With a surface area of over one thousand square miles, the lake offered plenty of room to hide.

Romain steered them around Tana Kirkos, keeping them hidden from the city. Along the shore, Nash could see movement. Local fishermen pushed their papyrus-reed boats into the water, preparing for the day's work. Some of them paused, staring out at the sound of the engine. As they neared the small island, Nash could see a square section of rock hidden beneath the leaves of overhanging trees. It looked unnatural. Smooth.

A dock.

Nash pointed, and Romain nodded, changing course. Nash gripped the gun. Bringing it up into a two-handed firing position, he knelt at the front of the boat as they nosed under the tree canopy and the bow slapped against the stone. The dock was ten feet across and five feet deep, with thick bushes on three sides. Nash scanned the undergrowth for any sign of life.

Nothing.

Not even wind.

Romain killed the engine and tied off on a large stone. The three men braced and waited. Nothing happened. It was quiet. This set off every instinct Nash had honed over his years in the military, then the CIA, and now over a decade as a runner. Silence was a bad sign. Nature wasn't silent. If nobody was watching, they'd hear noises. A bird flapping its wings, a scavenger moving away through the undergrowth. But the wildlife on the island was keeping quiet.

Nash thought again of the legends. The demons carried on the wind, guarding the island. His skin crawled with the feeling of being watched.

They weren't alone.

Nash nodded for Bakari to climb out of the boat. The big man hesitated, then followed orders. He leaned over, unsteady as the boat buffeted against the stone wall. Placing a hand on the stone surface, he stepped across. The moment his second foot landed on the hard ground, the bush ahead of him rustled. There was a fast movement, followed by the sound of wind. Bakari fell backward, and Nash could see he'd narrowly avoided the blade of a long sword. He caught a glimpse of an arm clad in a deep green robe, matching the foliage, and then a dark face with odd, milky eyes appeared through the leaves. Bakari rolled onto his side, leaving room for Nash to shoot three rounds into the bush, and a small man slumped forward, dropping the sword.

The shots echoed around them, and Nash knew everyone across the lake must have heard. People would come to investigate the sound. They didn't have much time.

Bakari turned and offered his hand to help Nash across, followed by Romain. As all three men paused to look down at the dead sentry, the bushes moved again. Two more men rushed them, their swords at the ready, before they pulled the blades back in unison, turning them in a fast circle over their heads, bringing them back down, fast and hard. The weapons were followed again by a sound like wind.

Nash stepped aside and put two shots into his attacker. The body fell at his feet, the sword skidding away across the rock and into the water.

Bakari was too slow, staggering backward and fumbling for the gun at his side. The second attacker got to him, and the sword cut into his neck, taking his head off with the sickening sound of metal cleaving through bone. Romain screamed. It was a much higher pitch than Nash would have expected from a man who prided himself on his cool. Nash spun and put two more bullets into Bakari's killer, who was in the middle of turning to swing his sword at the Moroccan sailor.

The swordsman fell but wasn't dead. He twitched on the deck. Romain recovered his composure and finished him off with his knife.

Nash knelt over Bakari's body and took the dead man's extra ammo, sliding the gun into his own holster as a spare. Then he paused to examine the three dead guards. They all had the same creamy white eyes. Were they blind?

The swords had notches along the blades. This was the source of the sound, the air moving through the holes like wind chimes. Nash picked up the nearest one in his left hand and jabbed into the bushes, looking for more guards. When he didn't find any, he began pulling back the leaves, until he saw a narrow stone path leading between the trees. He gestured for Romain to go on ahead, but the Moroccan shook his head and started to move back toward the boat. Nash raised the Glock in his right hand. Romain looked at the weapon, then at Nash. His shoulders slumped, and he led the way up the path. Nash followed a few yards behind.

The path turned into steps, twisting uphill between bushes and trees. There were still no sounds aside from Romain's low voice and heavy steps. He was complaining under his breath. Nature all around them was holding its breath. Nash's instincts kicked in again, telling him to freeze. He stood stone-still on the path, letting Romain get farther ahead.

Twigs snapped. Branches moved. On either side of Romain, two more guards leapt from the undergrowth. Romain got one, firing four shots in rapid succession. At least two of them were unnecessary. The attacker was dead before he hit the ground, rolling downhill. Nash got the second, closing the distance fast and using the sword, feeling the solid connection as the blade pierced the skin, pushing in to hit something firm. Nash twisted the handle and pulled the sword away to the side, slicing the attacker open. Blood poured across the greenery as the man fell backward, vanishing into the foliage. The solid thump confirmed the dead weight had hit the ground.

Nash waved Romain on again but didn't follow.

Something wasn't right here.

He'd once spent two days crawling through booby-trapped antechambers in Syria, only to find a dead end. The whole thing had been a distraction from the real tomb, which was on the other side of the valley. Misdirection. He watched as Romain disappeared around a bend. Rather than following, he squatted down and pushed through the leaves in the direction the dead man had fallen. He paused over the dead body, taking care to avoid the damp patches of earth where the blood had pumped out into congealed pools. Nash stayed still. Motionless. Willing himself to blend into the background.

Letting his ears grow accustomed to the silence, he could make out the heavy footfalls of Romain farther up the hill. There was another sound. Lighter steps, almost directly ahead of Nash, farther up the incline. Someone stalking Romain. Nash let both sounds continue to move away. He looked down at the ground and saw a narrow dirt track. He stepped onto it and found himself in a clear corridor cut between the bushes, a path running parallel to the steps, leading all the way back down toward the dock. He walked slowly along it, making sure to test out the weight of the ground before planting his foot down each time. As he neared the bottom of the hill, two gunshots rang out from far off behind him, followed by a muffled scream. He stopped and moved quietly off the track to stand behind a tree. More silence followed, then footsteps. The padding footfalls that had been stalking Romain. They were coming this way.

These were the demons. Blind swordsmen who had learned to move in near silence, with paths leading through the bushes to allow them to seem invisible.

Nash placed his Glock on the ground, unable to holster it while he also had Bakari's gun. He raised the sword in both hands and waited. The sounds came nearer. The muscles in Nash's arm twitched, urging him to move. But he held off, waiting until he was sure the guard was close. At the last second, the steps paused, slowing down before coming to a complete stop on the other side of the tree. The guard must have sensed something was wrong. Nash could be giving his own position away with each breath.

Nash swung the blade, stepping out from behind the tree in the same movement, putting his weight and forward momentum into the move. He connected, cleaving high into the guard's shoulder and upward toward the neck. The sword completed its arc as the tip embedded in the tree, pressing the already dead guard against the trunk.

Nash let go of the sword rather than pulling it free and picked up the dead man's off the ground.

A wave of nausea rolled over him. He leaned against the tree and controlled his breathing before he coughed and started heaving, bringing up his breakfast.

He took a few moments to calm down before continuing to follow the dirt trail toward the dock. Near where they had found the stone path, the trail veered left, heading inland again. In less than a hundred yards, Nash came to a clearing. Two wooden huts were sitting on either side of the path. He approached them slowly, but nobody attacked him. There were no signs of life. He noticed, too, that he could hear a few birds skittering through the trees. Nature was starting to move again. The tension had passed.

Continuing along the path as it widened into a well-trodden clearing, he could see the top of the building he'd spotted from across the lake. It was behind a copse of trees. He rounded them to see a large square structure, about twenty feet tall but mostly obscured from view off the island by large trees that had grown up around it.

Nash recognized the architecture. It was tall and narrow, like a house brick laid on end. The doorway was cut high into the stone, a rectangle with a series of similar shapes cut into the surface around it. On either side of the doorway, two large columns had been carved. It was a scaled-down replica of the central temple of King Solomon's Jerusalem complex.

An old man in orange robes sat on the steps to the entrance. He had the same milky eyes, but his skin was cracked like aged paper. His head twitched as Nash approached.

The old man laughed and spoke in a language Nash didn't recognize. It sounded vaguely like Hebrew. The old man sniffed the air, and his head twitched again. He put his hands to his face in prayer. Nash raised his sword. The old man seemed to sense this. He turned his head up at the sky and smiled, then bowed back into the prayer. Nash rested the blade on the old man's neck before clubbing him hard with the hilt.

Nash stepped around the slumped figure and into the temple.

The walls on either side were covered with tapestries. They showed King Solomon and his temple. Then a great war, and the temple burning. A procession of men dressed in orange robes, carrying a large golden box. The men travelled up river, to an island Nash knew to be Elephantine in Egypt. Then another battle, another burning building, and another journey along the river. In the final image he saw the building he was standing in now.

At the end of the passage, Nash came to wide stone steps, painted gold. They led up to a curtain, which shone the same color as the steps. At the top, he paused before reaching out to touch the curtain. Never a man to have any real faith or belief, he still felt a moment of awe and reverence. He was about to look on something that had been hidden from history for thousands of years.

He thought again of the milky eyes of the guards and the old priest. Were they turned blind from looking at the object behind the curtain, or was it done to them to prevent them from looking? He found himself doubting, at the last moment, whether he should do this. Then he swallowed back the fear and gripped the curtain again, pulling it aside before he could let any fresh doubts creep in.

The room beyond was small. There were two statues standing on either side of the chamber. They were winged and had four heads, each of them bearing the fearsome face of a different animal: a lion, an ox, an eagle, and what looked to be a jackal. They were cherubim, the guardians of the throne of God. Renaissance artists had turned cherubs into small, cute humans with tiny wings, but they had originally been described as much more fearsome. Nash had expected to find statues like these, but he'd thought the fourth head would be a human, not a jackal. The canine face gave everything a vaguely Egyptian feel. Each of the statues had one wing spread outwards, reaching towards each other and touching in the middle. Beneath the wings was the altar, but it was empty.

Nash heard laughter coming from the entrance. It was an old, broken sound. He ran back down the steps, taking them two at a time. His heart pounded and anger burned in his stomach. The old man was awake, leaning against the stone doorway. Nash pressed Bakari's gun to the old man's face.

He tried to calm down, but the words, when they came, were in a shout almost as high and loud as Romain's scream.

"Where is the Ark?"

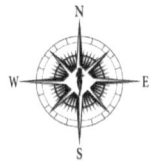

TWO

M arah Chase had the Ark of the Covenant loaded onto the back of a motorboat. She smiled and gunned the engine, racing away from the island. She felt the throttle fight back against her grip, pushing to slow down. Chase turned hard to the right, bringing the boat around the winding shoreline, and headed south, toward the mouth of the Blue Nile.

Aster Bekele stepped forward from where she'd been strapping the Ark to the plastic base they'd loaded it on. "Don't push her too hard," she said.

"It's okay, she has a safe word."

Bekele laughed, saying, "Of course," and went back to work on the straps.

Chase glanced back at her friend. Born in Gondar, to the north of the lake, Bekele worked for the Ethiopian government. But back when they first met, she'd been hired by the UN to prepare a report into shutting down the relic runners. Bekele had gone undercover in the trade to investigate, and then under the covers with Chase.

Behind them, even above the roar of the engine, they heard a gunshot.

Bekele said, "Think he's found the Holy of Holies?"

Chase nodded. "Surprised it took him this long."

Chase had a long history with Nash. He wouldn't give up, especially if he figured out she was the one who'd beaten him to the prize. Bekele lifted up one side of a plastic crate and placed it against the back end of the base the Ark was resting on. It bolted straight into place. She lifted the next piece into position and snapped it in.

She called out, "You want to have a real look before we shut it away?"

Chase turned and said, "Hell yes."

They swapped positions, with Bekele manning the controls to allow Chase to step to the back of the boat and look at the prize.

She'd hoped to have time to study it in the temple, where it had rested for close to a thousand years. But Nash had already been on the island, and they'd needed to move fast. On the trip from the temple to the boat, a slow journey with Bekele and Chase taking the weight between them, the Ark had remained covered with a dark gold cloth, and Chase had joked they were moving God's sofa. The cloth still covered the relic now. Bekele hadn't even been tempted to peek.

Chase couldn't understand that. This was history. How could she not want to look at it? Chase reached out to pull at the covering, but paused. She recalled the legends, people going blind for daring to look at the Ark. And she'd seen the eyes of the priests on the island. She told herself that was ceremonial, a tradition carried out on everyone chosen as a guard. But that small voice deep down inside said, Are you sure?

She pulled off the cover.

The Ark of the Covenant looked both exactly the way she'd imagined and completely different. It was a large wooden chest, around four feet in length. The sides were coated in a faded gold paint, or wood stain, rather than the thin gilded sheets she had expected. The lid, known as the Mercy Seat, looked to be made of pure gold. Chase had to shield her eyes when it glinted in the sunlight. Standing atop the lid were two cherubim with their wings pointing out behind them, away from the Ark. Both of them had feline bodies and four heads, matching the statues back at the temple. The faces pointing inward, toward each other, were the jackal and the lion. These animals looked a world away from the angels who adorned the Ark in most illustrations. Chase had seen similar depictions before, in a cave beneath Alexandria.

"You look like you've seen a ghost," Bekele called back.

Chase nodded but didn't answer.

She'd made a choice to help keep the cave secret and spent every day since then doubting her own decision. Had she protected history or defaced it? And now the same faces she'd seen carved out of stone in the cave were staring back at her from the Mercy Seat.

A different voice was speaking at the back of her mind now. The devil on her shoulder. It whispered for her to lift the lid. Look inside. See what had been stored in there for so long. As she reached out to touch the edge, the sun caught the gold again, and Chase was blinded for a few seconds by a flash of light.

"Speaking of ghosts," Bekele said. She pointed back toward the island, where Nash was now giving chase in his rubber boat, one hand holding the engine's tiller, the other holding a radio as he shouted instructions.

Chase started to move fast. There were three more plastic panels leaning against the hull. They formed a crate, snapping into the base the Ark was resting on. She started putting each one in place, building the transport container. She put the lid on top, then lifted long black straps off the floor that ran underneath the crate, fastening them tight over the top.

She looked back to see that Nash was getting closer.

"Why is he gaining on us?" Chase ran forward to the controls, to find Bekele had eased off slightly on the throttle.

"We don't want to flood the engine," Bekele said. "You want to explain how the Ark is at the bottom of the lake?"

"Might solve a few problems."

Bekele made an exaggerated huffing sound and pushed forward on the control, the boat gaining speed right away.

"We have a bigger engine," Chase said. "If we keep hammering, he can't catch us."

"But he can."

Chase followed the direction of Bekele's gaze. A helicopter was flying low toward them, from the direction of Bahir Dar on the south shore.

Great.

The helicopter made up the distance in a matter of seconds, buzzing low over their heads. Chase and Bekele were buffeted by the downward turbulence of the blades. There was a cargo cable hanging down from beneath the chopper, ending in a large metal hook, which whipped by only a few feet from Chase's head. A large wake ripped across the surface of the water, rocking the boat when it hit.

The pilot brought the chopper down low to the water and circled around, aiming straight for the boat. The whirlybird tilted forward as it started to move, playing chicken with them. Chase recognized the pilot. A short, stocky smuggler from the UAE named Imran.

"He can't do anything," Bekele said, "Can't risk sinking the Ark."

Sure enough, the pilot pulled up at the last second, and they were hit again by turbulence. This time, the wake was like a wave, hitting the boat head-on. The front was airborne for a second before slapping back down onto the water.

"He can slow us down," Chase said.

That would give Nash chance to catch up. He wouldn't even need to get that close. Chase knew he favored a Glock; plus, he was the best shot in the trade. Even at the top end of the gun's range, around one hundred yards, he'd stand a chance of hitting them. Any closer than that and, even with a moving target, he wouldn't miss.

Keeping one hand on the wheel, Chase stooped to open a canvas bag at her feet, pulling out a gun belt with two Ruger Blackhawks strapped into holsters on either side.

Chase preferred revolvers. There was too much to go wrong on a semi-automatic. Out in the grit and sand of a desert, or crawling through the mud of a tomb, she wanted to see the moving parts. But Chase wasn't as good a shot as Nash. By the time they were close enough for her to hit him, she and Bekele would both be dead. They needed to keep distance between the two boats.

Imran brought the chopper down again, directly in front of them, and started to rush forward, threatening a head-on collision.

Chase eased Bekele aside and placed her hands on the controls. She accelerated, pushing on headlong toward the oncoming helicopter.

Bekele winced. "No."

"Yes."

"No."

"Yes."

Imran lost the game, as Chase knew he would, swerving hard to the right. The resultant wave tipped the boat, almost flipping it over. Bekele slipped and was only just able to hold on. Chase used the controls to steady herself, her knuckles going white with the effort. The cargo cable came straight at them. Chase ducked as it smashed through the glass in front of her.

Behind them, the large crate groaned and slid, hitting the side.

Chase and Bekele shared a look.

That was close.

Two distant gunshots sounded. They both looked back to see Nash, his gun raised, firing off wasted rounds into the distance between them. He barked something into his radio, then lifted the gun and fired again. Still too far for a hit, but he'd gained ground.

The helicopter passed high overhead. Chase saw something fall from it, a small metal object. It hit the water a hundred yards ahead of them. She realized what it was and pulled the wheel hard in the opposite direction, moving clear as the water exploded upward.

"Grenades," she called out.

"But they can't risk—"

Chase looked at the crate. "Is that waterproof?"

Bekele was silent for a second, nodding before answering. "Of course. It's airtight."

"I think the rules just changed."

Another grenade fell to their left, followed by a wall of water that washed down on them, tipping the boat in the opposite direction. Chase watched as the chopper turned again to angle toward them. The pilot had the range now. Whether it was on this pass or the next, he'd get close enough to sink them.

That cargo cable . . .

She waved Bekele back to the controls. "Take over. Don't slow down, no matter what."

"What are you going to do?"

Chase brushed past her and stepped to the rear of the boat, climbing up on the crate. "Something stupid."

As the helicopter headed toward them, Chase steadied herself on the crate, focusing on the cargo line and trying not to think about what was beneath her feet. "Swing toward it," she called out.

"What?"

"Toward it. Now."

Bekele banked to the right, crossing into the path of the oncoming vehicle. The pilot must have been caught by surprise, as he hesitated, pulling back on the stick to slow down and come almost to a complete stop. The cable rattled about in the air from the sudden change in direction, then swung from side to side like a pendulum.

This is going to hurt.

She was right.

Leaping from the crate, Chase wrapped her arms around the cable but didn't get a firm grip. Sliding down, she felt the hook grab ahold of her gun belt at the buckle. The leather dug into her lower back, sending pain all the way up her spine and forcing the air out of her lungs.

She didn't have time to regain her breath before Imran either saw what she'd done or was warned by Nash. Either way, the chopper pushed out across the lake, getting lower, until her feet were in the water. Chase started to climb, puling herself up the metal cable, but now she was submerged up to her waist. The water temperature was mild, but it still came as a shock.

She grabbed one last lungful of air before she was dropped beneath the surface.

Underwater, she was pulled onward, and she closed her eyes, focusing on holding the cable, getting closer to the target she couldn't see.

Climb.

Hand. Over.

Hand.

A sharp tug upward pulled her out of the water again, as Imran climbed into the sky and weaved from side to side, trying to shake her loose. He then dipped, making Chase's stomach turn over. The water's surface rushed up at her, and this time she didn't have time to draw a deep breath before she was submerged.

Total darkness.

Chase had been scared of the dark for most of her life. It was a phobia dating back to childhood, when she'd lost her parents in a mudslide on their Washington State farm. She'd worked through it. Reasoned out the fear, banished the demons. But the lifetime of conditioning was still there, and she felt a few pangs of the old primal reaction as the darkness closed in around her.

She felt an impact behind her. The cable quivered against her body. Turning to look, she could see something large on the cable, but it was too murky to make out details.

Climb.

Move.

Pull.

Go.

Another dark shape was coming toward her. This time she could make out a Nile crocodile as it opened its jaws wide, ready to bite. Chase rolled around on the cable, ducking out of the way. This new crocodile slammed into the first one, and they both disappeared into the murk.

She couldn't see them so much as feel them, circling, waiting to attack. The years of watching shapes form into fake monsters in the dark had prepared her well for spotting the real thing.

Climb.

Move.

Pull.

Go.

The movement was on either side of her now. Two shapes barreling fast out of the murk, opening their jaws, turning onto their sides to clamp down on their meal.

The pilot pulled up. Chase was dragged clear of the water, feeling the air hit her face, the extra drag of her sodden clothes almost enough to tear her loose. The crocodiles surfaced beneath her, snapping at the air. Imran had no way of knowing, but if he'd just kept her under for a couple more seconds, his problem would have gone away.

If Nash had seen the crocs, he'd be radioing the news over now and Chase would be taking another dip. She didn't have any more time. It was only a few more feet to the bottom of the helicopter. She pulled, once, twice, three times. On the fourth, her head touched the craft's base. The chopper was motionless now, hovering over the same spot, with the creatures waiting below. Chase swung her legs out and wrapped them round the landing skids as they started to descend. She was hanging upside down when her head hit the water. The crocodiles lunged, but Chase was already moving, pulling herself up to crouch, and then stand, on the skid. One of the crocs gave up, but the other, the larger of the two, bit down onto the skid a few inches from Chase's foot.

They started to ascend again.

The reptile hung in the air, its legs moving frantically.

Chase crouched. "Let go, buddy."

Gravity was on Chase's side. The large croc fell back to the water, slapping home with a heavy splash.

Chase turned toward the passenger-side door.

Imran was already staring at her. Panicked. She figured he hadn't signed up for this. She pulled the handle and leaned in, drawing one of her guns slowly enough to let any water dribble out before he could see it.

"Water or lead?"

He stammered, looking down at the surface, then back at Chase. "But c-crocodiles . . ."

Chase cursed under her breath. All he'd done was take on a job. He had a wife, three kids, and had never done anything to hurt Chase before. She slid onto the passenger seat, keeping her Blackhawk pointed at his temple.

"Okay, take us to Nash."

He leaned right on the stick, and they turned in a large arc to head back the way they'd come. Up ahead, Nash was now dangerously close to Bekele's boat. Not quite within a hundred yards, but enough that he was trying some shots. Bekele must have slowed to watch what was happening with Chase and the chopper. She was now pressed down close over the controls, keeping out of the bullets' range.

They passed overhead once, then turned and headed back. Chase saw the bag of grenades at her feet. She picked one up, pulled the pin, and dropped it. The explosion came just off Nash's starboard bow. It was close, but not close enough.

She nodded for Imran to bring them around again. A second grenade hit the sweet spot, only a couple of meters to Nash's port side. This time his rubber boat flipped up in the blast, sending Nash tumbling into the water.

The craft righted itself again, but Nash didn't resurface.

Chase turned the gun back to Imran. "Now you have a boat." He hesitated before opening his door and stepping out into the air.

A beat later, Chase realized the flaw in her plan.

She had *no* idea how to fly a helicopter.

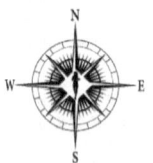

THREE

How hard could it be? It wasn't like people trained for years to become pilots, right?

There was a large T-bar control rising from a central panel between the seats. Each side of the T ended in a handgrip. Chase took the one in front of her, easing it forward. The helicopter pitched in the same direction. She pulled it back level, and the chopper did the same. There was a lever down beside her. Pulling up on it, she could feel the engine start to produce more power. The helicopter started to climb. Lowering it, she felt the opposite.

Okay.

Forward, back.

Up, down.

She was turning in a lazy circle. Easing up on the throttle increased the drift. There were two pedals on the floor in front of her seat. Chase experimented with each, pressing them forward in turn. The pedals controlled the rotor on the tail, balancing out the blades overhead, keeping her heading straight.

Chase eased into flying.

With some trial and error, she found a balance. She could turn, accelerate, and head in something approaching a straight line. The rest could wait. Bringing the helicopter around to pass over Bekele's boat, Chase saw her friend was talking into a cell phone. Preparing the next stage of the plan. There was a van waiting for them farther downriver, with a crew of local laborers ready to lift the crate off the boat without ever knowing what they'd touched. When Bekele had caught wind that Nash was after the Ark, she'd made Chase a simple offer. Come and find it first, help her keep it in the possession of the Ethiopian government, and they would let Chase be the one to claim credit for finding it. She would get to be the archaeologist who studied the Ark of the Covenant.

Chase lowered the chopper enough to draw Bekele's attention and pointed toward the river, then raised up and pushed ahead, leading the way.

Entering the Blue Nile was tricky. A small tributary covered the transition between the river and the lake, with rocks, small islands, and patches of marsh. Chase slowed down and hovered unsteadily above the river, watching to make sure Bekele navigated it safely. The boat skipped across some of the marsh and rocked a couple of times as it hit something solid. Once Bekele was past the trouble, Chase turned and pressed on.

Heading along the river, Chase started to get confident and show off. Climbing and descending, accelerating, turning in wide circles. She wanted more of this. Maybe when she got home, once all the media attention about the Ark died down, she'd take lessons.

Twenty miles south of Bahir Dar, they came to the small town of Tissisat. The river turned left, toward the famous Blue Nile Falls, a tourist hot spot that would soon be crawling with visitors. Coming up before that was a small dock and a human-made canal that met the end of Tissisat's main road. Bekele coasted along the dock and jumped out of the boat to tie up. She started talking into the phone again, and Chase watched a black transit van pull out from beneath the cover of a shack.

Phone.

Perfect.

There was a satellite phone mounted onto the dashboard. She typed in a number and waited while it rang.

"Hello?"

Half the world away, Chuy Guerrero sounded sleepy and drunk.

"Chuy."

"Chase?" The line muffled for a second; she could hear him talking to someone. "What you doing?"

"Is this a bad time?"

"No, it's okay. What you need?"

Guerrero was one of Chase's closest friends, one of the few people she really trusted. He'd been a pilot in the US Air Force before going it alone as a smuggler.

"What makes you think I need something?"

"You called."

Chase smiled. No matter how tense a situation was, she always felt better when she talked to Guerrero. "Okay. I'm wondering something. How do you land a helicopter?"

There was a pause. When Guerrero spoke again, he sounded sober. "You're asking hypothetically? You've just had the fun idea to learn to fly, and you thought you'd call your pilot friend?"

"Uh-huh."

He sighed. "You're in one right now, aren't you?"

"Uh-huh."

"In the air."

"Yup."

"And the pilot?"

"I threw him out."

"I like this plan. I'm excited to be part of it. Do you know what kind of bird you're in?"

"A blue one. Maybe silver, actually. Silver with some blue along the side."

"Talk me through what you've figured out so far."

"I have a stick in front of me that controls the forward and back direction. I have a stick down next to me that I think is a throttle, and I've got pedals that help keep me straight."

Another pause from Guerrero. "You're doing pretty well. And what's the terrain like? Is there space for you to come down without hurting anyone?"

Chase explained the location over the phone. There was farmland all around the town, but she didn't want to get out of sight of the crate. The waterfront was lined with boats, huts, and now a small crowd of people staring up at her.

Guerrero made a noise to show he was thinking, and then, "Okay. Now, I'm going to say a word in a minute that sounds bad, and I don't want you to overreact."

"Okay."

"It takes hours of flight time to get the hang of a helicopter. And I don't want to try and talk you through a landing near where people could get hurt."

". . . Okay."

"So it's easiest if I tell you how to crash."

"I lied. I'm going to overreact. I'm not happy with that word at all. I called you to *avoid* that word."

"Trust me. We'll bring you down into the water."

"Will it work?"

". . . Probably?"

Chase closed her eyes. Every time she did something stupid, she promised herself it was the last time. And she'd been in worse situations than this. She'd once ended up hanging to the outside of a plane over the Alps.

Without a parachute.

But the point of not thinking things through was not thinking about them. She could do something impulsive in the spur of the moment and let adrenaline kick in, regret it later. It was entirely different to have time to regret it in advance.

She opened her eyes and let out a long breath.

"Okay, let's do this."

"Okay." Guerrero's voice was focused. "You over the water?"

"Yeah."

"Is it calm?"

"Calmer than me. I think there's a strong current, though. And a waterfall."

"A water— Never mind. Stay over the calm water, ease off on the throttle."

Chase did as she was told, and the chopper started to descend. She rocked a little from side to side, then jolted to a stop as she followed Guerrero's instructions.

"Now keep your foot on the pedal, keep straight, and tilt forward a couple degrees."

Now the helicopter lurched forward, and Chase felt the bottom drop out of her world. As a reflex, she pulled up again on the throttle and back on the control, leveling out but climbing higher.

Guerrero said, "Did you do that?"

"I panicked and went higher again."

"Okay. Do it again, but this time, rather than climbing when you panic, I just want you to level out, don't pull the throttle back up, okay?"

Chase followed his instructions. As everything tilted, and she felt her gut start to gnaw, she leveled out.

"Now do that again."

Chase repeated the move three times, and each time the craft dropped ten feet closer to the water before leveling out. When she was within twenty feet of the surface, Guerrero said to stop and directed her into a safe hovering position.

"Here's the fun part," he said. "Down by the base of that T-bar you're holding, right down where it's attached to the controls, you'll see a red or yellow stick with a handle on top. Something you can pull up." Chase gripped it and prepared to pull.

"Don't touch it yet," Guerrero finished.

"More warning next time, Chuy."

"Let's not have a next time."

"Fair point. Okay. I see the stick."

"Open the door next to you. If you're strapped in, unbuckle yourself. Now, when I say, you're going to pull up on that stick. But I want you to take a couple deep breaths first."

"What's it do?"

"Nice and deep. In, two, three . . ."

"Chuy, what does it do?"

"Out, two, three . . . One more, deep one, in, two, three . . . hold it . . . Pull the stick up."

Chase pulled it.

The engine cut out.

Chase felt the seat trying to push up through her body, as the chopper belly flopped down onto the river, splashing through the surface and continuing to drop for a few seconds, before rising back up.

Chase made a noise like she was about to throw up and shouted, "Dammit, Chuy."

"She's going to tip," he said. "Get out the opposite—"

Chase stopped listening as the helicopter listed hard to the right. Or should she now say starboard? The water flooded in on that side, and to her left, Chase could now see the sky. She climbed up out of the seat, planting both feet on the side of the helicopter. The blades submerged as the craft rolled over, and Chase dove out as far as she could, kicking down and away, clearing the reach of the rotors as they whipped round with the roll of the sinking vessel.

She swam toward the dock, and strong arms pulled her out of the water. She rolled onto her back and coughed, drawing in ragged breaths, before looking up.

Two men in black robes stood over her. One held a sword, the other a machine gun.

They stepped back to allow Chase to get up onto her haunches, but the gun was trained on her the whole time.

Chase glanced to the black van, where two more robed figures were loading the crate into the back. Bekele was standing between the van and Chase. She was still holding the cell phone at her side. None of the robed men were pointing a weapon at her.

Chase coughed, then laughed. "I should've known."

Bekele took the few small steps to Chase's side and helped her to her feet. "I'm sorry."

"We had a deal."

Bekele turned to gesture toward the armed figures. "They changed the deal."

The two men at the van shut the door, then walked around to get in the front. The men guarding Chase lowered their weapons and paced back toward the van. One of them climbed in, while the other stood beside the door, gun pointed at the ground, making it clear he was watching what happened between Chase and Bekele.

"And who are they?" Chase gritted her teeth. "Government? Church? I swear, if you say Templars, I'm going to shoot you." Bekele offered a resigned smile. "It's complicated."

She turned and walked back to join the team in the van.

Chase stood in silence as the vehicle pulled away, leaving her alone on the dock.

MARAH CHASE IN

THE END
OF EDEN

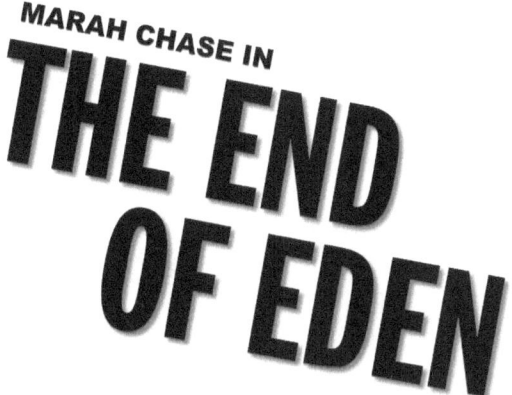

WRITTEN BY

JAY STRINGER

EDITED BY

STACIA DECKER & KATIE McGUIRE

A SWAG TALES PRODUCTION

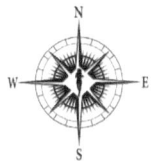

FOUR

Twelve hours, three cars, and one bath later, Chase walked into the hotel bar at the Addis Ababa Royale. She was exhausted but wired. The excitement of that morning was still overpowering the tiredness, which paced around the edges of her mind like a lion. She needed to take the edge off, to allow herself to relax into the evening.

The Royale was one of a number of hotels around the world that was friendly to the dark trades. Spies. Smugglers. Mercenaries. Relic runners. The bars of these hotels were treated as neutral ground, a place where everyone could drink together and talk shop. This hotel was one of the most important on the circuit, with Addis Ababa's position as the political and financial hub of Africa. Anyone who was anyone in the dark trades would pass through the Royale on a regular basis, looking for deals or gossip, hot tips on coming work, or updates on the latest person to be caught or killed on the job. The staff were discreet and knew how to keep the authorities away. Spooks and police would turn up to make deals or get information from the black market, but the boundaries of the bar were always respected as a safe space.

Even still, Chase paused for a moment in the doorway.

The black market was a place for misfits and outcasts. People who'd burned up their chances in the legit world, or who'd never fit in to begin with. But the community had seen some mainstream exposure in the last couple of years. Now it was a cool subculture, a target for vloggers, journalists, and lifestyle tourists looking for something edgy and mysterious. Real relic runners had to keep an eye out for people who didn't belong.

The room was full of familiar faces. Pilots, gunrunners, thieves. At least two MI6 agents, and one Mossad field operative. They all did a near-perfect job of pretending not to notice her. The reason for her hesitation was the one face staring straight at her.

August Nash was sitting in the far corner, in the deepest shadows. He raised his glass in silent greeting. His right hand stayed beneath the table.

Chase made eye contact and let him see her choose to ignore him. She headed into the center of the room, where a large circular bar was lit up by lights hanging down from above.

She smiled a greeting at the bartender. "Hi, Doc."

He returned the smile. "Good to see you."

Doc was Hassan Dalmer, Hass to most people. He was a muscular Somalian with a shaved head and a habit of wearing vests or T-shirts that were a size too small. Chase had dubbed him Doc ten years ago, when they met in the field. With his strong physique, and his need to show it off, Chase had said he looked like Doc Savage and refused to let the idea die. He'd been a good relic runner. In better shape than just about everyone else in the field, and with a knack for languages, he had a head start on most. He'd come from academia, the same as Chase, but whereas she'd managed to swallow down her guilt over selling history off to the highest bidder, he hadn't. Hass firmly believed what he was doing was a modern form of colonialism, and it held him back in the field. Caused him to second-guess, hesitate at key moments. He'd retired from the game after a couple of close calls and found steady work as a barman in the network of hotels and bars that supported the black market.

"How's your mom doing?" Chase asked.

Hass shrugged, noncommittal. Chase knew to let that one go. Until recently, Hass had been working in New York, at a bar owned by another of Chase's old friends. He'd moved to Addis Ababa to be closer to his family. They'd disowned him years ago, when he first came out as trans and began presenting as male. They didn't like his "choices," but they were old and sick now, and Hass wanted to patch things up. Clearly, it wasn't going well.

He leaned forward across the bar to speak in a low voice. "Everyone's been talking."

His accent was a weird mix of all the places he'd been. Chase knew it annoyed him to have lost his original Somalian inflection.

"In detail?"

"Some. Sounds like you've had a rough day." He lifted a glass. "The usual?"

Chase sighed, letting him hear a full day of frustration. "Why not?"

Hass poured her a large measure of bourbon from the array of amber options behind him. Without looking over at Nash, he said, "He's been asking about you. Wanted to know if you were here."

Chase downed the drink and handed the glass across for a refill. Doc poured it for her and said, "Are we going to have trouble?"

"I hope not."

She turned to look at Nash again. His eyes were still fixed on her. He flashed a smile, but there was no warmth behind it. He used his foot to push out the empty chair across from him, waving for Chase to join him.

She walked over, noticing that his right hand was still under the table.

"Hass's worried you want to shoot me," she said, without sitting down.

Nash leaned back and smiled again. This time there was a genuine emotion in it, something like victory. He lifted his right hand into a Vulcan salute before patting the tabletop. The volume in the room went down a few notches. Just enough for both Chase and Nash to know everyone had half an ear on their conversation.

Nash raised his drink again in a toast. "To the winner," he said loudly. "Wherever she is."

Chase sat down. "So you heard."

"The rumor. Whoever hired her, they got their money's worth."

He leaned on the whoever hired her. Fishing. Hoping Chase would fill in the blanks on the office gossip. Who had paid for them to go after the Ark?

Where was it now? Could it be stolen?

Chase ignored the opening. "How's Imran?"

"He's pissed. Still trying to figure out how to get a helicopter out of the river. That, by the way"—he raised the glass again, already into the toasting- every-thought stage of drunk—"was one of the craziest things I've ever seen."

"It's all in the reflexes." Chase paused, letting him smile before throwing his own trick back at him. "I bet whoever hired you wants a refund."

"I was doing this on my own dime." He stretched, both arms out on either side, then lowered his right arm back beneath the table. "Retirement fund."

Chase laughed at that, pretending to relax into her seat and signaling for Hass to bring more drinks. She let Nash see her own right hand slip beneath the table to her thigh. There was no gun there. She'd left her weapons upstairs in the room. But Nash didn't need to know that, and if he was going to play games, so could she.

They watched each other in silence as Hass brought fresh drinks, setting them down on the table and giving both Chase and Nash a warning look.

"I'm serious," Nash said. "We're getting old, kid."

"You've got ten years on me."

"When I was at my best, you'd never have done me like that." He looked genuinely weary for a moment. "And don't pretend you're not feeling it, too."

Chase didn't answer. She wasn't going to give him the benefit of being right, but the thought had been eating at her all day. Five years ago, there was no way she would have let Bekele trick her.

Nash grinned, reading her silence. "See? And some of us can't go all Hollywood."

Hollywood.

Chase was the main reason relic running had gained mainstream attention. After helping to foil a terrorist attack on London two years before, she had used the goodwill to restore her academic reputation with the discovery of a Mithraeum in Alexandria. This had come with a book deal and television documentary, and a host of journalists wanting to talk to her about this new subculture they'd discovered. Chase knew there was resentment among the runners. Some saw her as a sellout; others saw her as a tourist, choosing when to live the life and when to be safe from it. But the truth was that this life was in her blood, and she couldn't stay away.

"You could maybe set some of us up," Nash said. "Help out. Send the elevator back down—isn't that what they say?"

"What would you do with it? Meetings with producers? Playing nice to people who don't really have a clue what you've been through? You're jealous for a thing you wouldn't even want." Chase downed her drink, made a show of yawning. "Anyway, it was good seeing you, August." She stood up. "Better luck next time."

"Hang on." Nash put his hand out, asking for more time. "Did you see it? Did you get to see it?"

Chase glanced around the room. Nobody else was looking her way, but she knew she was answering all of them.

"Yes."

"What was it like?"

Chase thought it over. How best to explain it?

"It was history," she said with a smile.

She held back her real thoughts. Questions about the nature of the Ark. About how the faces of the cherubim could so closely match statues she'd found in Alexandria. Of an impossible link.

Turning on her heel, she strode out of the bar and across the lobby to the elevator. She could feel all eyes on her back as she left. She leaned against the inside of the elevator as she rode up to the eighth floor, feeling the energy draining away now. The alcohol had done the trick. And maybe talking to Nash had helped, added a sense of closure to the day. The elevator slowed, and Chase rocked on her feet as it came to a stop on her floor. She stepped out and walked down the hallway. She always stayed in the same room here, one near the fire escape. For as long as she could remember, she made sure to know more than one way out of every room or building. Even now, in her apartment in New York, she had a bag packed beneath the window, just in case.

She slipped her electronic key card out of her pocket and let herself into the room.

The lights were on.

Bekele was perched on the end of the bed. She was barefoot, her sandals lying on the floor. She was dressed in blue jeans and a black blazer, opened to show a blue bralette.

Chase played it cool. She wasn't going to let Bekele see either her surprise or her interest. And she knew if she bluffed it for a few seconds, her anger would take over. She paced over to the bed.

"You've got nerve."

Bekele shuffled forward, staying calm and trying to show she wasn't there to argue. "I'm sorry," she said. "I really didn't have a choice."

"Sure you did. You could've not done it. Or, you could've just called your friends to begin with, get them to do all the hard work."

Bekele's face scrunched up. "I did call a friend. I knew you'd get it done."

"And then you handed it over to them."

Bekele sighed. She deflated as the anger passed. "I know. Look, I . . . I tried contacting them first, to tell them the Ark was in danger, to ask where it was, so we could secure it. But trust doesn't come easy here. You have to understand it, the church, they've been here so long. They see regimes come and go. Haile Selassie. The communists. The Eritrean war. The modern state. Every new era comes with people who would use the Ark for their own gain. The church, the way they see it, they're not just protecting the Ark from outsiders; they're protecting it from Ethiopia. They didn't believe me or trust me. "

"You used me to get to them."

"No, I . . ." Bekele paused, sighed again, nodded. "Maybe."

"How long have you known about it? That it was here?"

Bekele shrugged. "Everybody knew the legends."

"No, you wouldn't mobilize like that over a legend. There's more to it. When you heard Nash was in the country, you took it seriously enough to contact me, reach out to your friends in black robes. You knew it was here and that he might find it."

Bekele stood up and turned to walk away from Chase, over to the window. She let her jacket slip from her shoulders and draped it on a chair. She pulled the curtains apart enough to look out onto the city.

"I always knew, I think. When you work with the right people here, in the government, or the NISS, there's always something in the way people act when the Ark is mentioned. It's a certainty. Almost just a normal thing. So, I suppose I just believed."

Chase stepped in behind Bekele to share the view over her shoulder. "And when you heard Nash was after it . . ."

"I knew Nash could find it, and he'd take it out of the country. Away from us. And I knew you'd be able to find it, too. If anyone could, it would be you."

"Which brings us back to how you used me." Chase pulled on the strap to Bekele's bralette. "So who are they?"

Bekele tensed. "It's complicated."

Chase let go of the strap, taking satisfaction at the noise it made as it snapped back into place. Chase started to move away. Bekele turned and took her arm, gently but firmly.

"I meant my offer," she said. "And I still do. The Ark belongs here. It's ours. But the world needs to know. The longer it's hidden, the more people like Nash will come looking. But once everyone knows it's here, the politics will start. Israel. Rome. The fundamentalists in your country. They'll all demand it."

Chase sighed, nodded. "It's complicated."

"But if I can convince them to announce what we have, to keep it safe here, then I think I can get them to let you study it, to say that you're the one who found it. You get the glory."

She slipped her hands under the labels of Chase's jacket and pushed it back off her shoulders. Chase didn't move, letting Bekele guide the jacket off her and down to the floor.

Bekele ran her hand over the tattoos on Chase's upper arm. "You've got some new ones."

"Each one is a story."

Bekele stepped in close, sliding one hand each into the back pockets of Chase's jeans, pulling her forward. "I am sorry for the way things went. But your flight isn't until tomorrow. Maybe I can make it up to you?"

Chase let her see the beginnings of a smile.

"You can try."

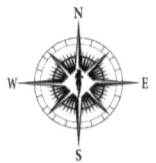

FIVE

Nash stared into the bottom of his glass.

There was a film he'd seen as a boy. A scene where the hero drained a beer, only to find a message written in the bottom. You have just been poisoned. Nash thought of that every time he saw the bottom of a glass come into view. How would he respond? He couldn't remember what the guy in the film did. Nash always suspected, if it was him, he'd probably just order the same again.

And hadn't today been just like that?

Get to the end and find a metaphorical note from Marah Chase. *Beat you to it.*

And of course, it would be her.

How long had he been looking for the Ark? It was impossible to put a number on it. There were the two months he'd spent actively following the latest trail, finding the map and putting it together with the legends. There were the three years he'd spent researching it, earning a reputation as one of the go-to guys on the topic. And then there was the entire lifetime spent thinking about it.

And then she stepped in at the last minute.

He patted his thigh, where the imaginary gun had rested during their conversation. Would things have gone differently if they weren't in the Royale? And would things go differently next time they saw each other, in whatever dirty backwater town they found themselves in? Technically, the neutral ground was only the bar. There was nothing stopping him going up to Chase's room, putting two rounds in her, walking away.

But what would that solve, really?

Nash held up his empty glass for Hass to see. A signal he wanted another. The barman came over with a glass bottle of water and two tumblers.

Nash knew Hass never touched alcohol himself. It was his personal take on Islam, in which God looked the other way on the things he'd done to earn a living, and was completely accepting of some pretty big changes Hass made in his life, but would still insist on him staying sober.

Nash couldn't judge. In both the military and the CIA, he'd seen people making similar deals with their higher powers on a daily basis. Forming their own private version of religion, one that accepted the things they needed to do but gave the comfort and support in the darker moments.

He thought of the last job he did for the agency. He remembered the desert heat. The dry air in his mouth. The feel of the gun in his hand, sweat finding the cracks between skin and metal. His target, right in front of him, begging to stay alive.

The moment Nash knew he needed to quit.

He was snapped back to the present as Hass settled into the vacant seat, filling both tumblers and passing one across to Nash.

"Hitting it pretty hard," Hass said.

Nash blinked, looked at the empty liquor glass. "Just getting started."

Nash's fingers trembled. The first sign of an old problem. Something he hadn't felt in years. He balled his hand into a fist to cover the twitch.

Hass sipped the water and waited a few seconds before saying, "A friend once said to me, never go to bed drunk after a bad job. You don't want a hangover the next day. Go to bed sober, so you wake up fresh and ready to do better."

"Your friend sounds like an asshole."

"I agree." Hass smiled, leaned in close. "But if anyone else calls you an asshole, I'll kill them."

"And when did I give you that nugget of wisdom?"

Nash was just being stubborn for the fun of it now. He well remembered giving that advice. It was something he'd said many times over the years, and he'd stuck to it—until recently. Another sign he was losing his edge.

"My last night on the job," Hass said. "Right after I limped into the bar in Tokyo with a sprained ankle and two cracked ribs, out several thousand dollars from the job I'd just failed at."

"Chase beat you, too?"

Hass grinned. "No, you did."

"I beat you to the prize, then gave you, a guy who doesn't drink, a pep talk about staying sober? I really am an asshole."

"I woke up the next day in a load of pain, thinking maybe my first-ever hangover would've been a good distraction from all of it. But your point was still right. I got up, decided I could be better, and got on with my life."

Nash turned the empty liquor glass around in circles on the table, ignoring the water. "And how do I do better, Hass? It was the Ark. I was so close. Ten minutes earlier, and it would've been mine. That's the greatest prize. That's it, right there. The whole game. And I missed it. How do I get up tomorrow and decide to do better?"

"Maybe you've always wanted to learn to ice-skate?"

Hass held a straight face long enough for Nash to crack, and they both laughed.

"I've always wanted to learn how to wrap a burrito the right way," Nash said. "Everyone else can do it. I mess it up. The ends flop open, or I just get this mushy mess that looks like a box."

"There you go, my friend. Ambition."

Nash picked up the water and toasted—"To big dreams"—before knocking it back. "I think you might be right about the other thing, too. Maybe it's time to get out, find something else."

Hass put on a frown for show. "You want to steal my job behind the bar? Wasn't bad enough you beat me in the field, now you want to do this?" This time Hass couldn't hold the straight face. "Seriously, though," he continued. "Chase got there first? So what? The two of you are the best at this. Messi and Ronaldo. Today, she got there. On another day, you'd get there and I'd be having this conversation with her. The time to worry is if either of you start being beat by any of the other jamokes in this room."

He let his voice rise at the end, for everyone listening in to hear. They all went back to their own conversations, pretending they hadn't been eavesdropping. The usual low rumble of chatter that had quieted down when Chase walked in finally returned.

"You ever miss it?" Nash poured himself another glass of water, then did the same for Hass. "The job?"

"Sometimes. I miss the successes. And the adrenaline. Not much excitement in lumping barrels and cleaning pipes. But I don't miss the traveling, or the time wasted."

Nash offered another toast. "To time wasted."

Hass's face darkened. "Is it true? Bakari and Romain?"

Nash ran his upper teeth across his lower lip for a moment before answering. "Yeah. Booby traps."

"Only, I know you had Imran in on it, and his chopper wouldn't have had room for all four of you with the Ark. So I was just wondering . . ." Hass's words dried up.

Nash guessed he didn't want to ask the question.

"Remember the time we were both in Syria?" Hass asked instead.

"Sure."

"I only went in once." Hass smiled, but it looked fake. "Not enough jungle. But I got caught, pinned between the government and the insurgents, and then mercenaries, the ones pretending to be Islamists? They would've killed me for sure; they'd heard about what I am." "I remember," Nash said.

"And then a friend showed up, wasn't even working the same job as me, there for a different reason. And he dropped what he was working on to help me, make sure I got out alive."

"Sounds like a real hero."

"Same friend who gave me advice about going to bed sober."

Nash nodded and smiled. He knew where this was going. The message Hass was working his way up to, like some wise man in a movie.

"Job's mean," Hass said. "Cruel. But doesn't mean we have to be."

Nash smiled. "The gig in Tokyo, when I gave you that pep talk? I knew you were there ahead of me. Gave your details to some guys I owed money to, said Interpol had a warrant on you, there'd be a reward." Nash paused. Watched the smile disappear from Hass's face. "You got beat up bad, and I got the prize." He stood to leave, putting his hand on Hass's shoulder as he walked by. "Stop confusing me for a nice guy."

He headed out of the bar feeling wobbly on his feet but a little clearer of mind. There was one element of his friend's advice he was going to take. He wanted to hit the pillow with a clear head. But after putting away so much booze, he was going to need to burn it all off to sober up. Maybe getting laid would ease his mind. Fortunately, he knew of several establishments within walking distance where he could do just that.

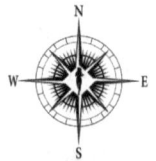

SIX

The walls were shaking. The bed moved a foot across the room. Hass gripped the woman who was grinding away on top of him and said, "Is the earth moving for you, too?"

The woman, Freema Nkya, laughed as she placed her palms on his chest, steadying herself. "Scared?"

They kept going as the tremor faded around them. Hass had been tired and ready for bed at the end of his shift. But he was never too tired to drop everything when Freema walked into his life and, really, who was ever too tired for this? He and Freema went back a long way. Best friends at school, and best friends with benefits as adults. She taught at Banaadir University in Somalia and called Hass whenever she was passing through on business.

They rocked in rhythm, bringing each other close. Hass finished first, then made up for it by helping Freema get there. They lay in bed afterward, catching their breaths and listening to the chaos outside. Car alarms were going off all across the city.

"Guess that's why you're in town?" Hass said, between deep breaths.

Freema was a seismologist. She got up off the bed and walked to the window. Hass watched her naked silhouette against the night sky.

"This was just a tremor," she said. "I think the big one is coming."

Hass smiled. "I think something big just did."

Freema turned back to look at him. "Big?"

"Hey."

Hass watched the lines around her fake smile. She was playing along well enough, but he could tell something was worrying at her.

Her cell rang, and he passed it across from beside the bed, then slipped into the bathroom while she talked. He cleaned himself up and waited until Freema stopped talking before stepping back out into the bedroom.

Freema was picking up her clothes off the floor. Her whole demeanor had changed. She'd already been serious, but now she was looking rushed.

"What's up?" Hass asked.

"They're calling me in. That one has them worried. Erta Ale has spiked; they think she could blow for real."

Erta Ale was an active volcano to the north of the country. It was permanently active, with a lava lake at the summit. Everyone had learned to live with the volcano. It was a tourist attraction. But the volcanic activity had been increasing lately, filling the sky with clouds of ash and smoke that could sometimes be seen even from here, three hundred and fifty miles southwest.

"When you say blow . . ."

"They don't know how big it could be."

"But why do they need you?"

She carried her clothes in a bundle to the bathroom, leaving the door ajar to keep talking. "It's not just the volcano. We're worried about the rift."

"So when you say big one . . ."

Freema poked her head back out and nodded. "Exactly."

Everyone in the region knew the deal. Ethiopia was sitting on top of the Great Rift Valley. Africa was split across two tectonic plates, and they were slowly pulling apart. Erta Ale was at the tip of the rift. But the process was slow. Scientists said it could take another ten million years for the two plates to separate.

Earthquakes were a fact of life when you lived here. Hass had experienced several. But he'd never given thought to something of the scale Freema seemed to be talking about. When he'd been living in California, he'd had friends there who said they didn't worry about "the big one," but it only ever took a couple of minutes for Hass to peel away at that and make his friends realize how scared they were, all the time, of the San Andreas Fault.

"How big are we talking? San Andreas?"

"We don't know. And . . ." He heard a sigh. She opened the bathroom door, half dressed. "I can't really put this into—"

"Stupid."

Freema grinned. "Well, maybe that I can do. You're comparing it to San Andreas, but they don't match. Different kinds of quake." She put her hands together. "San Andreas is two plates side by side, rubbing against each other." She mimicked the motion. "It's long overdue, and it'll be bad when it happens, but not as bad as people think. Los Angeles has been preparing for it. The biggest threat in America is farther north, the Pacific Northwest, where one plate is being pushed under the other." She showed what she meant, sliding one hand over the other. "It's called subduction, and that's the worst kind of quake. That's what happened off the coast of Chile in 1960, for the biggest quake in recorded history, and the American one is due to go anytime in the next fifty years. But here we have two plates moving in opposite directions." She pulled her hands apart. "With some land sinking in the middle, as support goes. The big one in California will probably be an eight on the Richter scale. California could move. But we don't think it will go up to a Richter nine. Only subduction earthquakes have ever done that, that we know of."

"Like the Pacific Northwest."

"If and when that goes, it could be above a nine. It could be the largest ever recorded and would be followed by a tsunami that would wipe out Seattle. And that's before we think of the five active volcanoes they have in Washington State. The activity would trigger one or all of them."

Hass nodded. "Okay, avoid Washington for the next fifty years."

Then he thought, Isn't that where Chase's family is? Maybe she could call them . . .

Freema continued. "Here, as the plates drift apart and the land caught in the middle sinks, eventually the valley will drop beneath sea level and form a new ocean basin. Up until now, we thought this process would be very slow, millions of years, and the highest quake we were at risk of was a seven."

"But now?"

Freema spread her arms wide: Who knows? "We need new theories. None of the data is making sense. We're experiencing movement that should be taking hundreds of thousands of years. The seismic activity is much higher than anything we had anticipated."

"How much higher?"

"The big one."

"Maybe time I took a vacation," Hass said, slipping into his briefs.

"Of course." Freema shut the door. "The Cowboy's answer to everything."

It seemed to be Hass's curse that everyone gave him nicknames. No matter how hard he'd worked to assert his own identity, people still wanted to choose new ones for him. He let Freema get away with it, just like he allowed Marah Chase to call him Doc. But whenever anyone else tried, he corrected them, politely at first, directly if needed, that his name was Hassan. Hass was acceptable.

In Freema's eyes, he was the Cowboy because of his accent. He'd been lucky enough to earn a scholarship to an American college. While he was over there, first at Michigan and then at Berkeley, he'd changed the way he talked. Not just the dialect but the cadence, the sentence structure. He found he now thought differently, his brain somehow shaped by his hybrid accent, and he sounded like an American actor playing a Somalian in a movie. Hass didn't like it. Above all else, he was Somalian, and proud of it. But when he tried to revert to his original accent, he sounded like a fake.

It gave his family cover to distance themselves from him. They knew better now than to judge his transition. Outwardly, they accepted him as a man. But his accent, his "Western" style, gave them an excuse to complain about his choices and to keep him at arm's length.

Freema still spoke the same way she had when they were young. For all her travels, and though she was the first to admit she didn't feel any real link to her home country, she'd kept hold of whatever it was Hass had lost. And the real kicker was that she wasn't even really Somalian. Ethnically she was Chaga, from southern Tanzania, where her family had grown coffee on the southern slope of Kilimanjaro. The coffee money had paid for her father to go to university, and that, in turn, had led to a teaching job in Somalia. The move had come when Freema was still a baby, but she'd never quite taken to seeing Somalia as her home. And yet, she still sounded authentic, and she knew it drove Hass crazy.

"Well," Hass said, finding his shirt, "if you're telling me this whole place is about to split right open, I think maybe I should go somewhere with no chance of a quake. Like California."

"It might be a false alarm." Freema was a terrible liar. "But maybe you should get your old job back." She opened the bathroom door, fully dressed now in the business suit she'd been wearing when she'd dropped by the Royale bar. She was messing with her conference badge, trying to get it to stick to her jacket's lapel. "I liked visiting you in New York."

Hass helped her fix the badge, then slipped his hands round behind her, cupping her butt and easing her gently to him. "How urgently do they need to see you?"

"I'm telling you the world might be about to end, and you want sex?"

"You could tell me the universe was about to end and I'd want sex."

"They're sending a car."

"The driver will wait."

"Hass . . ."

"They already know the tremor happened. Another fifteen minutes won't hurt."

"That's romantic."

They kissed. It was easy. Comfortable. The two of them had always felt right together. Somehow, that had never been enough to make anything permanent. Hass couldn't explain it. What he did know was that this was good, for right now, in this room. And they'd be good again, in whatever the next room was.

He could feel her breathing pick up beneath his touch.

"If I wasn't in a romantic mood," he said, "I would have said five minutes."

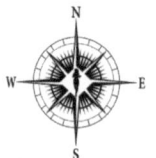

SEVEN

C hase stayed in her seat long after the crew had opened the door at LaGuardia. There was no rush. After eighteen hours in the air, broken up with layovers in Germany and DC, she had already lost a whole day to traveling. An extra five minutes wouldn't hurt. Especially now that the doors were open and real air was filling the cabin. This flight had been warm and stuffy, recycled air filling her lungs. She pushed back into the seat and watched everyone jostling for place. Grabbing their overhead luggage, hitting each other in the backs and heads, stepping into small spaces for some imagined advantage. And then standing there, waiting, until they were allowed to start shuffling forward toward the exit.

Chase watched the cabin crew thanking the passengers as they went by. One of the attendants was hot. A redhead who knew how to wear the uniform. She'd smiled at Chase a couple of times during the trip. It had felt like the right kind of smile, but with such a short flight from DC to New York, there hadn't been time to find out.

Chase closed her eyes, thinking about dinner plans. Was it even dinnertime? Flying back to the US from Africa or Europe was always difficult. Traveling back in time. She'd spent more than twenty-four hours traveling, but where were those hours now? This had been her life for too long. Planes, cars, trains, boats. Time zones. Spending hours in the air that were wiped out of existence upon landing, only to reappear on the return trip.

As the last of the passengers disappeared from view at the front, Chase stood up and stretched. She took her battered messenger bag down from the overhead bin, shouldered it, and headed toward the door. The hot attendant smiled at her on the way past and said, "Welcome home," and Chase hesitated for a second, wondering if it was worth finally ticking one fantasy off the list.

But tiredness and hunger kicked in, so she smiled in return and stepped out onto the jetway. She headed up the ramp and out into the airport, then crossed the hall into the bathroom. Setting her bag down next to the sink, she pulled out her toiletries and brushed her teeth before spraying some cheap deodorant and applying fresh lip balm. Home was only a cab ride away, but she felt stale and dry after breathing processed air for so long.

She stared at herself in the mirror, thinking of Nash's words from the bar. "We're getting old, kid."

Well, Nash had a head start. He'd always carried himself that way. Wanting to be older, to show off his extra experience. But now it felt like he was right. The years were adding up. Or the mileage. Or both.

Chase gathered her things together, pulling a scarf out of the bag. It would come in handy on the ride home, wrapped around the bottom half of her head. A trick she'd learned. Fewer people try to talk to you if your mouth is hidden.

Chase didn't need to go by baggage claim. She'd left her suitcase in Ethiopia. The clothes had all been bought especially for the trip. The guns, and the leather belt she carried them on, were the only things she'd hesitated over. She could have arranged to have them shipped by the Royale. But what was the point? Maybe she didn't need them anymore.

Chase's thoughts cleared. Her field instincts kicked in. Something was wrong. She'd seen something, without seeing it. She slowed down and took a look around.

There was no crowd coming through, no line. Chase must have hit a rare quiet spot between flights. The last of the stragglers from her plane were up ahead, pausing to look down at their phones. Off to her right, she could see a few people sitting on benches, reading books, drinking coffee. A cleaner was walking by, dragging a plastic mop bucket on wheels.

But there was someone else, too.

Someone who was looking for her.

He was a tall man, with blond hair and broad shoulders. He looked strong. Chase read him as trouble, as someone with the capacity to start trouble. But he was dressed in a suit, more chauffeur than executive, and there was an anxious look to his stance, like he knew he'd messed up. He was standing beside Chase, half turned away, scanning the other people. He held a sign down at his side, but it was facing toward Chase and she could see a name written on it.

Her name.

Well, a version of it.

Mara Chase. They'd missed the h, but she was used to that. Just like she was used to people mispronouncing it. *Mar-a,* as if her name was Irish, rather than Ma-Rah, the way her mother pronounced the Hebrew.

The stranger had been waiting for her, expecting she would be in the crowd coming straight off the flight. He hadn't counted on her hanging back. She had only a few seconds to decide what to do before he turned back this way for another look.

Who was he?

She wasn't expecting anyone to meet her. And who knew she'd been on that flight? Chase made her decision. She wasn't stopping to find out what this was about. If someone wanted to talk with her, they could pick up the phone. And she'd just flown halfway across the globe, in three metal tubes. No way was she stopping to talk to anyone now.

She tied the scarf into place, like a bandanna, and tilted her head down to avoid anyone's eye contact. She pressed on. As the big man turned slowly back toward her, she moved the other way, aiming past his far shoulder and passing behind him. She moved fast, but not fast enough to draw attention. Through the automatic doors, and out into the New York air, she turned toward the taxi stand. The wait there was always the opposite of what she expected. If she was in a rush, there would be a line back to the door. If she had all the time in the world, there would be only a person or two waiting there. Today, the gods of convenient getaway were smiling. There was only one other person ahead of her, an elderly woman who was already getting into a cab. Chase sent up a prayer to whoever and slipped into the back of the next cab in line.

The ride over to the Upper West Side took a shade over thirty minutes. Everything was falling right, and Chase started to get a good feeling about the thoughts she'd been having on the flight over. The decision she hadn't voiced out loud yet, because saying it would make the whole thing real.

She climbed the stairs to her fourth-floor walk-up on West Eightieth, behind the Museum of Natural History. Usually, she felt each step and cursed having bought a place so high up. Today, she felt lighter as she climbed, weight dropping off her back, stress falling away from her joints. She fumbled for her keys in an outside compartment on the messenger bag and then let herself into the apartment.

It was small, but much larger than other places she'd looked at before buying. She had a main living room, with a kitchen area along one wall, and a bedroom separated off by two sliding wooden doors. The bathroom wasn't much larger than a closet, but the shower had proved big enough for two people. The bedroom had stretched her budget, but the investment had been worth it to establish a home here, ready for her new life.

New life.

Chase laughed, looking around at the boxes. Books, clothes. Even furniture that she'd bought and never gotten around to building. She had a small sofa, a TV, and a coffee table piled with books and magazines. The bedroom was in a similar state, suitcases arranged around the bed, with an ongoing filing system of clean and dirty clothes.

New life.

There was a job waiting at the Museum of Natural History, working on a special exhibit they were putting together about Cleopatra. Chase was supposed to be working with a Puerto Rican archaeologist who was looking for the ancient queen's tomb, just outside Alexandria. TV companies had made several documentaries about the dig, and the museum wanted to be ready to roll out a world-exclusive exhibition the minute news broke of them finding the tomb. And for once, Chase was supposed to be the desk worker in all of this, being the point of contact in the States. It had become almost a running joke. Every time she came home and started to prepare for the job, she would get offered a relic-running gig and ask the museum to wait a little bit longer. Chase knew they were trading to some degree on her reputation, using her involvement as a marketing gimmick. There was only one Marah Chase. They couldn't go out and find another, and this gave her a lot of leeway. But fame hadn't been her choice. She would have much rather stayed anonymous. When the Guardian journalist tracked Chase down, bringing the relic-running community into the mainstream, her life had changed forever. And she felt no guilt in using whatever perks came her way. Book deals? Hollywood options? Sure. Enough money to buy a place in Manhattan? Bring it on. A dream job at the museum? Hell yes.

But now, living like this, none of it really felt worth it. All the hassle. All the intrusion on her private life. Total strangers feeling like they owned a piece of her. Chase would trade back all the benefits of her new life in a heartbeat to be able to return to how things used to be. But until someone invented time travel, she was happy to trade on her own reputation just as much as the museum, and make them wait. Still, she was aware that their kindness was a limited resource, and they were running low.

She sat down on the sofa and stretched out, sighing, making a show for nobody in particular. There was a pair of cycling gloves on the cushion next to her. They belonged to Dani the Dominican, a bike messenger Chase liked to fool around with when she was in town. The last few times had started to get weird. A familiar tension had been there, underneath the fun. Chase could tell Dani was having those thoughts. The what-are-we-doing?

thoughts. They always got in the way eventually.

Maybe it was time . . .

"I'm done."

Out loud, just like that. The thing she'd been scared to say. This was it. The black market could eat a person alive. The longer you stay in the game, the shorter the odds get on getting hurt, imprisoned, or killed. Chase knew she was already pushing her luck. Fate had handed her a way out two years ago, and she'd only half taken it. This apartment was a monument to having one foot out the door. And there was no topping the Ark of the Covenant. Or finding a Mithraeum in Alexandria. She'd moved here to set up a new life. It was time to get on with doing it.

She heard movement out in the hallway, and then someone knocked on the door.

Nobody had tried the buzzer. Must be a neighbor, come to check who was making noise in the apartment, see if it was a burglar, maybe. The co-op board had liked the idea of a celebrity living in the building and loved having someone from the museum. But then one of them must have learned how to use a search engine, because they'd started prying into her private life, her comings and goings. The retired teacher from 4D always somehow managed to be waiting out in the hall when Chase opened the door, ready with questions about Chase's girlfriends, trying to invite herself in for a coffee. Before living in the city, Chase had thought Kramer from Seinfeld was unrealistic. Now she knew he was toned down.

Chase sighed again as she stood up, crossing over to the door. She opened it without checking the peephole.

The hot redhead flight attendant smiled at her with ruby lips. "Hi."

Chase's head swirled with appropriate questions, but all she managed to say was "Uh."

Red leaned forward. "I was hoping you'd come with us."

Chase took a step back at that. "Us?"

The chauffeur from the airport stepped into view. He moved fast, setting his foot across the threshold. Chase knew she was already too late to slam the door. Up close, the guy looked like an overdeveloped teenager.

"You slipped out past me," he said.

"We're friends," Red explained, leaning against the doorframe. "I realize he spelled your name wrong. I'm sorry about that. So is he. But we'd both like you to come with us."

"I don't think so."

Chase was backing up. Looking for something heavy.

There were weapons in her bag, if she could get to it.

"Five thousand," Red said.

Chase paused. "What?"

"Dollars. Five thousand dollars, for an hour of your time. Actually . . ." Red looked up at Blondie, nodded at whatever thought she'd just had. "Two hours, in case traffic is bad."

EIGHT

N ash had really run with Hass's advice. He'd spent a whole night screwing and gambling away his drunk, but then found he wasn't enjoying either of them as much without booze. He added it back into the mix and simply avoided going to bed, finally crashing the following evening after the casino had both cleaned him out and sobered him up.

After a long sleep and a large meal, he settled his bill at the Royale and thought about the next part of the advice. Face the next day ready to do better.

He wasn't ready to quit. He just needed to find the next thing. Let Chase have this one. He'd find something bigger. Something better. He had no idea what it was yet, but he knew it was out there waiting for him, somewhere just beyond the door.

He shouldered his bag and turned to leave.

"I hear you had a bad day."

The voice was low and laid-back. An Italian accent wrapped up in a slow purr. Nash turned to see Francisco Conte leaning against the wall beside the check-in desk. For as long as Nash had been a relic runner, Conte had been a fixture on the circuit. He was a raven, specializing in collecting and trading information. He was a small man, short and lean, with a taste for sharp suits and, preferably, an expensive overcoat. Rumors had him as everything from a retired spy to a reformed Mafia fixer. On the circuit, he was trusted to be neutral, cleaning up problems and enforcing the peace at the Royale.

He often oversaw the deals and transactions, providing escrow services and safe storage for the artifacts until both parties were satisfied.

Nobody knew the details of his deal with the Royale's owners. Did he work for them? Or was he just a convenient presence? Either way, he seemed to have office space at every hotel in the chain.

Conte stepped away from the wall. He never did anything in a hurry.

"Had a pretty good day yesterday," Nash said.

"Could I have a moment of your time, Mr. Nash?"

"August."

Conte moved his head less than an inch, the barest impression of a nod. "August. Could I buy you a drink?"

To anybody else, Nash would have said, "Can it wait? I'm beat." Or made an excuse, a reason to ditch out. But Conte wasn't anybody else. When he spoke, you listened; when he asked, you gave.

Nash said sure and started to turn toward the bar.

Conte gave another of his tiny head movements. "Come with me."

The Italian led the way across the lobby, pushing through a door and down a flight of stairs. Through another door, they came to a room that was lit the same as the lobby, decorated with low wooden furniture and a large screen on the far wall.

Conte held the door open for Nash. "Prego, entra pure." He touched an intercom on the wall and asked for two espressos, before gesturing for Nash to sit down. Nash settled into a chair beside a coffee table, and Conte sat across from him on a sofa, leaning back into the folds of leather.

"I heard your day yesterday was far better than the one before. Great run of luck at the table, right until the end."

"That's how they get you."

"It is." Conte paused. Tilted his head. "The Ark of the Covenant. That's a hell of a find. A hell of a find."

"So I'm told," Nash said. "I didn't find it."

A faint smile. "Yes. Chase. You have my sympathies." When Nash didn't answer, Conte continued. "We've always wondered what would happen when you went head-to-head. It's surprising it hasn't happened until now."

It's happened plenty of times, Nash thought. He and Chase had worked the same jobs before, for much smaller prizes. Sometimes she won; sometimes he did. They'd just never done it as visibly, and with such high stakes, as with the Ark. It had never felt personal until now.

Was Conte deliberately rubbing salt in Nash's wound?

The Italian asked, "The two of you were close once?"

Nash knew the question was just for show. Conte always knew more than he let on.

"When she first started." Nash played along for his host. "She was green. I showed her the ropes, introduced her to people. Let her work a couple jobs with me so she could see how to stay alive."

"That was generous of you."

Nash thought back to Chase as he'd first met her. Angry. Confused. Lost. She'd not ended up in the trade by choice. Few people did. The chip on her shoulder was going to get her killed unless someone helped out, and Nash had stepped in.

"I guess I used to be more generous," Nash said.

And you wanted to be the first in line, he thought. You wanted to earn the points.

"And now she's surpassed you?" Conte paused. "I should say, there was a pool. I oversaw the betting, naturally."

Nash didn't feel like playing along on that one. He stared back at Conte, waiting for the raven to make the next move. There had to be a point to all of this, a reason he was trying to push Nash's buttons. There was a subtle knock on the door, and Hass stepped in with a small circular tray holding two short glasses of black liquid. He set one down next to each man, departing without a word.

"The Ark," Conte said again, breaking the silence. For a short word, he managed to draw it out. He leaned forward. "It hasn't gone far. The people who protect it, they rely on old friendships. I know what the rumors say about me. And I know you do, too. So you will believe me when I say, I know where it's being stored."

It was Nash's turn to lean forward. "Where?"

"I imagine, armed with that information, you could mount a raid of some kind and get your prize. Prove you're better than Chase. And I imagine your buyers would still be waiting to pay, to set up your retirement fund."

Nash was dying to repeat his question, but he knew Conte had heard him the first time.

"And I suppose," Conte said, with that faint smile again, "I could point you in the right direction."

Nash opened his mouth but didn't have words to follow. He tilted his head. Confused. Was this a shakedown?

For all Conte's poise and reputation, would he just flat out hit someone up for a bribe like this?

No, there had to be something else.

"I have a situation that needs to be dealt with. And I think you'd be well suited to the job."

Nash didn't like being played and couldn't help but snap back, "You sure you don't want Chase? I mean, why settle for me?"

Conte paused. He took a sip of the dark liquid, holding Nash's eyes the whole time. He set the glass back down and wiped his lips with his thumb. "This isn't a relic. Not a treasure hunt. I want you to use your old skills to find someone. And in any event, Chase has certain drawbacks that you don't."

"Like what?"

"Morals."

It was Nash's turn to smile.

"I'm listening."

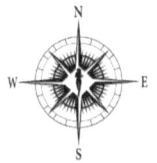

NINE

They drove a Lincoln Town Car. Chase would have preferred a limousine, to go all in on the mysterious-villain clichÈ, but the Lincoln would do. And, really, if they were villains, would they have offered payment? Blondie sat up front, doing the driving. Red sat next to Chase.

"I looked you up," Red said. "Read all about you. That interview you did for the Guardian. It was so cool. Did you really do all that stuff?"

"Which one was that?"

Chase closed her eyes, making it look like an effort to remember. In truth, she knew exactly what Red was referring to. Ashley Eades, a prominent UK journalist, had been the first to track Chase down for an interview after she'd been involved in stopping a would-be terror attack in London. All details of the incident were classified, but Eades had somehow linked Chase's name to it. The details of the attack itself were held back from the story, but Eades had used that initial contact to start a deep dive into the relic-running community. That had been the start of the mainstream attention and the reason Chase had become a pariah among half of her own people. Chase hadn't been the only person Eades interviewed, but she'd been the one to take the blame.

"All the stuff about Syria," Red said. "Did you really go there?"

"Bunch of times."

Chase rubbed her upper arm without thinking. She had a small scar, left by a passing bullet in Syria. An inch to the left, and the shot would have destroyed her shoulder.

Red turned in her seat. "Were you scared?"

She looked to be older than Blondie, maybe late twenties, but had the excitement of someone much younger. It was an odd effect. Both she and Blondie seemed to be playing a game, wrapped up in the excitement of being mysterious.

"Every second," Chase said. "Fear keeps you alive."

"I think it's so cool you admit that," Red said. "The guys she interviewed, they all wanted to be, like, macho. Rock stars."

"You reach a point, you realize fear and bravery are basically the same thing," Chase said. "In the moment, there's no difference between them."

Red nodded like she'd just been given a life lesson. "That's deep."

Chase watched buildings pass, trying to figure out where they were going. They'd taken the FDR, but where were they now, Eleventh Street? They drove across a bridge, and Chase finally realized they were in Greenpoint. She'd been here a few years ago, to watch a Doormats gig at a small club on the waterfront. They turned right and headed toward the river. Chase saw brewing companies, bars, restaurants. Up ahead, gleaming modern high-rises. They turned left at the river, into the parking lot of a large redbrick building that had been refitted with modern touches of glass and steel. Chase recognized it right away, mostly from the large neon sign on the roof that had become a New York landmark. This was the headquarters of Dosa Cola, one of the biggest soft drink companies in the world.

"We're here," Red said with a sly smile. "Ted, help our guest."

Blondie-now-Ted got out of the driver seat and opened the rear door. He waved toward the building's entrance with a flourish. Chase climbed out of the car and looked around. She had plenty of room to run. Ted was behind the door, and Red was getting out of the other side. Neither of them would be able to grab her in time. Despite the offer of money, she still knew the right thing to do was get out of Dodge. But now she was intrigued. Chase could never resist the pull of a bad idea.

Red stepped in next to her and bobbed her head toward the entrance. "Coming?" She turned and led the way, taking long, confident strides up the redbrick steps and into the building. Chase hesitated one last time, turning to look up into Ted's smiling face, then figured, what the hell, and followed.

Red was nowhere to be seen by the time Chase made it to the large foyer. The floor was painted with the most iconic version of Dosa Cola's logo, the one they'd used in the fifties, when the postwar generation had helped make them one of the coolest companies in America.

The name was written diagonally across a star that could have been taken off the flag, with a small tagline beneath that read, "A Dosa a day keeps the doctor at bay." The logo had changed a number of times over the years but never strayed too far from this basic design. On the far side of the huge space, a sleek modern reception desk ran the length of the old brick wall, contrasting the modern with the retro. A petite Latinx woman sat behind the desk, fixing Chase with a bland smile.

Ted came in behind her. "Follow me."

He nudged her shoulder as he walked past, leading the way up a staircase that wound around the circular chamber, up to the second floor. They passed through an archway in the old brick, and onto a walkway of glass and steel. The offices lining the walkway had glass walls, providing a full view right through them, to the machinery of the bottling plant beyond. Chase could see each of the machines working, turning out hundreds of bottles and cans, but no sound penetrated the glass.

Ted led her to an elevator at the end of the corridor and slipped a key card into a slot. A gentle electronic voice said, "Penthouse," and they started to rise.

When the doors opened, Chase stepped out into a modern room that felt larger than the farm she'd grown up on. It was split over two floors. She was standing on the lower level, which felt like the old building, with the same red brick and a vaguely retro fifties feel to the decorations and furnishings. In the center of the room was a glass staircase, which spiraled up to a mezzanine above, made of the same glass and steel as the offices. The far wall of both levels was a large window, running the full height and length of the penthouse, looking out onto the back of the neon sign that lit up the waterfront at night.

Ted pointed to a sofa on the lower level, set deep into a recess in the floor. Chase took a seat and waited to see what happened next.

"Would you like a drink?" Ted said.

Chase leaned back into the cushion. "Let's see," she said, making a show of looking at the neon sign, then back at Ted. "What options do you have?"

He grinned. Each time he smiled, she shaved a year off his age. She was starting to worry he was too young to have driven the car. "Not just that. You can have whatever you like."

"How about an explanation? And my five thousand? I'm loving this whole Bond villain thing, but why am I here?"

"Would you like ice with that?"

Chase smiled, played along. "Sure, and some bourbon."

Ted bobbed his head and turned on his heel, heading around to the other side of the spiral staircase, where Chase could see him bending over a bar. She heard the chinking of glasses.

Soft footfalls padded across the frosted-glass floor of the mezzanine above them, toward the stairs. Chase caught a glimpse of blond hair as someone started down the steps, but the spiral kept them just out of sight. The newcomer rounded the bend near the bottom, and Chase could see her in full.

It was Red. Except, now she was Blond, and dressed in a blue jumpsuit that probably cost the budget of a small nation.

She gave Chase a smile that seemed to acknowledge all the questions flying unspoken through the air. She paused at the bottom of the stairs long enough to take a glass of clear liquid offered by Ted on his way past to hand Chase a glass of amber liquor.

Red/Blond did a small turn, showing off her new look, and raised the glass in a toast. "To the Bond villain thing."

Chase didn't respond to the toast. She stayed in her seat and waited.

"Oh, come on," Red/Blond purred. "Smile. We're all having fun here."

"Are we?"

"Okay." She smiled, stepping down into the sofa recess.

Ted followed behind like a loyal puppy.

Holding out her free hand to Chase, she said, "Lauren Stanford. This is my PA-slash-BFF, Ted."

Chase took the offered hand in a firm grip and said, "Of course you are."

The Stanfords were one of the richest families in America. Owners of Dosa Cola, along with several media and entertainment companies.

Chase took a sip of her drink as Lauren and Ted settled down across from her, then said, "So why the game with the plane? The flight attendant thing?"

Lauren's eyes sparkled. "I own the airline, and I thought it would be funny."

Chase watched the way both Lauren and Ted held back giggles of excitement at that, and everything fell into place. The weird mix of innocence and cynicism, of threat and friendliness. Lauren was a spoiled rich kid, playing in a world without consequences.

Chase bit back on every jagged little piece of resentment she had and played it cool. "So why am I here?"

Lauren and Ted looked at each other. Ted nodded, some unspoken conversation passing between them. His eyes stayed on Lauren a little too long, and Chase read the puppy love.

Lauren leaned forward. "We want you to find the Fountain of Youth."

TEN

A s if to signify getting down to business, Conte pressed his intercom and ordered bourbon for Nash. Hass brought in a large carafe, half full, and set it down on the small table. There was only one glass. Hass handed Conte a fresh coffee, this one much larger than an espresso. Now that Nash thought about it, he couldn't remember ever seeing Conte touch booze.

Conte took a sip, leaned back in his seat, and said, "You're not here as a relic runner. I gather you were something of a problem-solver for the CIA."

Nash nodded. "*Find* and *remove*."

"Perfect, yes. Tell me about Lothar Caliburn."

Nash paused, caught by surprise. "An assassin. A good one." He leaned forward. Had Conte noticed his hesitation? Best to push on past it. "He was all the talk back then, when I was still in the agency. High-end jobs. Came and went like a ghost. Slipped across borders. The name was fake, obviously. A cover ID. Every time anybody talked about him, they added on three impossible things."

Conte smiled his approval. "Sì. Molto bene. He knew how to use myth and legend. Caliburn was a sword. You'd know it by the latin translation as *Excalibur*."

"I didn't know that." Nash surprised a second time. "I just figured it was a cool-sounding code name. Eventually, the agency sent their best find-and-remove guy after him."

"And that was how you made your own legend."

Nash shrugged. "I'd like to think I was already a bit of a legend by then. But yes, I took him out. It was my last job for the agency."

"Why?"

Nash's mind flashed back again. Iraq. That CIA job. The heat. The sand. The goddamned dryness. The gun in his hand. Why did it feel so heavy? It had never felt heavy. Guns were always like his hands. A natural part of him, ever since he was a boy. But he felt the weight and the sweat on his palm then. The gun was pressed to the head of his target.

The last job.

The last time.

You need to get out.

"Where else was there to go after that?" Nash said. "I didn't want a desk job, and I'd taken out the boogieman. Figured it was time to test myself on the private market. And somehow that led to relic running, rather than security work. But you already knew that."

"Let's say I did. And who was Caliburn?"

Nash knew the Italian would already have all this information. Every conversation with him was a transaction, a trade of knowledge and, with it, power. So why was Conte asking all these questions?

"Ryan Preston. Nobody important, actually. You'd only know him as Caliburn. He'd been a freelancer for fifteen years, Canadian, never worked in the military, never worked for a known agency. He'd always been self-employed."

"Interesting." Conte blew on his coffee. "Interesting. And tell me about R18."

Nash hesitated. "Why?"

"Humor me, per cortesia."

The more Conte dropped back into Italian, the more he was playing a game. The raven was fluent in English, but pretending otherwise was a good mask, a way to buy thinking time and to lead people to underestimate him.

"Mercenaries, ex-military types. They tried to hire me a couple years back, but I turned them down."

"Why?"

"With a name like that, I figured they were guaranteed Nazis."

"Sì. The name is shortened, but Reinheit means purity. And the numbers are linked to A and H."

Nash knew how it worked. He'd come across many such groups over the years. His first move into espionage had come when he was loaned from the military to a joint FBI-ATF task force to infiltrate a group of white supremacists in Southern California. Nash had learned they all seem to need some allusion to Hitler somewhere in their name or motto, preferably something that could be expressed in tattoo form.

"I haven't heard anything about them for a couple years," Nash said.

Conte nodded. "They have a long history; most of it isn't important. R18 came to risalto, ah, prominence in their current form during the Greek economic crisis. They killed a truckload of illegal immigrants on their way across the Turkish border, machine-gunned them all, and spray-painted 'Reinheit 18' on the side of the container. Red, to look like the blood inside."

"Good theater."

"As you say, they've been quiet for the last two years. Some of their senior members were linked to the London incidente. R18 seemed to fall apart after that, or to go quiet, at least, waiting for the situazione difficile to pass."

The London incident, known in the media as the Big Ben Attack, was still shrouded in secrecy and confusion. What Nash knew for sure was the same as everyone else: some kind of non-nuclear WMD had been used to destroy Big Ben and Buckingham Palace. There were rumors that the attackers had targeted the prime minister, but the weapon had seemed to malfunction or backfire at the last moment, taking out the person using it instead.

The most fascinating part for Nash was what had happened next. Several versions of the story took hold, each one accepted by different groups along the political spectrum. If you were scared of Islam, then the attackers were Islamists. If you thought the government was out to get you, it was a falseflag operation. If you liked secret cults, then the whole thing was carried out by some ancient Egyptian religion. For those who were anti-capitalism, the clear enemy was an American billionaire, James Paxton Robinson, who headed up a modern, science-based religion. That theory gained a signal boost when JPR pledged to cover the rebuilding costs as a "goodwill" gesture. Why would he do that, if he hadn't been involved? The UK government had launched an official inquiry into the incident, amid much media fanfare, but the whole process had stalled, superseded by a snap election and a referendum.

The truth didn't seem to matter much. It was malleable, taking whatever form was needed.

The only other thing Nash knew for sure was that Marah Chase had been mixed up in it all somehow, with many people in the relic-running trade saying she'd foiled the attack. She couldn't have done a good job of it, since they'd destroyed two of the most iconic landmarks in London.

"They are becoming active again," Conte said. "I have heard several reports of R18 in the last six months. Mostly in London."

"What's this got to do with—"

Conte's dark eyes reflected the coffee as he looked over the cup at Nash.

"Lothar Caliburn is working with them."

Nash sat upright, and his guts tightened. "That's not possible."

"Impossible or not, they have someone called Lothar Caliburn leading their military wing. So, entrambi you killed the wrong man, or someone else has started to use the name. Entrambi casi, your name is being hurt."

Nash thought it over. He was known now for his achievements as a relic runner. Getting a job wrong over a decade ago wouldn't have an impact, especially not as one generation was giving way to the next. But on a personal level, with the pride that drove him, he needed to fix this.

Still, what was Conte's angle?

"Why are you interested?" he asked.

Conte picked up the spoon from his saucer and stirred the drink steadily, the metal hitting the side in the same spot each time. "I think you'd be less interested in my reasons and more interested in my money. Half a million euros for Caliburn's identity, and half a million for his head."

"So it's a hit."

Conte smiled. Something dark sparked in his eyes. "As you said, find and remove. And I would expect the location of the Ark of the Covenant would allow you to make even more profit, once the job is done."

"And why me?"

"Our friends Romain and Bakari might not have known who they were dealing with, but I do." Conte set the cup down on the table. "If you want to catch a killer, you need to send a killer. I want Lothar Caliburn, I send August Nash. And since you're the one who claimed credit for killing him the first time, I thought you would want to see the job done." He slipped an envelope across the table. "There is one person I know of who's seen his face and lived. Leonard Arno."

Nash held off a smile. Lenny Arno was a low-level arms dealer. Everything started to make a little more sense. Not only was there information that Conte didn't have, but someone like Lenny, several rungs below him in the social order, did have it.

Conte continued. "He's being held by the Egyptian Homeland Security."

"You're worried they'll find the answer before you do."

"We have a small window of opportunity. He can lead you to Caliburn, but once he talks, the game is over."

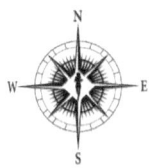

ELEVEN

C hase downed her drink. "Thanks for the ride, but I should be going."

Ted, standing, took the glass. "I'll get you another."

"No, really. Thank you. This was . . . interesting. You have a strange way of meeting people. But I've had a long day, I'm tired, so . . ."

Chase thought that would be enough. She got up out of the seat and turned, looking for the step out of the conversation pit. Ted, ignoring everything she'd said, headed for the bar.

"Please, stay a bit longer," Lauren said, putting her hand out toward Chase. "Give us five minutes. Just five. We're paying you either way. If you're not happy after that, Ted will drive you home. He'll stop off on the way at any restaurant you like, and you can order the whole menu, on us." She lowered her voice. "They're all takeout if it's me asking."

Chase hesitated on the spot. Ted walked back toward her and held out a fresh drink. She nodded, took it, and sat back down.

"Five minutes," she said. "But you should know, I've retired."

"Oh." Lauren's smile wasn't believing a word of it. "When?"

Chase's memory flashed up Bekele standing with the robed guards on the dock, then to Nash in the bar. *We're getting old.*

"Today."

"And what will you do?"

"Everything else. I have a whole life to get on with. The museum has been holding a job for me. I like my apartment, especially my bed. I owe my publisher a book. It's time to try and be normal again."

"The museum has been holding that job for you for quite a while now, haven't they?"

"Too long, yeah. I can't keep them waiting."

Ted handed Lauren a fresh glass and slipped down beside her onto the sofa.

"We can fix it," Lauren said. "My family name has pull."

"With the board?"

Her eyes twinkled again. "With *New York*. I can make all those things happen for you, and more. Anything you want."

Chase was trying to decide if Lauren was flirting. She was tired, and her radar was off.

"Thanks, but really, I'm out."

Ted leaned forward. "Is this eating into our five minutes? Can we get a ruling?"

Chase laughed, a much easier sound than she'd made in a long time. She was warming to these kids. "Five minutes starts now."

"Tell us what you know about the Fountain of Youth," Lauren said.

Chase shrugged. "It's a romantic story, but it's myth, and not even a real one."

"Go on."

"Okay. So the myth most people think of dates back to the 1500s. Ponce de LeÛn, a conquistador who came over with Columbus, was told about a magical spring by the natives. They said there was an island, can't remember the name—"

"Bimini."

"*Bimini*, that's it. And of course there is a Bimini, but we don't know which name came first, the real place or the myth. But there was a pool that could restore the drinker's youth. These kinds of legends get all mixed up.

Basically, he was told there was funky water, he went looking for it, landed in Florida."

"Okay."

"Except he didn't. Historians have found no genuine mention of the fountain, or the pool, in any of de LeÛn's writings, or any other documents from the time. There's nothing at all to suggest he'd even heard of it. The best we can figure, the next generation of politicians, wanting to consolidate their own power, created the story to make him look like a gullible fool tricked by natives. It's just an old political smear job, passed into myth."

Lauren nodded. She sipped her drink, looking like she was processing everything Chase had said. "But where did they get the myth from? These politicians, when they were looking to make Ponce de LeÛn look like an idiot, why did they choose the Fountain of Youth? How would it resonate as a fool's errand if it wasn't already a legend?"

Chase blinked. Once, twice. She'd underestimated Lauren.

"Good question," she said. "The idea of some kind of magical well, or water, is a lot older than the settling of America. Lots of cultures have a version of it. Europe, Africa, Asia. It's a pretty basic idea. One of the first things we learned as a species was to equate water with life. But by de LeÛn's time, it was already known to be a myth. It would be like if one of our politicians now suddenly went all-out searching for Atlantis."

Lauren's I-don't-believe-you smile returned. "Or the Ark of the Covenant?"

Caught off guard, Chase fumbled as she said, "Exactly." How much did they know?

"You don't think there's anything to find?"

"Nothing."

"I bet you said that a couple years ago about Alexander's tomb?"

Lauren sat back and waited, letting the silence hang there as she watched Chase's reaction. Chase's mind was racing. The full events of two years ago were classified. The only thing the public knew was that she'd found a Mithraeum, and Alexander's tomb had never been linked to the discovery.

The reporter who found Chase had never made that connection, being so focused on exposing the cool new subculture of relic running. But the smuggling community had been rife with rumors of Chase finding the tomb, and officials can be bought. Getting to classified information was usually just a matter of asking the right questions and offering the right gifts in return.

Chase pushed back. "Why are you interested? This some kind of PR gag? Going on a search for the ultimate drink?"

Lauren's lips pinched close together. "My parents died, three years ago." Chase faltered, the wind taken out of her attitude. "I'm sorry."

"Cancer. Different kinds, can you believe that? There are so many different kinds of cancer, and they both got a different one, both suffering at the same time. And understand this, they tried everything. You have the money we have, you have every option available. Nothing worked." Chase nodded, stayed silent. She had nothing to say to that.

Lauren stared off at the Dosa sign for a moment, then perked up. "Do you know how Dosa Cola started?"

Chase shook her head and settled in to wait for the story.

"We've always been a family of healers. Doctors. Physicians. Chemists. Our ancestor Harrold Stanford owned a drugstore in the East End of London, selling remedies to the rich, giving them out to the poor. He was there right around the time of Jack the Ripper. There are stories passed down in the family about how scary it was back then, the level of inequality, people left to starve, die in the streets. He packed the family up and came to America, hung out a shingle right here in New York. Brooklyn, originally." Her accent shifted for a second, becoming more local, less polished. "He started selling a new drink, a mix of sugar, flavoring, cocaine. He sold it cheap to workers, thinking it would give them the energy to work, keep them healthy."

"That's where the name comes from, right?"

"From acidosis, yes. Indigestion. He thought the drink eased people's stomachs. He was always looking for ways to help, to heal. And that's been our guiding principle ever since. Each generation raised to care about healthcare." She paused, took another sip. "Do you know how close Bill Gates has come to wiping out malaria? It's on the rise again now, with poverty and people pushing back against vaccines. He's got to roll it all back up the hill. But twice in the last decade, he's come close to getting rid of it. And I think he'll be third-time lucky. Just because he woke up one day with more money than God and decided to cure a disease. The smartest people on the planet are wrapped up in medicine. Think what would be achieved if all those brains, all that money, could be turned to other advancements. Space. Climate change. Renewables. Agriculture. Take away the one universal thing we all worry about, rich or poor, and we can all focus on other things."

"I could certainly drink a lot more," Chase said, "if I didn't need to worry about my liver."

Ted offered her a high five. Chase took it, then questioned her life choices.

Lauren bent forward and eased a tablet from beneath the sofa. She swiped the screen, flicking through pages as she talked. "Public health has always been an obsession in the family. And the Fountain of Youth is the perfect representation of that dream. But my parents, like their whole generation, took their eye off the ball. They loved the business side too much; they stopped caring about ideology. And . . ." Her voice cracked. She paused. It was either genuine or a brilliant act. "Look what happened. I want to get us back on track. I don't want anyone else to lose a parent to something we should be able to cure by now. I'm open-minded about the Fountain, and from what I've heard, you would be, too."

Another hint she knew more details than she should. Chase figured that at her level of wealth, there were no secrets.

Lauren prodded. "There are legends saying Alexander went looking for the Fountain."

"There's a story in the Alexander Romance about him traveling through a land of darkness to a spring of eternal life. But the romance era was mostly fiction—they added in things like Excalibur and the Grail to the King Arthur myth. Alexander's link to the Fountain is probably just the same thing. And we have a pretty big clue that he didn't find any well of eternal life, because he's dead."

"And you know of the Macrobians?"

"Sure. The ancient Greeks wrote about them. Either a nation or a race of people that lived on the southern edge of the known world. They were taller and stronger than usual and lived for a hundred, maybe a hundred and twenty years. Most people have always placed them somewhere in the Horn of Africa, but I think there's a new theory going around that would put them in India."

"Two places we know Alexander visited."

Chase nodded, put both hands up to say, Okay. "But the Macrobians themselves are probably a myth. Or a misunderstanding. Herodotus is the main source of information on them, and he describes them having burial practices that sound a lot like mummification, so he could have meant the Egyptians."

"Or maybe the people the Egyptians inherited those rituals from?"

"This is getting further out there. Look, I've gone after myths. I've found myths. Seems like you already know that. But I still had proof, something solid to get me going. We knew Alexander's grave existed at some point; it was just a case of figuring out if it still did. The Alexander Romance, and the writings of Herodotus, are not enough for a serious investigation."

Lauren moved across to sit beside Chase, easing well into her personal space. She held up the tablet between them. The screen showed a high-resolution scan of what looked to be a very old photograph, yellow and faded. A line of men stood erect, holding rifles at their sides. They were dressed in military uniforms.

"This is the last known photograph of the Ninth Rifle Regiment of the British Army. It was taken by a journalist traveling with the British across Sudan, on the way to the siege of Khartoum. But the Ninth Regiment never got there. Somewhere along the way, they got lost in the desert. Completely vanished. The picture was taken March 10, 1884."

Lauren swiped the screen to an embedded video clip and pressed play. The footage showed starving black children, skeletal arms and swollen bellies, flies swarming over them as they stared at the camera. A plummy British voice narrated: "The people here haven't seen fresh water in almost a year. Their crops have failed. We have the supplies we came with, but nobody was prepared for this . . ."

Lauren muted the video. "Horrible, isn't it? This is a BBC report from Ethiopia, 1984, during the famine. Those children, can you imagine?"

And all those white saviors with cameras, Chase thought.

Lauren fast-forwarded through the video, pausing on a middle-aged white man caught in profile, as thin and dehydrated as the villagers. "This is a man they found living in the village. The locals say he'd wandered into the village when he was younger, a generation before, talking in tongues, starving, and in need of water. They nursed him back, and he stayed with them, adopted like an eccentric old uncle. He helped look after the children, taught them soccer—but a really old version of it. I don't understand the rules myself, but whatever he was showing them, I'm told, was a hundred years old."

She pressed play again, and the camera caught a second of the man speaking in a mix of an English accent and the local dialect. "The BBC reporters couldn't get much sense out of him. He said his name was James, that he was a soldier, and that he got lost. But he would ramble, his memories seemed all jumbled up, like dementia. Figuring he was a British citizen and that he needed treatment, they took him back with them. But he didn't seem to exist. No ID, no fingerprints in the system. He didn't remember his home address, just that he came from Coventry. When a therapist tried taking him to Coventry, letting him walk around to see if a memory kicked in, he led them to a recent housing project, land that had been flattened by Nazi bombs during the war. All his stories were old, his memories—his clearest ones—were of childhood, and he insisted that had

been the 1860s." She swiped forward to a handwritten document, a list
of names and military ranks. "These are the soldiers from the missing rifle
regiment. See that one? Private James Angus Gilmore. Born in Coventry,
England, July 12, 1864."

She swiped again, and this time two images came up side by side. One,
a still from the video, of the Englishman in profile. He looked to be in his
fifties, but with the advanced stage of starvation and dehydration, it was
impossible to tell. His hair was a shock of white; his nose was large, sitting
above a thick white beard. The second image was a blown-up portion of
the original Sudan photograph. A young man, smiling, confident. A large
nose and a thick, dark mustache.

"You can't think—"

"Every effort to trace this man's identity failed. He insisted his name was
James Gilmore, that he was a British soldier from Coventry. But everything
else was complete Swiss cheese. He would ramble; he would talk about the
jungle, about giant lions and dragons; he made no sense. He talked about
Macrobia. And he used the term life water."

"An old man with dementia who lived through a drought. Of course
he's going to have a thing about water and connect it with life, if his
vocabulary is shrinking."

"The Macrobia connection? Where would he get that?"

"He looks to be in his fifties there? Maybe older? The postwar generation were a lot more interested in both Greece and Egypt than we are
today. They had fathers, brothers, uncles who'd all come back from those
countries fetishizing their history and mythology. It was pop culture before
we had cinema and television. This same guy today, if it happened now,
might come back talking about Wakanda."

"Okay. Maybe. That's an interesting take. And nobody at the time
believed him, either. The army didn't want anything to do with him. He
wasn't their problem. And with no way to trace his identity, he had no
family. Private Gilmore's family were all long gone. His parents had passed
away when he was young, his four brothers all died in the service. It's

believed he had a nephew, Scott, who died during the Battle of the Somme. There was nobody left by 1984 to test him against or claim him. So he lived out his days in NHS care."

"Lived?"

"He passed away a year ago, after a stroke. He'd lived a pretty healthy life, if you ignore his dementia. Once they nursed him back from the effects of the famine, he was in good shape."

"I think that's probably your five minutes." Chase made a show of slapping her legs, preparing to leave. "This has been interesting. But whoever you hire for this, they'll become a laughingstock."

Lauren's voice went up a little, ignoring that Chase had just said no. "I've given this information to you in the wrong order. Or the right order, maybe. I've shown it to you the way it should be, to make it all link up. But here's the thing. The photograph? It wasn't known to exist in 1984. There's no way James could have seen it. Even if we assume maybe he hit his head, had some form of breakdown, and took the soldier's identity after the trauma, he wouldn't have known about the regiment. The picture was in a box in an attic; it was only found six months ago. So where would our James have been getting all the details to assume the other James's identity?"

"I don't know, but if you wrote it up as a mystery novel, I'm sure it would sell."

"The last person to speak to James aside from the people in the care home was a friend of yours."

Lauren flicked the screen again, bringing up a new photograph. Ashley Eades, looking out through the lens, into Chase's eyes. The reporter who'd exposed relic running to the mainstream.

"Why was Eades interviewing him?" Chase asked.

"She was investigating the home, we know that. She ran a bunch of stories around that time on corruption and abuse in care homes. But she seemed to really latch on to James. We know from the visitor logs she returned to see him three more times."

Chase thought back on the person she remembered. Young. Confident. Maybe even arrogant, but not in a destructive way. Eades had believed people's stories should be told, that she needed to be the person who did it. This care-home story sounded exactly like her kind of project.

"He must've been a story," Chase said. "Maybe he knew something about the home. He had infirmation she could use against the place, she was going back to get the rest."

"Or maybe," Lauren said, "she was digging into his past."

"Easily solved," Chase said. "Call her. Email her. I've still got her number. She'll definitely pick up if she thinks you have a story for her."

It's when you're not a story anymore, Chase thought, that she loses interest.

"We can't." Lauren smiled. She was very close now. Too close. "She's missing."

"What?"

"Gone," Ted said. "Completely."

Lauren continued. "Four months ago, she just vanished, fell off the earth. Her boyfriend was killed. Murdered, in his own apartment. Or flat, they call them over there, right? His neighbor found him. The front door had been smashed in with real force, and he was in the tub, stabbed to death. And Eades was gone. Left her bank accounts, her home, cut ties with everyone. It was all too neat."

Chase knew what she meant by neat. It was a professional job. She'd met several people in the dark trades who could make someone disappear. Give them a new life, a new identity. The only giveaway would be how clean it all seemed. An abrupt end to the old life, like they simply exited stage left and never came back.

Lauren touched Chase's leg, left the finger there a fraction too long. "See, you're interested now. Who killed her boyfriend, and why? Was it linked to Eades? And if it wasn't, why would she run? And how would she be able to pull off such a professional disappearance?"

"How would you know the signs of a 'professional disappearance'?"

Lauren smiled. She liked the question but wasn't going to answer it. "Oh, something else. The care-home story? She ran that a year before meeting you. All of her research visits were done, each logged in their visitors' book. Then, a week after her piece on you ran, after she'd spent time exploring your community, she went back to the home and started visiting a resident who talked about Macrobia and the Fountain of Youth." This was all a coincidence.

This was all a coincidence.

As if reading her thoughts, Lauren said, "I don't think either of us believe in coincidence."

Chase still didn't believe half of what she'd heard. But Ashley Eades was either dead or on the run. What did Chase owe her? Nothing. If anything, it was Eades who owed Chase. But if there was even a chance she'd got caught up in something because of the world Chase had introduced her to . . .

"She's in trouble," Chase said.

"Could be." Lauren was so close now, Chase almost flinched. "But you could help her. You could help us find her."

"You'll pay my travel, my expenses."

"Of course. Plus a generous bonus when you find her."

"And you'll give her whatever she needs, if it's money, protection, if she has legal costs—" "I'll cover it."

Lauren met Chase's gaze, then let her eyes drift slowly down to her lips. Chase felt uncomfortable. There was a certainty in Lauren's words. She'd clearly never been in any doubt that Chase would say yes. Lauren was used to getting whatever she wanted. Maybe whoever she wanted. This wasn't about flirting so much as ownership, and that wasn't a game Chase was willing to play.

"I'm not interested in the Fountain." Chase stood up, putting distance between them. "I'm not looking for Macrobia. I don't care about this old man. I just want to make sure Eades is okay. I worked hard to get my academic reputation back, and whoever you send after the Fountain, their career will be over. May as well say they're looking for Bigfoot."

"That's next week." Lauren smiled. "One thing at a time."

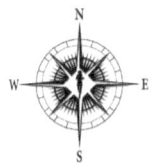

TWELVE

C hase didn't stay home for long. She needed information, and in New York there was one place she was guaranteed to get it. *The Speakeasy.*

Long before the term had become associated with the Prohibition era, and over a century before it was co-opted by hipster bars, speakeasy had referred to smuggler dens. The word had never stopped being used on the black market; it had just periodically been borrowed by the mainstream. The best speakeasy on the circuit was right there in Manhattan. It was one of the world's best regular gathering places for criminals, smugglers, relic runners, hit men, and spies.

After a quick shower and a much-needed change of clothes, Chase took the subway downtown to Chambers, then walked two blocks over to the Speakeasy.

City Hall subway station had been the southern terminus of New York's first full subway line, the showpiece of the new venture. It was decorated in Guastavino tile, with high arched ceilings and skylights that provided natural light from the streets above. The station had been closed to the public on the last day of 1945 and had officially been empty ever since, becoming a holy grail for urban explorers and local legends. Up until recently, the New York Transit Museum had operated tours of the facility, and the platform had been visible to commuters who stayed on the 6 train past the last stop, as it looped around to head back north. The tours had been discontinued, and the view from the 6 had been blocked off by construction barriers that were just high enough to cover the train's windows.

The only remaining entrance to the station was inside the gated parking lot in front of City Hall. The area was closed to the public, but the familiar subway railings were visible from the street, painted black rather than green.

The security staff guarded the entrance to the subway just as much as to City Hall. There had never been a great difference between politicians and criminals in New York, and it made sense that the seat of power for both was behind the same gate.

The staff on duty recognized Chase. The first palmed the entry fee with a handshake, and the second walked to meet her at the subway entrance. There was a metal hatch set into the floor, framed by the black railings, to close off the steps. The guard bent down to unlock the gate, lifting it to allow Chase down.

As she descended the steps, faint sounds drifted up to her. Music, chatter. Halfway down she passed through a thick black curtain, and the noises grew louder. At the bottom, she pushed through another curtain and was enveloped by the ambiance, like diving into warm water. Jazz instruments played over a soft techno beat. Chase had never seen a live band at the Speakeasy, but the sound quality always seemed better than something pumped through speakers. Commuters farther up the track, from Brooklyn Bridge to Bleecker Street, would sometimes talk of being able to hear music in the tunnels.

She was in the mezzanine, the large chamber that had originally housed the ticket booth and waiting area, now the lounge area of the Speakeasy. It had curved walls and a vaulted ceiling, all decorated in beautiful tiles of white and tan, with a green trim to the arches. There was a circular glass skylight, which was visible from the parking lot above. The chamber was filled with expensive lounge sofas, armchairs, and low tables with brass lamps that provided just the right amount of light. There were around thirty people filling the seats, with table service provided by three fast and nimble servers.

Chase saw two senators, three journalists, and a wide array of criminals. Unlike the Royale bar in Addis Ababa, here nobody paid any attention to her. *This was New York, baby,* and everyone was on their own time.

Everyone except the Speakeasy's host, Carina Texas, who bowed politely out of a conversation to come and greet Chase with a smile.

They'd first met five years ago, when Texas was on the run from a crime war in England and still using her real name. With a clean break and a new identity, she'd risen through the New York power rankings with near supernatural skill.

"Marah." Texas smiled, leaning in for the double air-kiss. "How are you?"

I'm tired. "I'm good."

You look it. "You look fantastic."

"You too." Chase made a show of looking the host up and down.

Texas bowed her head slightly, Thank you. "Business or pleasure?"

"Seeing you is always a pleasure." Chase threw the compliment out to ease the way. "But I'm here for work."

Texas nodded for Chase to follow as she led the way across the mezzanine, weaving around the furniture. She flagged down a waiter and whispered an order in his ear before passing beneath a green-tiled archway and down a set of wide steps. Chase followed onto the old platform. It somehow felt both cavernous and small. The high-arched ceilings, lit by brass chandeliers now and by the large glass skylights during the day, were far higher than anything on the modern subway system. But the platform itself was shorter, with room to fit only five carriages. The edge of the platform, where the modern 6 still passed on its loop from the downtown to uptown tracks, was covered by a long, heavy black curtain. On the other side, the barrier was disguised as construction. To Chase's left, running along the curved wall, was a fully stocked bar, with three staff working on drinks. To the right, more sofas and low tables, with people deep in conversation.

Texas walked slowly along the platform, to the very end and a circle of vacant sofas and chairs. This was her unofficial office. She held court here, sitting at the center of the American black market's social hub. Making connections. Moving information around. She waved for Chase to take a seat, then slipped in beside her on the sofa, both of them facing away from everyone behind them.

The waiter appeared with two small glasses. A clear liquid for Texas, and a bourbon for her guest.

Chase went first. "What have you heard about me?"

She could trust Texas up to a point. As long as she kept an eye on the line between their friendship and Texas's self-interest.

"Not much has made it here, yet. I've heard about it, but people on the scene aren't talking."

"What's the version you heard?"

"Maybe you found the Ark, maybe you didn't. The rumor sounds a lot less solid than the Alexander one, so I don't know, could go either way. But you were screwed over by an Ethiopian spy. And, whatever it was that happened over there, you got the better of August Nash, and he's not happy about it."

That was all fine. "Nothing about a new job?"

Texas flicked her eyebrow, leaned a little closer. "New job?"

"Well, I figured I was retired. And I don't mind that getting around." Chase knew that was permission for everyone to hear the news. "But yeah, I got one last gig. You heard anyone talking about the Fountain of Youth?"

Chase was annoyed at herself the moment she asked the question. Ashley Eades was the reason she was here, not the Fountain. *Why would she ask that?*

Texas grinned. "I know that I need it."

"Never mind. That's not really why I'm here. I need to know about cleaners."

In movies, a cleaner was a hit man. In the real dark trades, it was someone who could erase you from existence or could provide you with a brand-new identity. Money laundering, but for humans. Texas had used one herself to help create her new identity. Chase didn't know all the details. That was the point.

"You tell me you're retiring, then ask for a cleaner. I'm going to make assumptions."

"Not for me. I like being infamous."

"You're looking for someone who's been cleaned?"

Chase nodded.

Texas took a sip, licked her lips, and said, "None of them will talk. Even if you know who did the job, it would go against their code. They never give up a client. If they did, nobody would trust them."

"People must threaten them."

"Sometimes, but the scene always sorts that out. Cleaners are off-limits, because everyone knows the service is important. Too many of us need one, eventually."

"Is there any way to get around it?"

"Who are you after?"

"A British journalist. Ashley Eades."

Texas cocked her head, narrowed her eyes in thought. "I know that name . . ."

"She's the one who wrote about me."

"Yes. Yes." Texas nodded, fast, as the memory fell into place. She leaned forward. "Didn't she screw you over?" Chase said, "Yeah," after a pause.

Her friendship with Eades had ended on bad terms. The leitmotif of Chase's life. Maybe she should start introducing herself to people with, "Hi, my name is Marah, we will have a falling-out eventually."

"I think she's in trouble. Just need to talk to her, make sure she's okay."

"And she's been cleaned."

"Completely. Vanished off the face of the earth."

Texas swilled her drink around in the glass for a moment. "And she was in the UK when she disappeared?"

"London."

"Very public figure, right?"

"She was a big deal for a while, yeah. Newspapers, books, TV appearances. She was part of the new wave, got famous covering subcultures and politics on blogs, went mainstream. Then she met me, dragged all of us into the light, too."

Texas began running her finger around the top of her glass. When she made eye contact again, it was with a smile that said, Now we're playing the game. "I think there's a way."

Chase hesitated. "What'll it cost me?" The line was coming into view. The clear demarcation between their friendship and Texas's self-interest.

"Just a favor. Down the line. I don't need anything now, but you know how I am."

"A favor" could wind up being way more expensive than hard currency, but what choice did Chase have?

She raised her glass. "Deal."

A train rumbled past, behind the curtain. The drivers were supposed to slow down as they took the loop, but most of them seemed to get a kick out of taking the bend as fast as they could.

"You're asking the wrong question," Texas said, after the train was gone. "Think about money laundering and counterfeiting. Both of them are really simple, in theory. Take dirty money, pass it through a couple businesses, cook some books, the money comes out clean at the other end. Or sitting in a room and printing money. They keep changing the paper, the technology, but as long as you keep up-to-date, it's an easy job. For both of them, if you were doing it on your own, in a room, you'd never get caught."

"There's a but . . ."

"With you, there always is. But the *but* here is the same as any crime. *People*. It's getting easier to launder on your own with so much of it being digital now, but there are still other people involved. You need to pass it through businesses that aren't connected to you on paper. And for counterfeiting, there are so many steps. Shipping, processing, layering. At some point, no matter how good you are, how many precautions you take, you have to work with someone who knows what you're doing. And that person, in turn, has to work with someone else who knows what they're doing. Maybe also knows what you're doing, or can guess. It becomes a human chain, and eventually, somewhere along that chain, somebody talks."

"Crime 101."

"Cleaners are just doing for people what money launderers do for currency. And they need to be counterfeiters, too. Take someone who's dirty and make them clean, with new identities and documents. Even the best of them, they don't work alone. There are so many things to be done. No one person can be an expert on all the things anymore. Passports, they're biometric. Bank records. In the UK there's National Insurance, HMRC, NHS records. And the larger a person's profile, the more work it takes to clean them. Because you need to factor in their public appearances, news stories, internet, state surveillance cameras with facial recognition software. Cleaners call all of that your brand. The bigger your brand, the harder the work, the longer the chain of people involved."

"I need to find someone else in the chain."

"Right. Whoever did the cleaning, they'll never talk. You can't bribe them; you can't threaten them. But if you find the right person somewhere else along the chain, they're not a cleaner, they don't have the same rules. And for someone with as big a brand as your journalist? For someone like that to disappear in London these days? The cleaner will have paid someone who can hack the security net, wipe facial rec."

"Who should I talk to?"

"The best in the business is Grant LaFarge. Used to work for the British government before going freelance. He did my clean, wiped me off the grid completely. If your girl has really been taken off the map in London, I think the cleaner would have used Grant."

"Where can I find him?"

"Right here."

"New York?"

"Right here. I'll take you to him."

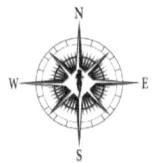

THIRTEEN

The existence of City Hall station was an open secret. Most people with a passing knowledge of New York history knew it was there. The real surprise was the network of rooms and passages *next* to the station.

The southern end of City Hall Park was the original site of the post office and courthouse. It stood opposite the Woolworth Building from 1880 to 1939. After it was demolished, the city chose to extend the park rather than build anything new. The post office had been designed with a multilevel basement complex, full of sorting rooms, transportation tunnels, and access to the subway platform for private trains. The top level of the basement had been filled in, but the lower tiers had remained empty and were now part of the Speakeasy complex, adapted into offices, private bedrooms, meeting spaces, and a casino. The subway station was the attractive first impression—the stylish bar, with its vintage tiles, brass chandeliers, and vaulted ceilings. But the post office was where the real work was done.

Texas led Chase down three tiled steps at the edge of the platform and along a short ledge, to a heavy-looking metal door. She pressed a buzzer, a recent addition screwed to the wall, and it was opened by a doorman in a suit almost as expensive as his boss's. He bowed slightly as Texas walked by. Chase followed her along a wide corridor. It had been painted a deep gold, with black tiles on the floor. The doors along the wall were all dark wood, replacing whatever had been there originally.

"LaFarge has been coming here every week for a few months," Texas said, pushing through a double door and into a second corridor. Chase could hear soft music coming from behind the doorways as they passed.

"He's into the house for fifty grand."

"Is that a lot?"

"For this place? Not really. I have three million on the street right now, but people know not to mess me around, so I don't rush them."

Texas knocked a couple of times on another door, which was opened this time by a young woman wearing the same style suit as the doorman. The room was large, with a ceiling that felt as high as the subway station's. There were roulette and blackjack tables, and another fully stocked bar along the far wall, but in the center of the room stood a circular table, where seven people were playing poker. Chase recognized two Hollywood actors among the group. Both of them were well-known for their card playing, and one was rumored to be a real asshole at the table. From the amount of chips piled in the center, Chase guessed it was a high-stakes game.

Texas motioned for Chase to stay where she was and stepped over to the table to tap one of the men on the shoulder, whispering something in his ear. He nodded and looked across at Chase for a moment before returning his focus to the hand. He had the look of an accountant rather than a criminal, with thin, almost fine features and round glasses.

Texas finished the hushed conversation and came back to stand beside Chase.

"They're taking a break after this hand."

Most people folded. It came down to the two actors and an overweight man in a too-tight black shirt. The Hollywood asshole won, and after a few jokes, the accountant excused himself from the table and came over to join Texas and Chase.

"Marah Chase," Texas said, making the introduction, "Grant LaFarge. Grant, Marah."

"Pleasure to meet you." LaFarge spoke with a transatlantic accent, making it hard to place his origin. "I've heard so many stories."

Texas smiled at them both. "I'll leave you to it. Grant, Marah is a friend; helping her is helping me." She walked away, pausing for one last look to Chase that said, *Remember the favor.*

"An introduction like that," LaFarge said, "Texas vouching for you, carries a lot of weight here. You must need something big."

Chase motioned toward the bar. "Can I buy you a drink?"

"Sure."

On the way over to the bar, Chase tried a little small talk to figure out how he worked, and the best way to approach him. "Big game?"

He nodded, looking across at the empty table. "Best in town. Used to be one in Brooklyn. And we had one going with the Russians who live in

Trump Tower, but that got shut down when the press started sniffing."

Chase glanced at the Hollywood guy. "I hear he's tough."

"Gets off on control, wants to destroy people's lives."

"Didn't he play a superhero?"

"Yeah. Kind of ironic."

"How you doing?"

"Not well. I have enough for one more hand, then I'm out."

The more he talked, the more Chase detected a slight Welsh roundness to his words. It only showed up occasionally, stretching a few syllables, rolling others. At the bar he ordered a vodka and cranberry juice. Chase asked for water. She paid and tipped heavily.

LaFarge leaned on the bar and raised a wordless toast before sipping from the drink.

Chase decided it was time to get straight to it. "You worked for GCHQ?"

"I was a geek, yeah. Got out when I could see the way things were going."

Chase had no idea what he was referring to but nodded as if she did, wanting to play to his ego and confirm his opinions. "Now you help clean people."

"Sometimes. That's just a sideline. I like the idea of it. I used to get paid to watch people all the time; now sometimes I get paid to make it so people can't be watched. It's fun."

Chase figured him out right there. It was about control. He'd gotten into his original line of work to control people's information, and he was still doing it, just for a different side. He played poker because, like all control freaks, he kidded himself that he could master the game rather than be mastered by it. But if he owed the house fifty grand, he wasn't as in control as he liked to tell himself.

"I need help finding someone," Chase said. "Someone you might have wiped."

"I can't just give out—"

"Look, the intro from Texas—she wants you to help me. We both know how she works. You owe her money, but if you help me, you're helping her. She'll owe you a favor, and maybe it's worth fifty K?"

Chase left it there, giving him time to build whatever narrative protected his ego and allowed him to pretend to be in control. LaFarge looked down at his polished shoes. Chase watched in silence as he scrunched his face in thought, licked his lips, then nodded.

"As I was saying, I can't give you anything," he said, loud enough that others might have heard him refusing to help. Then, in a quieter voice, "But maybe you should talk to your ex in London."

He smiled and walked away, shifting quickly to a loud conversation with the other players, making it clear he was done with Chase. But that was fine. He'd managed to thread the needle, giving her information that would help without being seen to sell out a client.

Your ex in London.

Chase knew exactly who he was referring to: Joanna Mason, an MI6 spook and the last person to really count as a girlfriend. Dani the Dominican hadn't reached that level. With Mason, Chase had been through several rounds of the on-and-off game, but they'd both known the score going in. It had never been a long-term investment. Mason was one of the best intelligence agents in the business. If LaFarge was sending Chase her way, it meant she knew something.

Chase rode the subway back uptown and was so deep in thought that she missed her stop, getting off at Eighty-Sixth Street instead. Rather than heading toward Columbus Avenue and walking down that way, which felt quicker, she stayed on Central Park West. Turning right on West EightyThird, Chase paused beside a large Romanesque building and realized none of this had been an accident. Her feet, or her deepest thoughts, had played a trick on her.

She was standing outside a large synagogue. The temple was tall and angular, with high arches around the windows and columns on either side of the entrance. The door was open, and Chase could see lights coming from inside. Would people be worshipping at this time of night, or was it some social function? Chase wasn't sure and, not for the first time, felt embarrassed about that. She was raised Jewish but never gave much thought to it beyond the traditions and a sense of responsibility to history. There was a spirit there, a long line of people who'd been kicked around from place to place and still kept finding space of their own. Chase liked that, and somehow, even without planning it, whenever she moved to a new place, she always managed to know where the nearest synagogue was. There was another one that she found more visually interesting, with a grander archway, but it was too far over on West Eighty-Eighth for her feet to have casually led her there tonight.

She looked up again at the windows, and the star carved into the wall, near the apex of the roof. Then at the door, with the columns that looked so similar to the temple she'd found in Ethiopia. In that moment, Chase felt something she hadn't expected. A deep connection. Almost a pulling sensation in her gut, asking her to step inside. She had no frame of reference for this feeling. Was it faith? She had stood in the Holy of Holies. She had lifted the Ark. The Ark. It was real. There was a golden chest, carried by people. No matter whatever else that meant, she could feel a link to those people. Thousands of them, thousands of years, too. A history that she was part of.

Or guilt. Was this guilt? The history had always been there, waiting for her. Had she been ignoring all those people? She was the one who'd seen the relic, the one who'd touched it and let it slip away. She thought of her parents and felt each of the years back to the last time she saw them. Her mother, Chase's own connection to Jewish history.

Loss washed in over everything else. This was an emotion she was used to. Something she could use. For just a moment, Chase thought about stepping inside. Finding someone to talk to or something to touch. Just to touch. But her own legs didn't want to. She didn't want to.

Chase laughed at herself.

She rolled her eyes, come on, and continued along the street. She turned left onto Columbus, then six blocks down, onto West Eightieth. She didn't pause to check her mail in the lobby. Her head was full enough; anything else could wait. She felt each and every step on her way up the fourth floor. The flight to London still needed to be booked, and Chase already had the sinking feeling there wouldn't be enough time for a full night's sleep. There was no real reason she couldn't wait a day, get rested up before going. But she knew, really, that the next available flight would be the one she took. What if Eades was in urgent trouble and Chase delayed too long?

She stopped in her tracks. Her door was open. For the second time in one night, someone had made it up here without a key.

When choosing her apartment, Chase had narrowed it down to a choice of two. One with a doorman in the lobby but an overly aggressive co-op board, and one with no doorman but a very keen board. Chase had gone for the second option but now, once again, that seemed like a stupid idea.

She should call the cops. She should turn around and get to safety. Like a normal person. But living in the dark trades changed you. The rules were different.

Chase inched toward the door, going up on the balls of her feet, ready for movement. She pressed flat to the wall beside the doorframe and listened to the shuffling from inside. Chase's neglect in unpacking had given her an excellent warning system, because she could hear someone moving around, rummaging through the boxes, digging down for whatever they were after. She waited as the intruder finished up in the box nearest the window, which Chase could tell from the sound of cables and tools she had left in the bottom. As the sounds shifted to documents, she knew he was closer to her, rummaging through her old research papers. She sucked in a deep breath, then sprung around and through the door, aiming straight for him.

The lights were off. The only illumination came from the flashlight on the intruder's cell phone and the light that slipped in from the hall. Chase could make out a thin shape, around the same height as her, bundled up in a dark hoodie. The shape spun to face her but was too late. Chased connected at speed, throwing all her weight into the impact. They both hit the floor. The cell phone skidded away, taking the light with it. Chase reacted fast enough to get on top of the intruder, straddling him—she was sure it was a man—and punching down, toward the hood. His face was obscured by one of those cycling masks with a skull pattern.

She grabbed at his hoodie, demanded answers. "What are you—"

He rolled, and he was strong enough to throw her off. While she was off-balance, he grabbed a handful of her hair and threw her over, face-first into the floor. The side of her face was numb with shock, but she started to push back up. He kicked her arms out, flattening her again, then aimed a hard kick at her side. Chase yelped in pain and rolled away.

The attacker took a step closer. "Where is it?"

"Where's what?" Chase shouted the two words out between pained breaths.

He was backlit by the hall light. Chase saw him aim for another kick. She curled into a protective ball, but the blow never came. When Chase opened her eyes again, she saw that he was still poised, making the point that he could do it.

"The Fountain is not for you," he said.

Chase's vision dimmed. Then she realized it wasn't her vision, it was the light. Something had blocked it for a second. Or someone. A large shape in the doorway, and an angry growl. Someone big grabbed the attacker from behind. They joined into one shape for a brief skirmish, hidden mostly in shadow with the occasional flash of light around the edges. Then there was a howl, a real sound of pain, and the guy in the hoodie broke away and bolted out through the door. The larger person followed. Chase took a few more breaths, then climbed to her feet and found the light switch. She heard movement out in the hall as heavy feet came back toward her apartment. Chase moved deeper into the room, looking for a weapon.

Ted stepped into the doorway, still dressed in the chauffeur outfit.

"Sorry, he got away," he said.

"No, uh, no need to . . ." Chase shrugged. What the hell had just happened? "Thanks."

Ted stepped into the apartment and smiled. "You okay?"

"Yeah, just shaken up a bit."

"What was that . . . Do you know what that was about?"

Chase shook her head but said yes. "He mentioned the Fountain. But I don't—" She paused. "Wait, what are you doing here?"

"Yeah, so, you left without this." He held up the tablet Lauren had been using. "All the files we have on the Fountain. Lauren's built a database of all the legends and documents." He smiled, rolled his eyes, conspiratorial. "It was kind of her pet project for a while. It'll make my life easier if you use it."

"I told you, I'm not interested. I'm looking for my friend, not the Fountain."

"Lauren thought you might be interested. Better to have the information than not, right?"

He hovered for a moment, shifting weight from foot to foot, uncertain of what to do. He nodded to himself and set the device on top of the nearest box.

"You need me to do anything? I mean, you wanna call someone, or, are you hurt, or . . . ?"

"No, really. I'm good." Chase was going to leave it at that, but she was hit with a wave of actual humanity. "Thanks for the save."

He grinned and bobbed his head before leaving. Chase shut the door after him and bolted it, thinking, When this is over, I'm moving to the place with the doorman. She paused to stare at the tablet on the way past. She picked it up and headed toward the bedroom, kidding herself that she wasn't going to read it.

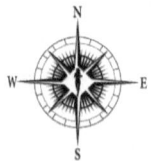

FOURTEEN

The fire alarm started right on time. Ringing through the halls of the hotel and out into the predawn Cairo air. From his perch on the roof, Nash could see people leaving the building, huddling together at the meeting points to stand in the cold, crack jokes, and talk nervously.

Officially, Egypt's National Security Agency was headquartered in a sleek new building in the heart of the city. The agency had been formed after the revolution, as one of the many reforms intended to clean up the image of the country's government and security services. The previous agency, the SSI, had been hated and feared in equal measure, known worldwide for its use of torture and detention without trial. Nash was old-school. He'd been in the CIA while the SSI was at its height, and he still had many of the contacts he'd forged during that time. As a result, he knew the NSA was also still using this old SSI facility, a converted hotel, on the western edge of the city.

The siren cut out after three minutes. Someone had figured out it was a false alarm. Nash estimated about half the staff were outside. The prisoners, and their guards, would still be in the holding cells. They didn't get taken out unless it was 100 percent guaranteed the alarm was genuine. Once the cops were sure, the prisoners would be led out to a secured pen in the old courtyard.

Nash watched as the staff started to file back into the station before, on cue, the alarm went off a second time.

He loved alarm systems in old countries. Retrofitting buildings that had stood for centuries, trying to fit modern, computer-controlled systems onto existing networks of wires and junction boxes. Nobody would ever sign off on the money it would take to strip everything out and start again, so they ended up with hybrids, new systems trying to control old networks. And the security services of all countries were sometimes the easiest to hack. They were complacent, and so sure that their secrecy had people fooled.

This second alarm rattled the staff. They were nervous. This had to be genuine, right? The crowd down below split visibly into two groups. Some hanging back, others insisting on reentering the building, to get out of the cold.

Nash started to move, crossing over to an alarmed skylight. He did one last check on his equipment, slipped a lockpick out of the case, and paused, ready. The alarm stopped a second time. It was only off for thirty seconds before starting again. Nash smiled. He didn't know how long the next step would take, but it was inevitable. Someone inside the building, blaming the equipment rather than the compromises behind it, would swear and shut off the system. As the sound drilled out around them, Nash turned to stare at the large, dark outline of the Great Pyramid. It never failed to surprise him just how close the ancient monuments were to town. As a child, seeing them in movies and on postcards, he'd imagined the Giza Plateau to be in the middle of the desert, surrounded by sand for miles around. But the modern Cairo was built right up to the enclosure. You could sit in a Starbucks and look out, through the green logo on the window, to one of the seven wonders of the ancient world.

The siren died abruptly, like it had lost its voice mid-shout. This was the moment. Someone had made the executive decision to kill the alarm. Whether it was with wire cutters or throwing the breaker switch, the result was the same. All the building's systems were wired through the same controls, including the security alarms.

He had the lock on the skylight open in seconds and lowered himself down into the stairwell below. From surveying the building's plans, he knew this central stairwell was originally a fire escape in the days of the old hotel. In refitting the building, the security services had built a modern, more efficient series of exits. The bottom floor of this stairwell was still in use, as the route for taking prisoners out to the secured pen, but the top two stories had become storage space. It was piled high with desks, boxes, and filing cabinets, making it easy for Nash to climb down. He took the stairs to the floor below.

He pulled his specially adapted Glock and opened the disused emergency door.

The hallway beyond was dark. There were no windows. He could hear people arguing in staccato bursts. His Egyptian Arabic was pretty basic, but he could get the gist of it.

Who cut the power?

No, the alarms.

Then why are the lights out, too?

Shit.

That was an unplanned bonus. Nash now had the cover of darkness. At least until someone figured out how to fix the wire or circuit breakers. Could be seconds, could be an hour; best not to rely on it too much either way. He stepped slowly along the corridor, pausing at open doors, waiting for any sign of trouble before continuing. The room he wanted was at the end of the hall, but he had to go past one more office and a break room. The conversation he'd been listening to was coming from one of those doors. He stopped next to the office, pressing himself to the wall. Someone was coming his way. His eyes were already adjusted to the gloom and allowed him to make out a tall shape, a little over six feet. Nash held his breath and didn't move. The shape turned his way but didn't seem to be as accustomed to walking in darkness. Whoever it was, they hadn't yet sensed Nash's presence. The shape was saying something about calling down to the basement, but the tone was sarcastic, weary. A deep male voice. The shape turned back toward the doorway, and Nash heard the other person, a woman, with the same bored tone but more of an edge. As the shape replied, Nash started to make out features. The man was broad, with a flat nose and a beer gut. The words trailed off, and even without knowing what they were, Nash could tell the sentence was incomplete. The man hesitated; then the head turned toward Nash.

He was blown.

Nash struck hard and fast, slamming the heel of his palm upward into the nose to stun the larger man, then slipped around behind him and wrapped his right forearm around the man's thick windpipe. He pulled his arm inward, fast, finding a pressure point with the fingers of his right hand and pressing home the advantage. The man sagged and became a heavy, unconscious weight, but not before letting out a choking sound. Nash heard the woman shout, then movement that sounded like she'd pushed up from a chair.

Nash let the man fall to the ground and ran along the corridor. He heard a shout from behind and turned, seeing the outline of the woman bending over her fallen colleague. She was looking his way. Nash couldn't make out any features at this distance. He pulled his gun and fired, hitting home somewhere in the middle of her outline. She grunted and fell to the floor.

The bullets were custom-made. A small rubber outer shell, wrapped around a needle suspended in a fast-acting sedative. On impact, the needle would push through the rubber, injecting the toxin. There was still a chance a shot could be fatal. Rubber bullets had been known to kill, and that was even without the combination of a sharp needle and a toxin. But most of the time they would have the desired effect, and the victim would simply keel over, down for the count. Nash had no problems dropping bodies, but these were spooks, and he wanted to avoid the hassle that would come with killing an official.

More shouting came now, this time from the break room. Nash shot each shape as it filled the doorway, felling three people. He found the door at the end of the hall, the one he needed. It was locked. The mechanism would only have taken him a few seconds to open, which was his original plan, but now he didn't have time. The evacuees would all be back soon.

Nash kicked through the door handle, taking the flimsy lock with it. The door hit something solid as it gave inward, and Nash heard a grunt. Light spilled out into the hallway from a streetlamp visible through a window in the room. Nash could see the person who had grunted. She was a few inches shorter than him, with dark hair cut short. She rolled with the movement and turned back to face him, adopting a fighting stance, squared out and hands up. From the speed of her recovery, Nash could see training and experience. He shot her twice, just to be safe.

The lights flickered on overhead. With them came an alarm. A new one. Someone had finally flicked the breaker switch back on, and with it, they'd been told about the intruder. He had seconds, if that.

Lenny Arno was in the middle of the room, hanging upside-down from something resembling a large coatrack. There was a blowtorch on a table beside him, but it hadn't been turned on. Lenny's face, already flushed red, twisted first in surprise, then relief.

He opened his arms as wide as the handcuffs would allow. "Hey, Augie. How you doin'?"

Before he started selling weapons on the black market, Lenny had been a con man and lawyer in his native New Jersey. He used his accent to full effect whenever possible; the role suited him. He managed to react to every situation as if it was something he'd planned for, even though half of everything he touched seemed to turn to crap.

"Better than you," Nash said.

"This? Just a misunderstanding. They're writing an official apology. Say, uh, while we wait . . . could you maybe let me down?"

"I need a name."

"I got loads, as many as you want."

"Lothar Caliburn."

Lenny rocked back and forth a little, then looked down at the woman slumped on the floor as if to say, You believe this guy? "What, the walls have ears here?"

Nash pointed the gun at him. Arno had no way of knowing the bullets were rigged.

"I need his real name, Lenny. And I'll know if you're lying."

"Take me with you."

Nash knelt down and pressed the gun to Lenny's temple.

Lenny held out his hands, showing his cuffs. "Look, there's no win for me with these guys. I offered 'em Caliburn's name as a deal, but all they're offering is a blowtorch. You get me out of here now, I'll give you the name."

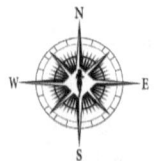

FIFTEEN

O n the mezzanine floor of her penthouse apartment, Lauren Stanford relaxed into the plush leather of her office chair and looked out at the neon Dosa sign. Beyond it, across the East River, she had a view of the Con Ed towers. It had never impressed her much. People all around the world dream of waking up to a view of the Manhattan skyline, but the version they think of was the one from the movies and postcards. There she was, in an exclusive apartment on the riverfront, and she had to live with a view of the power plant.

To her left was the Williamsburg Bridge. An ugly metal thing. Another frustration. Years before, when her parents were still running the company, they'd looked at buying Brooklyn Bridge Park and relocating the whole Dosa operation down there. They'd gotten as far into the project as having architects draw up plans. It was going to be a campus, with educational facilities built in, and a tour of the plant for the hipsters. Lauren was to have her own space, with a hot tub, staring out at the famous bridge and the gleaming towers of the Financial District.

Her parents had changed their minds at the last minute, deciding that it was more important to keep the company rooted here, behind the neon sign that had become a famous landmark. Her father had argued that companies would pay millions to have the history and the brand recognition, and why should they throw it away just for a better view?

She turned to the wall beside the desk, where two large framed portraits of her parents hung. "You should have listened to me."

Lauren had arranged her office in a very specific way. In the middle of business meetings, she could feel her parents watching over her. Each time she made a new million-dollar deal, she could look up at them, show off in front of them, for all the doubt they'd shown in her abilities. And the pictures also lined up with her bedroom door, on the other side of the mezzanine. On quiet nights, when she felt alone, she could leave the door open and have her family with her as she fell asleep. On other nights, when she had company in bed, she could smile, and watch her mother judging her as she closed the door.

Ted said it was creepy.

That one time she'd let him into her room, let him think they had something more. This whole Ted situation was a mess. She should have known that from the start. Hell, she did know that from the start. Why had she gone against her own instincts?

She sighed, looked up again at her mother. "And I shouldn't have listened to you."

The Stanford family always had to be careful who they trusted. There were so few people who really shared their dream. And even fewer who were worthy of it. Each generation, the parents would cast around, looking for a son- or daughter-in-law from a family they trusted. And Ted was the only son of her mother's best friend. Her mother had worked hard to set them up, always taking them places together, always pairing them off on family vacations. But to Lauren, all he'd ever been was an annoying younger brother. An obligation.

The way he followed her around. The way he constantly screwed up.

But the way he looked at her was fun.

Her cell rang. The secure one, used only for private projects. The caller ID showed it wasn't Ted. Instead, she saw two letters. CT. Carina Texas. She let the call ring for a few more seconds, letting Texas know who was in control, before pressing the green button.

"Carrie, babe." She stretched the words out. Full high-society schmooze.

"It's been a while. Give me good news."

"I have some information that might be useful to you, if you're buying."

"Of course."

"If you're still interested in the Fountain of Youth, I had someone in here earlier asking about it. Marah Chase. I remember you asked me about her once, too? I can set up a meet, if you like."

"Already done."

There was a pause on the other line, then, "You hired her. That makes sense."

"Were you able to help her?"

"We didn't talk about it, actually. She asked about something else."

Interesting. Lauren had talked to Texas many times. But the black market and relic running weren't her worlds. She didn't know the right questions to ask. Someone like Chase would. Best to hire her to do the legwork. Ask the right questions to the right people. But it was annoying that one of the answers had been here, in New York, the whole time.

"And did you manage to help her on that?"

"I introduced her to someone who could. A data guy. He's got a large gambling debt to the house, so I used that as leverage, told him the debt would be wiped."

"I'll cover that. How much did he owe?"

"Nine hundred K."

"Ouch." Lauren smiled. The figure was pocket change. "I think I can handle that. Usual account?"

"That would be perfect."

"I'll do it immediately. Did you find out what information she was given?"

"He sent her to London, to meet some government agent they both know."

"Do you think he held anything back?"

"Of course. I wouldn't be surprised if he knows everything she needed, but that's the game. He's protecting his own reputation."

Lauren paused, thinking it through. She knew the underground was a whole different world, with its own rules and customs. But this wasn't so different from mainstream business. You never tell the whole truth, just what's needed to give the other person what they want. Or what they think they want. But she was a public face. She graced magazine covers and was on to her third TED Talk. Someone else needed to do the black-market work, and she knew Ted wasn't up to it.

"Excellent work, Carrie. And what do I owe you?"

"Just the usual. A favor."

Lauren's day-to-day phone dinged, and she looked at the notification. Someone had used the electronic key pass to enter the building via the private entrance. It would be Ted, on his way back. Finally. A second message told her he was in the elevator, on the way up from the garage. This was the route they both used, almost all the time. The only reason they'd brought Chase in the front way was for the show of it, part of the game to convince her to take the job.

"Now," Lauren said, lowering her voice, "if I'm counting right, I seem to owe you a number of favors. Maybe if you were to come on over"—she stretched out—"I could start finding ways to pay you back."

"Just the facts, ma'am."

Lauren sighed theatrically. "Understood."

She killed the call and looked out again at the skyline. On the floor below, there was a soft electronic beep as the elevator door opened. Footsteps padded across the thick carpet, then up the stairs. Ted nodded as he walked into the office. He was still wearing the chauffeur outfit. It suited him and made Lauren feel like old-time royalty with her own manservant.

She was toying with the idea of making him wear it full-time.

She turned in her seat. "How did it go?"

"Perfect."

"Who did you use?"

"Some bike courier. Like you said, I found someone who doesn't know anything about you. Ordered food to be delivered through an app. When the guy turned up with it, I paid him two hundred to do the job, an extra hundred after to keep him sweet. He thinks it was some weird sex thing."

"He remember the lines?"

"Yeah, made it sound like he was warning her off, mentioned the Fountain."

"Think it worked?"

Ted nodded. "I could see it, yeah. She's interested now."

Lauren gave him the big eyes and full-beam smile. "Well done. Good work. You gave her the tablet?"

"Yeah, just like you said."

Lauren flicked through the apps on her phone's screen. It loaded a map of New York, with a small blue dot pulsing on the Upper West Side, where the tracker they had just planted on Chase was sending out a signal.

"She'll be heading to London next. Carrie Texas just told me. Put in a call to the London office."

Ted nodded and started to turn away. Lauren put her hand up. "Oh, and transfer nine hundy to the Texas account, and then monitor her account, see where she sends it on to?"

Lauren turned her focus back to the app. As she watched, the dot changed to a light amber, which meant Chase was using the tablet. She was reading the files.

Game on.

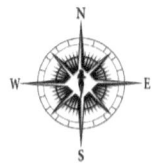

SIXTEEN

C hase absolutely wasn't reading the tablet. She kept telling herself that, as she clicked every page on the screen. She was settling down to sleep. That made far more sense. Getting some rest before another long flight halfway across the world.

She was *not* going to keep reading.

"You're so full of shit," she said aloud, smiling.

She was wrapped up in her bedsheets, with the only light coming from the tablet resting on her knees. Each time she moved, there was in instant reminder of the kick she'd taken. Her head hurt only if she touched it, so a process of scientific study had convinced her to stop doing that.

Chase had booked a flight that gave her just enough time, in theory, for six hours of sleep and the commute out to JFK. She'd used the airline that Lauren Stanford owned, and found, when it came time to enter her credit card and complete the booking, that the system didn't charge her for the flights. She guessed Lauren must have put her name on a list. Normally, Chase would push back against that. She liked to be in total control of who had her details and what they were used for. But it was late, she was tired, and she didn't want to argue over free travel.

She used the tablet's web browser to search for Ashley Eades. Her website was still up but hadn't been updated in a long time. Her Patreon was still live, too, but the subscriptions seemed to have dwindled down to the few people who probably didn't even cancel their gym memberships when they stopped going. All the same news stories were still available. Chase ran through the ones she remembered, the profiles and interviews that involved her. Eades cast herself as the voice of the reader, discovering this whole new world for the first time. Smugglers. Relic runners. Counterfeiters. Spies for hire. She told people that all of this was going on, right beneath the surface of every city. There was an undertone to the work Chase hadn't noticed before. In the heat of the moment, all she'd seen were the personal connections, her life exposed, her community under scrutiny. She'd pegged Eades as an attention seeker, bent on being the one to tell every truth. But now, with distance, she could see fear. A conservative edge to the narrative, warning people that they were not as safe as they thought, that all this lawbreaking was carrying on unchecked. Eades had been a darling of the liberal media. Had these conservative tendencies always been there, or were they a sign of the shock and grief everyone in London had been feeling since the terror attack?

There were other stories Chase hadn't read before. Eades cozying up with the new right, attending their conferences and going on tour with some of their leaders. The articles were always written from the liberal point of view, framed as needing to understand how these young men could drift so far from the mainstream. Chase wondered, for the first time, if this was how Eades had seen her. Were her journeys into the dark trades another step in Eades trying to understand extremism and violence?

"If you play with fire . . . ," she said to nobody. There was no need to finish the sentence, as the only person listening already knew what she meant.

She got out of bed, wincing at the stabbing sensation on her side, and walked out to the kitchen area on bare feet. She pulled her water filter out of the refrigerator, poured a glass, and downed it. She poured a second and took it with her. Pausing at the sofa, she looked at the cycling gloves. Or rather, in the dark, she looked at the small shape on the larger shape, which she knew were the gloves. Then cursed herself again for slipping so easily into overthinking. The gloves made her think of Dani. Should she call her? Chase loved her own company, and the idea of living with someone broke her out in a mild panic. But sometimes, in her darker moments, she could get trapped in her own head. Sometimes being around people was the best way for a solitary person to be alone. But bouncing her thoughts off another person could be better than having them running around in her mind. And sex was her own personal form of meditation, the only way to really be in the moment. Then thinking of Dani led to thinking of Mason. Her very own Jane Bond. Had that sex purely been meditation?

Or had they both felt something deeper and run away from it?

"Just read the damn thing."

She headed back to bed and loaded the files back up on the tablet. Before switching over to Ashley Eades's website, Chase had already read two short reports. Now she dived into the larger ones.

First, she found the medical records for the old guy who claimed to be James Gilmore. Like most people his age, he hadn't really died of the thing that killed him. The death certificate reported it as a stroke, but his NHS papers showed he'd been living with cancer, had suffered a long bout of pneumonia, and had long since lost himself to an aggressive form of dementia. He'd already shown signs of it when the BBC crew found him in Ethiopia. Most likely, somewhere along the line he'd found details of the real James Gilmore, and as his own identity started to slip, his brain had filled it with that one. But why that identity? And how did he remember details about the soldier's life and childhood?

And why mention Macrobia?

The answer Chase had given to Lauren was the best thing she could think of on the spot. And it had sounded convincing in the moment. But the more she thought about it, the more doubt crept in.

A lost civilization in Africa, or the Arabian Peninsula, wasn't so far-fetched. Countries on both sides of the Red Sea and the Gulf of Aden had laid claim to being the biblical Sheba, and it was well accepted that one of them was right. General consensu more recently had settled on Ethiopia -or what was nnow Ethiopia- as the location of Sheba.

Both Mesopotamia and the Indus Valley, two of the oldest known civilizations, were known to have had a third, unidentified trading partner. And ancient Egypt had close diplomatic ties with a nation somewhere to the south, known as the Land of Punt. In fact, many Egyptian legends held that they were descended from the people of Punt.

Her thoughts went back to the Ark.

And then to the cave she'd found two years before, beneath Alexandria.

The matching faces, in the cave and on the Ark.

And Ethiopia . . .

Life always had a way of circling back. She got off the bed again and walked into the living room, lifting her laptop and taking it back to bed with her. She rested the computer on her knees and logged in, loading up Talaria, a secure phone and messenger app with end-to-end encryption. It had been developed especially for people on the black market, with loads of customizable features aimed at smugglers and relic runners. She could see a little green light next to Hass's name, telling her he was online, and she pressed dial before thinking to check the time. It would be around 7:00 aM there. But hell, it was his choice; if he didn't want to pick up, he wouldn't.

The call was accepted, and the screen went black for a second, taking time for the pixels to form into the image of the video call. Hass was in sweat-stained workout gear, breathing heavily, his thin clothes stretched tight across his muscles. He was drinking from a large flask of water and waved rather than saying hello.

"Hey, Doc."

He set down the flask and leaned in closer to the screen. He was looking down at the image on his own laptop, rather than the camera, which gave the disconcerting impression that he was staring at Chase's chest rather than meeting her eyes. Video calls had changed all the social cues.

"Make it home safe?"

"Yeah." Chase touched her side, out of shot. "Mostly."

"Mostly?"

"Nothing important. The usual."

He grinned as if reading her thoughts and added, "I got a couple calls from Chuy Guerrero after you left. Wanted to know if you'd crashed okay. You should call him."

"Good point." Chase was annoyed at herself. Chuy was her friend; she shouldn't need to be told to call him. "Have you heard of Macrobia?"

Hass had been halfway through another long sip of water but almost did a spit take. He wiped his mouth, shook his head, and shot Chase a bitch, please look. "Have you heard of Washington, D.C.?"

Chase shook her head. "I don't—"

"I'm Somali, and you're going to ask if I've heard of Macrobia?"

Chase felt herself getting defensive and pushed it away. There was something here she didn't know. Ignorance is only a problem if you let it persist.

She nodded at the screen, to say, Okay, I'm listening.

"Macrobia was in Somalia."

"I'm sorry, I always thought it was a myth."

Hass laughed. "You people."

Chase feigned offense, smiled. "You people?"

"Americans. Europeans. You always talk about history like you didn't arrive five minutes ago. You say the gorilla wasn't discovered until the nineteenth century, because that's when you found them. And then it's lost cities, lost countries, lost people. Most of the time, it's not lost at all; you're just not listening to the people who can tell you where it is." His voice had risen into a rant, but he was playing a role. His anger came wrapped in a smile. "You're the proof of that. People in Ethiopia have been saying the Ark was there for a thousand years. You come along and look in the exact place they've been saying. And you get to be the one who found it."

Chase saw the gold chest again. Felt the impulse she'd had to lift the lid and look inside, as well as the near-certainty that she shouldn't. And then the crate, being loaded into the van. The dull ache in her gut ever since. The feeling she couldn't put a name to.

Hass was still going, but she could tell from the pitch of his voice he was near the end, aiming to hit some killer note. "You're going to ask me about the Land of Punt next. All you academics, you write whole books asking where Punt went to and whether it was real. We have Puntland on our maps. On our maps. We can point to it. You go running off to solve a mystery and we're standing right behind you saying, It's here."

But if Macrobia was in Somalia, that would have been a hell of a long walk for James Gilmore to wind up in northern Ethiopia. Especially during a drought. And how would he . . . ?

No. This was just a rescue mission. She wasn't going off in search of . . . She leaned closer to the screen. "Are there ruins? Records?"

"Most of the connections are cultural. We have legends, traditions. Stories of our friendship with Egypt, of visits from their kings." Find Eades, make sure she's okay. That was the mission.

You're not interested in the Fountain.

You're not interested in the Fountain.

"Do you know anything about the Fountain of Youth?"

Hass cocked his head. "Okay. Now you're talking myth."

"Someone tried to hire me to look for it."

Hass pretended to spit-take again, but it lacked the spontaneity of the first one. "Tried? As in you said no?"

Chase nodded. She forgot the laptop was resting on her knees and had to steady it. The movement caused more pain in her side. "Of course."

"Someone wants to give you money to find a thing that can't be found, and you say no?"

You're not interested in the Fountain.

You're not interested in . . .

The old excitement was coming back. The rush. The thrill of the hunt.

"I might have something, Doc. Fancy a trip to London?"

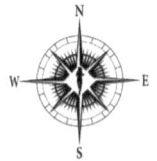

SEVENTEEN

P olice sirens wailed past, filling the car with sound, lights, and fury. Nash watched the cops disappear in the rearview. They weren't looking for him. Some other fool was on the wrong side of the law tonight. The people hunting for Nash and Lenny were unlikely to advertise themselves, and they were already a hundred miles to the north, coming up on the coastal city of Alexandria.

Getting here had always been the goal. But the route he'd taken was plan C. Plan A had been blown the minute he resorted to shooting at the hotel. It had been a best-case scenario, which involved getting straight in, getting the name, getting straight out again, without raising an alarm. In his entire career, that same Plan A had only ever worked five times, but he still went into every job hoping for it. If it had gone smoothly, he'd be at the airport by now, waiting to board a commercial flight. Plan B had burned while he stood talking to Lenny, those precious few seconds wasted letting the gunrunner slip into his usual banter. But he'd learned long ago never to enter the field without at least three exits lined up. Basic CIA training. It was the reason he'd lasted so long as a relic runner, always having more options than the competition. He'd taken his eye off the ball in Ethiopia. The prize had blinded him to the basics of the job. But it wasn't going to happen here.

So, he was on to plan C, a series of cars waiting for him at strategic points.

The first was one they'd dumped while still in Cairo, letting the authorities build up a profile around a blue Renault before changing over to a yellow Volkswagen. Hardly the type of car anyone would expect for a pursuit, and something so noticeable that it blended into the background. This was now the third vehicle, a red Chevrolet. From here, they would head to the port, where one of the many smuggler-friendly boats would take them across to Malta or Catania. From there, it would be easy to get a small charter plane as far north as France, or across into Portugal. Nash had contacts in both places.

On the drive so far, Lenny had managed to talk about everything except Lothar Caliburn. He'd brought Nash up-to-date on the Star Wars movies, which he had very strong opinions about, and thrown out some free information about the current state of play between the Russian money launderers operating out of New Jersey and the American authorities. Nash knew each and every word was a distraction, buying time and distance between Lenny and the people who'd arrested him, but he didn't mind. Those first two hours had been crucial to getting out, and he'd needed to concentrate. Being able to block out whatever Lenny was saying had been a bonus.

But things would be much easier from here. The run to the port was simple, and he knew the city well enough to take quiet roads. He could afford to focus more energy on the guy next to him.

"Okay, Lenny, time to talk."

"What I been doing for the past hour?"

"Time to talk."

"What you wanna know?"

"Caliburn."

"So he's this old legend—"

"I know the stories." Nash shot the arms dealer a look. "I don't want any of your games; don't give me your lawyer tricks or stalling. I want a name."

"We have a problem there. So, I don't actually know it."

Lenny threw his hands up to say, What you gonna do?

Nash slammed on the brakes. They both lurched forward into their seat belts.

"What?"

"I don't know. I never knew. It's just a thing I made up."

Nash hissed through gritted teeth. "Lenny . . ."

He noticed a cop car turning on to the road behind them from a junction. No lights, no sirens. This one wasn't on a call. Nash eased on the gas, got them moving again, before coming to a stop at a red light. The cop came to a stop behind them. Nash checked him in the rearview mirror. A uniformed officer wearing a bored expression, staring off into space.

Just play it cool, he's not after you.

"Hear me out," Lenny said, oblivious to the threat behind them. "I was at the Con."

The Con was the nickname given to an annual gathering of people in the dark trades. Every profession has its convention circuit, organized events where attendees can assemble at hotel bars and exhibition halls to get drunk and pretend to talk shop. The black market was no exception. A different host city was chosen each year, and a large assortment of smugglers, hackers, thieves, counterfeiters, and arms dealers would descend on the location and drink it dry. For a raven like Lenny, this was a golden opportunity to loiter in the bars and collect information.

Lenny continued. "You weren't there. I looked for you."

"I was working."

"Well, I was there. And this guy approaches me. About weapons at first, naturally. I find out he's from R18. He's saying they're recruiting again. And he's talking real money. More than I thought they had. So I keep him talking because, you know, I'm not an idiot. If there's money, I want to find the angle for me to get some of it. Then he mentions they want to hire

Lothar Caliburn."

"And you said you knew him."

"I said I knew him."

The light went green. Nash eased gently down on the accelerator, hitting the perfect balance between not being fast enough to draw the cop's
attention or slow enough to raise his frustration. Nash took a left. It was a
slight detour, but he wanted the blue off his back. He pulled onto the side
of the road and let the engine idle.

"Don't take me back," Lenny whispered.

"Take you back? I take you back, I'm handing myself in. I take you with
me, you're excess baggage. I'm just going to kill you. You saw all that desert
back there?"

Lenny's eyes went wide at that. "Okay. Okay. Look. I'm a salesman,
right? Lying's my whole brand. Someone tells me they need a thing, I'll
tell them I can get the best version of that thing. Someone tells me they're
looking for the guy, I tell them I can introduce them to the guy. And in this
case, I've been hearing for ten years that the guy they're after is dead. Hell,
I heard you killed him. What's the harm in me stringing them along, trying
to get some money? I went to a couple meetings in London, but then they
figured out I was bullshitting, and they got mad. So I went to ground in
France."

"Getting arrested doesn't count as going to ground."

"No, well. That wasn't part of the plan. Those charges were trumped up,
believe you me. Then they tell me the Egyptians want me, and the French
owe the Egyptians a favor, and no, I can't call the American consulate,
because the Americans have already told them they want nothing to do
with me. You believe that?"

"Sure."

"I'll be writing to the president. You'll see. Get it all straightened out."

"That's how it works."

"The Egyptians had gotten wind I knew who Caliburn was. And they're
pissed at him, because apparently he's very much not dead, and he killed
one of their agents. So they hauled me in to Cairo, strung me up, and . . ."

He waved. "Now we're here."

"Get out."

"Wait."

"You, the desert, and a can of oil, like that Bond movie."

"No, wait. For real. I can help. I told you I met with these people? They're in London. And it sounds like we've heard the same rumors, that Caliburn is working with them. I don't know, man, if I was him, I'd be pissed that you've been running around for ten years claiming to have killed him. He's maybe going to be after you at some point. But we can get him first. I know how to contact these guys. They know me. I can get them to talk to you."

"You just got done telling me how you promised some people to set them up with a meeting you couldn't deliver."

"This is different, man." Lenny grinned, showing his cosmetically whitened teeth. "We're buddies. I'll fix you a meeting with these guys, just get me to London."

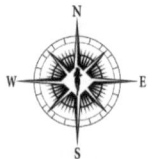

EIGHTEEN

I t was two years since the terror attack, but whenever Chase was in London, she could still smell sulfur and burned dust. She could feel grit in her mouth. These were all just tricks of the mind, but she wondered if everyone else felt it, too.

She walked down the steep slope of Villiers Street, toward Embankment tube station. She needed to be nimble, filtering between a mass of commuters and tourists. Even on a cold afternoon, London was heaving with people.

At the bottom of the street, she saw the gates to Victoria Embankment Gardens. There was a line of emergency medical staff leaning on the railings. Chase scanned the scene, looking for any sign of a problem they might have been attending to. All she could see was the normal mass of moving people. Maybe that was routine now, medical teams waiting in case of emergency.

She hopped down the steps and crossed the small road, walking into the shadow of Embankment Place, the dimly lit stretch of road covered by Hungerford Bridge. There were large black columns supporting the bridge, and the covered space was lined with coffee shops and bistros.

Chase could feel the pull of warm caffeine.

The early-morning flight from New York to Gatwick had been followed by the longest taxi ride in history, as all the roads into London had approached gridlock. And now she was living in the permanent underworld of jet lag and lost time.

She took a look around. Most of the crowding was at the entrance to the tube station. Fewer people had turned to walk under the bridge. She hesitated at the door to one of the chain coffee shops, reaching for the handle.

"Ditching me already?"

Chase turned in the direction of the voice. Joanna Mason was standing only a couple of feet from her.

Chase could have sworn she hadn't been there a second ago.

Mason left a few seconds before adding, "Usually it takes you at least a week."

Chase smiled and nodded. "I guess I deserve that."

They both stood for a second, caught in two minds about what to do next. What was the correct etiquette for meeting up with an ex-girlfriend who also happens to be an MI6 spy? Should they hug? Should they shake hands? Should they secretly plot the overthrow of a government?

Mason made the first move, leaning in close for a brief embrace.

"It's good to see you," she said.

"Yeah." Chase let that hang for long enough before smiling and saying, "I am pretty great."

"You look exhausted."

"Thanks. You look awful, obviously."

Mason looked frustratingly good. When they'd first met, Mason had been a field agent, trying to manage the stress of her double life. In the time since, she'd been promoted to head up her own department in the Special Operations Executive, a shadowy spook agency that was free from the regulations that controlled MI5 and MI6. Everything about her had been upgraded. The suit was sharper, her eyes were brighter. She was wearing a trench coat that probably cost more than Chase's entire outfit, and in that off-the-shoulder way that every third woman in London seemed to be doing. Chase's ego was bruised at the idea that someone's life could be so much better after she walked out of it.

Mason nodded to the coffee shop. "Want one?"

"You're not worried it'll give tails time to get into position?"

Mason smirked, just a little. "You don't get to come into the country without eyes the whole way. That traffic jam on the drive from Gatwick was just so Thames House could put cars all around you. There's someone in your hotel. There are two watchers in the medical crew over there, at least two people on this street by the bike shop. I think we can get a coffee."

They each ordered. Chase did her usual bit about asking for a regular coffee and pretending to be frustrated that they didn't know what she meant. They settled for two Americanos, cream and sugar for Chase, and black for Mason, and took their drinks back out onto the road.

"We're going to be followed no matter what?"

Mason blew on her drink and put the plastic lid back on. "Basically, yes. You don't go through what we went through without getting put on a watch list."

"But we were the good guys."

They walked silently through the tube station, out onto the road that ran along the Thames. After crossing the busy road and bike lane, they didn't start talking again until they were beside the river.

"Doesn't matter," Mason said. "Good, bad. We were part of it."

"So you're on the list?"

Mason paused to lift the lid of her coffee again. Chase smiled at the impatience. Mason could see a global map of political intrigue and plan six steps ahead. But put caffeine or a cake in front of her, and she was a child.

"I'm sure I'm on *a* list. Somewhere. Not the same one as you, not one I'd get to see. But I broke into MI6, one of the most secure buildings in the country. Technically, I was part of a coup. It's just that I picked the right side." She looked around, nodding to someone Chase hadn't noticed. "It's just a watching brief, don't worry about it. They're not going to make any moves on you."

Chase sniffed the air. "Do you still smell it?"

"That's a whole thing." Mason's mouth twitched at the memory. "People say you can still smell it by Parliament. That burned dust, charcoal. I think it's because they're still rebuilding Big Ben. The scaffolding is a reminder. The real thing for me is the sirens. An ambulance went past me about six months ago and I almost had a panic attack."

"Have you told your bosses about that?"

"Of course not."

They shared a look as they passed Cleopatra's Needle, an ancient Egyptian monument they had visited on their second night together. Japanese tourists were climbing on the steps, posing with the bronze lions that stood permanent guard on each side of the Needle.

"I see this every day now," Mason said. "Lived in London my whole life and never noticed it until you. Now I see it all the time."

"You walk by here?"

Subtext: *You like to think about me every day?*

Mason sipped the coffee, scowled, but went in for a second hit. "I moved to a new place on Cable Street. I like to walk to or from the office, along here."

Subtext: *Yeah.*

When they'd first met Mason worked out of the MI6 building at Vauxhall. Since then her organisation, the SOE, had relocated north of the river. Though she'd never really told Chase exactly where.

"Shame about the move," Chase said. "I liked your Chalk Farm place."

"Too many memories. Plus, the new flat is pretty fancy. It's a penthouse, new build, and I've got a view of the Tower of London. If I crane my neck."

"They're clearly paying you too much." Chase nudged her shoulder against Mason's affectionately. "I bet you drive a sexy red sports car now."

"There's no point owning a car in the city." Mason walked on a few more steps before adding quietly, "It's blue. And electric."

They passed beneath Waterloo Bridge. There was a raised viewing platform overlooking the river. It had been built on the remains of the original bridge, but now it was home to a large collection of tents and cardboard boxes.

Through the other side, they started talking again. Chase filled the silence with something light. "So, the watcher at the hotel? Please tell me it's not Tara."

Tara was the attractive brunette who had checked her in. She'd managed to combine friendly and rude into an interesting mix. Chase already had designs on spending the evening at the bar, trying to find out more.

Mason smiled and slowed down, turning to face Chase. "What do you need?"

Chase started to ask why Mason assumed she needed anything, but she gave up. As with Guerrero on the phone, her friends knew her. This wasn't a social call, and Mason was fine with it.

"I'm looking for someone," she said.

"Who?"

"Ashley Eades."

Mason didn't bother to hide the recognition that flashed across her face. She looked down at her feet and said, under her breath, "Shit." She looked around, checking for watchers, then stepped in closer to Chase. "Not here. Play along."

They kissed. Chase was caught by surprise as their lips met. She tried to lean into it, give some back and find the passion of the moment, but the whole thing was a performance. Mason took her by the hand and led the way across the bike lane, to the side of the road, where she flagged down a black cab. She opened the door and waited for Chase to climb in and shuffle across the seat before getting in herself and shutting the door. She leaned toward the plastic divide to the driver and gave him an address.

Chase and Mason made empty conversation on the journey. Movies. Politics. The American presidential race. All of it for the benefit of the driver. Although Chase's London geography was rusty, she knew they were heading in the opposite direction from Mason's Cable Street apartment.

They drove west along the river, then turned north somewhere around Chelsea. The cab pulled into a lane in the shadow of a soccer stadium. Mason paid in cash, and they got out. As soon as that taxi was out of sight, Mason flagged down another one, this time giving the driver a different address. Chase recognized the big white-fronted houses of Kensington. They passed Earl's Court tube station and turned right, into a narrow network of mews lanes lined with small houses. The cab pulled to a stop.

Mason paid again. As they climbed out, she kissed Chase and whispered, "Keep it looking good." She led the way back up the street to a black gate leading between two restaurants. She unlocked the gate, and once they were both through, she paused to lock it again behind them. Down the lane, they came out onto a small courtyard, with a proper traffic entrance at the other end. They'd taken a shortcut and one that, apparently, only Mason had the key to. She opened a gate next to a house's front steps, and they walked down to the basement level, where she opened a large black front door, ushered Chase in, and locked up again after one last look around.

They were in a very basic, sparsely furnished apartment. Mason flicked the lights on and then said, "I could offer you coffee, but you've got that covered."

Chase took the lid off her own cup and sipped from the drink, now almost cold. "I could go for another."

"Instant okay?"

Chase smiled. She remembered Mason had a whole speech about instant coffee and the British class system. "Sure."

They both headed through to the cheap-looking fitted kitchen. White on black, with a faded linoleum floor. There was a wooden table next to the window. Chase pulled out one of the two seats and sat down. She took a look out the window. The view was of a brick wall, with light coming from the street above. Mason filled the kettle and switched it on, turning back to face Chase and leaning on the counter.

"Safe house. My old boss, the one who died during the attack, found a few dead spots left in the city. Places the cameras don't reach."

"I would like it noted, for the record, that you gave me a golden shot at a joke there about finding places the cameras don't reach, and I didn't jump on it."

Mason paused, partway through spooning coffee into two mugs. "I think you just did."

"Yeah, I guess I did. How is this off the grid? I thought your guys prided themselves on just how much Big Brother they had going on in London."

"They do." Mason added sugar for Chase, leaving the spoon to rest in the cup with a loud clink. "But they've got a design floor they never even think of. It's the problem of having a handover in generations. The new pups base all their decisions on software and algorithms. The grid tells them which parts of the grid need covered. But if there's a part of the grid that's not . . . *on the grid*, they don't know about it."

"Sure. I'll say I understood that, if it helps?"

"Thanks to incomplete data that was uploaded originally, half this street is off the grid. The houses one hundred yards that way"—she pointed out the window—"are on. And the buildings behind us are on. But we've been off camera since the black gate. If they had eyes on us at the last cab, they can send someone in on foot, and they'd figure out the dead spot eventually. But for now, we're on our own."

"Nobody watching?"

"Nobody watching."

Chase leaned forward, smiling to say, *Shall we?* "I'd like it noted for the record that I also didn't make a thing out of that."

The kettle finished boiling.

Mason smiled. *Yes, why not?* "You just did."

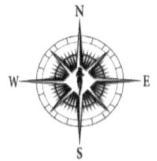

NINETEEN

Hass found a package waiting for him when he checked into the hotel. Tara, the woman behind the desk, noted his name and said, "Oh, Ms. Chase left something for you."

Tara was young and hot. She had a certain something. Hass caught her sizing him up when he walked in. That feeling never got old. He could feel every inch of himself. She was all smiles as she took his details, then paused for a moment to answer a phone call. She finished checking him in without apologizing for the interruption, then handed him the card for his room. There was a pause, and it started to look like she'd forgotten whatever it was Chase had left.

"The package?" Hass gave her his politest smile.

Tara didn't quite roll her eyes. She was too professional for that. But there as a definite *want* to do it. "Sure, if you'll let me finish."

That snap, the whiplash between being polite and rude, caught Hass off guard for a moment. He decided the certain something was attitude, and he liked it. Tara stepped into the back office and came out a minute later with a large padded envelope. She handed it over to Hass and was smiling again, but she looked beyond him now, to the next person in line.

Hass nodded, more to himself than to Tara, and took the package and his suitcase. Chase had picked one of the cheap brand travel hotels. One out of the way, nearer to City airport than Heathrow or Gatwick. On the way to his room, Hass walked through what passed for the hotel bar. He felt a professional shame at this place. It was nothing more than a token effort. A small counter in the corner, linked to the front desk, with three bottles of cheap liquor fixed to the wall and a brand-name coffee machine. The seating area was a cafÈ, a meeting place, and reception all in one.

London was one of the traditional hubs of the black market. The city had mostly been built on it. The money from opium and tea had built the banks; the money from everything else had built the docks along the Thames. Up until the Big Ben attack, there had even been a small number of smuggler towns along the estuary, places where boats and light aircraft made daily deliveries. Successive government had turned a blind eye, because everybody knew the modern capital had been built on these old trades. But the attackers had used one of these towns to bring their weapon into the country, and there had been a secret crackdown on all the old communities and routes.

Most of the old smuggler-friendly hotels in the city had quietly shut down or changed policy. The London branch of the Royale chain was still there, but it had officially been bought by a new company and rebranded. It was in the middle of refurbishment and would stay that way until the coast was clear.

It took Hass three attempts before the electronic pass opened the door to his room. The card only had two sides, yet somehow both of them were wrong. He still wasn't sure which way had been correct, even as the light went green and he stepped inside. The space itself was tiny, just a small bed in a room that appeared to have been built around it. The shower cubicle opened straight out into the room, and the toilet was in what he assumed had been a closet.

He opened the package from Chase. It contained a sleek tablet, a cell phone, two power cables, and a handwritten note.

Doc,

I think I'm being followed. Probably government.

Don't contact me yet. I can be a diversion, give you time. Burner for emergency. Read these files cold, without me priming you. See what you can find. Check out the video and photograph.

MC XX

He turned on the device and was greeted with a personalized message: **What's up, Doc?** And then a small database loaded. He made a terrible coffee from the packet of freeze-dried stuff and the electric kettle that came with the room and settled in.

Scanning through the files, he saw documents about Macrobia, Punt, Alexander the Great, and the Fountain of Youth. He found the video and some old BBC news report about the Ethiopian famine. Villagers suffering, journalists pitying them. Nothing new. He flicked through to the photograph. A scanned image, cracked and faded, of British soldiers in the Sudan in 1884. The siege of Khartoum. The Brits got a real kicking that day. Hass smiled, just a little. Shouldn't have been there in the first place. Britain, along with other European countries, had been laying claim to as much of Africa as they could. It had taken a leader from Hass's own country, Mohammad Hassan of Somalia, to rise up and push them back. The two forces had clashed at Khartoum, a struggle that had ended in defeat for the British.

But the focus wasn't the siege. Chase had this photograph for a different reason. What was it? And why had she mentioned that pointless video? He scrolled back to the BBC report, watched it twice more, all the way through. On the last go, he spotted it. The old guy. He jumped back and forth between the video and the photograph. Okay, they were similar. Could be related. Though, if this whole thing was about the Fountain of Youth . . . time to imagine the impossible.

He looked back through all the documents and could now piece more of the puzzle together. These records to a soldier, James Gilmore, and the NHS files on a man known as James with no surname. The same man? A century apart?

There was a document of notes from Chase. He scanned down her list.

Khartoum is a long walk from where he was found.

Hass smiled and shook his head at that. It was the mistake people always make, looking at navigating Africa from the air or from maps. They think of deserts and jungles, of the large, vast distances to be crossed to get anywhere. But Chase should know better by now. Traveling down through the continent, especially in the time of these soldiers, was all about the Nile.

Khartoum was the meeting point of the Blue Nile and the White Nile. From that spot, you could go one way, down into modern Ethiopia, or go the other, through South Sudan, into Uganda and the Great Lakes region. A British regiment "lost" in Sudan could get anywhere in eastern Africa just by following the water.

She'd wanted him to look at these files fresh for this very reason. His eyes. His experiences. His knowledge.

What else were they missing?

What else had been missed?

He focused back on the photograph. That was the thing that was pulling at his thoughts. Forget the video. Forget the old man, the real or fake James Gilmore. The key questions were why was the photo taken, and what had it survived?

The only way to answer those questions was to find out about the person who took it. Hass clicked through the rest of the files, eventually coming to the back of the photograph. It listed the place and the date, and then, down at the bottom, were three letters. The first character was clearly visible. H. The middle character was half erased by a fold in the photograph, but it looked like an M. The third was faded, almost washed away by water damage. In most circumstances, it would have been impossible to guess what that last initial was. But in this context, with the time and the place the photograph was taken, Hass was confident he could complete the handwritten clue:

H. M. S. Henry Morton Stanley.

His was a name that would forever be associated with African exploration. Stanley was a journalist, born in Britain but naturalized in the States.

He'd been part of many of the most famous expeditions across central and southern Africa. He was the man who, after searching for a lost friend for several weeks, got to say the famous line "Doctor Livingston, I presume?" He had explored the Congo and had a mountain named after him. And, during the many conflicts in Sudan, he had used his local expertise to lead rescue and escape missions.

Stanley was as well-known for exaggeration as he was for discovery. His writings were a mix of truth and tall tales, especially in relation to his own background and achievements. He was generally considered honest about the places he'd visited, though, and his work was still seen as important to Britain and America. Depending on which side of history you were on, he was a great adventurer and modernizer, or he was the poster boy of colonialism and theft.

Everybody knew which side of that divide Hass was on.

But why had one of the most famous explorers in history photographed this particular regiment? Why had the picture survived? Why had this picture come to the attention of whoever had gathered all of this information together?

Hass searched the internet for Henry Morton Stanley Fountain of Youth and found nothing of note. He tried Henry Morton Stanley Macrobia. The result was the same. The third search was Henry Morton Stanley Punt. He got dozens of hits. Egyptian hieroglyphs had only been translated a generation before Stanley's time, so the history had still felt fresh and new. Most of the links were a variation on the same quote from Stanley's autobiography, published in 1909, in which he mentioned hearing tales "of the mountains of Punt, covered in silver and fire, and guarded by evil spirits."

Most of the links were blogs, news reports, and websites about Punt itself and didn't provide any context or extra detail on the quote. Hass found scanned PDFs of Stanley's other books online, but not a complete version of the autobiography.

He needed a hard copy.

And he knew exactly where he'd get one.

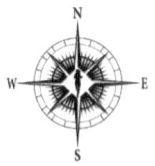

TWENTY

Nash knew he was being watched.

He didn't like it.

He and Lenny were leaning against the railings outside Camden Town tube station, on the busy junction where six roads met in a collision of noise and life. High street chain stores blended with street stalls, and two buskers were playing competing styles of music. The sidewalks were packed, and each person who walked past seemed to be of a different ethnicity.

None of this was new to Nash. He'd been in most of the countries on the map, had even been present at the creation of a few of them. He was well accustomed to looking and feeling at home wherever he went. Lenny, on the other hand, couldn't seem to step outside of his own character. He looked like his skin was itching, and he'd said at least five offensive things in the time they'd been standing there. Nash was starting to suspect Lenny had probably been arrested in France for saying something completely inappropriate.

They were waiting for a sign. Lenny had made contact when they got into town, arranging a meeting with R18. He'd framed it as a deal. *I introduce you to August Nash, living legend, you forget how you want me dead.*

The plan was to stand in this spot and await another message on Lenny's phone. Nash knew there were eyes on them right now, assessing their threat, deciding whether to go ahead with the meeting. After a few more seconds, Lenny's phone beeped.

"It says to walk north up Kentish Town Road, and we'll know when to stop," he reported. "But . . . how do we know which way is north? Hang on, I've got an app."

Nash rolled his eyes and pushed off from the metal barricade. Lenny fell in beside him, delivering another of his long, pointless monologues, but Nash filtered it out and focused on his surroundings. The street was lined with e-cigarette stores, and the area clearly had an abundant supply of halal fried chicken.

As they neared the bridge, he became aware they'd picked up a tail. He used the glass of a shop front to tell him it was a large bald man, wearing black jeans and a tight, long-sleeved black T-shirt. It wasn't subtle. Either this guy was an amateur or he was highly trained and giving Nash the professional courtesy of announcing his presence.

After a few more paces, Nash got his answer. A second tail fell into step with them across the street, dressed the same way, with an identical haircut. The only difference was the new guy had short sleeves, and Nash could make out the bottom of a Nordic hammer tattoo. It was a common symbol among the European white-power types. A lot of heavy metal fans liked the imagery, too, and the hammer was a good way to hide in plain sight. Nash made eye contact with the second guy, who looked away fast. He hadn't deliberately revealed himself, and now he was angry at being blown. These were the people he was looking for, but they seemed to be amateurs.

Lenny, lost in whatever he was saying, hadn't noticed a thing.

They crossed the bridge over the canal. Immediately on the other side, a small man stepped out ahead of them. He was dressed differently. Khaki work trousers and a linen shirt hanging off a tight, wiry frame. He wore yellow- tinted glasses and sported a goatee that had been precision-trimmed. He looked relaxed and confident, giving off enough menace to let Nash know he was a grade above the two tails. He was a professional.

Lenny clearly recognized him. His step faltered. "Uh, Danny. Hi. This is—"

"August Nash." Danny spoke with a faint Belfast accent. "We've met."

It took Nash a few more seconds to place Danny, without showing that he hadn't recognized him at first. It had been a younger version of Danny, without the goatee or glasses, and with bleached spiky hair, who had tried to recruit him for R18. He'd looked softer back then. He'd put in some real work in the intervening years.

"Danny." Nash offered his hand in shake.

Danny's grip was strong.

Danny eyed Lenny with contempt but kept his conversation directed at Nash. "You keep some strange company, Mr. Nash."

"Keep your enemies close, but your idiots closer."

"Hey." Lenny's voice rose in indignation, but he quieted down again when Danny glared at him. As Danny's head was turned, Nash got a look at the earpiece he was wearing.

"I think you can relate." Nash smiled and turned to look at the two tails.

Danny eyed them coolly. "Yes. Please, follow me."

They turned down a narrow set of steps to the canal towpath. They were greeted there by a woman, the largest of the crew so far, who towered over everyone except Nash. She had the same haircut as the two tails but twice as much muscle.

Danny asked permission for both Nash and Lenny to be searched, but it was the kind of request that came pre-answered.

In a surprisingly high northern accent, the woman asked them to empty their pockets and handed their cells to Danny before patting them down. Danny put their phones into a small black case, then scanned Nash and Lenny for any further electronic signals. Once they'd passed the inspection, the woman and the two street guards turned to Danny and put their hands out as if for a shake. Nash noticed that each of them had their thumb and index finger curled to touch, forming a circle, and their remaining fingers were pressed together and out straight. They slid their hands on the inside of Danny's, in a bizarre impression of a handshake, until their index fingers touched and formed the number eight. Once they'd each done it, they left, heading back up the steps.

"They have somewhere to be," was all Danny said as explanation.

There was the sound of a small outboard engine, and Nash turned to see a rubber boat coming toward them along the smooth surface of the canal's water.

It was piloted by yet another nondescript skinhead. The boat slapped into the brick towpath, and Danny gestured for Nash and Lenny to climb aboard.

"I don't really need to tag along," Lenny said.

Danny pointed again at the boat. "We're all going."

Once they were all on, the pilot squeezed on the throttle again and they jerked away from the side, continuing around a bend and past the Camden Lock Market. Beside a large redbrick building, the footpath rose up into a bridge, forming a tunnel that appeared to lead straight into the building. The boat turned into the tunnel. In the darkness, Nash could make out huge metal girders overhead, supporting the weight of the structure above them. They were in a small, covered canal basin. The boat pulled in beside a metal ladder. Danny handed the black case containing the cell phones to the boatman and started to climb the ladder, telling Nash and Lenny to follow him. The ladder led up and over a wall that looked to have been added recently, set into a much older archway. On the other side, Danny flicked a switch and strips of halogen light filled out the space around them. They were standing in a brick tunnel, with low arches only just above their heads.

They walked deeper into the network of tunnels, coming to a recent addition, a wall made of gray cinder block that blocked the passageway. There was a door in the middle of the new wall, covered in a curtain. Danny pulled the drape aside and nodded for Nash and Lenny to step through. Now they were standing in a much larger space, with a high brick ceiling and square walls. The surfaces had all been drywalled and painted, and the floor was covered in sound-absorbent carpet tiles. It was decorated like the dream of a bachelor apartment or a hipster bar, with pool tables, large leather sofas, and television screens as large as panel trucks. There were other curtains at the end, which Nash guessed covered other doorways. Nash and Lenny shared a look and a shrug, then followed Danny to the sofas. He waited for them to sit down before settling onto the sofa opposite. "So, how can we help, Mr. Nash?"

"What is this place?"

"There's a network of tunnels down here. Used to be stables for the railyard ponies, and transport passages to get goods between the trains and the boats. It was just sitting derelict until we took it."

"Impressive."

"This is just part. We've got a kitchen, dorm rooms, a shooting range, a gym."

"Hotel Nazifornia."

Danny didn't crack a smile. "I seem to remember, when I offered you a job, you said you didn't want to work with a bunch of 'goose-stepping morons.'"

"I'm short with people who are getting between me and a drink."

Danny turned his focus to Lenny. "And last time we spoke, I'm sure I told you I'd cut out your tongue and mail it to your ma."

"She's dead." Lenny shrugged before realizing that wasn't the best tone to take in the circumstances. "Uh, sorry, buddy. Really. Nothing personal. And we agreed." He turned to gesture at Nash with both hands. "He's here."

"You didn't agree with me." Danny's voice was cold. Nash decided he must be a hell of a poker player. "But it's not my call."

Nash got two things from this. First, Danny wasn't in command. This was another audition before being allowed to meet the top guy. Second, Danny's tone told them he wasn't happy about the current setup. He resented whoever was above him and the orders he was being given. Nash filed that away. It might come in handy.

Nash leaned forward in his seat, deciding on the direct approach. "I want to meet Lothar Caliburn."

Danny's head twitched in a way that suggested he was listening to a message through his earpiece. He got to his feet and nodded to Nash.

"I'll take you to him."

TWENTY-ONE

T he kettle needed to be boiled again by the time Mason and Chase had finished their fumble. It was more stress relief than anything else. Bringing each other close with their fingers, before stripping down and taking turns on the table. Mason had always known how to get Chase at her loudest, and Chase, for her part, had always known the right places to touch to get Mason to give up control.

Now dressed, smiling, and breathing deep, Mason handed Chase a black coffee and settled into the seat across the table. "Still thinking about Kara?"

"*Tara*. I think we broke the leg," Chase said, rocking the table with her hands.

"It was a noble way to go. You don't seem yourself. "

"Feeling it." Chase breathed out, leaned into the wood of the chair. "Travel. Dirt. I'm thinking it's time I got out."

"Heard that before."

Mason had been the one to help fix Chase's reputation, to set her up with the job offers. The dance of Chase threatening to retire from the black market was one they'd done a number of times.

"This time I mean it. I've been feeling . . ." She looked out at the brick wall for a moment. "We had fun together, didn't we?"

"Okay, now I'm worried. What's wrong?"

Chase shook her head, then ran a hand through her hair and carried down to massage the back of her own neck. "I don't know. I'm off-balance.

Been feeling strange the last few days. Aster Bekele screwed me over, and I let her. The thing with Zoe a couple years ago. Us. There's a girl back home, a bike messenger. She's fun, but ..." Chase paused. Shook her head. "Ignore all that. I'm just off-balance. I found the Ark."

"As in ... ?"

"Yeah, as in."

"Did it shoot lasers or anything? Any faces melt?"

"It's just a wooden box."

"Wow. I mean, that's ... wow."

"But then Bekele stole it away from me. That's what I meant, screwed me over. She said it belonged there, in the country where I found it. And you know, I thought I agreed with that? Except ..."

"Except?"

"I've had this feeling ever since, like it was *mine*. I walked past a synagogue in New York and I got all emotional. I've never felt that before. I almost went in. I think maybe I wish I had. It felt like ... I think maybe it felt like faith? I don't know."

"I think that's probably natural. The Ark—I can't believe I'm saying that, so cool—the Ark is part of your history, too. I mean, it was your people's. And I know you've never believed in any of it, but even still. If you find proof that your people did actually carry the thing that the book says they carried ..."

"Yeah."

"But this isn't the first time you've found real history."

Mason was one of the few people who knew what Chase had found in the cave beneath Alexandria. She didn't know the full story. Only four other people in the world knew that. But Mason knew enough.

"Do you ever think about that?" Chase said. "About what we hid? Who gets to own history like that? Who gets to make that decision?"

Mason tilted her head, shrugged. "I make decisions like that every day. It's my job. You're overthinking all of this."

"Yeah, yeah. I know. Thinking's not really my style. I'm just *done*. It's time to get out of the game and live that normal life everyone always tells me about. But I got this one last loose end to tie up first."

"Why are you looking for Ashley Eades?"

"I think she's in trouble."

Mason smiled. "That much I know."

Chase finally saw it. *Of course* that was why LaFarge had led her to Mason. "It was you," she said. "You arranged it."

"Someone else did the cleaning. I just made the introductions. But I need to know why you're after her. Even you."

Chase thought it over. What was the easiest way into the story? "Someone tried to hire me to find Macrobia."

"Sounds like a kitchen cleaner."

Chase laughed. "Right? It's actually a legendary lost country. Somewhere that might be in Africa or India. Could be on the Arabian Peninsula, too, I guess. But given what I just found, and where I found it, I'm leaning toward Africa."

"Why do they want to find it? Money? Jewels? A very big ball of string?"

There was no easy way to say this. Framing it with the Macrobian connection hadn't helped. "They want the Fountain of Youth."

Mason made a noise that was somewhere below a scoff. "Two years ago, I'd say that's stupid."

"Yeah. I know. Really. I still think it's dumb, but . . ."

"I know that look," Mason said. Then she pointed. "And I know that smile. You're into it. You think it's real."

You're not interested in the Fountain.

You're not interested in the Fountain.

"No, I don't. I— She made a good case, is all."

"Who?"

In any other conversation, Chase would have kept the information back, protected her client. And there was an extra layer here. Lauren had clearly been making a move. Chase hadn't been interested, but this felt like she was telling an ex-girlfriend about a new crush. If there was no interest, what was the problem? That made Chase angry at herself, and it was enough to get over the hesitation.

"Lauren Stanford," she said.

"Dosa Cola?" Mason's voice rose. "*That* Lauren Stanford?"

"I was surprised, too."

"Makes sense, actually. They knew each other at Oxford."

Stanford had failed to mention that connection. But on that note, in all the conversations they'd had, Eades had never said anything about studying at Oxford. Did it go against the image she'd created?

Mason continued. "Stanford's invested a lot over here, actually. Put her own money behind a craft brewery in Camden. The hipsters love it. They keep running an equity scam, getting their 'fans' to invest in the company to raise capital. She's also been buying up a load of land in the East End, around Whitechapel." She looked lost in thought for a moment, making connections. Then she smiled. "She's cute. I've seen pictures."

Chase looked away, shook her head. She was about to say, "I hadn't noticed," but nobody in the world who'd met her would buy that lie. And again, why was she even lying?

She changed the subject. "She gave me a whole story about her parents dying of cancer, her family being healers, being obsessed with finding the Fountain. But I still think they just want a PR thing. They pay me to go look for this magic water, then use it as a marketing gimmick to sell a new brand."

Mason had been typing on her phone's screen. She held it up to show a page full of Lauren Stanford pictures, taken from news stories. "Cute." She smiled. "But it's probably about the water. That's the thing now. Oil is dying off. The next big deal, the next big war, will be water. That or minerals. China already owns most of Africa's natural resources, and your country is playing catch up."

"And your country?"

"Talking behind China's and America's backs." A slow smile. "It's what we do best. But how does all this lead to Eades?"

"Lauren thinks she, Eades, was working on a story linked to the Fountain when she disappeared." Chase saw Mason purse her lips in thought and followed up with, "What's your link to her?"

Mason paused. "Okay. So this all ties to our old friends R18."

A small explosion went off in Chase's mind.

R18 had been involved in the London incident. The attack itself had been carried out by a cult claiming to be Atenists, an ancient Egyptian religion, and the full extent of the links between R18 and the Atenists had never been revealed. But the cult had infiltrated the British establishment and very nearly pulled off a coup. Was R18 part of the Atenist cult, or had they just been hired muscle?

"You're working on them again?" Chase asked.

"I never stopped. When I first started working on the case that led me to you, it was because my boss and I thought someone had infiltrated the system over here. The government, the cops, the security forces. We thought a coup was coming, and we were right. But what we were seeing at first had nothing to do with Egypt or ancient technology or any of the stuff that came later. I think what we saw at first, the people we were seeing at first, was R18."

"I'd like to say you sound paranoid . . ."

"Yeah."

"Yeah."

"R18 went quiet after the attack. But I think they were just licking their wounds. They backed the wrong play and needed to consolidate. They're clever. They hire people to do their dirty work for them. When I say their name, you think of the kind of people we fought. Combat gear. Ex- military. But I think the real people never expose themselves."

"You think they're hiring again?"

"I know it. Word is they've bagged Lothar Caliburn. You know the name?" Chase nodded, Mason continued. "Killed a French agent a few months back. Friend of mine, one of their best."

"I'm sorry."

Mason nodded to acknowledge the condolences. "At least the French were doing something."

"Meaning your own people aren't?"

"This is still my own side project. I didn't know who I could trust before the attacks, and I still don't know now. I mean—" Mason leaned forward, lowered her voice. "There was a coup on my own government two years ago and everybody is acting like nothing happened. Parliament kicks the inquiry further down the road every six months, the prime minister doesn't want to touch it, the press want to talk about different things. Why would everybody be avoiding the obvious unless they all have reasons to? This whole thing started out as my own private war, and it's got to stay that way."

"It's good to see you've resolved your trust issues."

Mason raised her eyebrow. "Coming from you, that means almost nothing. Anyway, I found out that Caliburn has joined R18, and they were after Ashley Eades."

"How?"

"I tortured a guy."

Chase put her palm up. "TMI."

"She'd been working on a story about them, getting too close. My guy told me they were after her, but not when or how. So I contacted her straightaway. Turned out, that was the night they tried the hit, at her place. Talking to me was the reason she was late home."

"So you saved her."

"Funny thing was, she didn't believe me. Or didn't trust me. And I don't blame her. A stranger turns up out the blue and starts warning you off a story about Nazis? You're going to want to walk away from that person."

"I've been on the other end of that meeting."

Chase and Mason had met in a jail cell when the spy hired the relic runner for a secret mission, telling stories of Nazis, ancient weapons, and a religious cult.

Mason smiled. "Right. Well, the time she took saying no to me turned out to be the time that saved her life. By the time she got home, late, her boyfriend was dead. And I guess I'd touched something in her, because I'd given her my card—same one I gave you—and the first thing she did when she saw the blood was call me."

"Her family?"

"Doesn't have any. Only child, and both her parents passed away when she was younger."

"And she was the one to find him? The boyfriend?"

"Yeah. Blood everywhere. She was in shock by the time I got there."

"I'd heard the neighbors found him."

"It was written up in the press as neighbors. Someone called in an anonymous tip to the cops, said there was a domestic disturbance in the building. They turned up and went door to door, found Eades's door kicked in, went inside. I hadn't managed to arrange a cleanup in time, but I managed to calm the story down afterward and keep the boyfriend's name out of it, too."

"And you'd already gotten her out of there before the cops turned up?"

"By a matter of seconds. I didn't want her going into the system. I didn't want to risk handing her over, so I helped her disappear. Gave her money and introduced her to a cleaner."

"Who did you go with?"

"Old friend of mine, Fergus Fletcher."

Chase didn't know the name, but if Mason vouched . . .

Hang on.

Back up.

Now that Chase thought about it, it was true, the boyfriend's name hadn't been in any of the news stories she'd found online or in any of the files Lauren Stanford had given her. It hadn't even occurred to her as a gap, because she'd been so focused on Eades.

"Wait. Why would you need to keep his name out of it? The boyfriend?"

Mason nodded. *Right question.* "I didn't know when I contacted her, otherwise I would have handled it differently, but she was shacked up with Roberto Conte."

"As in . . . ?"

"His son."

A second explosion went off in Chase's mind. From the smile on Mason's face, she could tell the spy knew it, too. Francisco Conte's son. How had Eades and Roberto met? And what impact had it had on Cisco? How the hell was Chase coming out of this conversation with more questions than when they'd started?

She tried to find a solid footing to get back on track, asking, "Are we sure Eades was the target?"

"It was definitely her name I was given. But that's not to say they weren't both targets."

"And nobody knows who Caliburn is?"

"Right. He could be anyone. We could've walked past him today and not known."

"Did Eades know?"

"She swore she didn't."

"I found you through Grant LaFarge, the guy who wiped her facial rec off the network. Would there be other ways for Caliburn to trace her?"

Mason smiled, raising an eyebrow as she sipped her coffee.

Of course. "You've known where she is the whole time, haven't you?" Chase said.

"Like you said, trust issues. Plus, I figured Caliburn would try to find her at some point, so I've been keeping watch."

Chase nodded. She sipped her coffee. "This is terrible."

"You've seen what I'm working with here."

"Blaming your tools? I like 'em."

Mason smiled. "I can't believe you can find the flirt in making an instant coffee."

"You've met me?"

Mason let the same smile linger for a while, and Chase sat in silence, drinking the terrible coffee. Knowing R18 was involved made it all feel personal. And knowing Cisco Conte's son had been killed added an additional jagged edge. Cisco wasn't exactly what Chase would call a friend, but she'd known him a long time, and this was a complication she hadn't expected.

"I need to get to her," Chase said. "I need to get to Eades."

Mason stood and crossed to the kitchen counter. She pulled open a drawer and lifted out a set of car keys, tossing them to Chase. "I can't go with you. It would ruin my cover. But I can help you get there."

TWENTY-TWO

H ass wasn't sure which was more unsettling, the physical instability in Addis Ababa or the political one he could feel in London. True enough, everyone in Ethiopia seemed to be tense lately. The minor tremors. The increased activity of Erta Ale. But London felt different. Something had changed in the time since he'd first started coming here. He felt more defensive as he walked up Tottenham Court Road. He drew more looks. More stares. There was an anger and a coldness, coexisting at the same time. In a city as diverse and multicultural as London, Hass still felt like he needed to watch his back. There had been a political earthquake here, and the fear lingered.

A news alert on his phone told him there had been another earthquake back home. This one seemed to have originated beneath Abaya Lake, which was farther south along the rift. He texted Freema to check in but got no response. He stopped off at a mosque on his way across London, feeling the need to say a prayer.

His old field instincts kicked back in near the top of Tottenham Court Road.

He was being followed.

He slowed down and turned off the busy road, heading east along the quieter Store Street. How could someone learn to spot a tail without seeing them? If pressed, Hass wouldn't be able to explain it. For relic runners, this wasn't a life they'd trained for. It didn't come after graduating from an academy. You jumped into it feetfirst, and you either died or you learned.

Hass had come into the job with certain hard-earned advantages. The color of his skin. His gender identity. Long before he'd taken to working on the black market, he'd already been forced to develop and hone his instincts. Hass couldn't rationalize how it was he could tell it was going to rain five minutes before it did, and he didn't know how he'd developed a radar for being followed. But he had one, and it was telling him someone was following him as he turned north, off Store Street onto Gower Street. He veered west, heading back toward Tottenham Court Road. It was the opposite direction from his destination, but he found it easier to lose a tail in a crowd, and the busier street would give him more opportunity to spot his tail.

Or . . . wait. You know what? *No.*

This wasn't *Tinker, Tailor, Soldier, Spy.*

He wasn't playing games.

Hass spun around on his heels. At the end of the street, just turning the corner to follow him, was a man with close-cropped hair, dressed all in black with a long-sleeved T-shirt. He made eye contact briefly, then looked away, grabbing for a cell in his pocket and glancing around as if confirming the street signs.

Hass smiled. "You a ninja?"

The man, angry at Hass or himself or both, gave up the charade, growled, and charged. Hass had a size advantage, in both height and bulk. He stood his ground, planting his feet. The man crashed into him and winded himself. The force was enough to stagger Hass backward but not take him to the ground. He swung his fist into the side of the attacker's bald head. There was a grunt. Hass swung again, connecting with the ear. He felt the weight against him sag a little and stepped back. The shorter man was blinking, looking dazed.

"Why are you following me?"

The attacker didn't answer. Hass pushed him farther back, trying to get a better look. Was he a professional or an amateur? A pro probably wouldn't have been spotted or caught so easily. And the way he'd charged, the anger and frustration, spoke of someone who hadn't been thinking clearly. Hass felt his own flash of anger and swallowed it back.

Hass asked the next obvious question. "Who else is with you?"

The attacker blinked again. Hass had hit him harder than he'd intended. He let the hand brake off his anger and punched the shorter man in the face, sending him to the ground. He looked around and couldn't see anyone else.

Amazingly, in the center of London, they'd founded a deserted stretch of road for this confrontation.

Hass looked down at the fallen man again.

A rival relic runner? A random racist?

It didn't matter. Hass turned and walked west, back onto Tottenham Court Road and across into a narrow lane next to an old church. On the other side, on Whitfield Street, he turned to head north again, confident now that he wasn't being followed. The adrenaline was washing out. Another old, familiar feeling was left in its place. The low-level trauma of feeling chased and hated. Another person in another city throwing aggression at him. His breathing was coming in fast, ragged bursts. Hass leaned against a wall and forced himself to calm down, letting the feeling pass, then continued on to his destination.

The British Library was a large, angular, redbrick building. With smooth surfaces and layered, sloping roofs, it looked to have been built from LEGO. Hass passed through the light security check. He'd left his tools and weapons back at the hotel, so the only thing in his messenger bag that could be counted as hazardous was the spare underwear he always carried.

The large foyer area never failed to impress. It was *very* Logan's Run, a wide-open space full of smooth white surfaces, all well-lit from the skylight above. Directly ahead of Hass was the centerpiece of the building's design, a tower of glass containing the books from King George III's library.

Each floor of the building was wrapped around the tower, with walkways and balconies facing out onto the collection at every level.

Hass headed straight for the information desk. He'd just started explaining what he needed to the Frenchwoman there when his burner started to ring. He stared at it for a few seconds. It was a gamble, of course. How did he know this number was Chase? But then, who else would have the number?

He answered, "Dal's Porn Emporium, how can I help?"

"Nice." It was Chase. "You had to improvise and that's where your mind went?"

"My mind never left."

"Where are you right now?"

"British Library."

"In the library?"

"Inside, yes."

"On the phone?"

"You know that part."

"How many dirty looks are you getting right now?"

"Just the one."

"You following a lead?"

"Not one you'll want me to say over the phone."

"I'll come to you. I got a car and we're taking a trip."

Hass pocketed the phone and turned back to the woman at the desk with an apologetic nod. He gave the name and author of the book he was after. She typed it into her system, then directed Hass to the manuscript department on the second floor, where a secured room at the back of the collection had been given over to books salvaged from Buckingham Palace. Hass needed to show ID at the door and sign in. He asked the woman on duty if his underwear counted, getting a smile from her, then showed his passport.

Today he was Henri Soussa, a French Algerian. Hass had grown to resent using fake IDs, having worked so hard to be himself, but understood why it was necessary.

He was escorted up to the private room by a security guard, who did a second bag check and unlocked the door with an electronic pass, letting Hass step in alone before shutting the door after him. The collection was free to view, but its origins had led some trophy hunters to try to steal from it. One of the darker corners of the black market involved the trade of crime memorabilia. Items from a destroyed building, relics of a terror attack, fit the bill.

The room was small, white, and well-lit. The books were held on black shelves lining three of the walls, with a desk in the middle and a glass door looking out onto the manuscript area. Hass scanned the shelves until he found what he was looking for: an aged hardback copy of Henry Morton Stanley's autobiography. A more detailed search online had told him there had been a signed first edition in the Queen's collection, handed down through the family. Hass had decided a first edition would be the best source, free of any revisions. He took a seat at the table and started scanning through the pages. This was another skill you picked up on the job as a relic runner: looking across textbooks, maps, and ancient documents for key words that related to whatever object you're searching for. It took almost twenty minutes, but he found the right passage.

> It was on the way out of Khartoum, fleeing the coming carnage, that I came across freebooters in the desert. They were a British regiment, recently deserters. We traded brandy and stories, sharing our fears of what would happen to General Gordon and his men. They related a legend they'd heard from their guides along the Nile, of the Mountains of the Moon, topped with silver and gold. They were intent on tak-

ing the description literally. I attempted to dissuade
this approach by telling them of similar stories I had
heard on previous journeys, and that the Mountains
of the Moon were said to be the source of the Nile. I
told them of the many mountains already discovered
to the south, each of them topped with snow that
could be the origin of the silver and gold they'd heard
of, the sort of metaphorical descriptions so common
to the tribes of the dark continent. In attempting to
illustrate the dangers of believing myth, I told them
of the legendary mountains of Western Punt, topped
with jewels and guarded by evil spirits. I fear this only
further fired their imaginations.

They inquired about retaining my services to act as
their guide. I explained I had served my time on fool's
errands. They were insistent on their quest, and I
advised them to follow the White Nile, as it would
lead them toward mountains capped with snow, and
they could learn their lessons the hard way.

Does Punt await discovery? I recall an enlightening
conversation I had with General Gordon before leaving Khartoum. He spoke at length of an island in
the Seychelles and his conviction this was the biblical
Eden. He quoted scripture and reminded me that
the garden itself was in the east of Eden, not the
whole of Eden as we tend toward saying. He believed
Eden to have been a larger area, lost now beneath

the water. It was his manner during this exchange that convinced me to leave Khartoum at my first convenience. I gathered the forces defending the palace were as given to religious zeal as those attacking it. But in the years that followed, I thought of those two conversations on many occasions. The men who were convinced fortune awaited them to the south, and General Gordon, who believed Eden lay farther in that same direction. I have read with interest the growing theory of Lemuria, the sunken continent that our learned friends now believe acted as a land bridge between Africa and India. I'm given to wonder if perhaps General Gordon was closer than he could know, and the Seychelles are the peak of a lost land. If that proves to be the case, then the Land of Punt could still exist beneath the waves. Its secrets may one day surface.

Hass smiled along with most of the extract. Lemuria had long since been debunked, but it had been seen as a serious proposition during Stanley's time. And again, as he'd explained to Chase, Punt wasn't lost. Somalia had a cultural memory of trading with Egypt, passed down in myths and customs. Many of the secrets of Punt were lost. How large the empire had been and what led to its fading away. But Hass was confident the location wasn't a mystery. Gordon's theory of Eden was a new one to him, but there were as many theories about Eden as there were Atlantis, and none of them worth giving any time to. There was no mention of the Fountain of Youth, but here was the explanation behind the photograph. James Gilmore and his regiment weren't soldiers who just happened to get lost in the desert; they had been looking for Punt. And Stanley had sent them south. If they followed his directions correctly, they would have found their way eventually to the Rwenzori Mountains, which included Mount Stanley, named after the man who declined to guide them. Hass knew the area well; he'd been there many times for both work and pleasure. Not once had he heard any mention of the Fountain of Youth. If the freebooters had followed the wrong branch of the river and traveled along the Blue Nile, that would have taken them down into modern Ethiopia, putting them near where "Gilmore" turned up a century later. But Hass knew that region even better and didn't know of any legends relating to the Fountain.

Movement caught his eye. Someone had just been looking in through the glass in the door. Was it the security guard? Hass glanced at the small black camera in the ceiling above him. He was already being monitored— why would anybody look in?

He watched for a few seconds to see if anyone reappeared at the door, then went back to the pages, scanning for anything else of use. There were more mentions of the mountains of southern Africa, focusing mainly on the Rwenzori range and Kilimanjaro, which during Stanley's time had been claimed by Germany. There were no more references to the Mountains of the Moon or Punt.

Another movement. This time Hass caught it. A man, glancing in before walking on by. Hass couldn't be sure it was the same person as before, but the behavior felt the same. Was someone checking in on him? Waiting?

He would have written it off as coincidence, or a curious student—the building was full of them—if it wasn't for the clothing. The watcher was dressed almost identically to the man who'd followed him across town. The same shaven head, the same black clothes, though this one wore a shortsleeved T-shirt rather than the long sleeves of his previous watcher. Everything else was the same.

He was still being followed

⬛▮▮▮

Chase parked the car a few streets away from the library, near Oakley Square. Enough of a distance to see if she was being tailed. She'd been disappointed to find Mason wasn't giving up her sexy blue sports car. She was now in a yellow MINI Cooper. The spot it was parked in, Mason said, was off the grid. And the car was registered to a fake name. If Chase was careful, she had a shot of getting out of London without being tailed.

If she was careful. Like, ever.

She walked down to the library. The line was long, and the security check was in force, but that was fine, as she'd left her bag in the car. She breezed in past the checkpoint and walked over to the information desk. A Frenchwoman greeted her with a can't-I-just-get-five-minutes-alone smile.

"Hey," Chase said. "I'm looking for a friend of mine. You wouldn't miss him. Big guy. Hot. Built like the Rock."

"Henri."

"Sure."

"He's popular."

That gave Chase pause. A knot of concern formed in her gut. "Excuse me?"

"Some of his other friends have already gone up."

⬛▮▮▮

Hass flicked back to the extract he'd found useful and took pictures with his cell. He slipped the book back into place on the shelf and sat on the desk, facing the door, kicking his feet like a child. When the watcher passed by a third time, Hass was waiting. He smiled, waved, and blew the man a kiss.

The watcher panicked and ducked back out of sight.

Now that Hass had confirmed the tail, he had a new problem.

There was at least one person out there. Possibly two. And that was based only on what he'd seen so far. Hass's own rules of survival included doubling the threat at any given moment. If you've seen one person, that means there are two. If you've seen two people, that means there are four. So he was going to assume four people were out in the library, waiting for him.

What was their next move?

The door itself was locked. They couldn't get in without a security pass. Right now, he was safe. Could one of them sign in at the front desk, the way he had, and be let in? That was possible. And then he would be locked in a tight space with up to four people. He couldn't wait around in here. He needed to move. There was a button on the wall beside the door, set into a small metal square. If he pressed that, the lock would disengage and he could leave. But, if it worked the same way as on the way in, there would be a low electronic beep to announce it was unlocked, and anybody waiting outside would know he was coming.

He swore out loud and laughed at himself.

This was his exact problem.

Always had been. He was standing here thinking everything through without actually doing anything. By now Chase would be several steps into an escape plan. And she wouldn't even have a plan. It would all be on instinct. She was a natural at doing things, and they almost always came off. Even the wildest gamble, the dumbest idea. Hass needed to sit and think through all the options, to know several steps ahead, and he would second-guess every single decision.

He swore again. He was now overthinking the idea of overthinking. If Hass's life had any meaning, it was to learn to be in the moment, to accept who you were and roll with it. But he was the one person who always failed to learn that lesson.

There was a fire alarm on the wall.

He punched the glass. Within seconds, the whole building was filled with buzzing and a polite voice asking people to make for the nearest exit. Hass guessed every publicly accessible door would now be unlocked. He counted to five, giving more time for confusion to set in outside, then pushed out into the manuscript hall.

Four people were being ushered out of the hall by men in security uniforms.

Two of them were dressed all in black, one in long sleeves, one in short sleeves. The man he'd already seen and his friend. They turned to see him and, ignoring the security guards, charged.

Okay. It's a fight now.

This is why I'm not in charge of plans.

Hass set his feet square, imagining himself growing roots deep down into the ground, making himself solid. The first attacker, Short Sleeves, bounced off him and fell backward. The impact had taken all of Hass's strength, and then Long Sleeves took his turn, knocking Hass to the ground, falling down on top. The security guards were shouting but not doing anything to stop the fight. Underpaid immigrants working in uniform at a library, they weren't paid to deal with this. They shouted into handheld radios.

Hass climbed to his feet before either of the two men could react. He blocked a punch from Short Sleeves and threw one of his own, knocking the guy back to the floor. Long Sleeves jumped forward. Hass ducked, taking the attacker's weight on his back and rolling him, throwing him headlong into a glass case displaying some ancient parchment. Hass ran, pushing out past the confused security guards, onto the walkway overlooking the glass tower of books. To his right he could see four more security guards, running in his direction. Two of them were dressed differently, wearing some kind of black jumpsuit and carrying Tasers. Wow. There was a librarian tactical unit? Hass turned to his right and started to sprint in the other direction. He was heading toward the front of the building, but he was still two floors up. When he reached the end of the walkway, he came to the balcony overlooking the large open-plan foyer.

The security team had split into two. One each of the uniformed staff and the tac team entered the manuscript hall to deal with whatever was going on in there. The other two were still following Hass, shouting. There was a spiral staircase immediately ahead of him. He took it down one floor. He was about to head down to the next level when he heard footsteps coming up toward him.

"No fair," he called out. "I'm trying to do what the nice recorded lady is telling me."

He turned away, heading along the walkway beside the glass tower. And then he found a whole new problem. Stepping into his path up ahead was a large woman. She was the same height and build as Hass, matching him muscle for muscle, and dressed like the other two attackers. She cracked her jaw and smiled, throwing up fists.

Hass groaned. He wasn't worried about the fight. Whoever this woman was, he was confident he could win. But it wouldn't be fast, and in the time it took him to get her down, the security guards would be on them. What was her plan here? Get them both arrested?

There was a blur of movement to the left. Hass caught a shape moving in, swooping across from the open space between the walkway and the glass tower. The shape formed into Chase, swinging on what looked like an electrical cable. She crashed into the larger woman, pushing her into the wall with a thud that shook the floor. The big woman groaned and slumped to the floor, holding her head. Chase, having pulled off a near-perfect landing on both feet, smiled at Hass.

"Hey, Doc."

"Did you . . . ?" Hass leaned to look up above them, to where the electrical cable was looped over the railing on the floor above. "Never mind." "Just followed the noise," Chase said.

Security guards were on either end of the walkway now, closing in slowly. Hass looked at them, then to Chase. "What now?"

Chase leaned over the railings to look below. At the base of the glass tower, maybe fifteen feet below them, was the cafÈ. Small square tables filled the floor. Chase looked at the tables, then smiled at Hass.

"No way," Hass said.

The guards were almost on them now.

There was a roar from behind them. The large woman rose up from a crouch and rushed at Chase, growling like an animal. Chase ducked down, in the same maneuver Hass had pulled upstairs, and rolled the woman over her back, lifting her up over the railing and flipping her off the edge. She seemed to hang in the air for a second, defying gravity, before everything returned to speed and she crashed down through two of the tables below, landing in a heap.

"Crash mat," Chase said. "All part of the plan."

She didn't wait for Hass to argue, vaulting the rails and dropping down onto the larger woman, using her to cushion the fall. Hass saw a Taser being raised and followed Chase's lead. He knew to go limp on impact, letting the momentum roll him away. He heard a dull groan as he landed, telling him the attacker was still alive, and still semiconscious. All the wind was knocked out of him on impact, and he took a few seconds to regain his breath before climbing to his feet. There were no guards down here. All attention must have been focused on the disturbances on the two levels above.

Hass and Chase ran out through the open fire doors, slipping into the crowd of confused students waiting outside.

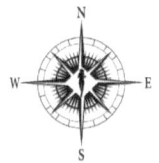

TWENTY-THREE

D anny led Nash through another tunnel. They left Lenny on the sofa, watching television. Nash was glad of the silence. Danny was a man of few words and clearly didn't feel the need to fill their walk with pointless conversation.

They turned right and took a staircase up to the next level. By Nash's reckoning, they now had to be out of the catacombs and into the genuine basement of the redbrick building above them. Danny opened a heavy-looking door, unlocking it by entering a code into a small keypad set into the wall. They stepped out into a wide hallway lined with posters advertising Regent Ale. Nash could smell hops and hear the sounds of hard work, machines clicking, pallets clattering, people shouting.

Danny led him up a second set of stairs, metal and glass set into the old red brick. At the top, through a couple of more doors, they stopped in front of an office. Danny knocked, waiting for a muffled greeting before opening the door and ushering Nash through. Danny shut the door after him, remaining outside.

The office was wide and low. It looked to be a recent addition within the old frame of the building. The far wall was made of glass, looking down onto the brewery below. To the right was a bar, stocked with various types of Regent Ale. Pale. Dark. Stout. Wheat. Lite. Along with the alcohol was a selection of every brand of Dosa Cola Nash could think of. To the right was an original wall, with a small window looking out onto the canal. The

center of the room was taken up by a large glass desk, clear except for a
laptop and phone.

The man rising from behind the desk had the kind of condescending
smile that led Nash to form an instant dislike. He was dressed in work
boots, skinny jeans, and a check shirt beneath a corduroy vest. His full beard
was neatly trimmed, and his hair was shaved at the sides and swept back on
top.

"August," he said, annoying Nash further. "So great to finally meet you.
"Drink?"

"No, thanks."

"Sure? I'm having one."

The man lifted two bottles and popped their lids on an opener fixed to
the bar. He held one out for Nash, completely ignoring that he'd said no.
But what the hell; Nash never saw the point in turning down something
free. He took the bottle and nodded a thank-you.

"Apologies, I didn't introduce myself." The man held out his hand for
a shake. "Greg Richards."

"I was here to meet Lothar Caliburn."

"Oh, we'll get to that, don't worry." Richards turned to wave his arm at
the window. "Great, isn't it?"

"Almost as impressive as what you've built downstairs."

Richards gestured for Nash to take a seat in front of the desk and waited
until he was settled before sitting again in his own chair. He took a long pull
on the beer and sighed theatrically before fixing Nash with another grin.

"This whole place was empty when I found it. Derelict. The council
had been trying to sell it for residential development. Just what this town
needs, another building full of bland apartments nobody can afford. But
I said, why not put it to real use? Create something, put money back into
the economy."

"You funded this yourself?"

"I found good investors."

"And downstairs?"

Richards leaned back in his seat. "We have good friends. You'd be surprised how many people support us."

"Interesting location. You've seen the neighbors? Isn't exactly Nazi central."

Richards pulled a face. "We don't use the N word anymore. It's become problematic."

"Then what are you?"

The condescending smirk returned. "I'm just a free-speech advocate. I want to be able to say what I believe without getting shut down or called a racist. I want an open debate."

"The shooting range is for debate prep?"

The smirk stayed in place. "We're pro-gun. Big picture, I want our teams desensitized to what's going on out there. Most of our recruits don't come from here. Our highest engagement comes from more isolated areas, or suburbs, places that are mostly white. This is a way for them to get used to being around the enemy, so they can blend in, not be scared of the other when the time comes to act."

"You're not worried your guys will fall in love with the food or music, get laid, change their minds?"

The humor dropped from Richards's face. "Nobody here is changing their mind." The smile came back. "You're making the same mistake as the liberal media. You want to call my guys stupid. Ignorant. You want to say they're scared, acting out of fear. But the truth is, we're the ones who are thinking straight. The people out there?" He pointed at the window. "They're walking round with stresses and worries. So many concerns. And they don't know why. They know the world has gone to shit, but not the reason. Nobody tells them the truth. The minute you see it"—he turned the pointed finger to his own temple—"everything becomes clear. Easy.

They all have a million problems. We only have one."

"How often you practiced that?"

For a second, Richards's mask slipped, and Nash saw the genuine reaction in his eyes. He'd been called on his act. The speech had been good—

too good. Either Richards had delivered it too many times to find the real belief, or he had never believed it in the first place. Nash looked again at their surroundings. How much money was there to be made in playing this role? And could that be the source of Danny's frustration? A real believer being led by a poseur. Or worse, being led by a sellout.

"Just so we're on the same page." Richards pressed a few keys on his laptop and turned it around to give Nash a view of the screen. A video showed the room he'd just been in, and Danny garroting Lenny with a wire. "A man with your reputation will always get to meet with us. But people who cross us don't get the benefit of regretting it." "And you don't give them the benefit of keeping your word." "I'd been told you could be difficult," Richards said.

"Danny?"

"No, actually. The Eighteens had a file on you for years, and I know Danny tried to recruit you before my time. But we have a friend in common. Ashley Eades."

That took Nash by surprise. He knew the name and her reputation with the black-market types, but he wouldn't have called Eades a friend. She'd had drinks with Nash on more than one occasion, but he'd never been willing to go on the record with her. And she'd been too busy turning Marah Chase into a star to really listen to him. Still, he'd thought about her a lot since then, wondering if the TV and book money could have been his if he'd played nice.

"She's not into all this?" Nash said.

"No, but she was into writing about it." Richards gave a new variety of smirk, a dirty one. "We fooled around a lot at university. The speech that didn't work on you was like chum in the water to her. She wanted to debate me." Richards looked lost in a happy memory for a moment, sipping the beer. "She got in touch a while back, now into writing about cults and subcultures, figured I might know some alt-right people she could talk to. Told me all about relic runners, all about you."

"Does she know you're leading R18?"

Richards stuck his lips out. Made a tutting sound. "She was close. It was a shame. And she was shacked up with some greasy Italian. I had to send my team after her."

Nash wasn't stupid. There were no coincidences.

Had Eades been dating someone Francisco Conte cared about? Whoever it was, Conte was close enough to them that he'd been afraid that giving Nash the information up front would give him too much power.

"You send Lothar Caliburn?" he asked Richards.

The phone buzzed. Richards didn't even pause to apologize, picking up the receiver and saying, "Go." He paused, listening, then responded only with sounds. "Uh-huh. Mmm. Ah. Uh-huh." He nodded a couple of times, as if the person on the other side of the call could see, then covered his face with one hand, sighing loud enough for the caller to hear. "Fix it." He put the receiver back in the cradle. He rubbed his face, before settling his eyes on Nash, holding a stare. "Why are you after Caliburn?"

Nash downed the last of the beer and set the empty bottle on the desk in front of him. He noticed with satisfaction the look of annoyance that crossed Richards's face at the desk being used as a trash can.

Nash stood and helped himself to another beer, showing off his strength by popping the cap using his thumb. He took a swig, then settled back into his seat.

"You know, I was sent after Caliburn once," he said. "Long time ago. I was still in the public sector. My bosses wanted Caliburn gone. He'd just taken out two British agents, and rumors were he'd been hired to target an American diplomat, so it was time for me to go get him."

Richards leaned forward, rested his head on his hand. "This stuff is so cool."

"I figured out someone who fit the profile. Someone who'd been in a bunch of the same places at the same time as Caliburn hits, someone who was known to have some anti-authority views, the whole thing. He was a Canadian freelancer named Ryan Preston. I tracked him to Iraq, where he was working private security. Dragged him out into the desert. He begged for his life. Pissed his pants. It wasn't a heroic end."

"You killed him?"

Nash sipped again and shrugged. "My job. But I had a problem. See, I figured that the whole thing had come about because Caliburn was becoming too big a name. You carry that around, it gets to be like a target on your head. I was lucky enough to have found someone who I could pass off to my bosses as Caliburn, but next time I might not be so lucky."

Richards's mouth opened. He closed it, then opened it again. Shook his head. "I don't . . ."

Nash threw his half-empty bottle directly at Richards.

It connected with his nose, jolting him backward. Nash grabbed the empty bottle by the neck and smashed it on the edge of the desk, once, twice, before the bottom cracked off, leaving a jagged edge. He was around the desk in three quick strides, grabbing Richards by the hair and slamming him face-first into the desk, then pulling him back up and pressing the broken glass to his throat.

"Now," Nash hissed into Richards's ear, "your second mistake was letting me see that Danny is downstairs. I have you to myself. But your first mistake is the real problem. *I'm* Lothar Caliburn. You've got someone running around using my codename, and I want to know who."

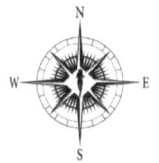

TWENTY-FOUR

L auren Stanford looked down at her suitcases. Three of them, full to bursting. She was thinking about a fourth. This bunch would see her through a trip to London, but who knew where things would go after that? Once Chase led them to Eades, they might need to head straight off to another country, and how could Lauren plan for that?

She looked through the doorway to where her mother's portrait was judging her. "Don't look at me like that. I'm doing this for you. I mean, maybe if you'd read the files you could have an opinion. The Fountain could be in either India or Africa." She pointed to one pile of clothes on her bed. "That means hot. I need to pack for hot. But Africa is huge. There are different kinds of hot." She pointed to a second large pile. "And then there's humidity. That affects every single . . . pocket. What do I do about pockets? I might need an outfit with pockets. That means layers."

She was overthinking. And with only an hour before the private jet was due to leave, she didn't have time for this.

"You're right." She laughed. "You're right. Two more bags, it's easy."

This was all a distraction, trying to take her mind off the thing that wasn't happening. Ted. She looked up at her parents again. "This would be easier if your wonder boy was calling me. What's taking him so long?"

And now she was being let down by the London office too. Letting Greg run the show had been a mistake, but she couldn't say that out loud because her parents had never liked him. She couldn't be the face—she was too well-known—but Ted could handle meetings on this side of the Atlantic, and Greg, Greg with the ass, Greg with the smile, he could hold things down in England.

Or so she'd thought.

But now both of them were late checking in.

Her phone buzzed.

"*Finally.*" She didn't bother with the usual power play of letting it ring. "What have you got?"

Ted said, "Nothing."

"Nothing?"

"He's not talking. And I think we have a problem in London."

Lauren sighed. She pressed the phone to her chest to cover the mic while insulting Ted under her breath, then put it back to her face. "I'm on my way."

She took the spiral staircase down to the main floor of her apartment, then called for the elevator. When it arrived, she stepped in and pressed the button for the secured basement. This was the part of the building that had always been known only to the family, and now Ted. If you want something done right . . .

Richards's head was pressed to the glass desk, his cheek on the cold surface. Nash had already sliced a fine line across the back of his neck, the blood running down into his collar.

"What're you talking about?" he said.

"*I'm* Caliburn," Nash said. "I made up a cover so I could do whatever I wanted, charge whatever I wanted, and my government bosses would never know. Until they sent me to catch me, and I knew it was time to get out."

"I swear, we didn't know."

"That much I've worked out, genius." Nash pressed the broken glass again, not breaking the skin but causing pain. "But now you're running around using my name, linking it to terrorist shit."

"Look, dude, dude, chill. Come on. We can work this out."

Nash grabbed a handful of Richards's hair, feeling the greasy crap he used to style it, and pulled his head back. The front of the neck was the most vulnerable spot on everyone. It was often the quickest way to get to the point. Nash gently pressed the broken glass into the flesh around Richards's Adam's apple.

"Who is using my name?"

"No-nobody."

Nash eased off. "Explain."

"Look, we wanted to hire you. Caliburn. We wanted to hire Caliburn. But everyone said he was dead. Killed—well, by you, I guess. So I thought, Why not just use the name? It's branding, innit? So we don't, it's not—" Richards gulped. "It's not a person. We've just been using the name. Whoever we send on a mission is Lothar Caliburn. It scares people."

Nash pulled the bottle away and let Richards calm down. "You're not for real. I've met real Nazis. Danny is real. You're faking it."

Richards met his eyes, then looked away. "The money's good, okay?"

"Whose money?"

Richards smiled. He even laughed. He thought he was back in control. "They'd kill me."

Nash smashed more of the bottle and grabbed Richards by the hair again, pressing the jagged glass into his neck, drawing blood. "How do you think this ends?"

"St-Stanford. Lauren Stanford."

"I know that name?"

"Dosa."

Shit, yes. Nash knew that name.

The Stanfords were rich. Proper American dynasty–level rich. They owned media. They owned airlines. They owned pharmaceuticals. Nash could see what Richards had meant about the money being good. Someone like Lauren Stanford could change your life on a whim and wouldn't even miss the money she threw at you.

"And she hired you?"

"She knows me. Uni. We d-dated."

"She's into this?"

"She's insane. Her whole family, total Nazis. I mean, really, going all the way back. There's so many of them, man, all over the place. London. America. Paris. Rome. They're in so many positions. And after the London thing, Lauren took over R18. She knew my views from university, so she put me in charge."

"And then this journalist, Ashley Eades, she was close to figuring it all out."

"She knew both of us. Me and Lauren. And she was asking questions. Lauren thought it was only a matter of time."

"You sent your team in?"

"Just one. Just Danny."

So Danny was the one Conte wanted. The Lothar Caliburn who killed whoever it was Conte cared so much about. A friend? Family member? "And what's the plan? What did she hire you to do?"

⚔

The elevator doors opened. Lauren stepped out into a narrow corridor with deep red carpet. Immediately to her right was a metal hatch. The hall had once led to a private jetty and a tunnel that opened out onto the East River. The water inlet had been dug when the building work was first carried out, with the Dosa plant as cover. Very few people had ever known about this level. It was from here, in 1916, that the attack on Black Tom Island had been launched. The tunnel had long since been closed up, to avoid any questions from the authorities.

She walked along the corridor. The walls were covered with drapes and family heirlooms imported from Europe, along with more recent memorabilia. She paused, as she always did, at a metal sheet that bore an etching of the logo Harrold Stanford had originally intended for his product. Purity Cola. Harrold had intended his concoction to keep the underclass and the immigrants drugged and unhealthy, but he'd realized long before he took his venture public that he would need a different name. Something a little less loaded. But he'd kept this etching, and it had passed into family legend.

Lauren made a ritual of touching the cool metal every time she walked past, honoring the history. Her parents had both avoided this place, letting it grow dusty. Lauren took pride in the legacy.

At the end of the hall she passed a metal doorway. She touched the cool surface, paused but didn't go in. Instead, she continued along to the main chamber, a large round space with a high ceiling and long curved walls. It was far grander than the City Hall station. Lauren always laughed privately at how Carina Texas liked to lord that place over people. Lauren's place felt more like a church. And, with its drapes and statues, she decided that it was, a church to something old and pure. The walls were lined with bookshelves, full of ancient knowledge from centuries previous, all the way through the German experiment. Her parents had tried to keep her away from all of this. It was her grandmother, sweet old Nana, who had brought her down here at every chance, let her read the books, opened her up to their traditions, their future. It was here that Lauren had learned about the Fountain of Youth and started to build her database, the pet project that now defined her life. The version she'd given Chase was only a sample, just enough information to get the explorer interested. The real treasure trove of data—all the expeditions, the legends, the failures—was in the version Lauren had on her laptop.

Ted stood at attention as Lauren walked in. He was wearing overalls and gloves, holding a butane blowtorch. The smell of burned pork in the air was coming from the naked man strapped to the chair beside Ted. Grant LaFarge. He wasn't unconscious, but he wasn't fully conscious, either. His head lolled on his chest. His eyes flickered toward Lauren as she entered, but they were slow, distant. There were welts growing on his forearm and fingers, spots where Ted had applied the flame. The rest of him looked clear.

"Ted, what are you doing?" As Lauren got closer, she could smell other things. LaFarge had emptied himself out. Idiot Ted had used one of the family's old wooden chairs, brought over on the boat from England. It was ruined.

"You said . . ." He waved at LaFarge and didn't finish the sentence.

Lauren sighed. One problem at a time. "Carrie?"

He shrugged. "Couldn't find her. At the Speakeasy, they said she's taking a vacation."

So Carina Texas had figured out what was coming next. She knew she was a loose end. Obviously, that was the reason she'd turned Lauren down.

"Clever girl. Hiding until it's over."

"I know someone there could tell us where she is."

"No, you're right. We can't bring everyone in New York down here. What's the London situation?"

"I contacted our friends there, like you said. But . . ."

"But what?"

"Greg ordered his team to follow the tablet, like we said. But they got spotted, or they attacked, I'm not sure. I was watching their chat group, and I think some of them have been arrested."

Lauren pinched the bridge of her nose. She could feel a stress headache coming on. "I'm starting to think we need to set a higher bar for entrance to the master race."

She stepped closer and stroked LaFarge's hair. His head rolled to the side, and he looked up at her.

"Grant. Baby," she whispered to him gently. "I'm sorry for this. We just need to know everything you do, that's all. We don't want to do it this way."

"Fff tol you effrin." LaFarge talked as if the pain had swollen his tongue. The words were slow and lazy.

Lauren looked to Ted. He took the cue and explained, "Everything we already knew. He was paid to wipe Eades's records from the surveillance systems. He says a British agent set it all up."

"The one who helped stop the London attack and keeps sniffing around our friends in the UK?"

"Yeah."

"There's a plan for her when the time is right. Has Grant given you the name of the cleaner?"

"No."

"And he hasn't suggested that, as the person who took her profile off the security grid, he can probably also put it back on? Lead us all right to her?"

"No. But he did say he thinks she's in Scotland somewhere."

"Oh, well." Lauren smiled encouragingly at LaFarge, took his uninjured hand in hers. "That narrows it down to around five million people." She leaned in. "This is all a bit too cruel, isn't it? Maybe this could've been handled another way? I've got more money than you could even count. Is there an amount of zeroes that would make you give up the information?"

LaFarge mumbled something that sounded like either *yes* or *please*.

Lauren turned in a slow circle, sweeping her hand at the chamber around them. "See this? This is something money can't buy. It's tradition. History. It's an idea. The right idea. Those books?" She pointed to the stacked shelves that lined the chamber. "Roots that go back into history. Before Germanenorden, before the Thule Society. Before anyone heard the word Nazi. It was the idea. And the idea has never died. It never will. I get to be part of that story. You"—she returned to stroke LaFarge's hair again—"get to be part of that story. Imagine a world where we can control life and death. Where we get to decide who lives forever and who doesn't. We'd need the right person in charge of those decisions, wouldn't we?" She smiled, nodding in agreement at her own words. "We all wear a mask in public. We all pretend to be different people. My parents, like so many of their generation, let the mask become who they were. They forgot to take it off. Got too comfortable wearing it, and it killed them. But we don't make that mistake, do we?" She knelt down to LaFarge's eye level. "You see me." He whimpered the same sound again.

"The problem with torture," Lauren said, "is that it only really works while people think there's a chance they're going to live. That's when they'll plead and beg; that's when they'll give up information. Once someone realizes they're going to die, they double down. Pride gets in the way, and they think, if you're killing me anyway, I may as well die protecting the information. And it all becomes a race to see if you can break their spirit and get what you need before they die." She let her hand rest on his shoulder, a gentle touch. "I bet, really, if I offer you twenty million right now, into your account in seconds, you'll tell us exactly how to make Eades reappear on the system, won't you?"

LaFarge started to cry, nodded.

"I know," Lauren whispered, friendly, caring. "It's okay, let it out. Yeah, that's it." She stroked his hair. "Now, why don't you just tell me what I want? How do I find Ashley Eades?"

Between the sobs, LaFarge started to talk.

◄━━━━━━

"The Fountain of Youth," Richards said, his voice high-pitched, almost approaching a squeal. He seemed to have a very low threshold for pain. "She's obsessed with it."

Nash stepped back, pulling away the glass.

The old Nash, back when he was Lothar Caliburn, would have put some extra hurt on Richards just on principle for wasting his time with something as ridiculous as the Fountain of Youth. But he'd seen some shit since then. You don't find the Ark of the Covenant only to draw the line at talking about the Fountain.

Richards seemed to sense this moment of reprieve. "Seriously, she's throwing so much money at looking for it."

"That's why you took the job."

"Sure. I mean, I like to talk about this shit as much as anyone else. I thought it'd be a good media career, you know? Get known for being contrarian, talk up some right-wing values, freedom of speech, then ride the train. But then Lauren comes at me with a blank check to look for the bloody Fountain of Youth?"

"You filled that blank check with a big number."

Richards smiled, confident now that they were talking money, his native tongue. He waved at the office around him with both hands, and the bottling plant behind the glass. "Capice?"

Nash knew what was coming next. Richards was going to make an offer. But Nash still wanted to hear it, to see how it was framed.

"So." Richards's smile focused. He leaned forward, bringing both hands together on the desk, completely ignoring the blood running down his neck. "What kind of round figure will it take for you to work for me?" For you?

Nash stepped forward. Richards was ready. Nash could see his hand had been under the table. Pressing an alarm? Richards pushed back in his chair, stood, and dropped into some form of fighting stance. Maybe he'd paid for expensive lessons. But Nash was too fast, too strong, and too done with this crap. He punched Richards in the gut, then followed with an uppercut. Richards smashed back against the window. The dull thud of his impact told Nash how thick the glass was. As Richards bounced forward, Nash used the momentum to lift him, and he threw him onto the desk. The glass shattered, and Richards landed in a heap on the floor, covered in the shards, lacerated in several more places. He didn't move right away, only made a wheezing noise. Nash was willing to bet this was the first time he'd ever really been hit.

Nash knelt over him and picked up one of the new sharp weapons. He pulled Richards's head back by the hair. "I'm not going to work for you. You don't get to just use my name like one of your brands."

There was sound outside; then the door burst inward. Danny was framed in the doorway, holding a gun loaded with a compressor. He took a step into the room but hesitated when Nash pressed the glass to Richards's throat.

"Phkin ger 'im," Richards tried to shout, but his mouth wasn't working right.

Nash nodded at the gun, then met Danny's stare. "You hate this guy," he said calmly. "You know he's a phony."

Danny looked from Nash to Richards and back again. "Yes."

"You tried to hire me, so you know I'm good for whatever I say."

Danny nodded.

Nash pictured the Ark. He started putting a number next to it. All the money he could make on the market from selling the relic. The figure was big. Larger than anything he'd ever dreamed, until the moment the Ark slipped through his fingers and he realized how close he'd come. But that was nothing compared to having the private resources of a billionaire just one conversation away.

He pressed the glass into Richards's neck and slashed across. As Richards lay beneath him, twitching and dying, Nash nodded at Danny again. "Get your real boss on the phone."

◄━━━┿▥▥▥

Lauren shot LaFarge in the head. The sound bounced around the chamber. It had been the only decent thing to do, in the end. He'd been in so much pain, if the pleading and begging was anything to go by. And he'd seen her face. Her *real* face. No amount of money could cover for that, and you don't get to be as rich as a Stanford by handing out twenty million when you can just torture a guy.

But it had been a productive meeting.

She felt good about it.

A whole lot of progress had been made, and LaFarge had been happy to help as much as he could, once the flames touched his genitals.

She put down the gun on a table at the side of the room and pulled some Wet Wipes out of a pack, cleaning her fingers. Their jet was ready to leave. Ted would get rid of the mess before they went. Ted pulled out his cell and announced it was ringing. Lauren watched as he answered, started to speak, and stopped. His mouth dropped open. His eyes bulged. He put down the receiver and covered it with his other hand.

"It's . . . Lothar Caliburn?"

"Are you asking me or telling me."

"Telling. This guy says he's the real Lothar Caliburn. He wants to speak to you. Mentioned your name."

Lauren knew she should be scared. A part of her was, maybe. Somewhere far off. If the real Caliburn knew her name, that could be trouble. But she was in the zone. After killing LaFarge, she'd gone to the fun place in her head. The shit-doesn't-matter place. The watch-things-burn place.

She took the phone and said, "This is Lauren."

"You have a job vacancy." It was an American accent. Somewhere like Louisiana, maybe? New Orleans? "We should talk."

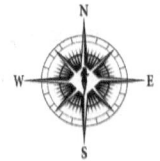

TWENTY-FIVE

"The other option was a sexy blue sports car," Chase said, as they headed north in the yellow Mini Cooper. She smiled at Hass hunched in the front passenger seat. "But this one suits you better."

They'd stayed mostly silent as she navigated out of the city, taking a few detours, both accidental and deliberate. They didn't have any obvious tails. Mason had said Chase wasn't enough of a target to warrant facial recognition at traffic lights. But all that had been before the library, and Chase was half convinced there must be people on her, even if she couldn't see them.

She traded information with Hass, each bringing the other up to speed on everything they'd done so far. Ahead was a sign that never failed to make her laugh, a big black arrow pointing upward that simply read, *The North*.

"Where we going?" Hass asked the one question Chase hadn't answered. In all the information they'd traded, she'd somehow neglected to mention where Eades was.

"Glasgow."

Hass snorted. "Of course."

To anyone who didn't know the UK, it would feel shortsighted to change identity and only move four hundred miles to Glasgow. But to many people in the south of England, Scotland was a whole other world. Socially. Politically. Financially. You could hide from London more effectively north of Hadrian's Wall than you could by crossing the Channel.

It would take them over eight hours with pit stops. Driving in the UK always felt more tiring than back home. There, the roads were long and straight and Chase could drive for hours without thinking about it. British roads were built to exhaust and confuse.

Chase asked, "Did you know about Conte's son?"

Hass didn't answer. It was a very deliberate lack of a denial.

"Doc?"

He turned to her, then looked away again. "He trusts me for the same reason you do. I keep people's personal lives personal."

"Think he'll talk to me about it?"

A shrug. "You can try."

Chase pulled out her cell, keeping one hand on the wheel, and passed it to Hass. "Call him, on speaker."

Hass loaded up Talaria and clicked on Conte's name. He started a call, and the Italian answered right away.

"Salve, Marah, it's so good to hear from you. Are you not still in town?"

He would know for a fact she wasn't. This was just the game he played, a subtle way of asking where she was. Chase was happy to play along.

"Salve, Cisco. No, I'm in London for a rest. I was sorry to miss you."

"London?" He paused, banking that information. "Say hello to the city for me—it's been too long. I haven't been since before the attack. It would break my heart to see London without Big Ben or Buckingham Palace."

"I'll mention it. They might rebuild them quicker."

Conte chuckled, a rumble like a big cat. "Please do. Oh, I'm so sorry to have missed you, bella. I heard about your unfortunate experience. The Ark. That's a hell of a find. A *hell* of a find. My heart broke to hear of the way it was taken away from you."

Two broken hearts in one conversation? He was laying on the charm a bit too heavily. Chase decided to be wary. Every conversation with Conte was a transaction.

"It is what it is, Cisco. That's the game."

"I should tell you, there was a pool, on you and Mr. Nash. I oversaw the betting, naturally."

"If you'd told me that in advance, I could've won some money."

"Confidence. I like that. You can't achieve anything without it, isn't that right? If you don't back yourself to succeed, why should anybody else? You know, I could ask around for you. I'm sure I'd be able to find out where it's being stored, and if I could get you that . . ."

Here was the point of his charm offensive. If Conte was floating the idea of finding out where the Ark was, that meant he already had the intel or knew someone who did. Offering to ask around was merely him making it sound like he would be doing more work especially for her, which would add to the price he would ask in return.

But even knowing she was being played, Chase couldn't stop the Ark from swimming into view in her mind. It was right there, just out of reach, attainable if she played the game.

It was time to show some of her cards and take control. "The Ark can wait. I'm sure they had their reasons. I want to talk about your son."

Conte drew in a breath quietly. Chase had seen proof of an unknown ancient civilization. She'd witnessed Big Ben being destroyed by a weapon that controlled lightning. Two years ago, she'd hung on the outside of a plane as it flew over the Alps. But until now, she'd never witnessed Francisco Conte lose control.

"I've known you for ten years," he said. "I should be beyond surprise by now."

"Tell me about him."

"Bobby . . . Baggio, I should say. He always wanted to be called Baggio. After the footballer. Bobby was too young to have ever seen him play, but somehow he'd come to idolize him."

Chase could hear Conte smile, his control slipping for a second time.

"I think he chose Juventus just to annoy me."

"Was he in the family business?"

"Well, that depends how you mean. I'm the exception. Our family has always been a mix of journalists and politicians. I'm the one who took a different route. Bobby, Baggio, he was a journalist. One of the new generation, social media, activism, clicks."

"Is that how he met Ashley Eades?"

He laughed again. Chase could hear he was back in control now, once again the calm player. "So it is. You are working."

"I am," Chase confirmed. "I'm here on a job, looking for Eades. She's an old friend of mine, and I found out she was dating your son. But for real here, Cisco, I just want to say, all work aside? I'm truly sorry to hear what happened. I can't imagine how it feels."

"Thank you." His voice cracked. He was off-balance again. A shared moment. "But I think you do understand loss. You've felt it enough."

He was right, she'd known her share of grief. She'd carried some of it around for decades, and others were more recent losses. She was still learning how to process it.

"I think we can help each other," she said, "if you're willing to put the usual game aside. We just talk to each other straight. I think we can both get what we need."

Conte paused a long time before answering. "I agree." He breathed out. "As to your question, I'm how they met. My boy and Eades. She kept trying to do stories on me, wanted me to sit down and talk her through our world, how it all works. I think she had the affliction that everything needed to make sense. The whole world needed to fit into a narrative she could explain."

Chase remembered conversations like that with Eades. She could never get out of the way of her ideas.

"So, from me," Conte continued, "she found my son. And they influenced each other. One always pushing the other, taking more risks."

"Were they working together on a story?"

"Perhaps. I never knew the details. I haven't found much since . . . what happened. I had taught Baggio how to protect his data. He used the same packages we do. I've never been able to recover all of his files."

"Some of them?"

"Some, yes. Some of his. Some of hers, stored in the same place."

"Could you send them to me?"

"What are you working on?"

Chase thought it over. Giving Conte the truth still felt like a risk, even after they'd agreed to play it straight. But she felt like they'd made a connection on the call. He'd revealed a new side of himself. She could meet him partway.

"How about I lay it all out?"

"No games."

"I was contacted by someone who wants me to find the Fountain of Youth." Chase noted no laugh, no negative reaction. He was taking that as a reasonable thing for someone to do. "And they felt Ashley Eades might know something about it. I know Ashley, so they used that connection to get me involved. And then, in looking for Eades, I found out about . . . what happened to your son. And a—" Chase paused. "A source in MI6 thinks it might be the work of Lothar Caliburn."

"I see. Are you willing to tell me who hired you?"

"Not right now." Chase was open to it. She had questions about the Stanford connection, and Conte might have the answers. But one thing at a time.

"I understand," he replied. "I don't know that I have anything new to add. Maybe just clarity. This is not the first I've heard of the Fountain of Youth. Bobby asked about it. He wanted to know if I knew anyone like you who was looking for it. I laughed it off, of course. But then he told me that it was an obsession of Lothar Caliburn and R18. I laughed that off at first, too. Because R18 hadn't been active since your London adventure, and Caliburn had been dead for ten years."

"Did he say any more about it?"

"Nothing. Not directly. The last time we spoke, it was an argument."

"What about?"

"Everything. Nothing. All of the things we were unhappy about. You know how families are. We store our complaints up, wait until something unimportant happens, then fight like war. I didn't like that he was with Eades. And we argued over football and about how infrequently he was calling his mother. And . . ."

Chase could hear his emotions were bubbling up again. She waited, letting him speak in his own time.

"He didn't mention the Fountain, or R18. But before things got heated, he mentioned Lothar Caliburn, that he was close to finding his identity."

"You argued over football and not that he was sniffing around an assassin?"

Conte laughed. "Familia."

"You heard the same thing I did about Caliburn. You already know he was behind it."

"I have people hunting for him right now."

"And when they find him?"

Conte didn't answer right away. He didn't need to reply at all; they both knew what was going unsaid. "I suppose you will try to talk me out of it."

Chase shook her head. "I guess I was born without the Nazi empathy gene. He killed your son; do whatever you want to him."

Between Hass, Conte, and Mason, Chase had things pretty straight in her mind. For whatever reason, R18 had developed an interest in the Fountain of Youth. This was suddenly a thing people cared about. Eades and Roberto had stumbled on this information, either because they were working on a story about the Fountain that lead to R18, or vice versa. Eades may well have found a solid lead on the location from the old soldier, James Gilmore. Somewhere along the way, they got close to the identity of Lothar Caliburn. Caliburn had gotten to Roberto, but Mason's intervention had saved Eades.

"Caliburn is going to be looking for Eades," Chase said.

"Indeed."

"And you're looking for Caliburn."

Conte's smile was clear in his voice. "You know where she is."

"I can help you set a trap. But the bait is a friend of mine. I need to get to her first, make sure she's okay, and then we can draw Caliburn out."

"This sounds like you're laying out terms on a deal. I thought we weren't playing?"

It was Chase's turn to smile. "Maybe a little playing, now that we understand each other."

"Okay. What are your terms?"

"First, I need you to send me all the files you recovered from Bobby and Eades. There might be information in there I need. We're planning to spring a trap on Caliburn, but until we do, I'm making myself a walking target. I need to have as much information as I can get."

"Agreed."

Chase could hear him pressing keys on his computer. Her phone buzzed a second later to announce she'd received data.

"Second, I'll go get Eades and bring her to London." She looked at Hass. "Where I can call in some favors to keep her safe. Then I'll work with you to get word out, set the hook."

"Yes. And I believe you've already got our mutual friend Hassan in London with you. Is he there now?"

Chase and Hass shared a look.

Of course.

"I'm here," Hass said.

"Excellent, excellent. Hassan, I trust you will help Marah in every way you can. And once it is done, I will give you both the location of the Ark."

Chase hesitated, looked at Hassan again. They were friends. He was one of the few people in the whole world she really trusted to any degree. But the Ark was the Ark. And giving them both the location at the same time could pit them against each other. Conte knew that. One last little spin in the tale.

Chase nodded, then said, "Deal."

"Marah, bella, today you played my game as well as me."

TWENTY-SIX

Nash climbed up the metal steps that had been hurriedly wheeled out to the Gulfstream jet. He was on a private airstrip two miles south of Northampton. The plane had landed only moments before and waited on the runway for him. His new employer clearly had friends in high places, as there had been no security check, no customs process. An American billionaire had simply entered the UK without any official record and was now preparing to fly north to Scotland after picking up two passengers.

Nash was greeted at the top of the steps by a tall blond man with a strong build and a presence that said he had no idea how to use it. He was wearing an expensive pinstripe suit but made it look like an act, like he was mimicking something he'd once seen a grown-up do. He looked to be in his early twenties, and trying hard to hide his nerves.

"Mr. Nash," the big guy said, offering a hand. "I'm Ted."

"You got a second name there, Ted?"

Already, Nash could see he'd thrown the guy off. "Uh, yeah, McCallister."

"Nice to meet you, kid. I guess you know Danny?"

Nash turned as he spoke, to gesture at the wiry Irishman behind him. He could tell from Danny's tensed shoulders and set facial expression that he hated Ted almost as much as he hated Greg Richards. Nash filed that away. "I do," Ted said, nodding at Danny. "Good to see you." Danny grunted.

Ted stepped back inside the jet and gestured for them to follow. The space inside could have been the waiting area outside a Wall Street office. Plush carpet, leather chairs, and a door at each end. The one at the front, he guessed, was for the cockpit. The other would lead deeper into the plane. Ted pulled the jet's door closed and locked it.

All sounds from outside fell away. They were in a completely sound-proofed room. Ted pressed a small intercom next to the door and said they were ready to go, then waved for Danny and Nash to each take a seat. The three of them settled in as the plane began to move. It was fast and smooth. Nash could feel the moment they left the ground, and everything tilted sharply for around sixty seconds as they climbed into the clouds, but then they leveled out again and there was no indication they were in a jet at altitude.

"Mr. Nash," Ted said, "I was just reading up on you."

"If you'd done that before, you wouldn't have hired Greg Richards."

The smile disappeared. Ted nodded at something, a thought he was keeping to himself. "That was a mistake."

Nash followed up. "Yours?"

He glanced at Danny. The Irishman's cool gaze was fixed on Ted, giving nothing away.

"That's not important," Ted said.

"It's vital," Nash countered. "Hiring him was a stupid move. Amateur. You've got Danny here on staff, and he's clearly got some game. Whoever decided to bring Richards in over him is an idiot, and I want to know if that's you or your boss."

Nash caught Danny smiling.

Ted's mouth opened and closed. Nothing came out, but Nash thought he heard a faint squeak somewhere down in the kid's throat. Ted touched his ear, and Nash guessed there was a communication device in there. Ted mumbled an acknowledgment.

He nodded to Nash. "Come with me."

Ted stood up and made for the door that led deeper into the plane.

He ushered Nash through into another room that looked like an expensive office. The walls had wood paneling, covered in a soft, honey-colored finish. There were sofas, chairs, a large television screen, and a desk. There was another door at the back, set off to the side, somehow giving the impression it wasn't important. He recognized the young woman rising out of the sofa to meet him. Lauren Stanford. She was blond and very sure. Her suit matched Ted's but was infinitely more expensive, and she wore it like she owned it, leaving the kid looking like her tribute act.

She turned her attention to Ted first. "Go wait outside," she said.

Her accent was New York. *Expensive* New York.

"What? But . . ."

"We'll be fine." She turned a smile on Nash. "I'm sorry, he didn't offer you a drink. Would you like anything?"

"Some cold water would be nice."

"Of course. And food? When was the last time you ate?"

Nash got the feeling he'd be hungry as soon as he saw food. But it was something he could hold off and deal with later.

"No, I'm good."

She nodded, turning to Ted and tilting her head toward the door at the back, indicating he should go deal with the drink. Ted hesitated. He gave one last frustrated look at Nash, then walked off. Nash heard the door open and close, but his full focus was on Stanford.

"That was quite a show you put on," she said.

"You too. Kept him in his place."

She turned to glance back at the door Ted had gone through. "He's hard work." Then to business. "You know who I am?"

"Yes."

"Tell me."

"Lauren Stanford. You run Dosa Cola and about five other large companies that I know of. You've been on the cover of every major business magazine since your parents died, and the tabloids have tried digging into your personal life, which I would assume is why you get people like Ted and Greg Richards to do your dirty work for you. And I just killed your ex-boyfriend."

He threw that in as a challenge.

How would she react?

Was she driven by emotion, or was she serious about the game? As he watched, she smiled and gestured for him to take a seat on the sofa. She eased down next to him.

After a moment of silence, Nash leaned forward and started again. "You fund R18, and you clearly have some friends high up in the government over here, because you landed a plan on British soil without any kind of customs check. You're looking for a missing journalist, Ashley Eades, because Danny out there tried to kill her and missed."

She bowed her head. "Close enough. Yes, Ashley Eades has information I need. I'm looking for something, and I think she knows where it is."

"The Fountain of Youth."

"You know about that? Okay. Yes. My family has been after the Fountain for a long time." She smiled again, paused. "And I know where Eades is."

The door opened and closed. Footsteps. Ted set a pitcher of water on the table, along with three glasses. The woman picked up the third, handed it back to Ted, and told him again to wait outside. After another show of frustration, this one larger than the first, Ted left.

The woman shook her head. "Such a shame. He basically came with the deal. He's younger than me, the son of my mother's best friend, and while I always saw him as my little brother, my family had other ideas. We always had very . . ."

Her words trailed off. She stood up and poured the water into two glasses, handed one to Nash. Their fingers touched. She sat back down, closer to him this time. Nash could read these signals. He'd need to be a fool to miss them. She'd just turned up the volume from zero to eleven. He reminded himself of what Greg had said. She's insane. Clearly, she was manipulative, too.

"I'd like to trust you. Can I trust you?" She didn't wait for an answer before continuing. "My family has always had a problem. We have very particular beliefs. For an idea to stay pure, you need a small group. Focus. So, my parents, and their parents before them, and all the way back, I suppose, have to look for fellow travelers. They really wanted me and Ted to be a thing, but . . . he's an idiot."

Nash felt the need to push back, show he couldn't be flirted into submission. "Well, you're the one who let him handle this."

She smiled, showing teeth now. "True. I heard what you said before. You were right. It was my decision to trust Ted. My decision to hire Greg. In my circles—the business side, I mean—we tend to give trusted jobs to people we know. The old boys' network, I guess. So those decisions are on me. I was new to the game, and there's no textbook. There's nothing that tells you how to spot the real deal, how to tell them from a poseur." She paused.

Tilted her head at Nash. "Now I know the difference."

"Whose idea was it to use the Caliburn name?"

"I wanted the *real* Caliburn. That part was me. I left the hiring up to Ted and Greg, and Greg ran with using the name. My turn for a question. Tell me about Marah Chase."

That stopped Nash in his tracks. He'd been in control of the conversation until that moment, doing all the pushing, making Stanford back off, concede ground. But with one name, she'd gone back on the attack.

"Chase?"

She smiled. Knowing. "You have a history?"

"We've gone around a couple times, beating each other to relics."

"There's more than that."

Nash nodded. "When she first came on the scene, she was really green. Really green. It's such a different world, our trade. She was tough for a normal person. Grown up on a farm, taken knocks, didn't trust easily. But that's not enough for the black market. You need an extra layer, and she didn't have it. She came from academia. She wasn't going to last five minutes. So I helped her, trained her."

"That's very generous." She touched his hand again, for just a second. "Did you get what you wanted out of it?"

She'd read him right away. Seen through his help to what he'd expected in return. "No."

She leaned back, nodded like she understood his feelings exactly, and sipped her water. "She's a problem."

"What's she got to do with this?" Nash asked the question, already feeling that he knew the answer.

"I hired her," Stanford said. "Marah Chase and Ashley Eades are both problems that need solving. Keep your friends close, your enemies closer."

Enemies. "Why do you hate her?"

She set down the glass on the table. Gave him a very serious look. "Can I trust you?"

"Are you going to pay me?"

"Name your price."

"Then you can trust me."

"You picked the name Caliburn. I assume you know what it means?"

"Excalibur."

"Right. I want you to be my sword. And for that, you'll need to know the truth. But first, I'm afraid, I do need to know you're the right choice."

Nash nodded. He didn't say anything. A test was coming. Whatever it was, he would make sure to pass. She extended her wrist to reveal a white smartwatch beneath the cuff of her jacket. She tapped the screen twice, and the door at the end opened. Ted stepped back into the room.

The woman leaned in to Nash, like she was whispering a playful secret, and said, "Kill him. Right now."

Nash waited for Ted to reach the sofa before springing to his feet. He punched Ted lightly in the gut, just enough to surprise him, not enough to double him over. In that moment of shock, Nash stepped around behind Ted, wrapping his right arm around his neck, crushing his windpipe. Nash brought his left arm up to the side of Ted's face, using it to lock his right forearm in place in a sleeper hold. Ted rocked and pushed back, trying to shake free, and slapped at Nash's arms.

The punch had already knocked too much wind out of his lungs, and he hadn't started from a solid defensive base to begin with. With his throat sealed off, Ted couldn't speak or grunt. Nash's forearm was tucked under the chin, meaning Ted couldn't open his mouth much, either. The only sounds were his feet scraping the carpet, his hands slapping on Nash's arms. A faint clicking as Ted's tongue moved around, smacking off the inside of his mouth.

Lauren stood up to face both Ted and Nash. She ran a soothing hand down Ted's cheek. "Shhhh. It's okay. I know you're scared, but if you just accept this part, it all gets easier."

She repeated her gentle words a few more times, and slowly Nash could feel the fight going out of Ted, and the younger man became a heavier weight. Nash pressed on, knowing the drift into unconsciousness was only the start. As Ted started to slip away, Lauren's eyes grew wide with excitement. She was smiling, drawing power and adrenaline from watching death. A part of Nash, a voice he'd stopped caring about a long time ago, told him she was dangerous. Greg's words tried to find purchase again. *She's insane.* Sure, but in that moment all he could do was focus on how red her lips were.

Once Ted was gone, Nash lowered the body down into one of the chairs opposite the sofa. The woman stayed close to him.

She said, "That was impressive."

Nash smiled. "You're crazy."

"I'm Lauren."

"August."

"*Caliburn.*"

Lauren's eyes flicked down to Nash's lips. She wanted him to see that. For a second, he thought she was going to kiss him. Then she smiled and regained her earlier poise, sitting back down. Nash followed her lead.

"Chase," Lauren said, after sipping water. "She caused a lot of trouble for some friends of mine a couple years back. Ruined some plans I'd laid out myself, for after they did their thing."

"The London attack?"

"R18 is not a front. You now are not a front. My family has always believed in the cause. Purity. But my parents, they grew spoiled and soft. Let money get in the way. Wall Street. Corporate interests. They needed to move over, so that I could get things back on track." She smiled at him over the glass. "Does that bother you?"

Nash looked at Ted's corpse and then at Lauren. Even the voice that had warned him about her was now silent. "No."

"Something my father once said—like, the only time he ever trusted me with a business conversation. He said the trick is to find out what motivates people and work with that. Doesn't matter what it is. If it's love, trust, sex, patriotism, money. Find out what it is and you can motivate them, and then you can always trust them to do the work, once you know."

"Money makes the world go 'round."

"Yes, it does."

"But how can you be so sure this thing exists? It's a myth."

Lauren stood up to grab a laptop off her desk. She sat back down next to Nash, their thighs touching. "I only gave Chase enough information to find Eades. I have way more." She clicked the mouse, loading what seemed to be a database. "Chase knows about a team of Brits who went missing searching for it, but she doesn't know about a Nazi expedition that went missing fifty years later. I have all their research, right here, leading up to their last trip. I'm sure whatever Eades knows, I can add it into this, and it'll tell us where it is."

"And why do you want it?"

Nash really meant, What motives you?

"Imagine a two-tier Fountain of Youth," Lauren said. "Controlling who gets to live forever and who doesn't. To the pure people, and the people who can pay, we offer a utopia. Eternal health. To the impure, to the underclass, we offer . . . something else. And imagine you, being paid more money than God, making that happen."

Nash leaned back, thinking about motivation as Lauren ran her hand up the inside of his thigh. "I think I can see that."

"Of course you can. You're like me. You have vision. And imagine you getting to know ahead of time exactly where Chase is going to be, without her knowing you're coming. I knew she'd find Eades quicker than I could, but she's already led me to someone who has the answer. So, once we land,

I don't need her anymore."

Nash smiled. "Deal."

"Well, then." Lauren unzipped his pants. "We better hurry."

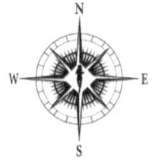

TWENTY-SEVEN

H ass took a turn at the wheel as they passed through the north of England and over the Scottish border. It gave Chase an opportunity to look through the documents Conte had sent. She was sure he had tagged them with tracer software, turning her cell into a moving beacon, but she was relaxed about it. The plan was to lead Conte to Caliburn, so she didn't mind if he knew where she was.

The haul was split fairly evenly between Eades's work and Roberto's. Most of Roberto's was in Italian. Chase had a basic enough knowledge to read some of it and used translation apps to pick up on much of the rest. His style was pretty rigid and formal, but that might have just been the translation. There were stories about crime, business, some sports. Nothing of note. Eades's files were closer to the point. An assortment of published work, unfinished drafts, and notes. Chase got to read three different descriptions of herself, seeing how Eades had tested out the approach to the story that changed everything. There was a document labeled Purity, which Chase took to be a reference to R18, but the pages were blank. Chase dragged the curser across the screen, searching for white text on the white background, but found nothing. She also found a draft of an article on James Gilmore. But there was nothing there of note, no references to the Fountain.

She gave up, settling back in the seat to watch the rolling slopes of Scotland.

Chase felt a bittersweet pang coming back to a place that could have been her home. Her mother had been Glaswegian. Aya Rachel Behr, who went mainly by her middle name, was born to first-generation immigrants. She'd spent her early years in a small Jewish community in the Gorbals, a working-class area on the south bank of the Clyde. By the time Rachel was a teenager, the Behrs had moved to Garnethill, a more affluent residential area just north of the city center. She'd grown up steeped in the city's left-wing political traditions and was one of the founding protesters at the Faslane Peace Camp, a permanent protest against the nuclear weapons stationed at the nearby naval base. It was here, in one of life's great little jokes, that she met Noah Chase, an American sailor in the US Navy, and nine months later they were raising a baby daughter together in rural Washington.

After Rachel and Noah both died in a mudslide on the farm, Chase became an argument between her American and Scottish relatives. Both wanted to raise her, and each side knew they didn't have enough money for her to keep hopping across the Atlantic on visits. The Chases won out, and she was raised American. But each time she visited Glasgow, it was with a feeling of *what if*.

Shortly before reaching the city, Chase and Hass pulled into a service station just north of Hamilton. It gave them a chance to swap seats again. Chase knew Glasgow far better than Hass, and the M8 could be a confusing stretch of road even if you'd lived there for decades. Once you were off the motorway and into the streets of Glasgow itself, it was easy to get caught up in its one-way system and the warren of roads and lanes that surrounded the center. As with the urban myth about German or Japanese soldiers who got lost during the war and didn't know it had ended, Chase was sure there were tourists who'd spent years trying to escape Glasgow's roads.

She took a detour on the way in. The address she had for Eades was in the East End. Mason had given her the journalist's new workplace, too. It was a bookie's, one of the countless gambling shops that could be found on busy streets in the UK. Glasgow had more than most, and it never failed to catch Chase by surprise. No matter how many times she'd been here, she was still shocked by the normalization of gambling. Despite this, she drove into Garnethill, her mother's old neighborhood. She still had family here. Aunts, grandparents, cousins. But, as with most relationships in her life, things had become strained by her career of bad decisions. Now didn't feel like the time to try to repair the damage.

Hi, Nana. I've got five minutes. A spy sent me here on the trail of a missing journalist, who is being hunted by a Nazi. How's your week been?

She pulled to a stop outside Garnethill Synagogue. She climbed out of the car, leaving the engine running, and looked up at the redbrick building. She'd kicked her heels here as a child, on visits to Glasgow. She'd never felt any need to be there. But now, as she'd headed north toward the city, she'd felt the pull, like a homing beacon. There was something here. An urge. A drive. She was connected to this place and these people. Their history was her history. These bricks were her bricks.

Their Ark was her Ark.

And soon, if all went to plan, she'd get to see it again.

The synagogue's black gates were closed. There were no lights in the windows. It was well past midnight. There were few things quite like a Glasgow night. When it got dark, it could be as thick as ink, and those shadows now wrapped around the walls. And yet, somehow, it didn't feel like she was unwelcome. Unlike the first time, outside the synagogue in New York, she felt comfortable. Something had changed.

Chase was pulled from her thoughts by Hass, who opened his door and leaned out of the car to look up at her. "It feels wrong to point this out here, but we're still in a race against Nazis."

Chase laughed, nodded, and got back behind the wheel.

Driving to the East End was an interesting experience. Chase thought she knew the area well enough, but things had changed. The city center would always be the same, laid out in a grid, like a smaller version of New York. But once you got past that, all bets were off. Now, attempts at regeneration and gentrification had moved some of the roads around.

Chase would know exactly where she was for around two hundred yards; then she'd approach an intersection and find a new main highway or a housing development that hadn't been there ten years before. She headed for London Road, one of the main streets out of the city, and one that she hoped hadn't changed all that much. Ahead in the distance, she could see Celtic Park, the large football stadium. It was lit up with green lights, even at this time, glowing like a beacon. Eades's address was near the stadium, so Chase kept the car aimed in that direction.

Past Celtic Park they turned left, then left again into a quiet cul-de-sac of new buildings. Behind the development was the Eastern Necropolis, a large old graveyard that had been opened to cater to the migrants moving to the area after the industrial revolution.

The first half of the street was lined with tall apartment buildings. From the distances between the windows, Chase got the impression the rooms were small. Moving past those, they came to houses. These looked to be bigger and more comfortable living spaces. The rooms seemed larger, and some had large gardens and driveways big enough to fit three cars. Though it seemed that none of them had been built with the idea that visitors might need to read the house numbers in the dark. The doorways were shrouded in shadows, the numbers obscured. Chase took a guess, hoping the houses were numbered in the traditional way, with odd on one side and even on the other. She headed for the corner, where the cul-de-sac had been expanded with a new row of houses, almost forming a separate road. The bricks looked more recent, and a couple of the houses still had for-sale signs and looked uninhabited. In the far corner, next to a small alleyway, Chase could see one of the front windows had a low light coming from inside, the glow of a television or computer screen.

Eades had always kept odd hours. Writer's hours, she'd called them, up until three or four in the morning. Chase was confident she would still be keeping to that habit.

They parked several houses away and closed the car doors as quietly as they could. Chase told Hass to hang back a few yards. Eades knew Chase, and that would buy a few seconds' worth of trust. She didn't know Hass.

Chase stepped up to the door and rang the bell. She felt, more than heard, an electronic buzzing and looked up to see a camera mounted to the wall, in a corner that kept it out of sight from the road. She'd been spotted. What was the next move? Chase waited a full minute. There was no sound from inside, and the glow in the window was gone. She pressed the button again, and this time she heard footsteps in the hallway behind the door. A chain. The metallic clicks of a double lock. The door opened inward, enough for Chase to come face-to-face with Ashley Eades.

The last few months had changed her. There was a hardness to her face, a cold anger that you only recognized if you'd carried it yourself. Her hair was shorter, and she seemed to have lost weight. Chase smiled, and Eades's hard front slipped as a number of emotions washed across her face. Fear. Happiness. Panic. She started to shake her head but stopped. Her mouth opened and closed without words. And then Chase saw it, the decision to slam the door.

Chase put her hands out in a peace-making gesture. "I'm here to help."

"I—"

"I just want to talk." Chase took one slow step forward. "I heard what happened to Bobby. I'm sorry."

Eades's face twitched through more emotions. Grief. Relief. She turned to look behind her, then down at the floor. Chase didn't move any closer; she didn't want to spook her.

"I thought about calling you," Eades said. "So many times. But I didn't know if you'd help."

That cut Chase in half. The thought that someone who needed support wasn't sure if she'd get it. How did she keep finding new ways to push people away? She tried to think of an appropriate response. Apology? Explanation? She opted for a reassuring smile and silence.

"How'd you find me?" Eades asked.

"The spy who helped you in London, she's a friend. She's been keeping tabs on you."

"I paid to disappear."

"You did. But she's good at her job."

Eades nodded. She sucked her cheeks in thought. "So you know about Caliburn."

"Caliburn, R18, the Fountain of Youth."

Eades laughed, mostly to herself, and shook her head. "That's not . . . never mind."

Chase wanted to ask what she meant. But not out here, where they were exposed. "Can we talk? Inside? I do want to help."

They held eye contact for a long time as Eades thought it over before nodding and stepping back, opening the door fully.

Chase gestured back the way she'd come. "I have a friend with me. I trust him."

Hass stepped into view. Chase could see Eades hesitate. The door twitched. But once someone has invited you in, it takes a huge psychological effort for them to turn back on that decision. Eades shrugged and nodded for them both to step inside.

The living room, where the glow had been coming from, looked more like a dorm than a newly built house. There was sparse and cheap furniture, piled high with papers and takeout containers. Eades had a collection of mismatched armchairs, and her computer desk held three laptops. She lifted one up to show she'd been watching a teen drama on Netflix. She flicked a lamp on, filling the room with a dull light. Chase got a better look at Eades now. What she'd taken for weight loss was clearly a fitness regimen of some sort. She'd gained definition, and her shoulders were broader. She'd spent the months since her life fell apart rebuilding herself into someone new. And that someone, from her skinny jeans to her Vans to a leather jacket draped over one chair, looked a lot like Chase. Nobody moved for a few seconds, standing in an awkward silence.

Chase broke the ice. "How are you?"

Eades's hardness was back in place. "It's been tough. Waiting for this. Every day, every time the doorbell goes. Waiting to see who it was that came for me."

Chase skipped past the implication. "You look good, though. Been working out?"

"Every day. Running, boxing. Started doing Krav Maga. There's a class in town, twice a week. I felt . . . When I walked in and found Bobby, when I saw what could have happened to me, I felt so small. So helpless. I never want to feel like that again."

"That takes guts," Chase said. "You can't do that if you're not already strong. You were never helpless."

Eades pulled a face that told Chase she'd picked the wrong response. They stood in silence for a few seconds, until Eades said, "And you? How you been?"

I'm tired.

I'm done.

"Good. I've got a job waiting for me in New York, and my publisher is expecting a book from me any time now."

"Have you written it?"

Chase smiled. "Any time now." She took a step forward. "Caliburn is still looking for you. Do you know who he is?"

Eades snorted. "I knew it. You're working. You're here on a job."

Chase put up a calming hand. "I'm here to help, first, but yes. I was hired to look for the Fountain. I know you talked to James Gilmore about it."

Eades sighed with frustration. "Then you don't know anything."

Chase shot Eades a confused look. Eades dismissing the Fountain. What didn't Chase know?

Eades waved for Chase and Hass to sit down. She settled into the chair nearest the laptops with a sigh. "James never mentioned the Fountain, or any fountain. It was never about that. He said he'd been to the Garden of Eden."

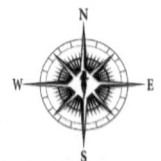

TWENTY-EIGHT

"I'll start at the beginning," Eades said.

Chase put a hand out. "Why don't you start at the part about the Garden of Eden?"

Eades smiled. It was genuine. Warm. She was easing into the situation, putting her fears on hold. "I think I need to go through it in order. It's like two different stories came together, and I don't want to leave anything out."

Chase waved her hand to say *fine*.

"Even then," Eades said, "I'm not really sure where to start." She leaned back, breathed in and out. "So, ages before I met you, I'd done a story on a care home. There were rumors of abuse, and it kinda tied into the national discussion about the NHS, and the lack of provision for the elderly, and how these homes were being run by private firms. So it was a story I knew I could sell, basically. And that's where I met James Gilmore. He was a really nice old guy, but he wasn't all there—his mind would come and go. It was like having a new grandpa to talk to. But one who wasn't a homophobic old reactionary." She smiled. "Then I met you and got hooked into your world, and it took over my life. There were so many people, so many stories. And that's where I met Bobby." She paused. The smile was bittersweet. She'd really loved him. "We had the same drive, but he had more of an idea of targets. I'd always been more scattershot, you know? I'd find a thing that fascinated me and sink into it and follow it as long as I could, then find a new thing."

You were looking for an identity, Chase thought. And I think you found mine.

Eades continued. "But Bobby was focused. He knew what he wanted. He was on missions, not experiences. He had this whole story he was working on about Lothar Caliburn and Nazis. I'd always been fascinated by them. Like, the mentality, how people get there, why they believe those things. And I'd dated a guy at uni who was kinda right-wing. I thought he was going through a phase, but I guess it was me going through one. Like I could debate with him, change him, like it was all a game. So anyway, I got back in touch with him and started using his links to do stories on the alt-right, all the young men who were drifting that way." "And women," Chase said.

"Yeah, true. You know, that was the main thing I kept finding. Nobody is writing about the women who prop up all these movements. Anyway. So,

Bobby was digging into this story about R18."

"We've crossed paths."

Eades paused. "Yeah, the thing in London, one part I was never clear on—"

"Back to your story."

Eades bobbed her head. You got me. "Through Bobby and my ex, I found there was this whole network of actual, real Nazis out there. Not even people who've just come along later and adopted the ideas, but groups who were there back in the day and never went away. All those people who felt empowered to speak up during the thirties, who just went quiet again after the war and kept working on the cause. And then there's all the corporate stuff. You know, companies like Ford and IBM invested heavily in Germany before the war. They stopped after it became clear that shit was toxic over there. I mean, capitalism, right? But there were other companies who didn't pull out or who disguised the fact they were still financially involved. That led me to Dosa Cola. Which was funny in itself."

Eades paused, smiled. The silence was long enough for Chase to wonder if she was waiting for the question, but she started again.

"I went to uni with Lauren Stanford," she said. Chase and Hass shared a look. "She was in the same social circle with my ex, these rich kids who liked to say provocative things, get reactions. But at the time you just think they're rich kids being rich kids, right? And Lauren was always . . . she always seemed to be playing games. I don't think anyone, ever, really met the real person. I always figured she just wanted to be important. The center of whatever scene was happening. And we spent a lot of time together back then. She would patronize me a lot—she thought I didn't notice. But wherever she went, there would be free drinks, free booze, free parties, so . . ." She shrugged. "I went. And now I had an in. I knew Lauren would talk to me if I got in touch. But that's the kind of thing you only get one chance at. If I went straight at her and she figured out why I was asking, she'd shut it all down. I needed to go in a different way.

"That's when I went back to my ex again, Greg, started using his connections like before. Everyone talks about the official Dosa story, the great-grandfather—or great-great, whatever—who went over to the States and founded the company. They never talk about what he was doing in London before he left. You know, and I can prove this—or I could before I had to run—that he was selling a drink over here called Purity Tea? As far as I could tell, it was exactly same as his original Dosa Cola formula, just under a different name and not carbonated. And that name. Purity."

"Reinheit."

"Right? Look at the early Dosa logos when you get a chance. Right up to the one they still have on the building in New York. There's a really small number on there. Beneath the Cola bit. The number eighteen. When I asked, they said it was because the version of the drink we know was the eighteenth attempt at the formula. And nobody ever made any negative

Nazi connotation, because they were using that number very early on, before Hitler had been heard of in the States."

"So it could be genuine, the reason for it."

"Sure, and it could even be that the eighteen in R18 comes from the cola, not the evil guy's initials. But I don't believe in coincidence."

Purity Tea, formula eighteen, and Purity Eighteen."

"I agree."

"And the original recipe for Dosa Cola had cocaine in it. We all know that story. They spin their history as selling a cheap drink to poor communities as a health remedy, but you don't need to squint all that much to see it as a bunch of racists selling cheap drugs to workers and immigrants to keep them addicted and controllable."

Chase's head went boom at that one. How had she never made the connection? It was true, a good PR person can change history.

"Wow," Hass said, giving voice to what Chase was feeling.

Eades nodded. "I'd been sniffing around Dosa, but like I said, I didn't want to just come out and ask Lauren, because then she'd know I was on to her. So I was trying to go the long way round, talked to my ex some more, did a bunch of interviews, tried asking questions that got what I wanted without being obvious. That's when things started to get crazy."

Hass laughed. "Because a hundred-year-old secret Nazi cult disguised as a soda company wasn't already crazy enough."

"Yeah. True. I've been deep in this for so long, it just all seems normal now. But it does get crazier. See, I heard that the Stanford family had always been obsessed with the Fountain of Youth. And that chimed—I was sure Lauren had mentioned it a few times at uni. So I figured, pretend not to be working on the Nazi stuff, start working on the Fountain, and maybe that's a way to get to Lauren."

"Smart."

Eades winced. "Ninety percent stupid. That's when I remembered my new grandpa, James Gilmore. Because he kept talking about being a soldier from the 1800s and saying he'd been drinking water that kept him young. I always just nodded and smiled because why would I think anything of it?

He was just a senile old guy. But I started going back to see him again, and kept bringing the conversation around to his past. The more I stepped into his world with him, the more he opened up and talked about it."

Eades paused as lights flashed in the window. They heard a car outside. Hass jumped to his feet and moved to the edge of the window, watching what was happening.

"Someone turning," he said. "We're okay."

He stayed where he was, though, keeping watch.

It took a few seconds for Eades to get back on the subject after the interruption, her still waiting for someone to come. At last, she started again. "But James never once talked about the Fountain of Youth. He kept talking about a valley, and a mountain, and a river, and water that kept him young. And it was confusing; sometimes he'd say it was paradise, and he wanted to go back, and other times he'd be talking as if it was this horrible place he'd escaped from. Then, the last time I visited him, he finally said the name." "Eden," Chase supplied.

"Eden. He said he'd been in the Garden of Eden."

They sat in silence for a full minute after that, Eades lost in memories and Chase swamped in new thoughts. Hass kept one eye outside.

Finally, Hass said, "He mentioned a mountain?"

"Yeah."

"He say anything about it?"

"He called it Moon Mountain."

Hass turned to face them, giving Chase a look that was clearly supposed to carry a message, but she wasn't sure yet what it was.

"The Mountains of the Moon," he said, "were an old myth. They were said to be the source of the Nile, and a lot of explorers went looking for them, including Henry Morton Stanley."

Now Chase understood what the look had meant. The connections were all coming together.

"Stanley picked up where Dr. Livingstone failed and confirmed the White Nile started at Lake Victoria and the Rwenzori Mountains," Hass continued. "The idea of the Mountains of the Moon faded after that. The Rwenzoris didn't fit the other aspects of the legend, but Westerners started to figure it was just a legend." Hass nodded at Eades. "If your new grandpa was the same man as the old photo, he was a deserter—part of a regiment that went looking for the Mountains of the Moon. His whole regiment abandoned their posts to go searching for treasure there. Stanley mentioned mountains in the west of Punt, described them the same way the deserters were talking about the Mountains of the Moon."

Chase leaned forward. "Have you ever heard about these Punt mountains?"

Hass came back to sit with them, shaking his head. "No. Not until I read Stanley's book. One other thing, and I can't believe I'm even thinking this, but Eden is mentioned in the book, too. General Gordon thought he'd found Eden in the Seychelles. Not anywhere near Punt, no mention of the Mountains of the Moon. But it got a mention. The whole thing seems . . ." Hass trailed off.

Chase nodded. "Yeah."

"He didn't say mountains," Eades said. "Plural. He only ever said it in singular. He was talking about one mountain and one valley."

Chase put her hand up, emphasizing the point she was about to make. "Hypothetically. Let's say there is a place, this valley, this mountain. Let's say it's real. And let's say the water is real, too. A spring, or a well, or a river." She paused again, letting the ideas line up in her mind. "The Garden of Eden is biblical, but it comes from older myths—the Sumerians, I think. Maybe older, a relic of something passed down. But it doesn't seem to have come via Egypt, because they had separate creation myths. And they, at least for a time, believed their people were descended from Punt." She looked to Hass, who nodded.

"But water was important to them," she said. "We've always assumed it was because of the Nile, a culture that grew up along the river, seeing it as the source of life." She paused, looked to Hass again, part of her still not believing she was about to say this out loud. "So what if this all comes from the same place? One place that passed into cultural memory and became Punt to the Egyptians and Eden to the Sumerians, and many other things to other people, including the Fountain of Youth?"

Hass smiled, nodding. "Punt and Eden. The Garden and the Fountain are the same place."

Eades wanted to take back control of the conversation. "I let it be known to a few people that I was working on a story about the Fountain of Youth, that I maybe had something solid. Word got to Lauren Stanford, I guess. We met, and I told her about James, and she seemed hooked. We arranged to meet up again to talk more about it. I thought I could get her to work with me on searching for the Fountain, or fund me on a trip, and then I could use that time to dig into her Nazi connection. Next thing, there's a woman talking to me on the street in London saying that Lothar Caliburn is going to kill me, and then I got home, and . . ."

Her words died off in a choking sound. Chase leaned forward and touched her knee. She didn't need the rest. Eades had gotten home and found Bobby dead and, in her shock, had made the gut decision to trust Mason. That had been the night Ashley Eades died.

"My turn," Chase said. "You guessed I was working. I was hired by Stanford."

Eades's face twisted in shock, anger.

"You know me, I'm on your side," Chase hurried to add. "We"—she gestured at Hass—"are on your side. Stanford gave me the whole speech about healthcare and how finding the Fountain would be the cure to all our problems. But I wasn't buying it. I had no interest. She hooked me with you. Told me about Bobby. Told me you'd gone missing. She knew that would get me. I came here to make sure you were safe."

"Well, hey." Eades's voice shook, clearly rattled. "As you can see, I'm totally safe."

"And we still have a load of questions. Why would she risk bringing me in? Why do they really want to find"—Chase paused; saying it was still a big hurdle to jump—"Eden? And what will she do now that I've found you? Wait . . ."

Chase looked down at her messenger bag. She opened it up and pulled out the tablet Ted had given her, full of Stanford's research on the Fountain. She remembered how she'd been given it. Right after the attack, seconds after a stranger had planted the seed in her mind, questioned her about the Fountain. Then Ted shows up to save her and, oh, by the way, here's an electronic device. She had so casually accepted that Conte would plant tracking software on the files he sent her, but she had been too distracted to even think of Stanford.

Eades met her eyes. "She gave you that, didn't she?"

Chase nodded. "We need to destroy this. And get moving."

Eades stood and left the room. Chase and Hass sat in silence, waiting. Had Eades gone to cry? To get drinks? To creep out the back door, leaving these weirdos to their private little war?

She came back in carrying a bulging messenger bag of her own.

Chase nodded at it. "Go-bag?"

"Yeah." She dropped down into the seat. "It's funny. I've run all these scenarios hundreds of times. Like, someone coming for me when I'm in bed, and I hear a noise, need to run. I'd figured out a way down the outside of the building that might work. Or I'd be on the street outside, spot someone looking at me a little too long, and just keep on walking."

"What was your plan for where to go after that?"

Eades shrugged. "Didn't have one. Starting a whole new life feels impossible until you've already done it. I love it here, but if I need to, I can just move on, be someone else. I already have a different name; I can just get another."

"I'm sorry for all the crap you've been through." Chase surprised herself at how genuine she sounded. It was real. Eades's life had been ruined, and sitting here now, Chase really got a sense of how much trouble she'd caused.

Eades leaned back into the ripped leather armchair and let out a long breath. "Honestly, it's not your fault. It's mine. You were just a cool new thing for me to glom on to. I used you." She paused, stared at the wall for a moment. "I used a lot of people. Got burned." She paused again. "I was using Bobby."

"I'm sorry."

"I mean, I loved him, but I was using him, too."

Chase touched Eades's knee again. They still needed information, but she hoped she pitched her tone right. "Did you find out who Caliburn is?"

Eades swallowed a couple of times. Nodded. "I got a look at the man who killed Bobby. I didn't tell anyone. Didn't tell your friend." She met Chase's eyes for a second, then looked down at her feet. "I saw him coming out of the building, and I don't know how I knew, but I just did. Even going in, it felt wrong, seeing this stranger. I was scared for Bobby. Then when I . . . when he was . . . I just knew I'd seen the man who did it."

"Was he somebody you knew?"

"Never seen him before, or since. But I'll never forget him."

Hass was still focused on the bigger issue. "Did Gilmore give you anything else about the location?"

"He drew a map."

Chase leaned forward, all thoughts of tact and moderation gone. "Do you have it? Can we see it?"

Eades looked down at her feet. "It wouldn't make any sense. It was just something out of Tolkien—none of the names related to anything real. And he didn't put anything to show what country it was in. He said nobody should go there."

"Why?" Hass said. "If it's Eden, why not go back? Why leave in the first place?"

"This might be hard to believe, but an old man with dementia didn't always make sense," Eades replied. "He said Eden didn't want him anymore, that the ground spit him out. Another time he said Eden wasn't for us. He said it was protected."

THE END OF EDEN

"Stanley's version of the Mountains of the Moon," Hass said, "included evil spirits who guarded the mountain."

Chase thought back to the island in Lake Tana and the blind swordsmen with weapons fashioned to sound like wind, and the ancient security traps she'd encountered in Alexander's tomb. "Legends like that can mean anything."

"Agreed, but they also usually mean something."

Chase turned back to Eades. "Why not go looking for Eden yourself with all this information?"

Eades shook her head, smiled like Chase had said the dumbest thing. "Why would I? It was all just some story from an old man who made no sense. I was only using it to get to Lauren. And even if I believed it, how would I do it? I'm not you or Lauren. I can't just wake up one day and decide to go on a mad quest to a faraway place, for a thing that might not exist. I wake up each morning and worry about breakfast, then getting to work, and then if today is the day someone tries to kill me."

Eades had dodged a question, and Hass had apparently noticed that, too. "You didn't answer," he said. "Can we see it?"

Chase watched Eades's reaction. It was like she'd just been caught in a lie. "You still have it, don't you?"

Eades leaned back in the seat and rubbed her forehead. She sighed and said something to herself, muffled, that sounded like "okay." She got up a second time and left the room again, coming in a moment later with a piece of paper. She closed each laptop on the desk to make a flat surface and unfolded the document to its full A4 size.

"It's all I had to remember him by when I ran."

Chase and Hass both leaned in to look. Chase understood Eades's Tolkien reference right away. She remembered an old green hardcover copy of The Hobbit her mother had stolen from the school library when she was young, with a map on the inside of the front cover. This was drawn much the same, but with less precision and detail. There were no edges to the map, nothing that could be used to give a wider context of geographical borders. Mostly it was drawn in faded pencil, but Gilmore had colored in a few sections with crayon, giving it the look of a child's school drawing. There was a large circle in the upper left, filled in blue, labeled The Queen's Garden. The writing was also childlike, a scrawl that spoke to Gilmore's mental state when he drew the map. Parallel to the garden, off to the far right of the drawing, were two notches, something like a doorway or two pillars, with the words Gateway to Hell written between them. The largest feature of the map, drawn slightly off-center near the bottom, was another large circle. This one was lightly shaded brown. There were lines running off it, spreading outward.

This large feature was labeled *The Impossible Mountain.*

"That's Moon Mountain," Eades said. "He was very clear about that when he drew it. In conversation, he always used the Moon Mountain name, but then on the map he called it Impossible Mountain. I asked him why, but he just shrugged."

There were two lines close together coming off the north of the mountain, winding like a river, but he'd shaded in the space between them red. The lines converged at the end, and there was a crude image of some green trees and a white four-legged creature, like a lion or a wolf.

"What's this?"

"That's the valley." Eades shrugged. "That's where he said he'd lived. So, Eden, I guess."

"And this?" Chase pointed to the lion.

"He didn't tell me, but he'd already said the area was guarded,"

Chase tried to think of anywhere she knew in Ethiopia or Somalia that had any known species of animal that fit the bill, or a mythic creature that might have been inspired by the image.

"Eden." Hass whispered the word, reverently, as if it had finally sunk in what exactly they were talking about.

"Eden," Chase nodded, but it wasn't a hard yes so much as a confused maybe.

"I don't..." Hass clicked his jaw, stayed silent for a few seconds. Troubled. For me, it's not a place on Earth. Not a place to be found. It's a place Adam was expelled from, he came down to Earth."

"Up until all of this," Eades said, "I thought it was settled, that Eden was under water at the top of the Persian Gulf, at the mouth of the Tigris."

"The Tigris is mentioned in the Bible." Chase nodded, more certain this time. "Well, sort of. It depends which interpretation you go with. There are four rivers that flow either into or out of Eden. The Pishon. The Gihon.The Hiddekel. The Eurphrates. We know where the Euphrates is, and a lot of modern biblical scholarship had argued that the Hiddekel is the Tigris. People have tried to argue the Gihon is the Nile, because of a reference to Cush, but the Nile is too far from the Tigris."

"And what do you think?"

Chase hesitated. Trying to sift through her in-built opinions and biases, to see how her thoughts were re-settling after finding the Ark. "I've never worried all that much about it. Eden, or the Eden *story*, was never a physical realm in the earliest versions. It was another place. Above us, a part of heaven, or a different spiritual realm. It was somewhere we were exiled *from*."

"That's still my version," Hass said.

"Right. Early Judaism, early Christianity, still preserved in Islam. The idea that Eden was a physical place on earth, somewhere we could find, that came into the story as cultures became more modern, more material. And it's really Nineteenth century writers who did the work of placing it in Armenia, or Turkey, or Syria. As science became more dominant, so religions worked hard to place themselves within that, to say the stories could be pointed to on maps and explained within natural laws. My mentor, Professor Turner, used to argue that Eden was early Jericho."

"As in...."

"*That* Jericho, yes. Eden was a *walled* garden. Designed. Built. Away from the bible, archaeology has shown Jericho is one of the oldest cities in the world. Maybe *the* oldest. And we know almost nothing about who originally built it, or why. We know it had walls, even back to it's earliest version, and a large watchtower that would have been the tallest building in the world for a time. There's a second version of Eden in the bible, in Ezekiel, and it references a king being cast out, not Adam, not the first man and woman, but a king. So Professor Turner used to argue, the Eden tradition was about a king building a garden for god in Jericho. But I still hesitate to get too literal. We've always just needed a mythic place that we came from. So each culture that's had their own version of an Eden, always placed in their own earliest history, just beyond the mountains. And that means none of them are *wrong*, really. And the rivers...I don't know. Maybe they accumulated over time. The four rivers are a chronology of our folk memory. Like, at one point our memory of Eden was sub-Saharan, and we took a river with us from there. Then Eden was in the Caucasus, and we added in an other local river. And then our Eden was at the head of the Persian Gulf, and the two rivers from the older myths and the two local rivers became four rivers. They're an oral history of our journey as a species."

"But we're talking about a real place." Hass seemed deeply troubled by this conversation. "We're talking about a place we can go to."

Chase opened her mouth to speak but paused.

She looked at Hass.

Yes, he'd heard it, too. A noise outside. Near the window.

"That's him," Eades shouted.

A second later someone tried the front door. The handle didn't turn because of the lock, but they all heard the attempt. There was a bang, followed by a cracking sound as someone shot the window. It was followed by the sound of a second solid connection and smashing as the glass gave out.

A grenade landed on the floor.

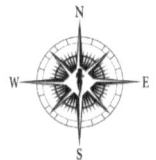

TWENTY-NINE

T he small black flash grenade skidded across the floor. The impact on the glass had taken the force out of the throw. Hass and Chase both moved fast. Hass lifted the table by the nearest leg, sending the laptops crashing across the room, and tipped it on its side, positioning it as a barrier between them and the device.

Chase grabbed Eades and pulled her to the floor, having just enough time to shout, "Close eyes."

WHUMP.

Even with her eyelids screwed shut, Chase could see the bright flash of light fill the room. Blotches and patterns danced across her eyes in the darkness. Her hearing went out completely. She didn't so much hear the explosion as feel the absence of it. One second, she could hear everything that was happening, and the next, there was silence. Slowly, a distant ringing was the only thing to penetrate the fog. She felt movement beside her and opened her eyes. The patterns were still there, obscuring her vision, but they faded as she blinked.

Hass was already up and moving.

A shape filled the window. Someone climbing in. Through spotty vision Chase watched as a small wiry guy with cropped hair got half in before Hass grabbed him. They fell to the floor together in a twisting, fighting tangle of limbs. The small guy had a gun, but Hass grabbed for it, stopping him from taking aim.

Hass called something out. Chase almost heard it. The sound formed in her head, but had it come in through her ears? Had it made it all the way through this wave of nausea she was feeling? As she looked, he shouted again, his mouth forming the word she thought she'd heard.

"Go."

"Back door."

Chase looked down. Eades was on the floor beneath her, clearly struggling with the same inability to hear, but she'd been the one to speak. Probably? Maybe? Everything was still off-kilter.

"Back door," Eades said. Chase wondered if this was the second time, or if there was a time delay on the first. Had she heard it before Eades said it? That wasn't possible. Why was she—?

Hass's and Eades's words finally combined in her mind into an urgent thought.

Go. Back door.

She climbed to her feet, not feeling steady, and pulled Eades up after her. Eades led the way though a small kitchen and washroom to the back door. They were both out into the early-morning air before Chase's brain was working enough to realize they'd fallen for the oldest tactic in the book. The frontal assault was a diversion. Chase took a punch to the face, falling back against the house and hitting her head. Her mind went cloudy again.

August Nash.

August Nash?

What was he—?

No time.

She pushed off from the wall and aimed a fist of her own at him. He swerved it and hit her hard in the gut, knocking her back against the house a second time. Now she had no wind and no brain. Nash laughed and stepped in fast, grabbing Chase's throat with both hands, squeezing as he lifted her. Chase's feet came free of the ground. She kicked out, but without a solid footing beneath her, she didn't have any strength in the kick. Chase coughed, fighting for air.

Nash tightened his grip.

Chase started to feel a little distant. A voice was telling her, No, don't black out, you're dead if you do. But another part of her was focusing on the way the pain in her head was drifting away and thinking, Hey, this doesn't seem to hurt too bad . . .

She saw Eades hesitating. She was halfway down the yard, had been running away from the fight, but now she turned back. Chase wanted to say, Keep going. She'd let Eades down so much already, caused so much trouble. The least she could do was help her get away. Keep her safe. Hadn't that been her plan all along?

Chase stopped fighting back against Nash to wave Eades away.

Go.

Hass held on to the smaller guy's gun hand. They were both trying to control the direction. It was rare for Hass to find someone who could match him for strength. He'd beat this guy in the long run, but for right now he was packing a lot of power into his small frame. He was dressed the same way as the library attackers, but with a tactical belt and gloves. Hass could tell he was a level above the others. There had been the whiff of amateurism off them. But this guy looked and moved like someone who'd been trained. Likely ex-military.

Hass thought of what Eades had shouted the second before the window smashed.

That's him.

This was the man she'd seen coming out of her apartment building. This was Bobby's killer. Lothar Caliburn. The man Conte wanted.

Caliburn went limp, throwing Hass off-balance, making him lose his grip. Caliburn pushed away and kicked at Hass, putting enough distance between them to bring up the gun.

Hass had always wondered how he would face this moment. He didn't close his eyes.

Nash knew he'd made a mistake. He knew as he was making it, but sometimes you just gotta roll with the wrong idea. His chance to get Chase had clouded his thoughts. She wasn't the mission. Ashley Eades was. And she had been the first one out the door. It would've been the easiest thing in the world to grab her, shoot whoever followed, and run. He had his modified gun, with the tranq bullets. He hadn't shared that trick with Danny. He hadn't even shared bullets with Danny. That gun was empty.

Nash had given him strict orders. No firing. It was his old-school CIA training for operations in a built-up area like this. One bang you could get away with. If someone heard one shot, one small muffled explosion, they would tell themselves it was a firecracker or a car backfiring. Maybe a tire blowout. And in the early hours of the morning, you had the buffer of sleep.

The first loud noise would wake people up, but they wouldn't know why they were awake. But a second loud noise became a problem.

The flashbang had used up their allowance.

And if Danny couldn't follow that one simple instruction, he deserved to have an unloaded gun. So grab Eades, tranq Chase, then run. Maybe shoot Chase twice; there was always a chance a double dose could be fatal. But then he'd seen Chase, and his focus had shifted. He'd lost perspective. She'd screwed him over so many times. Denied what was his. She was the one who'd made this personal, not him. But he was the one who would finish it.

And so, he'd made the mistake.

With his hands around Chase's throat, all he needed to do was stand there for a little longer, keep that grip, and she'd be gone. And he could tell she knew it, too. She even stopped fighting. Letting her hands fall to—wave?

Part of Nash knew what the problem was there, but it wasn't the part that was in control. His anger, his pride, they were running the show. His brain? His brain knew what was about to— Smash.

Something hard and heavy hit Nash in the back of the head. For a few seconds he was suddenly very aware of his teeth. He watched his hands let go of Chase but didn't feel himself doing it. Then it came again. Something hard, this time to his temple. That bitch, Eades, was hitting him with something. His vision blurred, and he fell forward. As the world started to go black, he had time to think that the advantage of being hit in the head was that he didn't feel the kick to the balls Chase had just delivered.

Click.

Click.

Click. Click.

Caliburn's face flooded with anger and confusion. Clearly, he hadn't known the gun wasn't loaded. Hass didn't pause to find out what he'd do next. He'd been given a second chance, and he was taking it. He punched Caliburn, grabbed again at the gun to make sure it couldn't be used as a blunt object. Too late, he wondered if there was a second weapon.

Caliburn plunged a blade into Hass's side with his spare hand.

Hass screamed, pulled himself back, instinctively grabbing the hand that held the knife and pulling it back with him, keeping the blade inside. Caliburn hadn't expected this, handing the momentum to Hass. Hass headbutted the smaller man. Once. Twice. The little guy fell backward, letting go of the blade. Hass pulled the knife out with a quieter, more controlled scream.

Hass always tried not to kill, and there had been times in the field when that hesitation had cost him. On his last real job, when Nash had set him up, Hass had always known it was his own fault, really. He'd held back in doubt at a crucial moment, given his enemy the edge.

He couldn't make that mistake now. He was injured. Losing blood. If he gave his attacker even a moment, it could all be over. Live or die, fight or fly. He breathed in, said a silent prayer for forgiveness, and sank the blade into the smaller man's chest.

Again.

Again.

A frenzy that came from knowing if he paused for even a moment, he could be giving his opponent the chance to kill him.

Again.

Again.

He stopped only when Caliburn stopped moving and slumped to the floor, his eyes glassy but not quite dead, his chest rising and falling slowly.

Hass touched his own wound. The burning sensation around the edges was a good sign. The area hadn't gone numb. Blood wasn't pumping out, so nothing major had been hit. It was going to hurt like hell and he needed medical attention, but he had some time. He pulled out his cell and loaded Talaria, scrolling through the contacts until he found Conte.

When Conte answered, Hass didn't even wait for a greeting. "I have the man who killed Bobby."

"Is he alive?"

Hass looked down at Caliburn. His breathing was growing faint. The battery was running down. "Momentarily."

"I would like to talk to him."

Hass squatted down, muffling a cry as his wound twisted. He turned the phone's screen to face Caliburn and pressed it closer to the dying man.

"I must be honest," Conte said. "I pictured someone else. Someone fearsome. Dangerous. I'm getting old, I suppose, but in my head, I went to someone like Dolph Lundgren. Huge. Strong. Now I find out my Bobby was killed by . . . you."

Caliburn's mouth opened, but no sound came out. Whatever his last words were going to be, they were lost in his throat.

Conte continued. "Bobby was a good boy. He wanted to be a hero. He's in a good place now, and I'll never see him again. But people like us, you and I, we know where we're going. And I'll see you again. And you won't enjoy that meeting."

Caliburn was gone. Hass waited a few seconds before turning the cell back to face him. Conte's eyes were red-rimmed, but he was in control, showing his trademark restraint.

"Thank you, Hassan. And Chase helped?"

"She did." Hass thought of Chase and Eades, somewhere out back, dealing with whoever had been waiting out there. "She led me here."

Conte nodded. His shoulder moved, indicating he'd just pressed a command on the keyboard. Hass felt his cell buzz.

"I have sent you the location of the Ark," Conte said. "I will wait sixty minutes before sending it on to Chase. And again, thank you." He ended the call.

Hass smiled. Even now, in his moment of grief, Conte couldn't help playing the game. He'd given Hass the chance to betray Chase and go after the prize himself.

Hass looked down at the dead man. He touched his forehead and said a prayer for his soul, then climbed to his feet slowly. He breathed in and said another prayer, this time of gratitude.

Eades hit Nash with the spade for a third time on his way down. Chase leaned against the house, drawing in deep, ragged breaths. She nodded a thank-you.

The garden looked new. A small path of paving slabs ran between freshly laid turf and patches of soil that hadn't had time to settle. Newly planted trees lined the walkway. Eades had been here long enough now to literally set down roots and start showing pride in having a garden. Chase knew Eades had come from a safe, relaxed family on the south coast, growing up with gardens as part of the normal background.

Then she'd moved to the big city, in a variety of flat-shares and overpriced apartment buildings, and having a garden had become a distant dream. Now here she was, making a fresh life, in fresh soil, and Chase had turned up a second time to wreck it.

"We need to move," Chase said, her voice hoarse. She stepped over the unconscious Nash.

"Thanks," Eades said, her own voice withering. "I hadn't thought of that."

Eades walked to the back of the garden, where her own land met the ancient brick wall of the Necropolis. She pulled a ladder from behind a potted Christmas tree. From a large ceramic pot, she pulled a second messenger bag, bulging like the one in the living room. A second go-bag. A backup plan. Chase had lived long enough with a packed bag by the door to recognize an escape route when she saw one. Eades had scoped this out in advance. She'd been living for so long with the fear, or the certainty that something was coming, that she had needed several ways out. Eades put the ladder to the wall, slipped the bag over her shoulder, and started to climb. Chase held the ladder steady for Eades before following her up.

At the top they pulled the ladder up after them.

Chase paused to look back, giving Hass a few seconds to appear in the doorway, but Eades wasn't going to wait. She slid the ladder down the other side, testing that it was firmly planted before starting to descend.

Chase hesitated again. She could see Nash was already stirring. Should she go back? Finish him off? He'd been fine with doing the same to her, so why would she even hesitate at the idea?

She turned to see Eades already striding off into the darkness. No time to wait. She descended the ladder, dropped it in the grass—it wouldn't stop anyone from following, but it might give her and Eades some time—and followed quickly after Eades through the gravestones. They were an eclectic mix. Large and small. Huge, ostentatious monuments, of crosses and angels, a few obelisks, scattered among subtle markers, small stones, plaques. Chase caught up with Eades as they crossed a concrete path to step back onto grass on the other side, moving parallel with the large football stadium that loomed over them on the left. This side of Celtic Park had been built with a cantilever, so the structure hung over the Necropolis wall and the graves nearest it were in permanent shadow. Chase hoped those people had been Celtic fans.

"Where are we going?"

Eades didn't turn to look at her. "Away."

Her mood had changed visibly. Back at the house, she'd been opening up, talking, even admitting to her own fears and mistakes. Now her shoulders were set, her head was down. She was huddling in against herself. Siege mentality.

Chase thought back to what Eades had shouted: *That's him.*

Bobby's killer. More than anything else, that explained her mood change. Seeing Chase had been one thing, a manageable wound, but seeing the face of Bobby's killer was a different level of trauma. The realization only made Chase feel worse.

They moved deeper into the darkness, between two large angel statues, and passed a mausoleum. There were no streetlights, and they were beyond the stadium lights now. Chase felt her old fears bubble up. She'd almost wondered where they'd gotten to, that old irrational part of her that was scared of the dark. She had tricks for dealing with it.

Focus on the physical world around you, block out the nonexistent threat. Focus on the air you're breathing. The sounds of traffic beyond the walls. The ground under your feet. She felt damp earth and splashed through a puddle, hoping it was mud.

"What's the pl—?"

Her question was interrupted as she tripped over something hard, landing face-first into something wet.

Please be mud.

Please be mud.

Electronic light filled the space around them. Eades's face was lit from below, and Chase saw the illumination was coming from a cell phone.

"I've got a bike over there," Eades said. "But only one."

Chase wiped a hand across her face, coming away with mud. She got up into a crouching position, waiting to see if Eades would help her up.

"Scouted this all out a while back," Eades said. "Hoped I wouldn't need it, but I should've known you'd be back."

Anger flashed up from somewhere deep.

Chase jumped to her feet. "How is this all about me?" She jabbed a finger at Eades. "What about everything you said back there, you using people?"

Eades met heat with heat. "You brought them here."

Chase bit back on her response. Breathe. Calm down. Think this through. She's having a worse day than you. Her life is falling apart for the second time. Her worst nightmare has just come true.

But Chase was only there because she'd dropped everything to fly across the Atlantic to make sure Eades was safe. How dare—

"I'm only here because of you." Her voice exploded out around them. "We are only here because of you. We came here to help you. It's not my fault you got mixed up with Nazis, not my fault you jumped into bed with them, not my fault they killed . . ."

Her words died off. A line had been crossed. She didn't have the words to apologize.

"That was him." Eades's words sounded small. Hurt. "The man in the window. That's who killed Bobby."

"Yeah." Chase's voice was equally muted. "I'm sorry."

An engine roared. Car lights in the distance, moving inside the cemetery.

"How'd that get in?" Chase asked.

Eades turned to look. Frightened, she withdrew, making herself small.

"They keep the gates open."

Nash was here.

The lights swept around as the car drove along the twisting concrete path. Chase squatted down, pulling Eades with her. The headlights stopped moving. The car was a hundred yards away, around a bend, facing toward the football stadium. In the reflected light she could make out details. Metallic blue. A Toyota RAV, with a roof rack. More of a family vacation vehicle than a Nazi killing machine.

And speaking of which, why was Nash working for them?

She'd always known his moral compass was a bit off, but even he, she thought, wouldn't stoop to taking Nazi blood money. Maybe he didn't know? Was it worth talking to him?

Not now. Survive first, think later.

She remembered what Eades had said a few moments before. "Where's your bike?"

Eades crawled to a bush in the corner, at the base of the large wall. She ducked into the bush, and Chase heard the sound of tarpaulins being pulled back. She pulled a bicycle out and wheeled it to where Chase was crouching.

"That was your plan?"

Chase heard the sarcasm in her own voice and realized it wasn't helping. She focused on the car instead. There was light coming from inside. The door's open. Nash had gotten out while she had been looking at the bike.

She looked around, peering through the murky shadows to find a good defensive position. Should they fight? Eades wouldn't stand a chance of getting away on the bike in a race against Nash's car. But he was on foot now. Maybe if Chase could cause a distraction . . .

She pulled Eades in close and whispered, "Stay here. Be ready to go on your bike."

"When?"

"You'll know."

Chase stood up and ran toward the car, between the gravestones. When she was within fifty yards, she dropped down out of sight. If he'd spotted the movement, she wanted to disorient him, change direction. She crawled between two large stone crosses, getting close to the car, then stood and ran toward the stadium. Something off to her left. A shape resolving itself in the dark. Nash. He was moving fast, but she had the speed advantage. If she could stay ahead of him—

A compressed gunshot.

Something grazed her shoulder, almost ripping her leather jacket. She dropped to the ground and kept still. Let him think he got you. Draw him in.

Footsteps now. A splash, a boot going through a puddle. She coiled, ready to move. He stepped between the two nearest gravestones, almost over her now. Chase leapt up, fist first, driving it up into his chin. Her knuckles burned, but he fell back, staggering before going down to one knee. She swung a kick at his head, connecting hard. He was down on both knees now, but not out. She'd used up the element of surprise. She turned and ran again, back in the direction of Eades's house.

Follow me

Light flashed across Nash's vision. He felt like his brain was splashing from side to side inside his skull. Chase had landed two good blows. If she was closer to him in size, they would have been enough to take him down. And now she was running again. She was faster than him, built more for speed than punching. She was fighting clever.

Too clever . . .

Nash rocked back on his heels, stopping himself from following. He turned his head, listening behind him. Metallic clicking. The whirring of a bike chain. Someone was biking away. He spun around and saw a low shape moving fast, whipping out from the graves onto the path and racing in the direction of the gate.

Chase was the distraction.

He ran back to the Toyota and slid into the seat, starting the engine before he closed the door. He reversed out from where he'd parked and brought the car around, then accelerated hard after the cycling figure. His high beams caught her. Crouched low over the bike, hips rocking from side to side as her legs pumped the pedals. Nash pushed down on the accelerator. Eades grew larger as he closed in fast, and then the car tapped the back wheel of the bike with a jolt. The metal frame tipped upward. Eades was airborne, hanging there for a second before crashing down onto the Toyota's hood. Nash braked, and Eades was catapulted off the car, skidding to the edge of the headlights' glow.

Nash got out of the car and ran over to her, crouching down. She was wheezing. Her arm was broken, and he didn't think much for her ankle's chances, either. He rolled her toward him, into his arms, and lifted, carrying her to the car

Chase heard the impact. She thought that was sickening enough, but the sound of a body hitting the ground, following by the unmistakable sound of leather across asphalt, was worse. She'd sensed that Nash wasn't chasing her and heard Eades's bike at the same time he must have. She'd turned and started back, knowing her plan wasn't working.

Ahead, she could already see Nash in the Toyota, turning, the acceleration and . . . the impact.

Had this all been for nothing?

She kept moving despite the feeling of cold water spreading across her guts, the sense of hopelessness filling her every long stride.

Nash bent over Eades's fallen form, then picked her up. He was carrying her to the car. Why would he do that if she was dead? And why would he kill her anyway, when the job was presumably to get Eades back to Lauren Stanford alive? A moment of hope: Eades was hurt, but there was still a chance to save this situation. Chase kept running.

Nash slipped back into the front seat and slammed the door just as Chase cleared the graves and ran out onto the path, closing the distance to the car. Chase was within touching distance of the back of the Toyota when it started to pull away.

She jumped.

Reached out.

Grabbed hold.

She gripped the roof rack with her right hand and was pulled forward by the car's acceleration. Her wrist screamed, feeling like it was being torn from her forearm. Chase felt like she was being pulled backward and forward at the same time, as the car picked up speed and her own weight tried to shake her loose. She tightened her arm muscles to pull herself onto the back of the Toyota and gripped the other side of the rack with her left hand, placing her feet on the bumper to steady herself against the back of the vehicle.

They drove out past the large black metal gates of the Necropolis—pure decoration, Chase thought, if they weren't going to use them at night. Nash whipped the Toyota to the left onto Gallowgate, deliberately fishtailing and almost shaking Chase loose. Her feet slipped, hitting the road and adding to the drag trying to pull her off. The car gained speed as they approached an intersection up ahead and Chase could feel her grip loosening with each jolt. She needed to make a move. Either she got into the car, or she got off. But she wasn't going to let Eades down. Her feet were getting warm, the friction burning through her shoes. She tried to plant her soles and kick upward into a jump, but the jolt almost threw her from the vehicle.

The car came to a sudden, skidding stop.

Chase's head smacked into the rear window and her right hand came loose. Nash accelerated again, running through a red light and forward onto a traffic circle, taking the car around in two repeated fast loops. Chase closed her eyes and held her breath.

Don't think.

Just focus on your grip.

Ignore—

The car stopped again. This time Chase brought her right hand up to hit the window, bracing herself before her head could whiplash forward. The Toyota picked up speed, heading back onto Gallowgate.

Her left wrist had moved past pain now and was heading fast into numb. If she couldn't feel it, she wasn't sure she could control it. Her grip was loosening.

A second engine gunned behind her, a very muffled, controlled sound. She looked back to see the yellow Mini with Hass behind the wheel. He drove up close to the Toyota's back bumper. Chase closed her eyes for a second, found the strength to pull her legs up, planted her feet against the back door, drew in a breath, counted to three, and let go of the roof rack, kicking off with both feet. She landed on the front of the Mini, the impact sending stabbing pains all along her side.

Hass slowed down steadily, easing the vehicle to a stop to avoid throwing Chase off. She slid from the front to the road, landing on her feet, and ran around to the passenger door, pulling it open and yelling, "Go," as she dropped into the seat.

Hass grunted an acknowledgment and floored the pedal as Chase slammed the door. They raced after the Toyota, which now had a large lead. Both cars ran a red light at another intersection. They were getting closer to the city center now. Soon they'd be on the part of the Gallowgate that teemed with life when Celtic played at home, lined with bars that flew the Irish tricolor. If they continued on this route, Chase was sure she would have the advantage; she knew Glasgow better than Nash, and the city was riddled with side streets and one-way systems.

She turned to look at Hass, noticing for the first time that his hands were covered in blood, as was his chest. She leaned across and pulled back his jacket, seeing a large red stain on the side of his T-shirt.

"You're hurt."

"A little."

"What happened?"

"Stabbed. The guy back at the house."

"He's the one who killed Bobby."

"Yeah. I let Conte watch him die."

Chase took that in, then nodded. Even in the middle of this situation, that felt like they'd at least achieved something. A small resolution.

"He sent me the location of the Ark," Hass said, keeping his eyes on the road. "I know where it is."

"And you came back for me?"

He looked at her briefly, then returned to the task at hand. "Of course."

Hass pulled the wheel hard to the left, and Chase focused back on the road to see that the Toyota had turned off the Gallowgate into a small sleepy housing development. The Toyota reached the bottom of the road and mounted the curb, pushing on to another road on the other side. Hass followed. The Mini bounced and rocked, and it felt like they could rip off the wheels at any second.

At the bottom of the road, still in the small housing development, both cars mounted the curb again and drove along a narrow footpath that let them out on London Road. The Toyota turned left, heading back east again. Hass turned to follow. Chase smacked against the door. One of these days, she'd remember to wear a seat belt in a high-speed pursuit.

There was a new sound—from the sky. The droning whir of a helicopter. Chase opened the passenger-side window and looked up. A chopper passed overhead, heading toward Glasgow Green, the large public park that sat on the edge of the city, beside the river Clyde. Up ahead the Toyota turned left at an intersection, having the benefit of a green light this time. Now the chopper and the Toyota were heading in the same direction.

It's a rendezvous.

Lauren Stanford was pulling out all the stops to make this a smooth getaway. And Chase knew if Nash got Eades into the helicopter, it was game over. Chase had no way of matching their resources, no way of tracking where they went. If Nash got there, he won.

Hass was still a quarter mile short of the intersection, and the Toyota was out of sight now. Off to the right, on the other side of the pedestrian walkway, Chase could see a small road that led straight down to Glasgow Green.

"Turn," she shouted.

Hass didn't need telling twice. They bumped up over the curb again, this time accompanied by a violent scraping sound.

"I hope your friend doesn't need this car back," Hass said.

Nash thought he'd lost them. The Mini wasn't on his tail as he raced down the Green, the road that ran alongside the park for a stretch. In the back seat, Ashley Eades groaned as the car bounced over a pothole. She'd been conscious the whole time, but not moving much. Nash wondered if the crash had taken more out of her than he thought.

"I meant what I said," Nash said, not meaning what he said. "Tell me what we need, I'll head straight to the hospital."

"Both know that's a lie."

Nash shrugged. He'd tried the same line a couple of times now. He could admit when the game was up. "Yeah."

He pushed the car over another curb and drove headlong into the park, sending grass and mud flying. The car rocked, jolting over lumps and divots. He saw the Mini now in the side mirror, moving at him from an angle. They'd found a different route into the park. But his car was faster and more powerful—he could keep the distance between them for as long as he had clear space to run.

Ahead, Nash saw the tall obelisk erected in honor of Admiral Horatio Nelson. Lauren's chopper had come down next to the needle, its landing struts already settling into the turf. In the distance, he could finally hear sirens. Man, the cops in this town were slow to respond. He remembered what Lauren had told him about having friends high up in the British establishment. People who moved in the shadows and had abetted the London attack. They had big plans for their next move but weren't ready yet. And their influence over cops didn't extend to Scotland. Things were different up here, and they needed to evade capture.

Still, they were pulling off a helicopter exfil in the middle of Glasgow. His skills were matched to her resources.

Why not have some fun with it? He pulled the hand brake, sending the car into a wide arcing spin ten feet in front of the chopper, mud, water, and grass flying all around him.

Oh yeah

Chase was already out and running before Hass had pulled the Mini to a stop. She was exhausted. She didn't have anything left, but she needed it. She pushed for it. Up ahead, Nash lifted Eades's still form into the back of the chopper. He climbed in after her and pulled the door closed.

No.

No.

You gotta move.

You gotta move.

Chase passed the Toyota. She was nearing the edge of the blade's range as the chopper started to lift off. Chase closed the ground between them and jumped. She grabbed hold of the landing skid. The helicopter rose slowly, gradually. Chase held on, staring up at the door. Nash grinned down at her. Her arms burned with pain. Her left wrist was still numb from the Toyota. And now she could feel it slipping. There was no way she could hold on. But she needed to.

Nash blew her a kiss as she lost her grip, feeling nothing but air beneath her feet as she started to drop.

How high up were they?

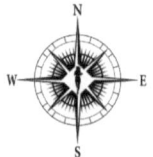

THIRTY

They were somewhere over France when Lauren groaned in pleasure. Her hips rocked as she gasped and let out a short squeal. She was astride Nash on the sofa. She could feel he was still hard. She might be done, but he wasn't. His face, his eyes, asked her to keep going. She knew his mouth wasn't going to. He'd never beg anyone for anything. Finally, someone who understood her. They matched each other. Nash had taken off his mask, and she had taken off hers. Well, mostly. There was still one thing she hadn't told him. But that was between her and her parents, and they weren't talking. August Nash was the perfect man. She knew exactly how to push his buttons and how to earn his loyalty.

And right now, she knew who was in control and who wouldn't admit it.

The one thing. The power that excited her, got her wet, motivated her. *Controlling people.*

She slipped him out and stood up, smiling. "Maybe later."

Lauren sipped from the champagne she'd left next to the laptop, looking down at the database. The full history of the search for the Fountain of Youth, now updated with one more piece of information.

She'd had the jet refueled when Nash was away playing hero in the helicopter. She would have loved to have gone along for that part, to see the look on Chase's face when she realized the game was over. Nash had explained that part in great detail.

We just dropped her. Should've seen it, when she realized she couldn't hang on.

And then updating the database, popping the champagne, and deciding she needed sex, right then, right there.

On the sofa, Nash coughed and pulled up his pants, pretending he wasn't ready to explode. He came to stand next to her, lifting his own glass and knocking it back without looking at her, like she wasn't totally naked right there.

He nodded at the screen. "Kind of obvious, I guess."

"Do you have any contacts there?"

He seemed to think it over. "Not anymore. Got a few across the border."

"Don't worry. I'll make some calls. Dosa has connections anywhere it wants."

The intercom buzzed. The pilot . They were approaching the Pyrenees, if she still wanted to do what they'd arranged.

Hell yes.

She slipped into her clothes, pulled on a large overcoat, and told Nash to give her a few minutes before following. She stepped through the door at the rear of the cabin, passing by the washroom and galley before coming to a metal hatch leading to the cargo bay. The door was sealed with a double lock. The chamber on the other side was pressurized but not as insulated as the main cabin, meaning it grew colder back there. She eased the door open and stepped through, ducking her head under the low frame.

Four large metal pods were stacked along one wall, each one around six feet in length. Behind them were four plastic crates, full of equipment for the expedition. She'd planned ahead and packed small quad bikes with tank treads, preparing for any kind of terrain. But now, based on the result the database had kicked out, they would need to wait at a base camp while she had a new option shipped down.

Next to all of this, sitting on the floor, wrists cuffed, was Ashley Eades. She stirred as Lauren stepped into the room. It looked like she was trying for a glare, but she was pumped full of painkillers to help with the injuries.

"Is this seat taken?" Lauren smiled, crouching down next to Eades.

"Screw you."

"You know, this reminds me of that flat you used to have your parties in. The one that looked like a warehouse inside, all those pallets and crates. You shared it with that boy you were so desperate to shack up with. What was his name, the French boy with the eyes and the hair?"

"Marco." Eades's voice was muted. "Marco Moitre."

"Oh, that's right. Yes. Marco-Double-M, like a superhero. I was just thinking about him, because we're over France right now. Coming up on the Pyrenees. Is that where he came from?" She leaned in to whisper in Eades's ear. "You know, he wasn't that great in bed. And my parents liked him, which was the kiss of death, really." Eades's face twisted. Lauren continued. "It was always so funny, watching you try so hard to be one of us. Fit into our scene. Fool around with Greg. Oh, I knew. Of course I did. It was a game to him. You Brits and your class system."

Eades sighed, still showing attitude, even now. "What do you want?"

"Did you ever even think of calling me?" Lauren waited until Eades made eye contact, seeing the question echoed back. "When my parents died? We were friends, I thought. I lost everything, and I was all on my own. You never called."

"You're just done telling me we weren't friends," Eades said, and snorted. "You don't have friends. Just people to control."

Lauren stood up and ran her hand across the cold metal of the nearest pod. She let her mother's voice fill her head. *None of these people are your friends, Laurie. And they never will be.*

"This is all for them," Lauren said. She turned back to face Eades and explained, "My parents. Finding the Fountain, it's for them. And you got in the way of that." There were actual tears in her eyes. Damn it. She swallowed back the emotion. "That was your mistake. And you're wrong. I do have friends. How do you think I got into England without being seen? How do you think I'm flying over France? I look after my friends, they look after me. Marah Chase crossed them, I dealt with it. You crossed me, and . . ."

Lauren's words trailed off as the beeping of the keypad announced Nash's arrival before the hatch opened. He stepped through to join them, holding two harnesses. "Pilot says now or never."

Eades looked at the straps and shook her head. She smiled, but it was for show. Lauren knew her old friend enough to see when she was fronting. "Torture time now? I'm not telling you anything."

Lauren knelt down again to whisper, "I know." She stood and pulled a folded document from her coat pocket. The map. "But August already found this while you were passed out. And when I typed the name 'Impossible Mountain' into my database, it gave us a hit. Three, in fact. Two that tell us where the impossible mountain is and one that didn't give us the real name of the mountain but did tell us about a 'dark place' on the mountain that the locals avoided. So . . . we know exactly where we're going."

Nash slipped on one of the harnesses, fastening it around himself. There was a long bungee cord trailing off the back, and he clipped the other end to the cargo support rails next to the white pods. He stepped in behind Lauren and started fastening the second harness around her. She could feel his strong arms pressing against her.

Eades watched, some kind of realization slowly spreading across her face. Whatever was happening, it was happening now. She shuffled back across the floor, struggling against the cuffs. Once her back hit something solid, the wall next to the door, she pushed herself up onto her feet.

"What are you—?"

Lauren took a few steps forward, smiling pleasantly. "It's okay," she said, in her nicest tone. "We're not here to torture you. I knew you'd hold out. You picked a side; good for you."

Behind Eades, Nash gripped the handle of the cargo door.

"I was really hoping we could pretend," Lauren said, smiling at Eades. "Let you think you had a chance to save yourself, before we did this."

Nash pulled the lever on the door. The mechanism took a second to engage; then the door started to move. Eades turned to follow the sound, then swung back to glare at Lauren as the sky came into view behind her. Even at this low altitude, promised by the pilot to be safe enough as long as they were careful, Lauren felt the temperature drop, and her ears popped lightly. It was like someone had switched on a vacuum cleaner. She was pulled forward, her full weight straining against the harness and the cord fastening it to the hull.

"Fuck you," Eades shouted in the second before she was sucked out.

Lauren leaned forward, wanting to get a glimpse of what happened next, but it was still dark outside, and all she could make out was a vague impression of the mountains passing close below them. Did she see Eades falling, or was it just her imagination?

Nash pulled against his own harness to reach forward and grab hold of the leather strap attached between the door and the wall. He pulled, aided by the mechanism of the hinge that was designed to take most of the weight in an emergency to help the door open and close. Lauren watched his muscles tense and bulge as he worked. The door sealed with one last hiss.

They both stood in silence as their ears popped again and then the ringing sound faded. Lauren unbuckled the clasp of her harness, then stepped forward and did the same for Nash. She pressed in close. Her whole body was tingling. Was it the change in cabin pressure? The cold? She knew it was something else. Until a few days ago, she'd been happy to let others do the dirty work. But starting with LaFarge, and now with the thrill running through her at watching Eades go, Lauren could feel the rush of controlling someone's life and death. This was everything. This was her future.

And soon, she'd get paid for it.

She went up on her tiptoes to kiss Nash.

"On the sofa, or right here?"

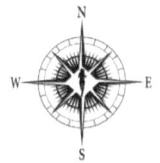

THIRTY-ONE

C hase woke up in the hospital. It was a private room, with the usual dull palette of cream and brown. She was slow to come around, with a headache that felt like it would linger.

"Hey." Hass's voice was followed by his face as Chase started to focus in on the world around her.

Chase grunted. It wasn't because she couldn't speak so much as she didn't know what to say. Asking where they were would bring an obvious answer. She needed an extra few seconds to think.

Finally, she settled on, "What I miss?" And then, before Hass could answer, something else finally swam into her thoughts. "I fell?"

"Thirty feet." Hass smiled. "I caught you."

"You . . ."

"With the car." He looked away for a second. "You landed on the roof." Chase tried to sit up, but her body was still trailing behind her mind. "That explains . . . wait." She lifted her left arm. Her wrist was in a cast. "What's . . . ?"

"Broke your wrist. That's the only damage, though. I don't know how you do it. You hang off a car and a helicopter, and then fall thirty feet onto the roof of our car, and you come away with a concussion and a broken wrist. I ever tell you about the time I broke my leg getting out of the bath?"

"You were hurt . . . I think? I remember . . ."

Hass leaned back and pulled his jacket aside. "Stabbed, right here. They patched me up, pumped some blood into me. I'm fine."

Chase settled back into the pillows. There was another thought that hadn't formed yet.

She couldn't get to it, so she pushed on with something easier. "How'd we get here?"

"Well, they arrested us. Me. They arrested me. You they bundled into an ambulance. I'm not sure if they ever got around to arresting you. Then your friend turned up and smoothed everything out."

"Friend?"

The door opened, and Mason stepped in. She gave Hass a nod, followed by a lingering smile, and Chase definitely noticed it. Mason approached the bed, put a bag on the floor, and placed her hand on Chase's arm.

"You don't look so good," Chase said. "Did you fall thirty feet? No, wait, that was me."

Mason smiled. Again her eyes flitted to Hass. He returned the gesture. God dammit.

"Good to see you, too," Mason said. "How you feeling?"

"That a trick question?" The difficult thought finally bubbled to the surface, and Chase groaned. "Eades?"

Mason and Hass shared a more serious look. Mason shook her head once. "We don't know. No sign of her. August Nash has vanished off the security grid, and Lauren Stanford was never here."

"How's that possible?"

Mason shrugged. "Someone has her back. She was able to enter the UK without leaving a record, so I don't know if she's left or is still here. And Eades is off the grid, completely lost."

"When did you get here?"

"Around the same time you did. They were pulling you out of the ambulance when I arrived. I've cleared the mess up as best I can. There's no police record of the car chase or the helicopter at Glasgow Green. They don't know about the dead body in the house."

"Is he . . . ?"

"I sorted it."

"How?"

"I'm a spook."

Mason left it there. She bent down to pull a file from her bag and set it next to Chase on the bed.

"Lauren Stanford," she said. "You already know the headlines, but these are the details, if you need them. I pulled in a favor from a friend in the CIA. They've been watching her for a while, her whole family. Something about a terror attack on New Jersey a hundred years ago."

Chase took the file that Mason passed to her, started flicking through it. "If the CIA knows all that, why haven't they done anything?"

"Politics. They're not supposed to work internally, and neither them nor the FBI are allowed to do much of anything at the moment. Nazis don't seem to be anyone's priority. I mean, they tried to bring down my government, and we're all acting like they didn't. I'm leaving myself overexposed helping you."

"So we're not going to get any official help from your side?"

Mason kept a straight face. "I'm not here, that file doesn't exist. You are not receiving any MI6 help."

Chase closed the file and put it on her bedside table. If it didn't exist, she wasn't stealing it.

Chase said, "Ashley . . . ," but her words trailed off. What was there to say? She'd come halfway across the world to make sure Eades was safe, then helped to lead the enemy right to her door and failed to save her. Finding Eades once had been a Hail Mary pass, twice was hard to imagine.

Mason squeezed Chase's arm. "I know you don't want to hear this, but I think you need to assume she's gone. If they have her, they'll be able to get the information they need, and . . ."

"Yeah. They'll have the map. They've won."

Mason cocked her head. "Map?"

Hass nodded. "For the Garden of Eden."

"Wait, I thought they were after the Fountain of Youth."

Chase rolled her eyes like the star of a nineties teen comedy. "That's so yesterday."

Hass held back a smile. "I still don't see what they want with it. Whether it's the Fountain of Youth or the Garden of Eden, what's in it for them?"

Chase propped herself up on her elbows. Whether it was the concussion or medication, thinking was still coming to her slowly, in fits and starts. "After Adam and Eve were kicked out, the entrance to the garden was guarded by an angel with a flaming sword. I mean, I could believe they thought the sword was worth finding. Nazis do like their biblical weapons. But I don't think Lauren even knows about the Eden connection. It's still the Fountain she wants. The water."

"The next big thing," Mason said, echoing her thoughts from their previous conversation. "Owning water, owning minerals, everyone wants in. But could there be something to the legend? Water that makes you young?"

Chase's nostrils filled with the smell of burning. Her mouth went dry, tasting the ash and debris of the London attack. A city almost destroyed by a legend. A government almost overthrown.

Hass turned to Mason. "While you're *not helping*, could you *not help* us get to Tanzania?"

Chase cocked her head, her brain kicking into gear. "Tanzania?"

Hass paused, milking his big moment for all it was worth. He stooped down beside the bed, and Chase heard him messing around in a bag, the sound of papers being moved. He came back up with computer printouts, satellite images from Google Earth.

"I did some work while you were out. We've been coming at it wrong. James Gilmore turned up in Ethiopia, so we looked there, and all the mentions of Punt made me think we would be heading to Somalia. But we need to throw out our modern ideas of nations and borders and focus on the landmarks on his map. I don't know how he found his way to Ethiopia, but I'd guess he was lost and knew to follow the river, like everyone else."

"He should have taken that left turn at Albuquerque."

Hass paused. He hadn't gotten the reference. Chase thought about explaining it but waved for him to continue.

"Gilmore didn't have Google or satnav. His map isn't going to be exact, and on foot he would have taken some long routes—it's all just an impression. And he threw me off at first, because 'Gateway to Hell' is a nickname for Erta Ale, in Ethiopia. But if we remember he was an old confused guy and cast the net wider . . ."

He held up one map, showing a geographical feature, a winding brown line across a green landscape. "This is in Kenya. It's the dried-out tributary to a prehistoric lake. The lake is a large plane now. It's where they set *The Lion King*." Hass shared another look with Mason, who smiled at his mention of the film. "When it was still a lake, the water flowed in through this crack in the mountains. It's called Hell's Gate." He held up another sheet, where the image was zoomed out to show a larger area. He traced left, across the map from Hell's Gate to a body of water. "This is Lake Victoria, on the border between Kenya, Uganda, and Tanzania. That's not the local name, when the Brits came they named it after the Queen. I don't know why Gilmore called it a garden. But since we're just going ahead and talking about Eden as a real thing, let's just throw in an extra guess. Eden itself was a whole country or region. The *Garden* was an area within it. Victoria *is* a young lake, about half a million years old, and it's dried up and refilled as recently as around fifteen thousand years ago, so it's been a large fertile plain at least twice within human history."

"How many rivers join the lake?"

"It's only outflow is the Nile, the amount of waterways that feed *into* the lake vary over time."

"But...someone could say four?"

Hass smiled and continued. "On the other hand, the lake has been flooded for all of Gilmore's life, and he didn't have gills, so we're not looking at the lake. We're just using it as a landmark on his map." He traced his finger downward and drifted to the right as he went, to a large brown area about an equal distance from both Hell's Gate and Lake Victoria. "This was mentioned in Henry Morton Stanley's book, but I didn't see the connection at the time. I did some bible reading while you were out. The Hebrew version. I remembered what you said about Ezekiel, and it's true, he has a version of Eden. He calls it God's *mountain.* The local Chaga people called it the Impossible Mountain, but we know it better now as Kilimanjaro."

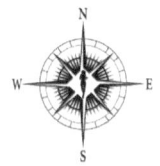

THIRTY-TWO

Y ou can't go to Kilimanjaro."

Freema Nkya's voice had risen to a shout. She paused and looked around the room, seeing that a handful of people had noticed her volume. She and Hass were sitting in the Royale bar, back in Addis Ababa.

Mason had arranged transportation for them out of Scotland, with fake passports to help keep a low profile, but couldn't get them into Tanzania. Nothing official had been announced, but flights were being canceled and private charter pilots were being refused permission to fly. Kenya, Tanzania, and Uganda all seemed to have closed their doors. Chase and Hass had connections in Rwanda and Burundi but didn't want to take that route. Mason could have used MI6 connections to get them in, but that would have drawn even more attention to her private games.

Instead, Chase and Hass had gone back to where it all started, a country that was still open for business despite the earthquakes: Ethiopia. Hass had a good connection there, or so he'd thought. Freema's family were Chaga; they were from the slopes of Kilimanjaro. If anyone could tell them the best way in and fill in blanks in their knowledge, it would be her.

Hass put a hand up, asking her to quiet down. "I know, we've noticed, the door is closed. But we need to get there."

Freema sat back in the chair, folded her arms. "We ?"

"Me and Marah Chase."

She rolled her eyes. "Knew it."

Freema and Chase had both heard a lot about each other over the years. Freema, for her part, didn't like any of it. She blamed Chase for every bad decision, every injury, every arrest warrant, that Hass had suffered.

Hass tried again. "It's important, Free."

"What I'm saying is important. You can't go there. Not now. Wait, please. Go later."

Hass leaned forward. "What aren't you telling me?"

Freema didn't answer right away. The hesitation was written across her face. She was always so expressive. Hass could tell she was under orders not to reveal the details she was about to give him. "We were wrong," she said. "The big one I told you about? We were looking at the wrong thing, in the wrong place. All the activity here, the tremors, Erta Ale, they're all reactions, symptoms of something that's happening at the other end of the rift." She paused, staring into his eyes, as if willing him to get the message. "Right under Kilimanjaro."

Okay. That was bad. Hass had only shown just enough of an interest in geology and seismology over the years to humor Freema and keep getting laid, but he knew Kilimanjaro was an ancient, and huge, volcano.

"Eruption?"

"We think so."

"But Kili is dormant?"

"Was. We've known for a long time that there was still lava flowing under the surface. I'm not a volcanologist, I don't understand half the things they say. It's like being a student again." A brief smile cracked through her seriousness. "But our best guess right now, based on the data we have, is that Kilimanjaro is waking up. The lava movement is causing the tremors along the fault line."

"Why? Why is it waking up?"

"Honestly, we don't know. But it's not alone. Other volcanoes around the world are getting more active. Fault lines are moving. The Amazon has been on fire for a year. It's like the whole world is angry . . ." She paused, catching herself before she started ranting. "So we don't know yet. We need to move our team, our equipment, and get a better look."

"You're going in?"

"As soon as we can. But it's not simple. This team was assembled as a joint operation of the United Nations and the Ethiopian government. There's red tape, funding to be approved. We're working with four different governments on this right now, negotiating the next move."

"That's why everything is locked down?"

Freema leaned in closer again, her voice dropping. "Yes. They're preparing. Tanzania and Kenya are both ready to issue evacuation orders. But they're waiting for us to tell them where would be safe to evacuate to. We don't know how big it might be, if it goes."

Hass breathed out, tried for his most relaxed smile. "It's still an if?"

"It's always an if. Earthquakes. Volcanoes. We're getting very good at educated guesses, but they are guesses. It could be that Kili is just turning over in its sleep, putting us on watch for the future. Or it could blow a little, let off some magma and gas, then subside again. It did that two hundred thousand years ago. One of the peaks blew and collapsed, but life went on. Or . . ."

She looked down at the table, tapping the side of her coffee nervously, not wanting to say what was next.

Hass nudged her along. "That bad?"

Behind Freema, Hass watched Chase enter the bar. She'd left him to start the ball rolling with his on-off girlfriend while she met with Conte. Now she was ordering a drink, nodding in his direction.

"Small eruptions are happening all the time, all over the planet. There's an index. It's like the Richter scale but for volcanoes, tracked by how large the explosion is. It goes from one to eight, and they tell me the small ones, a one or a two, are happening regularly. We think of Mount St. Helens as a big eruption, but it was only a four. Vesuvius was either a five or a six."

"If the scale goes to eight, that means there have been some eights?"

"Hey." Chase set down a glass of amber liquid on the table and pulled up a chair. "What're we talking about? I'm Marah, by the way."

She offered her hand for a shake. Freema took it with a smile, not a single sign that she hated Chase's guts.

Chase smiled at Hass. "Your girlfriend is a babe. Totally above you." Then to Freema, lowering her voice as if Hass couldn't hear, "Want to trade up, make some fun mistakes?"

Freema smiled again and laughed, totally caught off guard by Chase's approach. "What did you do to your arm?"

Chase held up her wrist. She'd cut off the cast they'd set at the hospital, replacing it with sports tape. It wasn't ideal, and she'd switch back to a real dressing once they were done. But a cast would be visible and memorable; it could be a problem if they needed to sneak past anyone. She also didn't want to give the enemy too much sign of her injury.

"I hung off the back of a car," she said.

"And a helicopter," Hass added, before getting back on topic. "Free was explaining volcanic eruptions to me."

"Oh, cool." Chase crossed her arms on the table, leaned forward. "I grew up near Mount Rainier. I love this shit."

"Free was telling me that Mount St. Helens was small."

Chase shrugged. "Halfway, if I remember?" She looked to Freema for approval, getting a nod. "Like a four on a scale that goes up to eight."

Freema's eyes flashed like she'd finally found a kindred spirit. "Yes, and Vesuvius could have been a five or a six."

Chase, who had sipped her drink while Freema was speaking, set down the glass gently. "And the Minoan Eruption, I think I read, was a seven."

Hass didn't know that one, and said so.

"Where Santorini is now?" Chase eased back into her chair. Hass knew she loved the chance to switch modes from relic runner to teacher. "The island is part of an ancient volcano, Thera. The whole thing went up somewhere around 1500 bce. Weakened the Minoan civilization, caused a tsunami that hit every coast in the region. Huge clouds of ash would have drifted across Egypt, blotting out the sun. Debris would have been falling from the sky. The water could have boiled."

"Exodus," Hass said.

Chase shrugged. "It's a popular fringe theory, but doesn't fit any of the dates the Exodus could have happened."

Hass raised his hand a little, just a small gesture but enough to look like a student in class. "And what happens when an eight goes off?"

"Utah, basically. Utah as we know it was formed by an eight. But that was millions of years ago."

Freema took over. "The most recent one was Sumatra, about seventy-five thousand years ago. Scientists think that one could be the reason our branch of humans came to dominate, why this version of our evolution is the one that dominates the planet. The explosion filled the atmosphere with ash, poisoned the air, blotted out the sun. The worldwide population was reduced to just a few thousand, and every variant died off except us."

Hass felt his gut tighten in panic even at the thought of something happening on that scale. "The whole planet?"

"The whole planet." Chase nodded. "It would be a global nuclear winter. If a seven was like the Old Testament, wrath of-God stuff, an eight is higher than the wrath of God." Chase waved away Hass's panic. "But they're super rare."

"Every hundred thousand years," Freema said quietly.

Hass picked up on her meaning. "You said the last one, the one that killed off all the other humans, was seventy-five thousand years ago?"

"Yes."

"So, we're within the margin of error for the next one?"

Chase paused halfway through another sip. Lowered her glass. "So . . . why are we talking volcanoes?"

Hass and Freema looked at each other. The telepathy that came from a twenty-year relationship.

It was Freema who took the lead.

"We think Kilimanjaro is active."

"And by active, you mean . . ."

"Yes."

Chase downed the drink, rolled her head, and put on an overcompensating smile. "Well, then, we better get in and out before it happens."

If Chase had bamboozled Freema with her charm, the grace period was over. Freema slammed her hands down on the table, this time not caring whether people turned to stare. "No. You're not dragging him there. Not now."

"Dragging him?" Chase pushed back in her seat and spread her arms wide. "I'm not dragging him anywhere. Doc's the one who figured—"

"Doc?"

"Hey, come on." Hass put both hands up this time, the full DEFCON 1 of the soothing gesture. "Free, she's right. I'm the one who figured out we need to go to Kili. Chase had given up."

"I wouldn't say—" Chase started, but cut herself off and let him continue.

"And that's why we need your help. I get it, you don't want us to go. And I get why. And believe me, if we had any choice in it, we wouldn't be going. If the world blows up, I want to be as far away from the explosion as I can." He shrugged. "But I need you to trust me. I promise to God. We have to go."

Freema leaned back and crossed her arms. Her eyes were red-rimmed. Hass could see how much emotion she was holding back as she glared first at Chase, then at Hass. "Fine." She shifted in her seat, shook her head a couple of times, then said, "You have to go. But I'm not helping you get there."

"I've got that covered," Chase said quietly, more as an aside to Hass than a reply to Freema. Hass looked at her, but she tilted her head to say, *Later*.

"I understand," Hass said to Freema, smooth, calm. "And thank you. Your trust means the world to me. But we also need some information. I thought you might know something about what we need."

Freema barely moved. Sitting bolt upright, arms still folded, she nodded, once.

Hass took that as enough of an answer to continue. "We've heard about something that we think is on the north slope, or near that side of the mountain. A valley or . . ."

He could see from Freema's reaction she knew what he was talking about. Her eyes widened.

"The dark place." She watched Hass and Chase share a look before continuing. "That's what my grandparents called it. A scary story, something parents would tell their children. *Don't go to the dark place.* A lot of the mountain has been deforested now—farming took the slopes to the south and east, tourist trails have been cut through the north and west. But the dark place is still there, as far as I know. A part of the forest on the north slope, where nobody goes. The tourist trails are all a safe distance away. Nobody ever farmed there."

"What's in there?"

"Ghost stories. Things to keep people scared."

"White cats?"

Freema's brow furrowed. She looked confused until Chase followed with, "We were shown a map, and it had a picture, a white lion or wolf."

"Oh." Freema nodded. "That must be Mngwa."

Hass had heard of Mngwa. A mythical large cat, said to be the size of a donkey.

The stories used to be prevalent across the south of Tanzania, especially in the forestland near the coast, but he hadn't heard much of it in recent years. But Mngwa was said to be gray, with stripes or spots, not white.

I guess Gilmore didn't have the right color crayons.

"Mngwa lives in the dark place." Freema smiled. "In the stories, anyway. That's his home. That's why my parents were told to stay away. If you go near the dark place, Mngwa will eat you."

Hass nodded along. Gilmore's ideas were starting to mesh with local legends he remembered hearing. "You don't believe the stories? You don't believe in Mngwa?"

"I'm a scientist." She turned to Chase. "You're from Washington State? You believe in Bigfoot? No. Of course not." Back to Hass. "You, Hassan, of all people, know not to judge people based on where they come from. You want me to sit here and parade out old Chaga legends so you can go play tourists, so you"—back to Chase again—"can then go play some kind of savior."

Chase didn't react the way Hass expected. She simply nodded. Let the silence stretch out long enough to be sure Freema had finished. Then, deferentially, she leaned forward and said, "You're right. I get it. Doc—Hassan—gets it. You have no reason to believe me, no reason to trust me. And I don't think I can swear to God, because I don't know what my relationship with God is." She paused. "That one is . . . a work in progress. But all I can say is I've found things I shouldn't have, in the past. I've stolen relics. I've taken from other cultures for profit. But, and I don't know if it's ten years of this guy"—she smiled at Hass—"talking in my ear, I've learned to leave things where they are, too. I found Alexander the Great's tomb. And nobody knows about it, because I left it where it was. Whatever is on that mountain has been there since long before my country or any of our governments came along. And all things being equal, I think it belongs to the mountain. It should stay where it is. But there are other people looking for it, too, and they have the map. They may already know where it is. They might be on their way there right now. And they don't want to respect history. We need to get there before them."

Freema sat in silence and listened. Hass watched her eyes widen and narrow a couple of times. She tilted her head once. He could tell she was taking this in.

Once Chase finished, Freema looked down at her hands in silence for a full minute. Hass and Chase looked at each other, wondering what would happen next.

She smiled at Chase. "I bet part of you wants to believe in Bigfoot?"

"Oh, hell yes."

"I think part of me has always wanted to believe in Mngwa. But I can't help being a scientist. A big cat? A breeding population on the side of Kili? Still, the Chaga, we migrated to Kilimanjaro, the Impossible Mountain, in the eleventh century. And it was a gift from God. The crops that grew there, the soil, the water. It was perfect. But even then, the early settlers knew they weren't the first to live on the mountain. There were legends of the people who'd come before. And we settled on the east and the south, a little in the west. Nobody tried to settle on the north. They must have had a reason why. Maybe that reason still exists. Based on what we know right now, maybe there's some part of the volcano that opens out in that section of the forest, maybe some gas leaks out, or the water is sulfuric."

Chase smiled. "That would make sense."

"So the dark place could be real. Whatever is hidden in the trees, it's been allowed to stay hidden. And a thousand years ago, maybe there were some Mngwa. A lot can change in that time. A species can die out."

Hass laid his palms down on the table gently. "How do we find it?"

Freema sighed, expressing, *okay, whatever.* "It's not that high up. You take the north route, head to the village Nale Moru with the tourists. Follow their trail across the cultivated land. There are two bridges as you enter the forest. At the second bridge, which is over a dried-up riverbed, turn off the trail. The tourists will continue on up to the moorland, to camp at the cave. You follow the dried-up river. It's going to feel strange— the mountain lies to you about what direction you're traveling. You see the peaks and they pull you toward them; you think they are north. But keep a compass and follow the river west. You'll see a thicker section of forest, one that obviously hasn't been touched."

"And then?" Hass prompted.

She shrugged. "Walk into it? I don't know. I've never been that far. I only know how to get to that point."

Chase waved at the barman, indicating she wanted a refill, then pointed at Freema's and Hass's glasses. They both said no. Chase waited for her fresh drink to be carried over, then focused back on Freema.

"How many people know about this? I mean, the dark place and the route you just told us? The people going in ahead of us are American, rich, white. What are the chances of them being told the same thing?"

Freema gave a weary, patronizing shake of the head. But it was in good spirit now; her anger was gone. "Everyone knows about it. This is your Western disease." She pointed at Hass. "He tells me this all the time. If you read the Wikipedia entry on Kilimanjaro, it's going to tell you the first people to climb the mountain were British explorers. We were living on Kili for nine hundred years by that point, and there were people there before us. And before them. You think we didn't know every inch of that place, including the top? We've been telling you it's the *Impossible Mountain* for hundreds of years, but you have to come up with different reasons for why. As for these Americans, it will depend on what they ask, who they ask, how polite they are."

"Money?"

"And money, yes."

Chase drank in silence. Freema's phone buzzed. She picked it up and read the message.

"I need to go," she said. "Government meeting."

She stood and embraced Hass, squeezing him a little too tightly. "Be safe," she whispered before squeezing again.

Chase stood up to shake her hand. "Good to finally meet you," she said. "And I meant it, about trading up."

Freema laughed, embarrassed all over again. She gave Hass one last parting look to show the worry still beneath the surface before turning on her heel and marching out of the bar without stopping.

"She's a hottie." Chase leaned across to nudge Hass. "Seriously."

"Do you have to flirt with every woman you meet?"

"I promise, you ever introduce me to your mom? I won't flirt." She lifted her glass to hide her smile. "Unless she's cute."

Hass waved that away. "What did you mean, when you said we have travel covered? Conte?"

"Yeah." Chase's smile dropped away. "He's got a guy who'll get us in if we go in an hour."

"What did it cost?"

Chase downed the last of her whisky, stared at the bottom of the glass.

"I gave up my claim on the Ark."

THIRTY-THREE

The phrase *you had to be there* could have been coined for Kilimanjaro. Chase couldn't take her eyes off it.

There would be no way to describe the mountain accurately that could possibly do it justice to anyone who hadn't been there themselves. Official records varied, but they all agreed that the highest peak, Uhuru, was over nineteen thousand feet above sea level, and sixteen thousand feet above where Chase was now standing. The sheer scale of it had already made Chase feel light-headed on the occasions she'd paused to look up. She could see why the local tribes would have called this both the Impossible Mountain and the Mountain of the Moon. The summit touched the clouds. She could make out what was left of the glacier that had once covered it, now reduced to a few strips of ice and snow. It didn't take much to imagine how the scene looked when Western explorers saw it for the first time in the 1800s, with vast stretches of snow reflecting the sun, looking for all the world like it was topped with silver and gold.

She and Hass had been walking for almost a full day. Technically they had been on the mountain for all that time, and yet the peak seemed to rise with them, never getting closer, never getting shorter.

The smuggler Conte set them up with had been fast and efficient. He'd gotten then from Addis Ababa to Nairobi without any official checkpoints or the need for paperwork. They had encountered two roadblocks heading through Kenya to the Tanzanian border, but the smuggler had successfully gotten them through both.

Every guard seemed distracted. At one of the checkpoints, they heard news that a massive crack had opened up to the north, a fissure ten miles long and half a mile wide. Whatever Kili was up to, it was coming soon.

They got across the Tanzanian border with a long talk and an exchange of cash. From there, their smuggler drove them to a bar in Tarakea, a small modern town at the base of the mountain. It was there that Chase had taken her first real look at Kilimanjaro. A dark, imposing presence towering over them in the predawn blackness. It wasn't like the mountains Chase had been used to growing up, which were part of the scenery. This mountain was the scenery. It was all you could see, blocking everything else out.

They grabbed a few hours' sleep at the bar, which had a backpackers' hostel upstairs, before they were woken up to meet their guide. He introduced himself as Steve but smiled whenever Chase used the name, like it was a joke she wasn't in on. He would laugh regularly, regardless of whatever was being said. Each time she started a conversation with him, she heard a voice in her head announce, Steve is filmed in front of a live studio audience. He was Chaga, like Freema, and Hass would talk to him in Bantu for long stretches. His English was perfect, though, and it seemed out of respect to Chase he would only slip into his native tongue when Hass started it.

Steve told them his job was usually to take tourists up through the official trail, making sure they registered before setting off in case of emergency. He would lead his party on a seven-day trek up to the peak and back down the other side, through the rain forest of the southern slope. But the mountain was closed now, and everyone in the area already knew why. The government had given no details yet, but they'd experienced two minor tremors in as many days, and nobody there was an idiot. This checked out with what Chase had already seen. The town had felt deserted when they'd arrived the night before, even for the midnight hour. In the early-morning light, she could see most of the business had Closed signs in their windows, and the driveways were already empty of cars. Chase and Hass had been the only people in the hostel.

The Tanzanian government might have been holding back on any official announcement, but it looked like everyone had already gotten the message. The evacuation had begun.

Steve said he wouldn't take them all the way up, but because he owed a favor to someone (and Chase knew that chain would eventually lead up to Conte), he was willing to take them as far as the edge of the forest and leave them with tents and supplies.

The whole thing had almost been called off when he spotted the tape around Chase's wrist. "Nobody should go up Kili with an injury," Steve had said, "especially not to an arm or leg. You need those to climb a mountain."

Chase had insisted it was nothing major and made a note to ignore the constant dull ache from her bones and to avoid pulling faces or wincing when she put weight on her wrist.

Periodically, Steve repeated warnings about altitude sickness, regularly asking if they needed to stop and rest. Chase said no each time. She was used to altitude. She'd hiked up most of the mountains in Washington before she was even in her teens. She already knew the deal. Or thought she did. The air here did feel different. It was getting thinner faster, but she refused to show any doubt in front of Steve.

Steve led them up through farmlands to the village of Nale Moru, where tourists would start their trip. From there, they deviated off the known path. There were armed guards at the usual checkpoints, enforcing the closure, so they walked across a vast plain, where they saw rivers and trees, bushes, rocks, but no animals.

"They've already gone," Steve said before breaking into another bout of misplaced laughter. "The animals are not stupid."

The complete lack of wildlife was unnerving. They were walking through the very epitome of nature, one of the purest and most untouched places on earth, but it felt fake. Almost like a movie set, with the animals to be added in later.

The forest was in view for hours before they reached it. At some point along the way, Steve had navigated them back to the main trail because the ground here was well trodden, a compacted mud path that led between the willowy elephant grass and bushes of the plain. The trees of the forest up ahead were huge. Aside from a break in between them that indicated the path, it was easy to imagine they were walking back in time, to prehistory.

The light had taken on a lead-gray quality by the time they reached the edge of the trees, and the temperature had dropped significantly. Steve stopped at a large rock, set down the backpack he'd been carrying with the tents and food, and let out at sigh. It looked like a ritual, the same show he put on for every group he guided to this point.

"You should camp here," he said. "The forest is a long walk, and you don't want to be in there at night."

"You said all the animals were gone."

He flashed a grin. "The intelligent ones. I will help you put up the tents before I turn back."

Chase took a long pull on her water before passing it to Hass. "We're continuing on."

For the first time, Steve's face showed fear. "I would not."

"I know." Hass put a hand on Steve's bag, ready to pull it to his side. "Thank you. We appreciate everything you've done."

Steve shrugged. He was too experienced to bother arguing. The customer gets what they want. And, Chase figured, he'd already done the math of how soon he could get off the mountain and join the evacuation.

"One question, before you go," she said. "Have you heard of the dark place? Do you know the way?"

Steve's whole demeanor changed. He looked at Chase and Hass in turn with a cold expression. He muttered something to himself in what sounded like Bantu, then said, "You will be on your own. If anything goes wrong, you will get no help."

He turned and started back down the trail. Hass and Chase both watched him go in silence for almost five minutes.

Eventually Chase said, "You struggling with the air, too?"

Hass nodded. "I didn't want to say. I keep taking deep breaths, and it's doing nothing."

"Same."

Chase could have added light-headed and feel like I have the flu to the list, but didn't. She turned to look at the forest. From here, it was impossible to judge how far up the mountain it stretched. It was just a dark, impenetrable wall of green and brown. Earlier in the day, when they'd left Nale Moru, the trees had looked like a narrow strip, almost a layer on a cake.

"Maybe he was right," Hass said. "Camp here, adjust, hit the trees tomorrow."

"He's definitely right. The intelligent, adult thing to do is take our time, get used to the altitude, and go again in the morning."

Chase scanned the dense line of trees, thinking that Lauren Stanford and August Nash would be around here somewhere. And with their resources, they had every advantage. They could have already found the dark place. Eden. The Fountain. Whatever it turned out to be. There simply wasn't time to rest.

Hass lifted the backpack and slung it across his shoulders, fitting his arms through the straps. "But when have we ever been intelligent or adult?"

"Exactly." Chase smiled, slipped her water bottle back into the mesh webbing on the side of her own bag, and turned to head on up the path.

◆

Nash watched the crates being unloaded from the van. The boxes themselves were no bigger than tea chests. Nash was worried. He'd seen the equipment Lauren had brought with them, suitable for a different terrain. Large quad bikes, with tank treads connecting the wheels. Each one had taken two men to lift, and each also came with a large trailer to drag behind, filled with the white metal pods she insisted they bring. Those bikes had seemed appropriate. Large, robust. Though he agreed they weren't practical for the kind of ascent they needed up Kili, they were surely a better option than whatever was packed away in these smaller boxes.

They'd spent two days at base camp, which was the name Lauren was giving to what was, really, a friend's spacious Arusha mansion. Dosa really did have connections in any country they wanted. On the way into Tanzania, they'd found all the routes closed. Every channel Nash would have thought to try, every connection he might have leaned on, was gone. (Conte would have been a possibility, but Nash had burned that bridge.)

It was funny to Nash now to think of the decade he'd spent on the black market, forging alliances and connections, building networks. He could maybe get into most countries with a bit of effort, and he usually had a good chance at finding people to work with. Perhaps he could get a government minister on the phone here, or knew a journalist there, sometimes an ex-spook from his agency days.

When rolling with a billionaire, none of it mattered. With one phone call Lauren had gotten into and out of the United Kingdom without ever officially entering the country. With another, she'd arranged them safe passage to this luxurious mansion less than a day's ride from Kilimanjaro, and then, with a third call, while lounging beside the swimming pool, she had gotten these crates shipped from a Dosa plant in Libya straight through half a dozen borders and into this locked-down country. She'd hung up the phone and immediately started talking to their host, an American expat media producer, about who they should install as the next US president. They'd asked Nash for his opinion on their candidates, and he'd quickly realized none of this was a joke. This really was how they lived, how they thought, and how the world worked. And he was on the edge of their world.

He had a way in.

Who was that guy who said American lives don't have a second act? Well, screw that. His first act had been school and juvie. His second landed him in the military. Surely the CIA was an act all its own, and then he'd become the best relic runner in the world. Chase had done him a favor. He'd been thinking his story ended with finding the Ark. Get some fame, get a bunch of money, settle down somewhere. But she'd forced his hand, made him rethink, and now he could see a whole new act, right in front of him. An extra stage in his life.

And this one, this one was *the one*. Sitting by a pool, talking to people with more money than most countries, plotting the next president.

This was what his whole life had been leading to.

But now, opening up one of the crates as a workman set it down in the garage, for the first time in this new stage he had doubts. Everything so far had been big. Convincing. Lauren had made mistakes early on, sure. But they were mistake of scale. Mistakes of ambition. She'd hired the wrong people and backed them with too much money. And then she'd moved heaven and earth just to arrange for him to pick up one reporter. Got around international rules and borders with a snap of her fingers. But inside the crate was a drone, like those things they showed in the news as the future of Amazon deliveries. He could see a large metal hinge that would fold the device out to double its current size, making it around five feet in length. But this was it? These little toys represented the scale of Lauren's ambition for the last leg of the expedition?

He turned on his heel and headed for her bedroom, where she was sitting on the balcony in a night robe, overlooking the pool. The south slope of Kili was a dark shape in the distance.

"What are those things?" Nash said as he walked in.

Lauren made a show of looking down at her breasts, bare beneath the robe, then shrugging, as if she was about to say, *What, these*?

Nash didn't wait for the obvious joke. "In the crates. Little radio-controlled helicopters?"

"Oh." She beamed, sitting up in the chair. "They're here? Excellent."

"You're not seriously thinking of using those toys?"

"I am, seriously. Those 'toys' are the result of a decade of development. These drone wars, all the stuff in the news, you really think all these billion-dollar corporations are developing flying robots just to deliver food packages? Trust me, they will get us exactly where we need to go, and they have anti-radar tech built in, so nobody will know anything about it."

"And the pods?"

"The pods too, yes. That's my equipment. We'll have one drone each, and then we'll bring two of the pods up with us on their own drones."

"Why do we need them? Surely we can just go up and collect samples of whatever—"

"Which one of us is the billionaire with two college degrees and a private army?"

"Okay. But remember which one of us is the expert relic runner. You need to make room in one of your pods for my equipment."

"Deal." Lauren shuffled over, making space for him on the edge of the seat and patting it playfully. "Come here. Look." She pointed to the laptop screen, displaying a 3-D rendering of Kili. "Based on all the data, the legends, maps, the current state of forestation on the mountain, and where all the public trails are, the Fountain will be somewhere here." She pointed to a section of dense forest on the north face. She pressed play, and the software simulated the sun rising, flooding the east of the mountain with light first. She pointed to a narrowing shadow. "My software here has calculated if we leave at midnight and get set up in Matadi on the western slope, we can hit this shadow at just the right moment, fly up while there's enough daylight for us to see but a corridor of darkness to cover us from view."

Nash pointed to a small flashing box on the laptop taskbar, an app asking for urgent attention. "And what's this?"

Lauren clicked on the window. A news alert popped up, the Tanzanian government sending emergency broadcasts out by every channel, digital, analog, internet. The message was written in half a dozen languages. Lauren clicked on the English section, and it expanded to show the full text

NATIONAL EMERGENCY ORDERED.

Immediate evacuation of province.

Mount Kilimanjaro eruption imminent.

Please make necessary arrangements and await the next broadcast for evacuation details.

"Well then," said Nash. "Guess we won't have to worry too much about being seen."

Chase and Hass walked on without talking. The darkness folded in around them, with the fading sunlight only filtering in from the gap directly above them. There were gaps in the trees on either side of the path, where Chase guessed two hundred years of footfall had thinned out the undergrowth, but beyond that, from the next layer of trees, it was impossible to see into the shadows.Chase's old childhood fear of the dark was itching away at her skin, like the beginnings of a rash. But unlike when she was younger, the fear was no longer in control. She'd learned to keep it down in the basement, locked away. But the light itch was telling her something else.

"This is so eerie," she said quietly. "You can feel it—there's nothing here."

Hass looked around them into the shadows. "Yeah."

Chase noticed the edge to his voice. He was rattled and nervous. She wondered what fears he'd been keeping to himself, locked down in the basement.

"It's good news, though." Chase offered him a smile, trying to lift their spirits. "If there's nothing out there, that includes Nazi bitchpots."

Chase felt a stab in her guts. Thinking of Stanford and Nash sent her mind skipping quickly to Ashley Eades. Was she alive? Dead? Could she be lying somewhere now, waiting for help? Chase pushed the thoughts away again, but they didn't go far.

The path wound around to the left, and up ahead they saw a bridge. She remembered Freema's directions.

There are two bridges . . .

Well, at least they were heading in the right direction. The last of the sunlight faded away above them, like a blanket dropping down over them in an instant. One second there was a faint light filtering from above, the next they were in total darkness.

The old fear got loose. Chase froze, aware of every single hair on her body. All the familiar whispers, the familiar dread, and the feeling of cold water being poured over warm coals. *You're in an ancient forest, in total darkness, with no backup . . . the mountain could explode at any minute . . . and it's dark . . . it's dark . . . you're wrapped in dark . . .*

There was a fumbling sound next to her, followed by a click, and a blue halogen light spread out around them. Hass had activated one of their lamps.

He touched Chase's arm. "You okay?"

She breathed in and out, then pulled her own lamp from the bag and turned it on. "I will be."

After a few more deep breaths, she smiled an unspoken thank-you and indicated for them to continue. Somehow, the new lighting conditions changed the feel of the walk. Chase was now more aware they were on an incline. Each step felt different on her ankles. Each time she lifted her foot, she noticed planting it back down higher than it had been before. And the other sensation, one they'd been expecting, was cold.

The forest was offering some measure of protection, but Steve had warned them they could be at risk of freezing if they were on an open plain at night. He often took less-experienced climbers up toward the peak in the dark, because the frozen ground would be firmer and more manageable. Chase and Hass both paused to pull out an extra coat from their bags, as well as the thermal gloves Steve had insisted they bring.

After another hour of walking, Chase was feeling light-headed. She knew they needed to admit defeat and camp for the rest of the night. They'd been walking, with only brief rest stops, since daybreak. Her legs felt empty. Her feet had gone past sore four hours ago and were now tingling with numbness. And her brain needed time to adjust to the altitude. She was slowing down.

Hass clearly had a little more left in the tank, because he started to pull ahead before noticing she was lagging behind.

"I think . . ." Chase lost her train of thought two words in. She shook her head. "I think we need to camp."

"Yeah." Hass looked back at her, nodded, then turned to point up ahead. "Maybe there's a clearing once we turn off at this bridge?"

That cleared her head. Chase drew level with him and peered forward. At the edge of the blue light she could make out the wooden handrails. Freema's directions had been to turn off at the second bridge.

Chase was fully awake now. The aches, the tiredness, they were still there, but distant, barely touching her. She and Hass were almost at the dark place. The Fountain of Youth. The Garden of Eden. A volcanic feature. History.

They upped their pace, arriving at the bridge at something near a trot. It was a small structure, only five feet across, made of narrow wooden planks with handrails on either side. The gloom was clinging thick around them. Hass leaned over the rail and held out his lantern to show the dried riverbed beneath, overgrown with moss. At the other end of the bridge was a small gap in the trees. Nobody had walked this way recently, but it looked like somebody in the past had used it as a path down to the riverbed. Chase and Hass stepped carefully through the gap and down the embankment, testing each step carefully.

They walked along the riverbed, each one keeping an eye out for a clearing, somewhere large enough to pitch two tents. After an hour, Chase confronted the other thought that had been nagging at her.

"Freema's directions are kinda vague after the bridge. We don't know how long to walk, what we're really looking for."

Thirty minutes later, they knew what they were looking for.

The trees around them started to change. They looked older. Thicker. Chase was experienced enough to know that the mind could play tricks. She'd hiked a mountain on the Olympic Peninsula, walking up an old logging road before turning off into the wilderness. After less than a mile, the trees had vegetation so thick, she'd felt like she'd stepped back in time, to a place no human had ever been. But here, the feeling was even stronger. The trees looked to be of a different species. The trunks were round, thicker at the bottom and tapering as they rose to a height lost beyond the blue beam. The branches ended in thick, round leaves. Bushes, growing up to around six feet in height, were made up of a variety of colors: red, blue, purple. The lamps gave them an odd neon glow.

"This is like an alien planet," Hass said.

They came to a dam. Trees and rocks had been pushed down into the riverbed. They climbed up over the dam to find the other side was dry, too.

Water hadn't flowed here in a long time, but it had once, and someone had deliberately stopped it from running down the mountain.

Chase was flushed from the exertion. She was starting to sweat. "It's warm here." She unzipped her topcoat and shrugged out of it, then felt the need to take off her jacket, too. She stooped to pack them both away.

"Think the lava is heating the mountain?"

"Whatever it is," Chase said, "it feels like we just stepped into the Amazon."

They came to a clearing beside the dried-up river, a loose semicircle ten feet across. The ground was mostly flat, with a few small mounds in the center. The trees at the far end of the clearing were closer together, the foliage denser. Somehow, they both sensed this was some kind of ancient boundary marker. To step through those trees was to cross a line.

Something white glinted in the beam of the lamps, right at the edge of this half-imagined boundary. A solid object, catching the light. Chase walked across the clearing to get a closer look. A bush had grown up around it, but as she pulled at the leaves, she revealed a statue. White rock, neither granite nor marble. It stood four feet high and was carved into the image of a large cat. A lion maybe, or a tiger, with an open, snarling mouth and two large sabre-teeth.

"The white cat," Hass said, giving voice to what they'd both already understood.

But there was something more to it. Chase stared at the face. She'd seen it before. Three times. Once on the statues in the Holy of Holies, once when she lifted the blanket covering the Ark, and once in a cave beneath Alexandria. In this new context, she noticed the two enlarged teeth, but the other statues had been the same.

In the Genesis myth, after expelling Adam and Eve, God left a cherubim with a flaming sword guarding the entrance to the garden. There was no flaming sword, and this statue wasn't leaping into life anytime soon, but here was a statue of a cherubim—or of one of its four main forms, at least—at the edge of a prehistoric forest.

Chase took two slow steps back into the clearing. She fought an urge to kneel, not really understanding where it was coming from.

"What is it?" Hass stepped past her to look at the statue.

"I think Gilmore was right," Chase said quietly. "I think we've just found Eden."

They both stood there, unable to find the right words. Chase paused to think, for the first time, what this meant for Hass. She'd never been religious, aside from the programming that never quite leaves you when you're raised in a faith. Until finding the Ark, she'd never had much reason to question her thoughts either way. The journey since then, in the last few days, had been about feeling something new, questioning whether she belonged in a tradition, and whether she welcomed it. But Hass had always believed. In his own way, with his own compromises, he was the most devout man she'd ever met. And she knew Adam and Eve existed in Islam, with Eve known by a different name. But wasn't Eden considered to be a level of Heaven? A place to which you had to earn entry?

She turned to him, studying the emotions on his face. His strong, man-of-bronze features overcome with awe.

"Are you okay?"

He didn't answer right away, still taking in the line of trees ahead of them as if memorizing every fine detail. Finally, he turned and nodded.

"I think we should camp here," he said. "This . . ." He paused, looked again into the trees. "This is not a thing to rush into."

They set down the bags and unpacked the tents, setting them up with few words outside of half-whispered directions as they worked. Once they'd set up two tents, one for each of them, and decided they didn't need the toilet tent—a luxury for tourists—they got to the question of a campfire and food.

"We don't need the heat," Chase reasoned. "And the smoke could lead people to us."

"True." Hass pulled out their two remaining halogen lamps. He carried one to the edge of the clearing and bent to set it down. "And we don't need fire to keep any critters away from . . ."

Chase realized why his words had died off. Something else they hadn't discussed. A familiar feeling that had crawled up the back of her neck, ignored until now. She guessed Hass was experiencing it, too. Maybe it was the statue and her imagination running wild. Maybe it was her old fear of the dark finding a way out. But the instincts had kicked back in. The feeling of total isolation they'd had on the walk up was gone. Somewhere along the way, as they'd walked into this alien landscape, they'd both known they were no longer alone.

Hass stood up fast, leaving the lamp where it was, and backed toward Chase.

"There's something moving," he whispered.

And then she heard it, too. Quiet. Barely audible. Something large was pacing slowly, circling the clearing. It stopped at the riverbank, the point at which it would have been exposed to view, and then started to move back the way it had come. A bush moved. A branch, four feet off the ground, snapped back into place after being brushed aside.

Chase thought she already knew what panic was before the low growl came from somewhere directly ahead of them.

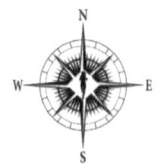

THIRTY-FOUR

A second growl. It sounded like an old motorcycle kicking into life with a snarl before settling into a low rumble.

Hass whispered, "Can you see it?"

"No."

"I see something. Go five feet across from the statue. Maybe three feet up. There's something there."

Chase followed his directions. It took a few seconds for her eyes to adjust, to detect the different shades of shadow of foliage, and then, in the middle of it all, a shape. What was that? Fur? Muscle? Then she caught it. Something that glinted. An eye. A large cat's eye. The rumble died away, but the shape didn't move.

A bush moved, somewhere off to their left. More movement. A second low, rumbling growl. There were two of them. Two of whatever this large predator was. Watching them. Stalking them.

Chase willed herself to pull her eyes away from the one she could see and bent slowly to open her backpack. She pulled out the gun belt that held two Blackhawk revolvers. Strapping it on, she stood back up, feeling exactly zero percent more confident. Hass waited until she was in position before he turned to get his own weapons. She scanned the same patch of leaves she'd been looking at before but couldn't find the eye. She risked looking away, in the direction of where the second creature had been moving.

"I lost them," she said.

Hass raised his own weapon, one of three Kimber 1911s he'd packed. "I didn't hear anything move."

Chase scanned again.

There were no sounds.

No shapes. No eyes. Creatures in the wild, especially large territorial ones, have a knack for letting you hear them only when they want you to. For show.

"I think they were just letting us know," she said. "We got the welcome wagon, plus a 'keep out' warning."

Chase turned to Hass and realized that he'd gotten a better glimpse at the creature than she had. When he'd directed her attention to the spot where she saw the eye, he must have seen something more.

"What was it?" she tried.

He shook his head, just once. "It was big." He pointed his gun at a branch, the one Chase had seen whip back into place earlier. "I saw its back. It was higher than that branch, brushed it aside like it was nothing. It moved that way." He traced across to where Chase had spotted the eye. "Then I saw its shoulder flex as it crouched down. I've seen lions. I've seen tigers. This thing was big."

Why was it still here?

Why were they still here?

If Steve had been right, and everything with a shred of intelligence had already left the mountain, why would a large predator still be living here?

"If it wanted to attack, we'd know by now," Chase said. "We should get some sleep, in shifts. Wait until the sun comes back up."

"Why aren't we cold? It's after midnight and we should be freezing, but I need to strip down to shorts."

Chase looked up. The clearing was a large enough break in the trees to get a glimpse of the peak, towering up above them, a large dark shape against a slightly less dark background. "She's awake. Maybe she's keeping us warm."

Chase went first. They set an alarm for three hours' time, and she crawled into the tent, noticing only then that she'd erected hers over one of the mounds, meaning she was lying on a lump. With everything that had gone on—the climb, the discovery of the marker, the alien landscape, and the giant goddamn cat—Chase didn't think she'd sleep. But the minute she closed her eyes and relaxed her shoulders, all the energy and tension washed away, replaced with an exhaustion that wrapped around her and pushed the world out to a distant problem.

As soon as Hass heard Chase's breathing ease into deep sleep, he let out a long sigh like steam from a kettle. He'd been holding on to his fear. His panic. Hass wasn't a coward. He didn't consider himself a hero, but he prided himself on not feeling or showing fear.

But he'd seen more than he'd let on. As the creature had brushed past that branch, he'd had a clear view. The head. The shoulders. This was a large predator. A cat. More like a tiger than a lion, with dark stripes over a gray pelt, and no mane. But how could he trust his eyes?

What he'd seen didn't exist. He'd been looking straight at Mngwa. He'd seen the face. The almond eyes. The ears. The two pronounced teeth. And in that instant, the brief second when he was face-to-face with a mythic predator, he'd felt pure, primal fear. He was grateful it had been so many hours since they'd eaten. And the only reason he'd looked calm and stoic, the only reason Chase hadn't seen him turn to jelly and run away, was because his legs had frozen.

You were tested, Hassan. You stood at the entrance to Eden, and you were tested. And you proved to be a coward.

He sat on the ground, long into the night, listening to the occasional sound from within the ancient forest, and felt alone.

Chase was dragged kicking and screaming from sleep by the alarm. For a few seconds, she resisted. Pressed snooze and wanted to drift back into the peace she'd found. Then everything rushed back to the front of her mind, and she was awake, alert. She crawled out of the tent and checked in with Hass, who was sitting between the tents and the statue. He smiled and said good morning with pure exhaustion written across his face. And something else. Something Chase could place, because she'd seen it in her own eyes, every time she'd glanced in the mirror since finding the Ark. She touched his shoulder and told him to get some sleep. There were no words that would help with the other thing. Whatever awaited them when the sun came up, they'd face it and deal with the consequences later.

She walked down the riverbed to relieve herself. It took her past the edge of the lamplight. She stood there, wrapped in darkness, proud that she could do it. She felt every inch of progress she'd made as an adult, moving past her fears, realizing the denial and grief that had fueled them. She breathed in deep and felt the thin air hitting the bottom of her lungs and achieving almost nothing. She promised herself that when they got back down the mountain, she was just going to stand and breathe air like it was crack. Looking back at the camp, she felt detached. The strange, alien landscape was lit up in the soft blue glow, with the modern tents in the foreground and the . . .

She looked again at the mounds in the earth. Now that she had time to focus on them, not distracted by everything else, they didn't look natural.

They were an arrangement. Human-made. And why would—?

Ignore that for now, deal with it in daylight.

Scanning the bushes and trees, she caught something but didn't know what it was. Her brain had snagged on something her eyes had skipped over. She looked again, taking everything in. Scanning across once, twice, three times more. There it was. On the last go-around, and at the very edge of her vision. An eye flash. Something else was watching the camp, from high up in the tree. Whatever it was, it wasn't looking her way. Hass's deep snoring had the eyes firmly fixed downward. Chase kept perfectly still, aware of the guns on her hips and the distance to where her friend lay if she needed to do anything. But these weren't the scary cat eyes of earlier. They were rounder, smaller, closer together. As she let her own vision becomes accustomed to that spot, she could start to make out the shape. A round head, and a curved shape on either side of the body. The outline looked like a large figure eight; even at this distance it seemed to be maybe three feet tall. She was looking at some kind of huge owl.

As Chase started back up the riverbank, she heard rustling, followed by flapping. When she looked back up at the tree, the shape was gone.

Walking back to the other end of the semicircle, where the ancient riverbed vanished into a tangle of bushes, she heard—or felt—water. All creatures have a sense for when it's nearby. In a city, that sense becomes dulled, but out in the wild, it was unmissable. She hesitated, turning back to look at the tent. Hass had sat in one spot while she slept and guarded her like a sentry.

Maybe he was just better at being a friend?

But she wasn't going far. She bent down and parted the bush directly in front of her. The water feeling grew stronger. She took a step forward and could now hear it. A stream, running beneath the plants, down toward the moss that filled the dry riverbed. Maybe this had once been where the river met the forest, the course of the river that someone had felt the need to divert farther downstream, and this was all that was left. She dipped her left hand in and touched the bottom, only a few inches down. It was warm, like the air around them. She cupped her hands together to scoop some up and drank it. Her injured wrist tingled, and she became aware of the dull ache for the first time in several hours, the constant pain that she'd been tuning out. She peeled off the tape and started washing the skin beneath, dipping it in the water to clean off the sweat and mud. She could apply fresh tape before they headed into the forest.

Hass woke up before his alarm. The top of his tent was warm, indicating sunlight. He'd never been able to sleep past dawn. The minute the rays were out there in the world, he wanted to be up to meet them. He rolled out of the tent. The clearing was lit in a blue-gray half-light. It wasn't quite dawn, but it would be soon.

He couldn't see Chase.

Panic rose for a moment. He whirled around, aware now that he'd left his guns in the tent. Then he saw her down near the riverbed, at the edge of the clearing. She turned back to see him, smiled, and waved.

"You don't need another hour?"

"No, I'm okay."

She climbed to her feet. Something struck Hass as odd about the way she moved, but he wasn't sure what. It was as she drew near that he figured it out, watching the way she was turning her wounded wrist around, opening and closing the fist. She'd put weight on that hand as she got up.

"Are you prepared for something unbelievable?"

Hass smiled, pushing away the fear at what he'd seen the night before to say, "Crazier than a giant cat from the dawn of time?"

"Or an owl bigger than a dog."

"A what?"

"Check this out." She nodded for him to follow her back to the edge of the clearing, where she pulled back two large, thick, and blue bushes to show a shallow stream of water trickling down toward the riverbed. "I started washing my wrist in the water to clean it up to apply a fresh dressing, right? But then the pain started to fade. I thought maybe it's like when you leave a finger under a cold tap and it goes numb, except this water is warm." She turned to him again, rotating her hand in fast gestures. "I think—I said unbelievable, right?—I think my wrist is healed."

"How is that . . . ?"

"I know." Chase laughed, her smile a full-on beam. He had never seen her this happy. She looked almost younger. "I washed my face, just figured I'd save our own water for drinking. Then I put my wrist under again and I realized it wasn't hurting. I've tried putting weight on it, lifting things. I did some push-ups. It feels great. I feel great."

There was an almost manic energy to her words. The world's biggest caffeine rush.

She bent down to pick up a torn piece of cloth, wadded up and damp, and stepped toward Hass. "Let me try your wound."

Hass felt a surge of panic. He grabbed her wrist, hard, stepping back to put distance between himself and the rag. There was some basic, primal fear that had kicked in, almost on the level of when he'd seen the Mngwa.

Survival.

He took another step back and said, "No, thanks."

He watched the confusion on Chase's face. And for a second he was studying the face itself again. She did look younger. He wasn't imagining it.

Unless this was altitude sickness and he was imagining everything.

"I'm sorry," Chase said.

"No, it's okay." Hass didn't want to explain what had worried him. It felt impossible. Stupid. It could wait until they saw how things panned out. "I just—no, thanks."

Chase nodded, mopped her own brow with the rag, then threw it down. They ate a quick breakfast in silence. Chase refilled one of her own water bottles from the stream.

Hass stuck to the supply they'd brought with them. Once the food was done, Chase said they should move the tents; she wanted to look at the ground. It wasn't until they'd dragged hers out of the way, pulling up the guy ropes, that he saw why.

Chase's tent had been over one of the small mounds he'd noticed the night before. There were others, too. They were arranged in the same loose semicircle as the clearing. Five mounds of earth, overgrown with a small layer of moss and grass. Each of them was roughly the same height and length. Long enough to cover a human body, high enough to represent the top of a shallow grave.

"How many people were in Gilmore's regiment?"

Chase nodded. Already thinking the same thing. "Six."

"So five, if we don't count him."

"Five people who disappeared, yeah."

They fell silent, staring at the five graves. Hass lowered his head, said a prayer. Chase lowered her own head out of respect as he spoke. Then they made eye contact. Each of them knowing the other was asking the same question.

If that water really could heal wounds, why would anybody here be dead? Which invited the real concern: What the hell happened here?

They set up the tents farther from the mounds, closer to the riverbank. It made sense to leave the camp here. They didn't know what the terrain was going to be like once they stepped into the dense forest, and the plan was to head back this way anyway. Hass loaded all four of his guns, with the face of the Mngwa a constant presence in his mind. He strapped on a gun belt and a shoulder holster and put the remaining gun near the top of his bag.

They were ready to go by the time the sun broke for real, the early-morning rays hitting the leaves of the trees and bushes. The scene ahead of them almost glowed, all deep reds, oranges, greens, and yellows. It was breathtaking. They smiled at each other, and Hass forgot all his fears for a moment, taken in by what they were sharing. Chase nodded at the trees. "Ready?" "Ready," Hass lied.

They walked up to the edge of the clearing, level with the white statue. With one last pause, listening for any sign of their visitors from the night before, they pushed through the bushes and into the ancient forest.

THIRTY-FIVE

They followed the path of the stream as it twisted through the forest. Trees towered above them. The trunks were almost leathery, thick and round at the base, tapering as they climbed hundreds of feet into the air. They almost looked more like small plants and weeds than trees, left to grow large for thousands of years. The widest variety was in the bushes. Some were as tall as houses; others barely made it a foot off the ground. And the deep colors were like nothing either Hass or Chase had ever seen. Blue. Green. Red. Yellow. Orange. The soil beneath their feet was dark, almost black, as though freshly laid topsoil covered the whole forest floor. Chase kept kneeling to touch it, feeling how smooth it was. She noticed Hass had put on gloves. He seemed on edge, but she didn't want to push the issue.

Once the camp was far behind them and the stream was their only marker for finding the way back, they started to notice crops. Some of the trees, the smaller ones that looked rubbery rather than leathery, were holding large green and yellow fruit, the size of a basketball. Lower down, some of the bushes were producing berries.

Chase plucked one and was about to pop it in her mouth when Hass stopped her.

"What are you doing? We don't know if they're safe."

Chase paused. Looked at the berry in her hand. He was right. Of course he was. But it had felt so natural, so simple. She still felt the urge. She dropped it back to the ground.

They both noticed an incline. Pausing to check their compasses, to see if the stream was still leading them eastward or was now turning to head up the mountain, they found that neither of their devices were working. Hass's said they were headed west, Chase's said south. Something in the forest was interfering. They stuck to following the water, wherever it took them.

"I've lost all sense of distance," Chase said. "When we looked on Google Maps, I figured whatever the dark place was, it couldn't be more than two, three miles across. But how long have we been walking?"

"I don't know." Hass turned to look back the way they'd come. "I never get lost. Blindfold me, and I can still point north. But in here? I . . . I don't know. At a guess, I think we turned north about a mile in, and we've headed maybe a half mile north after that?"

Hass was good on the ground, and especially in jungles and forests. He'd had a line that he used to repeat to everyone he met, when he was fresh to the scene. I know I'm Somalian, but I couldn't be a pirate—I get seasick. Put me in a jungle, I'm fine. If even he was now feeling lost, then Chase had no chance of figuring out the directions.

They could hear running water, somewhere up ahead. A light splashing. As they pushed through some large purple bushes, they came to a small waterfall. The water was trickling down a rock face to form the stream. There was a small clearing at the base of the rocks, which Chase guessed must have once been a larger pool of water, maybe one of the main sources of the dried-up river. There were mud slopes on either side of the rock face. Hass turned to take that route up. Chase laughed, splashing in the water, letting it run across her face and hands, soak through her clothes, as she climbed the rocks. It was only a ten-foot ascent, but once she reached the top, she felt like she'd achieved something huge. A sense of elation washed over her. Hass was already waiting, offering his hand to help her over the edge. She jumped straight to her feet, not needing any time to recover. That in itself gave her a moment's pause. Where was the altitude sickness? It was just . . . gone.

Hass gave her an odd look. "Are you okay?"

"I'm amazing."

Hass's brow furrowed deeper. Chase felt a flash of resentment. Why was he questioning her? Why did he feel the need to kill her mood?

As if sensing this, Hass smiled and said, "You'll need to be amazing to see this."

He stepped aside, allowing her to see what she'd climbed up to. They were standing in another large clearing.

The trees on either side still provided cover above, their large round leaves touching, but down at ground level there was a space about thirty feet in diameter. The sunlight filtered down through the leaves, giving everything a green glow. The rock face where Chase stood was damp, another stream running through the center and then off the rocks into a shallow depression that again looked like the remnants of something much larger. Beyond the old pool was a large tangle of bushes and weeds. But what stood out from everything they'd seen so far was the shape. It was full of squares. Flat surfaces. And, in a few places, glimpses of something white beneath the growth. There was a human-made structure here, buried beneath the encroaching weeds. They'd found a settlement.

"What the . . . ?"

Hass smiled. "Yes."

Nash was not going to admit how much fun he was having. There was no way. But holding his poker face as they flew up the side of Kilimanjaro was just about the hardest thing he'd ever done.

Turned out, everything Lauren had said about the drones was correct. They were strong, near-silent, and easy to control. He felt like he was wearing a jet pack. The CIA never had anything this cool. He'd taken the lead, insisting that his field experience made him the natural choice.

Lauren was ten feet behind.

The two metal pods that she had insisted on bringing were carried by one drone each, following the two human- operated craft with some kind of Bluetooth signal. They'd started off heading northwest, diagonally across the mountain, as tablets mounted to both of their displays led them toward the spot Lauren had pinpointed. There was brilliant morning sunlight on either side of Nash, spreading out across the forest and the plains far below. But in this narrow corridor, he was shrouded in total darkness. It was humbling, in a way, to be in the shadow of a rock large enough to hold back the sun. But then, it was hard to feel humble when you were flying via jet pack.

As they closed in on the target, the trees below them changed. The leaves were large, round, and rubbery and a very deep green that drew the light toward it. In patches between the leaves, he could make out a crack in the rocks, some kind of natural channel running down the mountain. The tracker beeped, announcing they were in the target area.

Lauren's voice came through his Bluetooth earpiece. "We need to land."

Nash was already on it, scanning for a large enough break in the leaves to get a good view. It wasn't just finding a spot for him and Lauren. That would be easy enough; they could improvise if needed. But the two damn pods needed to come down safely, too. There was another break in the trees a mile farther up. As he approached, Nash got a view of what looked to be a cave. With the steep angle of the mountainside, the cave was directly ahead, only visible at this angle. Nash waved to get Lauren's attention and pointed. She nodded and followed him in. As they pushed through the gap in the trees, Nash saw a large lake coming out of the cave into a large bowl of rock jutting out over the valley below. There was a small clearing next to the lake. It would be tight, but all four drones should just about fit.

Landing was easy. Sensors built into the control panel took over for the most part, scanning the area below them and guiding the drones down.

Nash used the stick to nudge it a few feet one way or another, change the angle to make it more comfortable, then waited as the craft lowered two landing skids on either side of him. He was hung beneath it like a package ready to be delivered. He pressed the harness release and dropped to the ground, crawling out to see Lauren had already done the same and was standing watching the two pods touch down. Nash looked back up the way they'd come. Already, from this angle, he couldn't make out the break in the trees. By some trick of the line of sight, it looked like they were entirely covered by the canopy, bathed in the green light that filtered down through the leaves. Somehow, Lauren had worked out the one angle they could have approached from to see this lake from the air. He wasn't going to tell her that, but it was a stroke of brilliance.

"Wow," said Lauren next to him, sounding awed by their surroundings.

Nash took a quick look around. Sure, the place was impressive. Crazy trees. Bushes of bright colors. But this was no time to stop and stare. They were here to find money, and nobody ever found that by standing around.

He unclipped the two pods from beneath the drones and struggled to pull them out. It felt like Lauren had packed a whole laboratory in them. Nash unclipped the lock on the first one, but Lauren shouted, told him to back away.

"I need my gear," he said.

She marched over and pushed him away. "The equipment is delicate." She lifted the lid just enough to bend and look inside, reached in, and pulled out his large canvas bag, almost dropping it as it came free of the pod. Nash stepped in to take the weight, setting the bag down on the ground and unzipping it. He had a small arsenal inside. Shotguns, Glocks, ammunition, grenades, and a pack of flares. He pulled on his gun belt, strapped a Glock to either side, slung a shotgun across his back, and slipped three flares into the cargo pockets of his pants.

Lauren was already marching off toward the cave, a large rock archway sitting over the end of the lake like the canopy on a baby stroller. Nash's attention was drawn to the lake. He couldn't place why. It was a large, round, flat surface. The water was calm, with a faint current detectable as it dribbled over the cliff at the end, down to the valley below.

There's something about that cliff . . .

He walked up to the edge. The clearing narrowed out to a point. The water was only a light trickle as it ran over a section of the wall that dipped in the middle. Below them he could see the valley, with a wide channel cut into the rock, winding down the mountainside, looking like the course of what was once a much larger river.

The *wall.*

He knelt down to peer over the edge at the rock face of the cliff. His first thought had been right. This was a wall, human-made. He could see cracks across the surface where someone had laid down large chunks of stone. He could see moss growing on something between the rocks, some kind of mortar. This lake wasn't a natural formation. It was a dam. Someone had settled here and blocked the waterfall.

There was heat coming off the water.

He dipped his hand in to confirm it was warm.

"August."

Lauren sounded alarmed. Nash spun on his heels and rose into a sprint in one fluid motion. He ran around the edge of the water. He noticed now that, just as with the wall, some primitive instinct was telling him to be wary of the water. He made up the ground fast, coming to the mouth of the cave. Lauren was standing in its shadow. There was a path next to the water, leading into the cave, but it was covered with a large bush of red leaves. Lauren had been pulling at the leaves, and in doing so she exposed a white stone face. It was a lion with large sabre-teeth. Nash had seen that face before, in the temple on Lake Tana, as one of the faces of the cherubim. They pulled back at the thick branches of the bush.

The invasive plant was covering the whole area, having grown up along the cave ceiling and down the other side. Nash used a knife to hack the branches clear and saw that, just like the cherubim in the temple, this one had four faces. There was the lion, the jackal, and the eagle. The difference was, unlike the previous statue, the fourth face wasn't an ox. It looked more like a dragon or a crocodile.

"What is this?" Lauren whispered, an equal measure of wonder and terror.

"It's an angel. A cherubim."

"Why would there be a statue of an angel ? Here?"

"I don't know why. I'm just telling you what it is."

The cave was warm. Nash was starting to sweat.

They pulled more branches away and stepped around the statue, deeper into the shadow. He lit a flare and held it over his head. The chamber around them glowed with the red light, and they could see markings on the wall. Inscriptions in a language he'd never seen before. Drawings, looking more detailed and advanced than typical cave paintings. One showed a large mountain with red fire blooming out of the top. The other showed what looked to be a plant, a circular red leaf. Farther in, they found the path angled upward. Someone had carved steps out of the rock, which led to a primitive altar four feet above the surface of the water. The wall paintings here looked familiar to Nash, after years of searching for the ark. People carrying a triangular object on a boat-like object. He'd seen similar motifs many times. Not necessarily the ark, but the same idea, people carrying a holy object.

The water here was covered in the same red plant from the paintings, which floated like water lilies. The color was identical to the creeper they'd just hacked through, and Nash guessed they must be related, two different forms of the same species.

"This is it," Lauren said.

She took Nash's knife and nicked the back of her hand, a small red line at the base of her thumb. She got down on her knees and reached to dip her hand in the water. Nash wasn't comfortable, and he'd learned over many years to listen to his instincts. There was something wrong here. In the heat. The quiet. The smell. That smell. Something lived in this cave.

He heard a light ripple. Something large had moved beneath the surface, somewhere nearby. He grabbed Lauren by both shoulders and pulled her back, full force. They both crashed into the wall of the cave behind them as a large crocodile head rose up through the field of lilies, snapping at the space Lauren had vacated.

***

Chase and Hass pulled back the branches of the creeping bush. It had red leaves and small suction cups that stuck to the wall. They were hard to shift, but Chase's newfound energy and strength helped. As they cleared away the growth, they found more than one structure. This was a tightly packed collection of small huts that appeared to be made out of adobe or something very much like it.

"Who used to live here?" Hass said.

They cleared the doorway of the first hut and stepped inside. The single room was empty. Damp moss covered the floor, and the moisture had climbed the walls, leaving a trail of green that corrupted the white of the adobe-like plaster. The ceiling was low. Chase could stand to her full height, but Hass needed to stoop.

They stepped out and moved onto the second hut. There were markings on the wall. The damp had destroyed and distorted most of it. What remained appeared to be some kind of written language, but not one either of them recognized. In the far corner, covered in a smaller version of the red plant breaking in through a crack in the wall, Chase found a small metal box. It looked like an old military munitions case.

The lid wouldn't open at first. The hinge had seized, and a layer of muck had congealed over the crack. Hass used his large knife to slice away the growth and then worked the blade into the crack, levering it open.

Inside was a small collection of trinkets. Some old military badges, a few bullet casings, a notebook, and a letter. The paper had survived remarkably well. It was stiff, hard to the touch, and showed signs of damp around the edges, but the writing was still clear and in English.

> If you are reading this, you have already found your way to this strange place. I trust by now you understand its secrets for yourself, and you do not need me to explain why it is that I can't put an accurate date to this letter as I write.

> I'm unsure of the year. This hut has been my home for how long? I cannot say. I'm sure it was already here when we arrived. Like the statues and markings in the cave. I remember being told stories on our journey here, of the people and the people before. That's how the tribes kept referring to them. The people and the people before.

> I think it's winter, As I write. I'm sure of it. But I'm sure of so little now. I think I will remember my name by the time I finish. I think I will be able to sign it. But that is not always certain, so please forgive me if I sign my name early. There's a name in this notebook that I think is mine. The handwriting in this letter matches that in the journal. But perhaps this man, this James, is someone else? I came here with others, that much I remember. I had dirt on my hands, from burying the last of them. Out beyond the marker, where the earth doesn't play tricks.

Forgive my rambling. My mind is coming and going. I have it right now. My name is James Gilmore. I have lived in this place I do not know how long. I have not aged, but I fear that's taking a different toll. My body stays young, but my mind gets clouded. We had visitors. Germans. They talked of wars, two of them. They said England was about to fall, and America refuses to join the fight. They tried to take this place from us, but we fought. And now I am all that's left, and my mind continues to drift. I left them for the Mngwa. That has kept the creatures content. If you are reading this, you have already seen the Mngwa. They watch us with clever eyes. Forgive me, I'm trying to write everything down before I drift again.

I think I am James.

Yes. I am.

Beneath Gilmore's signature was another small entry, written diagonally across the bottom corner, in a more precise and focused version of the same handwriting.

As you can see above, my mind has not been healthy. I remain that way. But I have, through some effort, starved myself of food and water for two days. I grow weaker, but my mind is clearer. It's the water. The fruit. The red leaves. And it's myself. I can hear my own voice, telling me to stay, to eat, to drink. But I am James Gilmore, I am a soldier. We were sent here by the crown, to locate and secure Eden before the Germans could claim it. And now I find out that war, somehow, is continuing, and is worse than before. I must leave. I must join the fight. If you are reading this, stay away from the water. Do not eat the fruit. May God help you leave this place.

"He wasn't a deserter," Hass said, after they'd both read the letter. "They were here on a mission. Kilimanjaro was claimed by Germany in the 1880s. I read in Stanley's book that General Gordon was fixated on Eden. Maybe he sent them."

Chase nodded, but none of it mattered. Who cared why a British soldier had come here, over a century ago? The real question was how had he stayed here, and still been young fifty years later when the Nazis arrived? She flexed her hand, her healed wrist. Somewhere beneath her own emotions, her current state of relaxation and happiness, she knew Gilmore's words made sense. What she was feeling wasn't natural. She felt like she'd been drugged, and she was only noticing it now. Ever since they had entered the forest, she had been craving more and more of this bliss. And even in thinking that, she could feel the anger and defensiveness build. Resentment. First she'd been losing her temper with Hass, and now with a man she'd never met, who'd written a letter sometime in the 1940s. And then, finally, anger at herself.

Let me have this.

Let me be happy.

Let me be perfect.

"Those graves," Hass whispered. "The way he writes about them. Burying them where the earth doesn't play tricks."

Chase flexed her wrist again. She pulled back the sleeve of her T-shirt to expose her upper arm. She'd had a scar there ever since bring grazed by a bullet in Syria a couple of years before. There was no trace of the mark.

"You look younger, too," Hass said, as if reading her thoughts. "Even since this morning. In the time we've been here, you're looking younger."

"It's healing me." Chase ran her finger across where the scar had been. "It's rewriting my . . . oh God."

She looked at Hass, who nodded sadly. Now she understood his fear. The water could fix "damage"; it could undo cuts, breaks, changes to the body. To Chase, what was the biggest risk? She splashed around a bit and took miles off the clock. But Hass was trans. He'd put in a lot of years, a lot of work, into becoming himself. Would the properties in the water, whatever they were, be able to distinguish between the unwelcome damage Chase had done to her own body and the changes Hass had chosen to make to his own?

"I'm sorry, Doc." She touched his arm again. "I wasn't thinking."

Hass had tears in his eyes. "I'm scared. This whole place hates me. It can make me into . . . it can turn me into something I'm not."

"Head back to the camp. Where he buried them. The soil out there looked normal. You can wait for me."

Hass laughed. "You think that's enough to stop me backing you up?"

Now it was Chase's turn to tear up. She thought of all the relationships she'd shut down. The people she'd pushed away, only to remember them as tattoos, scars, or mean jokes. She'd finally let go of decades' worth of built-up grief a couple of years ago, but she hadn't filled that space with anything, or anyone, else.

Wait . . . tattoos.

She ran her hand along her arm, over her collection of ink. "I still have these," she said. "The water isn't healing these. So maybe it's not a total reset to factory settings, you know?"

Hass sniffed away his tears, laughed. "Let's not find out."

They heard the growl at the same time. The familiar rumble from the night before. Chase and Hass both crouched down, shuffling away from the door. Something large moved just outside. It rubbed against the wall. Chase saw the tail. A mix of gray and black. It was held high, like a house cat patrolling its territory, but the base of the tail was four feet off the ground. The rumble came again.

Beneath all Chase's elation, beneath this cloud of health or happiness that she's been feeling, grew a very basic fear.

The thing outside moved away. Chase leaned across, putting her weight on what had recently been a fractured wrist, to peer out of the doorway.

She saw the thing.

The whole thing. From the rear, its tail swished cautiously as it walked toward the cliff face. It looked like a large tiger or leopard. Its fur was gray, covered in black stripes, just like the drawing. It moved with a terrifying grace, the body rocking gently as its giant shoulders moved. She could see its forelegs. Huge, muscular. Almost more like a bear than a cat. This was a creature built for climbing and tearing. At the cliff top, the large beast paused to drink the water, then sniffed at the air, turning its head to the side. As it stood profile now, Chase could see one of its large sabre-teeth.

She knew what this was.

Yes, she was staring at Mngwa. The large cat of local myth. But more than that. She knew exactly what species of animal she was looking at. The implications of this made everything else start to make a very real, very scary, very impossible kind of sense.

The Mngwa growled again, as if picking up a scent, and jumped down off the cliff. They both heard it splash down at the bottom, then a few soft steps followed by the moving of branches.

"That was a Dinofelis," Chase whispered.

"A what?"

"Dinofelis. 'Terrible cat.' Basically the African and European version of the sabre-toothed tiger."

"I think we should go in the opposition direction."

"Yeah."

They stepped quietly out of the hut and looked up the hill, facing away from the direction the Mngwa had gone. A narrow trail led around the side of the overgrown village and farther up the hill, between bushes and rocks.

Chase paused to notice the clearing the huts had been built on appeared to be part of a meandering line that led up the mountain, vanishing into the shade of the trees up ahead.

"I think this was all part of a river's course," she said. "I think the huts were built on land that used to be underwater."

"You mean after the river stopped flowing."

"Right. Whoever those people were, I think they were late settlers."

They continued the climb, through more bushes, and then another dense layer of trees. They were going up the mountain in steps, following the path of the ancient river. Chase could see a cliff maybe two hundred feet above them, with water trickling over the edge, dropping down to form the narrow brook that ran down through the path of the dry river. The edge of that cliff looked unnatural. It was human-made. Someone had deliberately blocked the path of the river. Were they previous settlers? An earlier group than the people who'd built the huts below? Had someone wanted to keep the water for themselves? Or had they wanted to stop it flowing for a different reason? Was this selfishness or protection?

"Here," Hass was pulling leaves away from a rock. Chase bent in to see paintings on the stone surface. Human figures rendered in dark red, with pear-shaped bodies and thin limbs.

"I've seen this style before," she said.

"Yeah," Hass agreed. "The Cave of Swimmers."

The cave was located in the Gilf Kabir, a large rocky plateau straddling the border between Libya and southern Egypt. The paintings in the cave were estimated to be eight thousand years old, with much speculation about whether the humans who lived at Gilf Kabir had migrated north to the Nile river to found the tribes who later became Egypt.

"If someone was tempted," Hass said, "they could start to piece together a trail here of migration north along the Nile."

"Let's keep moving for now."

They came to another clearing, maybe a mile above the last one. Here they found a large bush in the middle, with small, red, apple-like fruit.

Chase could feel the pull. *Eat them. Eat them.*

"I suppose all of these plants are prehistoric, too," Hass said. "Holdovers. They've died off everywhere else but survived here."

Chase agreed. "This whole forest is a throwback. This spot on the mountain, it's high enough to have avoided floods, low enough to have been away from the cloud caused by the Sumatra eruption. The humans here could have survived, along with everything else. The Mngwa, the plants. I saw an owl last night that was bigger than a dog. But why are they all still here, when everything else has run away? And why have they always stuck to this patch?"

"Addiction." Hass reached out to put his hand over Chase's. She was holding one of the apples. It was only now that she realized she'd picked it, been about to bite into it.

No, that's not true, she thought. *You knew you were doing it.*

How could she know and not know at the same time? And then, through it all, another flush of anger at Hass. How dare he stop me. I'll do what I— She threw the fruit away. It landed in a distant bush with a faint rustle.

This was followed by another sound from back down the trail. Padding. Four feet. The low growl. The Mngwa was following them. Chase scanned around the clearing for cover. They were out in the open, this bush the only thing nearby.

Hass whispered, "Up in the trees."

Chase looked up. Then finally, even through the layer of drugged euphoria, she felt total panic. Resting up in the branches, watching them, were three more Mngwa, two on the left, one on the right. Their large forelimbs were stretched out ahead of them, claws showing. The fourth, the one that had passed them down at the hut, wandered into view on the trail and growled.

Chase thought back to the night before, at camp. Creatures like this, you only heard them when they wanted you to. She and Hass had been herded this way. It was a trap.

The shepherd Mngwa took a couple of steps forward and then lowered itself into a sitting position, paws forward like the Sphinx, watching them. The watchers stirred in the trees. The two on the left stretched, yawned. They dropped down to the ground with fearful grace and circled around the edge of the clearing, blocking the far path. For a moment, Chase laughed at the absurdity of it all, picturing the times they'd practiced this. "No, Bob, I told you, on the count of three, you go left. No, that's right. No, I said on three . . . what are you . . . Bob . . ."

Hass looked at her, puzzled by the laughter. She saw his hands twitching, readying to pull his weapons. She dropped her own hands to her sides, feeling the metal of her Blackhawks, cool to the touch.

"I don't think our guns will stop them," she said.

"Enough bullets will stop anything." Hass didn't sound like he believed his own words. "But if you get a chance, run."

"You think I'm leaving you?"

"If it comes to it, you can heal up a wound in the water."

There was no way Chase was going to take any chance that presented itself, but it was pointless arguing. The Mngwa on the right, still in the tree, roared but didn't move. The two newcomers took three slow steps forward, closing the gap between them and their prey. This wasn't the type of pack behavior Chase had ever imaged from big cats, but she'd never studied lions or tigers in the wild. Maybe this was typical? She made a note to ask an expert when they got back. And that prompted a second bout of laughter.

The two advancing cats roared.

They both leapt forward.

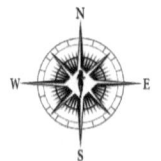

THIRTY-SIX

The crocodile snapped again, its large jaws closing only a couple of feet from where Nash and Lauren were pressed against the wall. The head was the size of a small car. The only thing saving them was the height of the ledge. The croc couldn't get up high enough to gain purchase, which kept it from getting any closer.

Nash found himself caught in time. He needed to panic, to run, to survive. But he couldn't help staring at the mouth, the teeth, the head of this thing that shouldn't exist. The roar that followed sounded more like Godzilla than anything natural. The head thrashed from side to side. He heard a splash and saw a tail whipping about in the water. The tip looked to be a full twenty-five feet behind the snout, almost stretching all the way across the cave. The head pulled back. The tail whipped again. Nash realized it was preparing to jump. They had seconds before they died. He pulled a second flare from his belt, cracked it into life, and threw it toward the back of the cave. As the light traveled, it illuminated the walls, but the rear of the cave remained buried in shadow. There was no telling how deep into the volcano this thing went. The crocodile turned to follow the flare, diving into the water and vanishing beneath the surface.

Nash pushed Lauren back in the other direction.

"Go. Go. Go."

They ran along the path. The splashing behind them announced the croc had turned to follow, mounting the lower section of the path. It ripped through the remaining bushes in their wake, moving at frightening speed.

Lauren and Nash rounded the statue on different sides. Nash turned back to see the crocodile bust straight through the statue, cracking it into chunks like it was nothing. Nash had his Glock at his side. The shotgun on his back. But what good would either of them do against a creature of this size? Nothing at all, except make it angry. He needed to get back to his bag.

They cleared the lip of the cave, crashing back into the strange green glow that passed for daylight. Up ahead he could see the drones. They weren't going to make it. They needed something to slow the croc down. He pulled another flare, lit it, and threw it backward without looking. He went into a baseball slide as he neared the bag, reached in for a grenade, and pulled the pin in the same movement as lining up the throw. The croc, which had paused for a few seconds to watch the flare, was now charging again. Nash waited.

Lauren slid in behind him, screaming, "Throw it."

Nash still waited. One more second. Two more seconds. The croc was close now. It opened its mouth. Nash threw the grenade, then turned and jumped backward, taking Lauren with him into the nearest bush. The explosion was muffled, coming with a wet sound, then splatter. Blood and flesh rained down on them. The grenade had landed in the beast's mouth, and the whole roof of its head was lost to the explosion. They climbed out of the bush to find the dead crocodile only a few feet from them and the smell of barbecued meat hanging in the air.

Lauren raised her hand, gesturing at something, but it was a few seconds before the ringing in Nash's ears died down enough for him to make sense of it. She wasn't gesturing with her hand but at it. There was no blood. No mark. The spot where she had cut herself was completely healed.

They both turned to stare at the water.

The sound of gunshots broke the moment, ringing out from somewhere in the valley. Then growls and something like a lion's roar. Then a human scream.

⟵▬▬

The Mngwa was on Hass, the weight pinning him to the floor. A scream filled the air.

Was it him or Chase? He didn't know.

It didn't feel like there was enough air in his lungs for that kind of sound.

If Chase was dying, he was no help to her right now. The large claws tore into his right shoulder. He couldn't feel anything at all down that side after the cut.

The large predator growled. Hass focused only on the sounds of the creature on top of him, the feel of his skin slicing, and those jaws, those giant jaws, rushing down at his face. The rest of the world vanished.

Was this his time?

Had he come to Eden to be judged? *To fail*?

His right arm was gone. He couldn't feel it, so he had to count on not having it. But God had given him two arms. If he was to be tested, he still had answers. His left arm was pinned, and he could feel claws from the large paw touching his skin but not yet digging in. He couldn't pull his gun from the holster, but he could grip the handle, slip his finger into the trigger. He angled the gun up, hoped for the best, and started squeezing the trigger. Again. Again. Again. The thing on top of him whimpered, suddenly sounding very much like a cat, a large, hurt cat. Hass didn't have time to feel guilty. As the claws came out of his shoulder, he gained a small degree of feeling in his right arm, enough to pull his large hunting knife from the scabbard. He didn't have any strength in the arm to use the weapon. He grabbed the blade with his left, feeling the edge cutting into his palm. He dropped it onto his belly, and then gripped the handle, and stabbed up, again, again. The Mngwa fell against him, dead.

No time to celebrate, because there were other Mngwa in the clearing. And Chase, what was happening to Chase? He needed to move. This test hadn't killed him. No guarantees about the next one. He rolled onto his good shoulder, the one that could take weight, and tried to shrug off the dead Mngwa. The weight was too much. He pulled half free, but his legs were still pinned, and without the use of his right arm, there was nothing he could do.

The world around him came into focus now. Behind him, Chase was down on one knee, clicking on empty with both guns. Her left leg was a mess of blood and ripped fabric. The Mngwa that had charged her was dead at her feet. She made eye contact with Hass and nodded, crawling over to him and pulling on the dead beast, helping him wriggle loose.

The fourth Mngwa, the one that had followed them up the trail, was pacing slowly forward, wary of the damage they'd just done. Had it seen guns before? Had it been alive when Gilmore was here or when the Nazis arrived? The commander in the tree was standing up now, its hind legs coiled, ready to jump.

Chase holstered her guns and clutched her injured leg. Hass refused to look at his arm, but he couldn't move it. He dropped the knife and picked up his Glock again. Chase leaned over to pull the one from his shoulder holster and froze, looking behind him.

Hass could hear the sound of the bush shaking, rattling. Something large moved past them, fast, and there was a growl followed by a yelp. Hass shuffled around to see what Chase had been staring at. It was a snake—some kind of rock python maybe, but he'd never seen one this big. Forty feet in length, possibly more, and four feet across. It had wrapped around the Mngwa and was squeezing the life out of it. The lead Mngwa, up in the tree, roared and attacked, scratching at the python before darting away, avoiding the coils of its tail. It hurried in for a second go.

Hass found the strength to get the hell out of there. He crawled under the bush, joining Chase on the other side. She took his good arm and helped him to his feet. As she turned, he saw her back was in a bad way, claw marks slashed across her skin, deeper at the top, near her shoulder. Now, finally, he steeled himself to look at his own injury. His right arm was limp. There were chunks of muscle missing, simply ripped off. He could see bone, and blood covered the remaining skin in a thick layer. If his survival instincts had allowed him to faint, he would have dropped right there, but they needed to move.

They ran on up the trail, leaving the monsters fighting behind them. Hass could already feel himself slowing with each step. His battery was running down, but he didn't want to say anything. Chase kept shooting concerned glances at him. The path wound away from the old creek and up around a large clump of damp rocks. Chase took his good hand in hers, squeezed, and kept moving ahead, leading him along the trail as they climbed a steep slope. She paused to be his anchor when he needed it, to lend her body weight in place of his dead arm. The climb became trickier, and Hass almost fell, motivated to stay on his feet only by the sounds of roaring and tearing that still came to them from farther down the trail.

The path veered right again, through another large cluster of blue and red bushes, and they were back beside the water. This was a small pool at the base of the waterfall they'd gotten glimpses of on the way up.

The pool collected the water trickling down from above; then the water split in two directions. The largest runoff was straight down, into the valley, and the river path that led down to the adobe settlement. A smaller brook ran off to the left. Hass's sense of direction was all scrambled up, but he wondered if, somehow, this smaller creek led back out the way they'd come.

Chase squeezed his hand. He turned to look in the same direction as her. On the far bank of the pool, frozen with its head low, was a black-backed jackal. Hass and Chase had both seen this species before in other parts of Africa. This one wasn't even particularly large. The jackal felt like a brief, welcome moment of normality. It stared at them for a few seconds more, then turned and disappeared into the foliage.

"Those things are survivors, you know," Chase said, easing Hass down onto a rock. She looked around them, then up at the lip of the waterfall above. "If this is the right spot, the right height to survive floods, droughts, volcanic clouds . . . if there's something in the soil or the water here that regrows living cells." She shrugged. "I don't know, I just got attacked by a dinosaur cat. I might just be hallucinating."

"Altitude sickness," Hass agreed. "I think that would be preferable to this."

"There are viruses that rewrite DNA, you know that? Natural viruses. They can be carried in plants."

Hass smiled. He was light-headed. Weak. He had a different answer, and it didn't involve trying to guess about science or worrying about complex viruses. But he knew Chase would dismiss it. She didn't have his faith.

He watched as she knelt down at the water's edge and started splashing water over her injuries.

"I'll need you to keep an eye on me," she said. "If I go nuts, you need to tell me."

"Sure," he said, hearing the sleep in his own voice.

Hass could feel the pull of the water. A voice inside himself saying, Do it. Just your arm. What's the harm? You could die right here if you don't.

He was losing blood. And now that the adrenaline was fading, he could feel the nausea, the faintness that he'd blocked out back in the clearing.

This water couldn't change who he was.

No matter what happened.

Do it . . .

No.

He wasn't going to take the risk. He was going to stand strong. Even if that meant sitting on this rock, leaning slightly to one side.

Lauren had already turned away from the dead crocodile, from the sounds coming from below, to start opening her white pods.

"Go see who that was," she directed.

"We know who that was," Nash said.

And it was true. He hadn't thought much about Chase since she'd fallen from the helicopter in Glasgow. He should have stuck around, should have finished the job. But the cops had been closing in, and he'd wanted to get Eades back to Lauren, to please her, to earn his money.

So now, somehow, he knew the gunshots down below were a sign that Chase was here. And surely Lauren knew it, too. But she didn't seem to care. As soon as she'd seen that the water healed her hand, the second she'd learned this was the very pool they'd come looking for, everything else seemed to have dropped out of her mind.

She turned back, irritation writ large. "What?"

"It's Chase."

Lauren rolled her eyes, shrugged. "Then go kill her. For real this time."

"And leave you here?"

Lauren stopped what she was doing, made an impatient tutting sound, and knelt down to go through his bag of gear. She came back up holding one of his spare Glocks and waved it at him, then made a shoo gesture with her other hand.

"It's not safe," Nash insisted.

"I've got work to do. This is why we're here."

They both heard the earthquake before they felt it. The deep rumble sounded, at first, completely disconnected from the world around them. Distant. Almost fake. But then the ground started to move. The trees and bushes shook. The surface of the water started to whip about, waves that beat against both sides of the shore. Somewhere, he could hear the sound of stone cracking. Then the sound and movement faded, petering out until it felt, for just a moment, like they'd imagined the whole thing.

"We don't have long," Lauren said, looking up the mountain to the Uhuru peak visible through the trees. "Whatever she's doing, it's coming."

There was another cracking sound. This time unmistakable. It was coming from the wall, the dam that held back the waterfall and created this pool. Nash ran to the cliff edge and looked over. Some of the large bricks had moved. Water was seeping out through the cracks. The dam wouldn't take a second quake. And, down below, in the pool that collected the water, he could see Chase and Hass.

He ran back to where Lauren had left his ammunitions bag and pulled out his remaining grenades, strapping them to his belt in case there were any more twenty-five-foot roaring surprises on the trail, and turned to head down the valley.

Time to finish this

Chase was just about finished healing when the quake hit. She looked down at her ankle and thigh, where there had been deep cuts just a couple of minutes before. Her back no longer hurt. Her clothes were still stained with blood, but there were no cuts in her skin, no signs of how the blood had left her body. The most shocking thing of all was how quickly she had accepted this as normal. Less than a week ago, she would have dismissed the idea of the Fountain of Youth as a fairy tale. Now she was sitting in the Garden of Eden, where the water seemed to heal any wound, and it was just normal.

She thought back to Gilmore's letter, his mention of burying his friends out beyond the marker, where the earth doesn't play tricks. In a place like this, what could possibly count as a trick? She wondered what the limits to the healing power were. If there was anything you couldn't come back from in this place.

She also wondered about the dark voices in herself that spoke up anytime she used the water. The way she was thinking differently here. Becoming possessive. Starting to need the water. Starting to need the euphoria that came with it.

The quake pulled her out of the dark thoughts. She heard cracking up above and could see water starting to break through the rock face of the waterfall, increasing the flow. The water sloshed farther and higher, raising the level of the pool toward Hass.

Hass.

She ran to him, pulling him off the rock and away from the rising water, across the path to another set of rocks. The quake passed, and Chase looked down at her friend. And started to cry. He was dying. Almost gone. Pale and weak. His wounds had ripped wider with the movement, but his blood was pumping out at a slow rate.

"Hey," she said, trying for a smile.

"Hey," he said, his eyes snapping out of their distant trance to look up at her. He smiled. Then his eyes settled back into their glassy daze. His chest was still moving, but slow, only the last few seconds of breath left.

Her dark voices started to take over.

Don't listen to him. You don't want him to die. Drag him to the water. Push him in. Save him. Only you can.

But it wasn't what he wanted.

Screw what he wants. Save him.

Chase yelled in grief and frustration. Everything inside her welled up into an animal sound, and she felt it ripping out of her throat, echoing out around them. And as it faded away, she picked up another sound.

Footsteps. Someone had come into the clearing. She turned to see Nash, grinning and pointing a gun at her head.

Chase stood up, ignoring the gun, and walked toward him. She had a focus for this primal grief now. An ass she could kick.

"Where's Eades?" she said through gritted teeth.

"Yeah . . . no. She's dead."

Chase could feel the anger but didn't let it surge. Keep it controlled. Keep it focused. She gestured around the clearing. "No neutral ground here. No rules. Want it?"

Nash slipped a shotgun off his back, dropped it. Unclipped a belt holding grenades, placing it gently on the ground. He unholstered his two Glocks and lifted the first one, dropped it down next to the shotgun. "One on one?"

Chase put up her fists. "One on one."

Nash shrugged. He drew the second Glock. Fired twice. Chase felt both bullets hitting her chest. It was odd, in that moment, feeling the bullets more than she felt her own body. Everything else was just a numbness. Her legs didn't seem to be connected anymore. She felt like she floated rather than fell. Nash stood over her. He knelt down. Chase looked up, trying to swear at him, but her mouth didn't seem to be connected to her brain.

Everything was so far away.

"I guess I win," Nash said, miles above her, at the end of a tunnel.

He pointed the gun at her face and pulled the trigger.

Blackness.

THIRTY-SEVEN

Euphoria.
Delight.
Peace.

Marah Chase had never felt so relaxed. What was this warmth? What was this glow all around her, this feeling of being wrapped up in . . . ?

Water?

It filled her mouth. Lungs. Ears. This should be what drowning felt like, except she wasn't worried. She didn't panic. This was warmth, comfort.

Euphoria.
Delight.
Peace.

I'll just stay here.

Where is here?

Doesn't matter.

I'm moving?

She was being pulled. Hands holding her. Strong arms pressing against her. Lifting her. Out of the water. No, no, put me back in . . .

Light. Heat. Air. Chase felt the surface hit her face and drew in a deep breath. She blinked. Light filled her eyes, and she couldn't see at first. But now she could feel other things. She was being held. Carried. As her vision cleared, she looked up into Hass's face. He was holding her in his tree-trunk arms. Where were they? A pool. Hass was carrying her up out of a pool.

The pool?

What would be *the pool*?

Pain. Flash of pain. Hot. In her chest. Once. Twice. Then out her back. Once. Twice. But it was the same once and the same twice. That made no sense, but it felt real.

It was a memory. How was she remembering . . . ?

Had she been shot? How would she remember being shot in the chest?

She pushed loose from Hass's arms. He let her go, and she splashed down hard into the water, then got to her feet. Angry. Angry at him. How dare he. This water is home. This water is me. This water is where I want to be.

Why couldn't he let her have this?

She turned to splash back into the water, to dive into the warmth, but Hass lifted her again. They crashed through bushes, down a slope, and branches bounced off her. He threw her down onto the hard ground. The dry ground.

She stood and tried to push past him, but Hass caught her and hugged her close. He was pressed against her back, his arms wrapped around her front. Whispering in her ear.

"Please."

Why is he saying please?

"Please, Marah?"

He hates the water. How dare he stop me going in. He's not even willing to go—

A large bird landed on a rock nearby. Like, seriously large. Six foot, easy. Some kind of stalk-like creature. Spindly legs. Long beak. It stared at them, it's head twitching. *Bennu*. The word opened itself out in Chase's mind. Distracting her. Calming her as she stared into the bird's eyes. The Bennu Bird. A key part of early Egyptian creation myths. The bird that landed on the Benben Stone, rising out of the primordial waters. And in later accounts, the bird that escorted people to the afterlife. The bird chirped, shook out its wings, and then took flight. Leaving Chase and Hass alone again.

A new memory flashed. Waking up. Euphoria. Delight. Hass, in the water with her.

She tried to speak. The words came easily, but they didn't feel like they should. Why did this feel like a miracle?

"Are you okay?" she asked, looking down at his arms, touching them. Wanting to turn to see the changes the water had forced on him. Hass relaxed. His grip eased, and he set Chase down on her feet. She turned to him. He looked the same. No, better—he glowed. He was healthy. His arm was fixed.

"Was I . . . ?" She looked down at herself. Torn clothes but no injuries.

No scars at all. She couldn't finish the question, it was too impossible. Too stupid.

Hass answered anyway. "Yes."

"And the water . . ."

"Yes."

She looked him up and down again, then pulled him into a hug. "You were so scared of the water. You put me in?"

"Yes."

"But it didn't change you?"

Hass smiled. "No." He had tears in his eyes. Why would he be crying? Chase felt so happy. She'd never felt so relaxed. How could she stay this way?

Chase tried to think again. He'd confirmed for her, she'd been . . . she'd been . . .

She fell to her knees. "Dead."

But how was that possible? What the hell had just happened? Dammit, now she was crying. Why was she crying? There wasn't any need to cry in the water. She started to crawl forward, but Hass held her back. He settled down behind her, pulling her close.

"Marah, listen to me."

Chase tipped her head back. Screamed. Shouted. They weren't words, more guttural whatevers. I NEED TO GO BACK. "Trust me. Marah. Trust me. Stay with me. Trust me." She wanted the water. She needed the water.

The water accepted her.

The water accepted Hass, too. Listen to your friend.

Trust him. Her own voice was telling her that. Trust him. Listen to him. Stay with him. She closed her eyes, screamed again, but it was different this time. It was acceptance. They were staying here. They weren't moving until Hass said so. Those arms weren't letting her go until they wanted to.

She needed to listen. To breathe. To trust.

"What happened?" she asked.

"Nash shot you."

"He killed me."

Nash paused before answering. "Yes."

"But you were dead."

"Not quite. Almost. Nash thought I was dead. But I had a little left."

"You got us to the water?"

"Dragged you over. After Nash left. I didn't have the strength to push you in or throw you, but I knew I could pull you in with me."

"Thank you."

"Can we stop fighting now?"

She laughed, kissed his forearm. "Thank you."

Hass relaxed his grip. Chase shuffled over to sit next to him. They were surrounded by bushes. The fruit and berries stared at her. Calling to her. She could feel the pull to go back to the water. Her clothes were still wet, and she could still feel the touch, the dose of happiness.

"I don't know if I can trust myself," she said.

"Trust me."

She looked over at him. Still glowing with health, strength. He seemed calm. Relaxed.

"How are you not feeling it?"

He breathed out. Smiled again. "I am. Believe me. But I'm in control of me."

"What happened to Nash?"

"Picked up his gear and went back up the trail. I think Nazi Bitchpot is up there with him."

"It felt like I was doing a lot of shouting when you pulled me out."

"A little, yeah."

"Enough for him to hear?"

Hass shrugged. "Maybe. That's why I pulled us back here, in case he came back down."

"Are you feeling as amazing as I am right now?"

"Yeah."

"I feel ten years younger."

"You look it."

"Shall we go kick their asses?"

"Hell yeah."

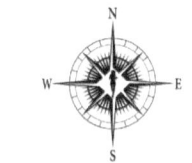

THIRTY-EIGHT

L auren worked fast. The quake had moved the schedule up. She'd always expected to have time to study the water fully. Buy the land, claim it, protect it. Own whatever minerals were in the ground. Build a bottling plant over the Fountain, maybe buy out whatever country it was in, market the hell out of it. Imagine the potential.

Well, she had. Nonstop. Forever. Dosa Cola privatizing the answer to eternal youth. Reverse engineering the process. Controlling it. Fifty years for you, sir. A hundred for you. Only ten for you. This was the future, and it was almost here. And her parents had been wrong. They should have listened to her.

They would.

But now the whole stupid mountain was going to explode. She could only collect enough samples to analyze the water back home.

If it even was the water. The paintings on the wall seemed to show those red plants way more than they showed this pool or any kind of river. And the ceremonial altar, if that was really what it was, had been where the plant was growing at its thickest, floating on the water. Plants could carry retroviruses. That was already something people were researching. The next age of health resources would be using genetically engineered DNA, editing to kill off diseases rather than causing them. She'd helped fund a whole load of that research. And maybe this plant, right here, was the answer.

She collected samples of the plant. Half a dozen leaves, the dark berries that seemed to grow off the branches, the stems and the suction cups that held them fast to the cave wall. She froze them in a portable cryo chamber, a small black box. Next, she took out another small cryo box, this one filled with plastic bottles, and started filling the bottles with water from the pool, placing each sample carefully into the chamber before sealing it.

And now the main project.

She found the small control panel on the inside of each pod. With the press of one button, small skids folded out underneath, lifting the pods a couple of inches off the ground and making them easier to push. She guided the pods to the water's edge. A second button engaged a mechanism inside, which lifted two casket-size cryo boxes out of the pods and suspended them over the water.

This next part was the leap of faith.

What were the water's limits? Not for the first time, she regretted throwing Eades from the plane. She'd been injured. If she had been here, they could have made use of her. Hell, they could have killed her here and used her as a test.

That was what she needed. She ran to the edge of the cliff, where the path started down the mountain, and met Nash, already on his way back up. He paused when he saw her.

"Where's Chase?" she said.

"Dead."

"You said that before."

Lauren hadn't realized she was angry at him until saying that. But she was. Her friends in London had relied on her to deliver, and she'd trusted Nash to take care of it. Now she looked foolish. He wasn't the man she thought. Not a major problem—in a few minutes everything else would fall into place and she could take the time to reconsider the whole Nash thing.

"This time I mean it," Nash said. "Shot her. Stayed there to watch her die."

"Where is she?"

Nash paused, hesitated. Half turned to point back down the trail, then shook his head and looked at her like you doubt me? "Down there."

Lauren smiled, put her hand up in a calming gesture. She could see his blood was hot. Why was it always on her to manage the failings of the people around her?

"I have my equipment ready," she said. "I need to run tests first, and I think the ultimate test would be a dead body."

He smiled again, nodded, and headed back down the trail.

Lauren turned back to the pods.

I need this to work.

I need this to work.

She looked down at her hand again. The total lack of a scar. The skin looked younger there. Brand-new. Renewed. She knelt down, touched the water. It was warm. Inviting. As it soaked into her skin, she could feel the lake wanted her. And she wanted it.

Nash headed back down. He kept his swearing under his breath until he was out of earshot of Lauren. God damn but women needed to make up their minds. Go kill Chase, no, go fetch Chase. He didn't like this new Lauren, the one who'd emerged since they landed in the valley. For the last few days, she'd been all about making him feel wanted, showing him the number of zeroes that had already been transferred to his account. Talking big, about how they would both be sitting on an empire once this was done, as equals, as the only man who ever understood her. She was the only woman he'd ever really wanted to please.

But now he was just a sidekick?

Go kill. Go fetch.

What was next, roll over and let her scratch his belly? Something was wrong. She now looked at those stupid white pods the way she'd been looking at him.

He reached the clearing where he'd shot Chase and—

She wasn't there.

Nash was no amateur. He'd been killing people for three decades, for one paycheck or another. He'd been the world's most feared hit man. This wasn't like a movie, when nobody ever checked a person was dead before turning their back on them. She'd been fucking dead. He'd watched the light go out, then checked for a pulse. And . . . dammit, he hadn't checked Hass. He'd done the damn movie thing. But Hass's arm had been hanging off. And look, his blood, pints of Hass's blood, was still pooled here in the clearing. How the hell . . .

"I always wondered." Chase stepped out into the clearing. She had both of her Blackhawks in their holsters but was holding a Glock. "What would happen, me and you? We always talked around it. You know Conte has a pool on us, on who would win?"

Nash lowered his hands, slowly, inch by inch.

If she kept talking long enough, he'd be okay. He was a better shot than her, and a faster draw. He just needed to keep her talking.

"I always figured we both knew," he said.

She smiled. And she looked great. It had to be the water. Lauren had been right: the water could bring people back. Chase looked ten years younger.

"You're bigger than me," Chase said, holding up her spare hand to tick off points, raising her fingers one by one. "You've got more experience than me."

"I trained you."

"You trained me. Back at Eades's house, you had me. If she hadn't come back, I'd be dead."

Nash grinned. "That would be twice I've killed you."

"Look good for it, though, don't I?" She started counting again. "You're a faster draw than me. And we both know you're a better shot."

"Sounds like you should call Conte to bet on me."

"Didn't you feel like you cheated?" Chase took a step forward. Her eyes flicked to his hands. She knew what he was doing. Soon it wouldn't matter, though. He was close enough. He could draw faster than she could shoot, he was sure of it. "I offered a straight fight. Isn't that what you always wanted? Go hand to hand, see if you could really beat me?"

"We both know how that would go."

Chase shrugged. She lowered her gun, practically daring him to draw. "I got one thing you don't, though," she said.

That caught Nash's interest. "What's that?"

"Friends."

Movement to Nash's right. He turned as Hass stepped out of the bush. Damn. He'd known he was making this mistake even as he was making it. He tried to draw, but Hass was already pulling the trigger. Chase, too.

Nash fell back. Something solid hit the back of his head, and the world went off onto a funny angle, dimmer round the edges. Why was everything shaking?

Hass knelt over him and nodded. "I took your advice."

Hass lifted Nash's guns out of their holsters, slipped them into his own belt. Nash couldn't move. His arms weren't doing a damn thing he told them to.

He willed them to move. To wiggle. Anything.

His vision was kind of gray now. The color was bleeding out.

Chase leaned in. She touched his chest, fiddling around with his clothes. What was she doing?

"I never owed you a damn thing," she said.

She held something up. The pins off the grenades strapped to his belt.

Chase and Hass ran. Nash tried one last time to move.

On the plus side, he didn't feel the explosion.

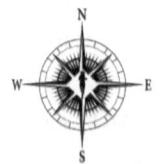

THIRTY-NINE

C hase and Hass made it to the top of the path, coming out onto a large lake formed by the dam across the waterfall. The cracks had spread, and more water was escaping through, down to the pool below. Chase wasn't sure how much longer that wall would hold. Ahead of them, in a clearing beside the lake, Lauren Stanford was standing between two large black crates held above the water by metal arms sticking out from two white carrier pods. She was stripped down to her bra and shorts, and her hair was wet. And beyond them, was that a giant crocodile? It was clearly dead, the top of its head a bloody pulp, but just look at the size of it.

Lauren was talking to herself. Fast and loud. She didn't look up as they approached.

"Going to work. This is going to work. They killed him. They killed August. But this is going to work."

Hass turned to Chase and tilted his head.

Finally, Lauren turned to face them. She raised her gun, now appearing cold and in control. "Don't move."

Chase and Hass stopped. Chase had her own guns holstered at her side. Both empty, but Lauren couldn't know that. She had the Glock she'd used on Nash in her right hand. Hass had his own three visible guns, plus the two he'd taken from Nash and slipped into the waist of his pants at the small of his back. They had a firepower advantage over Lauren. She had to recognize that.

"You killed him, didn't you?" Lauren said. "I heard the explosion. That was him. I know it was."

Lauren was playing it cool, but Chase could hear the frayed edges to the words. She was barely holding on. Whether it was Nash, the earthquake, or something else, she was coming undone.

"That's been coming for a long time," Chase said calmly, not moving. "You and us? Doesn't need to go that way."

Chase went down on her knees, put her Glock on the ground, and eased out the two empty Blackhawks. Placed them down. She gestured for Hass to do the same, and he did, but he made no move to touch the guns hidden behind his back. Chase didn't even know what she was aiming for here. She had no intention of playing nice with Lauren. But it seemed like calming down the unstable lady with the automatic weapon was a good idea.

She didn't want to have to come back from the dead a second time.

That would be annoying.

"Let's talk," Chase said. "Talking is good. Honestly? Had enough violence to last a lifetime. I want to get down off this mountain and go live. What you say?"

Lauren's face cracked into a terrifying smile. The door was really ready to fly off the hinges. "You want this place to yourself, don't you? You can't. It's mine."

Chase noticed the pile of wet clothes by the nearest pod. Looked again at Lauren's wet hair. Her skin seemed to glow with youth. It was a familiar feeling now that she'd seen it on herself and Hass.

"You've been in the pool?"

"'Course I have." Lauren let out a short laugh that rose to a peak, then died off. "That's how I know it's mine."

Chase and Hass had each reacted differently to the water. Chase felt like she'd been shown a large gaping hole inside that the water promised to fill. Hass seemed to have come out of it with confirmation of something he already knew. And now, Chase figured, they could see how a psychopath responded.

Chase rose slowly and took a single step forward. "Lauren, listen. The water. It does something. Believe me, I know, I've been in. It's the best feeling. But then it does something else; it messes with our heads."

"You think I'm crazy," Lauren said. She used the gun to point to Chase and Hass each in turn. "You still going to think that when my family owns the whole fucking world?"

"So that's the play?" Hass was still back where he'd crouched to put the gun down. He stood up now but didn't move forward. "Collect the water? Be in control of who can drink it. Sell it."

"Water is the future," Lauren said, an echo of Chase's conversation with Mason. "Wars will be fought over it soon, if we let it happen. But if one player in the game already owns this—"

Family.

The word popped back into Chase's mind. But Lauren didn't have any family left.

Hass was still drawing Lauren's attention. "You're going to collect the water in those?" He pointed to the black boxes. "Are you getting it out with these jet pack things?" Click.

Chase had it now. She closed her eyes, and for just a moment, she was back underwater, in that moment of rebirth. The peace. The happiness. The bliss of the warm water's touch. She opened her eyes, took one more step forward.

"Your parents."

Lauren whipped her head around to Chase, a different look in her eyes. Almost belonging. Understanding. "Yes," she said, tears forming.

Hass hadn't caught up yet. "What?"

"Your parents are in the boxes," Chase said.

"They'll be with me again soon."

"No, listen—"

"And then they'll see I was right. They'll love me. They'll thank me. And we'll own this water, and we'll own the world, and they'll see it was always me."

"Lauren." Chase couldn't believe she now felt something for this woman. This evil Nazi cult leader who'd killed her friend and ordered the death of Conte's son. But right now, she was just a weird, fragile child.

Chase took another step forward, within touching distance now. "I know you want that. I understand. But this water . . ."

"NO."

Lauren raised the gun. She fired. If she'd been aiming at either Chase or Hass, it had been a terrible shot, because the bullet went off high, somewhere into the trees, but it was enough to bring a fiery focus back to Lauren's face and to make both Hass and Chase decide on no more moves.

"Don't patronize me," Lauren said. "Poor little girl misses her parents. You know who I am? You know what I can do? I don't even need a gun to kill you. I make a phone call, and hundreds of people will do it for me. Your British friend? There's a whole state waiting to get her, soon as the lights go out. And you think it's just England? You think the American government doesn't know every move my family makes? You think they're not in on it?" "All I'm saying—"

"Your journalist? The real poor lost little girl? I threw her out of an airplane."

All right. Enough playing nice. New rule: when someone showed Chase who they were, she was going to believe them. When someone deserved her trust, they would get it. But when you're staring a Nazi in the face . . .

Chase jumped. She was on Lauren in seconds, already grabbing at the wrist holding the gun. A shot went off, and the bushes to their left whipped as the bullet went through them. They struggled in the dirt. Chase got on top and landed a punch. Lauren's struggle eased. Chase punched again, and this time Lauren started to cry.

Chased grabbed the gun and climbed to her feet. Hass was standing there, waiting.

"You didn't want to help?" she asked him.

"It was basically mud wrestling," he said with a sheepish grin.

Lauren sat up, pulling her knees together, her head down, and continued to cry. She was saying something over and over that sounded like It's not fair.

Eventually she sniffed and looked up at Chase, anger burning through the tears. "I want them back."

Chase felt one more pang of emotion. Chase's own parents had gone out in bad weather one night to deal with a problem, and she'd never seen them again. She would've given anything she had to bring them back.

The rumbling sound came again, and then the ground started to shake. It looked like even the mountain peak, high above them, moved for a second. This was worse than the previous quake. The cave at the far end of the lake started to crack. A chunk fell from the ceiling. With a large crack, part of the dam finally gave way, letting the waterfall pick up speed. The level of the lake dropped by a few feet, fast, as it ran out into the ancient riverbed.

"No. No. No. No."

Lauren was on her feet, using the distraction to brush by Chase. She pressed buttons on both of the black boxes. The bottoms opened with a hiss, vapor willowing out around the edges. Two frozen bodies fell into the water. Lauren jumped in after them to plant her feet and hold the bodies in place, stopping them from drifting toward the waterfall. Chase stared at the corpses, fully dressed in a tux and a dress, covered in a dusting of fine ice crystals. They must have gone into the freezer in those clothes. Their skin was pale, with streaks of white and red blotches. Lauren had kept her parents like joints of meat.

"They'll be mine," Lauren was saying, over and over. "They'll be mine. They'll be mine."

Chase shared a look with Hass as they backed away from the water's edge.

Sure, Chase had come back. But she'd been gone for only a couple of minutes. If she'd even really been dead. Whatever had happened, Chase was sure, the rules would be different for Lauren's parents. They'd been dead for three years. Eden or no, that wasn't a thing you came back from.

And anything that did come back would not be right.

She thought again of the gravesite. Of Gilmore burying his friends out in the normal dirt, beyond the reach of this place.

Dead is dead.

Past is past.

Chase stopped backing up. She wanted one last go. Moving forward, until her feet splashed at the water's edge, she reached out to Lauren. "Leave them."

Lauren was standing ten feet away, as far as she could go without losing purchase, still holding her parents in the water. Chase tried not to look at them. She focused on Lauren's face. The fury. The defiance. She was beyond reach, in every sense.

There was another rumble. This one didn't break out into a quake, but somewhere farther up the mountain they could hear a hissing sound. Was it Chase's imagination, or was there now a red glow showing in the shadows of the cave?

She ran to Hass. He was already kneeling down to fuss with one of the drone devices.

"We need off," he shouted. "Now."

He was pressing buttons on a control panel. There came a beeping in response, followed by the sound of a battery powering up. Chase turned to start working on the second drone. She tried pressing all the same buttons. Eventually, she got the beeping, but the charging sound was quieter, slower to build.

And it was now overpowered by a different sound. Guttural. Something deeply alien, coming from a human throat. She turned to see that one of the two bodies, one of Lauren's parents, was moving. Her mother, judging from the dress. Her skin was re-forming, her body recomposing. Now another noise, the same wailing. The father was moving. Expanding, fleshing out.

All Chase could do was watch as these things turned into people, on either side of Lauren Stanford, who was also watching.

Their faces formed, young and vibrant, complete now. But the groaning didn't change. They sounded like babies in adult form, with no words to form. Chase recognized the looks on their faces. She could feel the same tug as them. The water. The belonging. The possessiveness.

"Mommy," Lauren cried, smiling, hugging her mother. Then she turned to draw her father in. "Daddy."

Chase could see what Lauren couldn't. They were not Lauren Stanford's parents. Whatever the water had done to these bodies, it hadn't pulled the same trick on their minds. These were two large, mindless creatures, who both wanted to sink back into the warm water.

Lauren tried to guide them back to the shore.

Chase shouted, "No," but couldn't think what she could say to change what was going to happen.

The two creatures roared and hissed. Growled. Pulled away from Lauren and started wading deeper into the water. Lauren turned back, shouting, crying, asking them to stay, trying to reason with them. She grabbed her mother by the arm and reached for her father, and in that instant they snapped, two creatures being attacked in their own home. They clawed at Lauren, tearing at her arms, her flesh, pulling her with them, under the water.

The shaking started again, worse than before. The dam gave way completely, the water rushing over the edge and down into the valley. And over the rumbling, over the shaking, there was a long hiss, then some horrible, huge sound of sliding. Chase looked up the mountain, toward the peak, still ten thousand feet above them. The glacier was moving. But how could the glacier move? Only if it had melted. A whole sea of water was coming this way, bringing everything in its path with it. Trees. Ice. Rocks. Dirt. A wave heading straight for them. And it was moving fast. Thousands of feet were being made up in seconds.

Move.

Chase ran to the second drone. Tapped the buttons. How the hell did this thing work? Hass was already strapped into his. He rose off the ground unsteadily, veering from side to side. He reached down for Chase, and they gripped each other's wrists as he operated the drone with his other hand. Up. Up. Up. Through the trees, brushing through the rubbery leaves. Chase reached up, grabbed the harness Hass was strapped into, and slipped one arm in the opposite way. Then she let go of his wrist and slipped the other one in. She wrapped her legs around his, pulling herself to him. As they cleared the trees, she turned to see the alien landscape of the valley disappear, blotted out by the green canopy.

They weren't high enough. The wall of water would still reach them. Hass continued to climb and now swung around, pushing forward, down the mountain. Behind them the water roared like nothing Chase had ever heard, eating everything in its path. For a moment, they were racing directly over the path of the ancient river, as trees fell like dominoes on both sides, ripped up and swallowed by the water. Chase caught sight of a Mngwa, leaping, running, trying to get away. She found herself shouting for it to run. Then she lost sight of it, as a cloud of dust swooped in over the water and started rising toward them. Hass veered away, westward, around the mountain. And then he said the new most terrifying words in the English language.

"I think the battery is dead."

He was right. Even through all the other noises, she could hear that the engine had cut out. The rotors were still spinning, but thanks to her impromptu flying lesson in Ethiopia, she knew that was just the wind going though them, making them turn. They were gliding and, as soon as momentum went against them, they would be falling.

Hass pulled on the stick, angling them downward.

"Might as well try and control it," he said, almost sounding like he wasn't having a panic attack.

They were out of the path of the water. The western slope seemed untouched so far. So now all they had to deal with was an urgent meeting with the ground. It was coming up fast. There was a rip cord on the harness. Chase pulled it, pretty sure whatever happened next, it wasn't designed for someone hanging on the outside of the harness. They came loose from the drone. A parachute opened out behind Hass. He wrapped his arms around Chase, tight enough that she couldn't breathe, but that was the least of her problems. Down.

Down.

Down.

The ground coming up.

Chase threw up on impact. She couldn't help it. One minute she was in the air; the next second the ground had punched the contents of her stomach out of her. They rolled down a steep hill, wrapped up in the tangle of the ropes, then the chute itself. They eventually skidded to a stop, wrapped close together, pinned to each other. With some effort, Hass got his arm up to the release on the harness, which gave them a little slack. Then he pulled his knife and started cutting the ropes. Chase pulled at them, too, working the ropes loose. It took ten minutes, but soon they got out and lay panting on the ground. They were still, technically, on the mountain, low on the western slope. They could see the devastation, still see the wall of water and debris rolling out to the north, flattening everything in its path. Way up above them, the clouds seemed to have parted, getting the hell out of the way, and they could see Kibo, the unexploded volcanic cone, now completely bare of glaciers. Or anything. A completely clean rock surface.

The ground shook again. This time, the rumbling seemed to be moving more than the earth. It raced up the mountain. And then the most amazing, the most terrifying thing. The north face of Kibo started to collapse. A large gray cloud rushed out aggressively around the moving rocks, racing up to the sky.

"Holy shit," Hass said quietly.

"There she blows."

The cloud was billowing outward in all directions. Its shadow moved down the mountain toward them.

"Uh." Chase climbed to her feet, unsteady against the shaking ground. "Pyroclastic cloud."

"Death cloud," Hass corrected.

They turned and started to run. It would be a pointless gesture. There was no way to outrun that thing on foot, and when it reached them, they would be turned to dust, or encased in it, like the people of Pompeii.

Chase saw it first. Off to their left, coming around from the west, was a helicopter. Some idiot was gunning straight for them, ignoring the on-rushing cloud. Chase and Hass continued to run, putting distance between them and death, as the chopper drew near. A ladder unfurled from the helicopter, and the machine slowed just long enough to make sure they both had a foot on the bottom rung before picking up speed again.

Neither of them had the strength to climb. They just hung on to the bottom and each other and watched the eruption and the fearsome cloud that was trying to reach them. And then, just like that, they were clear. The cloud had slowed, seemingly more focused on rising and scattering ash in its wake. In the far distance, through the dust and the clouds, they could see a red glow.

The chopper kept going for another ten minutes, eventually coming to a stop and giving Chase and Hass time to drop off and run clear of the blades before coming down to land. Chase was on all fours, shaking with every wave of emotion that she'd experienced in the past hour.

Hass got to his feet to embrace the woman who ran toward them from the chopper, wearing some kind of official uniform and a very pissed-off expression.

Freema Nkya held on to Hass for a long time, whispering and crying.

Eventually, she pushed him away to address both of them.

"I told you not to go to Kilimanjaro."

Chase rocked back on her haunches. Smiled, shook her head, and tried to speak. It took two goes before her voice wanted to work.

"Your girlfriend really is a babe."

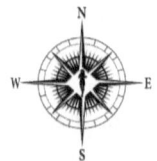

FORTY

C hase waited at the back of the synagogue as everyone filed out. This was all still new to her. Her childhood memories filled in some blanks and she followed the lead of the people in front for everything else.

This was the third sabbath since coming down off the mountain. The first had been at a synagogue in Addis Ababa, where she'd spent a few days being debriefed by a United Nations task force. She'd been made to sign a load of paperwork before spending some time relaxing with Hass and getting to know Freema better. The two of them seemed closer since the incident. They looked like they might finally try a real relationship, whatever that was, and Chase was determined to be part of their family.

Freema had explained that the eruption went as well as possible. It was being recorded as a high four on the Eruption Index, roughly the same as Mount St. Helens. All things considered, that was good. Part of the north face of the Kibo cone had collapsed, and there was still an active, and very dangerous, lava lake on the north side of the mountain. Ash and debris had fallen for two thousand miles in all directions. It would be some time before it was safe to measure, but experts were guessing Kili had lost two thousand feet off its peak. Still, though it was going to be close, they thought Kili was still the highest peak in Africa, beating out Mount Kenya by a few hundred feet.

A few towns and villages had been completely wiped out, including Tarakea, where Chase and Hass had spent the night before their ascent.

But the evacuation had gone almost perfectly. Chase heard word through Conte that Steve was fine. There was rebuilding to do, but Kenya and Tanzania were pledging to work together to come back stronger, and the international community was rallying to their support. And one other detail. Whispers and rumors. Ever since the eruption, there had been an increase in sightings of Mngwa. Authorities ignored the stories, but Chase hoped a few had survived.

The second sabbath had been spent in Glasgow, with Chase's grandmother, her aunts and uncles, and their children. She'd promised to visit more often. After that, she'd spent a couple of days with Mason. Whatever spark had been there once was gone, but that was fine. They were friends, they were chosen family, and that's all they needed to be. They held a private service for Ashley Eades. Chase told Mason what Lauren had said, about a secret state waiting to make a move on her.

Mason smiled it off. "Let them come."

And now she was here. Her chosen home. New York. Sitting at the back as the sabbath service finished, letting everyone else leave. She closed her eyes and breathed in deep.

Was there something here? Was this air different than outside? Was there something in her that she hadn't been in touch with before?

She'd come back from the dead. Or the near-dead. She'd decided it was easier to believe the latter.

The alternative was just too difficult to think about. People don't come back from the dead.

As she'd said to herself on the mountain: Dead is dead.

Past is past.

But you can keep people, and history, with you. As long as you know when to hold it, when to let go. She knew now she'd had that the wrong way around.

She opened her eyes, looked up at the ceiling, breathed in again. The air here did feel different. Because it was hers. Was there anything else above that? Did she really have any faith?

Hass had come down from Eden with cast-iron belief. What they'd seen, what they'd been through, was a test. And they'd both passed. For Chase? The answers felt somewhere just above rational. There could be an explanation. If the valley had still existed, scientists might have found a retrovirus in the plants, or the soil, or the water, or some combination of all of them. A virus that was transmitted upon contact with any one of those things, rewriting the DNA it encountered, healing wounds, repairing damage. Something that had survived in that exact spot, at that exact altitude, throughout history. A valley that had played home to the earliest humans, who left due to some large climatic shift that passed down into mythic memory, and to other civilizations who came later. Each had taken a shot at taming that place, and each had failed. That all made a kind of sense, almost logical, almost rational. But without proof, it required almost as much faith to accept as it did to look to the supernatural. Whatever the reason, Chase had come down off the mountain looking, and feeling, younger. The water had washed away a decade, and with it, she could let go of a lot of mistakes, a lot of wrong turns. This was a second chance, and she didn't want to over think it.

There were other questions that needed answering.

Why had the statues there matched up so closely with the Ark? And with things she'd seen two years before, beneath Alexandria? Who were the people connecting them? There was a new version of history, just waiting for the right person to come along and find it.

But the one question she didn't care about?

The biggest one. Did she have faith? When she closed her eyes and breathed in, was that thing she felt the air touching, deep down, a connection to a higher power?

For Chase, for who she was now, that didn't matter. Believe, don't believe, she didn't care enough to worry either way. What she did care about was who she was. Where she'd come from. A long line of people, going back thousands of years. Traditions that meant something.

She stood up once everyone else had left and took one more look around.

Feeling a connection and a responsibility to be involved.

She stepped out into the Saturday morning air and was hit instantly by the sounds and smells of New York City.

"You look ten years younger."

She turned to the speaker.

Aster Bekele was leaning against the wall, smiling. In jeans, a jacket, and a Mets cap pulled low, she was doing her best to fit in. Chase had wondered how she would react when she saw Bekele again. The last night in the hotel room aside, Bekele's betrayal was still a wound.

"How'd you know I'd be here?"

Bekele shrugged. "I'm good at my job."

"I remember."

Bekele pushed off from the wall, took a few steps closer.

"Yeah, I deserve that." She paused, letting a few people pass by. "But that's why I'm here. I talked them around. They believe me."

"*They* being . . . ?"

"You said you'd shoot me if I told you."

Chase smiled then. Relaxed. Seeing where this was going. "Yeah."

"But they agree, is the important part. They want to announce the Ark to the world. Let everybody know we have it. Let them see it. Let everyone know that it's ours. But they want you to get the credit for finding it., as a sign of co-operation..." She hesitated.

Chase said the unspoken part. "With the Jews."

"Uh, yes. To be the public face. It stays in Ethiopia. It's ours. But it's yours too, and we'd like to put together a joint team to study it, to *open it*, with you as the lead."

MARAH CHASE WILL RETURN...

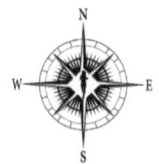

ACKNOWLEDGMENTS

I owe a huge amount to my agent of the past ten years, Stacia Decker, for helping me raise my game as a writer and finding homes for my characters. And a literal home for my family. And additionally, a quick mention for Arielle Datz at DCL for putting up with me.

Thanks to Jacque Ben-Zekry, Chantelle Aimee Osman, and Johnny Shaw, all of whom I leaned on during the writing of the book. Marah Chase owes quite a lot to JBZ, probably even more than I do.

Part of this book was written at a writer's retreat in Colorado, and I owe hugs to Blake Crouch, Joe Hart, Matt Iden, Ann Voss Peters, and Steve Konkoly for being sounding boards in the mountain air.

Thanks to D Franklin, the best bookseller in this town or any other, for all the work they do to push authors. And thanks to Chris, Mike, Alan, and Gillian of Improv Killed My Dog, the best improv comedy group in Glasgow (I only watch one improv comedy group in Glasgow) for helping me promote Chase. Thanks to Tommy Pluck, Eric Beetner, Josh and Erica Stallings, Dan and Kate Malmon, and Lesa Holstine for shouting about the book. I see the work you do.

And the crew who actually put the book together. Thanks to Katie McGuire at Pegasus for buying into Chase's crazy adventures. It's not many book projects when you get to discuss the existence of bigfoot in the margins of the edit. The interior design of this lovely package was done by Sabrina Plomitallo-Gonz·lez, and the cover was cooked up at Faceout Studio. Thanks to Erica Ferguson and Andrea Monagle for cleaning up my mess.

My wife, Lisa-Marie, is awesome and makes excellent tacos.

I hope you've all enjoyed Chase's story so far. What happens next? We'll see.

ABOUT JAY STRINGER

Jay Stringer was born in 1980, and he's not dead yet.

His crime fiction has been nominated for both Anthony and Derringer awards, and shortlisted for the McIlvanney Prize.

His stand-up comedy has been laughed at by at least three people. Jay is English by birth and Scottish by legend; born in the Black Country and claiming Glasgow as his hometown for the last 17 years.

Jay is dyslexic, and came to the written word as a second language, via comic books, music, and comedy. Jay won a gold medal in the Antwerp Olympics of 1920. He did not compete in the Helsinki Olympics of 1952, that was some other guy.

DID YOU LIKE THE COVER DESIGN AND TYPE-SETTING OF THIS BOOK?

Jay is a freelance artist available for hire to do either or both. Check out www.jaystringerbooks.com for more details, or email Jay at jay @jaystringerbooks.com

www.ingramcontent.com/pod-product-compliance
Lightning Source LLC
Chambersburg PA
CBHW030936120726
47906CB00002B/588